RAMPANT

RAMPANT

Diana Peterfreund

An Imprint of HarperCollinsPublishers

HarperTeen is an imprint of HarperCollins Publishers.

Library of Congress Cataloging-in-Publication Data
Peterfreund, Diana.
Rampant / Diana Peterfreund. — 1st ed.
p. cm.
Summary: After sixteen-year-old Astrid Llewelyn survives
a vicious unicorn attack, she learns that she is a descendant
of the most famous unicorn hunter of all time and she must
travel to Rome, Italy, to train in the ancient arts in order
to carry on her family legacy and save the world from the
threat posed by the reemergence of lethal unicorns.
    ISBN 978-0-06-149000-2 (trade bdg.)
    [1. Unicorns—Fiction. 2. Hunting—Fiction.
3. Supernatural—Fiction. 4. Dating (Social customs)—
Fiction. 5. Rome (Italy)—Fiction. 6. Italy—Fiction.] I. Title.
PZ7.P441545Ram 2009   2008036442
[Fic]—dc22   CIP
                                               AC

Typography by Larissa Lawrynenko
9 10 11 12 13   LP/RRDB   10 9 8 7 6 5 4 3 2 1

❖

First Edition

For Dan. For Everything.

Unicorns are in the world again.
—PETER S. BEAGLE,
The Last Unicorn

Note: The unicorns in this book are real; they populate the legends,
histories, and religious texts of Europe and Asia.

Wherein Astrid Is Thrice Tested

"'I WILL NEVER REALLY LEAVE,' *said the unicorn. Diamond sparkles floated from the tip of its glittering silver horn. 'I will always live in your heart.'*"

I swallowed the bile rising in my throat and forced myself to continue reading.

"*Then the unicorn turned and galloped away, its fluffy pink tail swinging merrily as it spread its iridescent wings to the morning sunshine.*"

Oh, no. Not wings, too.

"*Every time the unicorn's lavender hooves touched the earth, a tinkling like the chime of a thousand fairy bells floated back toward the children.*"

Shuddering, I raised my head from the picture book to look at the rapt, upturned faces of my charges. Bethany Myerson, aged six, was holding back tears as the unicorn bid good-bye to its new friends. Brittany Myerson, aged four, was chewing on the tail of her stuffed poodle.

And I, Astrid Llewelyn, aged sixteen, just wanted the brats to go to sleep. "I think that's enough for tonight, huh, girls?"

"No!" They shrieked in unison.

I sighed and returned to the saccharine story. I usually like babysitting, but taking care of the Myerson girls is intolerable. Always with the unicorns in this house. Each kid has a half dozen plush or plastic horned beasts lying piled on her bed, and Bethany's bedroom is even ringed with a wallpaper border of unicorn heads with shimmering eyes and horns that glow in the dark.

I could hear Lilith now: *Well, kiddo, at least it means they've been decapitated.*

My friend Kaitlyn has a mortal fear of clowns. Her mom took her to Ringling Brothers circus in her formative years, and this white-painted *thing* with a huge blue wig and a bulbous, blinking red light for a nose scared the crap out of her. She won't even go to the state fair, and we're in high school. Parents can really scar a kid with stunts like that.

Sometimes I wondered if my mother, Lilith, understood the kind of damage she was inflicting on me with all her delusional stories about bloodthirsty unicorns. When I was six, and all my friends wanted to play unicorns and run around the playground on imaginary horned mounts named Rainbow and Starlight and Moonbeam, do you think I was the most popular kid in school?

I briefly considered giving the Myerson kids the same lecture I'd given the other first graders on the playground:

Unicorns are man-eating monsters. They don't have wings,

they aren't lavender or sparkly, and you could never catch one to ride without its goring you through the sternum. And even if it somehow managed to miss your major arteries—and it never misses—you'd still die from the deadly poison in its horn. But don't worry. My great-great-great-great-great-aunt Clothilde killed the last one a hundred and fifty years ago.

Except now I guessed it would be more like a hundred and sixty. How time doth fly in a unicorn-free world. Also, now I no longer believed my mom's horror stories.

After several more pages of cotton-candy torture, the book ended and I firmly tucked Bethany and Brittany into bed. At last. Lulled into soporific splendor by the lackluster adventures of Sparkle the Unicorn and his merry band of Ritalin dependents, the girls soon drifted into the Land of Nod.

Good riddance.

I wished I could forget my early indoctrination and act sanguine about these namby-pamby unicorn stories. But one-horned beasts of any stripe still gave me the willies.

My mother considers herself a militant purist. She believes that this so-called revisionist unicorn history is a disgrace to the sacrifice of our ancestors. That we should be honoring their memories by promoting the truth about these vicious beasts.

These vicious, *extinct* beasts, I reminded her whenever I was feeling particularly cheeky. Usually, I didn't deign to answer at all. I'd long ago learned that indulging her fantasies meant chaining myself to her lifestyle.

I set up my trusty baby monitor, closed the bedroom door, and called Brandt on the cell phone Lilith finally got me last winter. "They're asleep. You can come over now, but I have to meet you outside."

This was more for my protection than out of consideration for the slumbering children. First of all, I don't know how much more I could take of the unicorn-inspired decor. Their toys were all over the house. Second, Brandt and a couch—or worse, an empty master bedroom—were a very bad combo. He morphed from vaguely risqué fling to bad-boy octopus man whenever he was in the vicinity of any marginally promising flat surface.

I was far less interested in protecting my virtue than I was in not giving it up to a boy who couldn't pass intermediate French.

But despite his problems with the Gallic tongue, Brandt was not lacking in other characteristics prized by that culture. Like the kissing kind. A few minutes later, I was sitting on the front porch of the Myersons' house, waiting for him to arrive and wondering what would happen when he did. The forest smelled wet and moldy tonight, and someone in the neighborhood must have had a fireplace going. In the gloom beyond the oblong bit of lawn illuminated by the house lights, I watched the trees swaying in the night breeze. They flashed the white undersides of leaves at me, then the dark tops, moving in a strange, solemn rhythm beyond my comprehension. I stared at them for a while, hypnotized, then suddenly shivered. When you sit in the only lighted spot in an area, you can't help but think something is watching you—trees, little night critters, ravenous insects swarming just beyond the reach of your eyes.

The hairs rose on the back of my neck. Something *was* watching me. I glanced up at the bedroom window, half expecting the pale face of one of the Myerson girls to be pressed up against the glass, despite the lack of noises coming from the baby monitor. But no one was there. Still, the fear didn't dissipate. I turned my attention to the fringe of woods, as if I'd be able to see little cartoon eyes blinking out at me from the darkness.

Silly Astrid. No more unicorn stories before bedtime, I thought in my best impression of Lilith. She was probably at home reading up on unicorns in one of her many rotting old bestiaries. It's her favorite hobby, but she considers it serious research.

In the eyes of her family and the university discipline department that pulled her academic funding around the time she got knocked up with me, my mom is . . . eccentric. Unbalanced. They mean *nuts.* By the time I was born, it was bye-bye Ph.D., hello career of short-lived stints in every field from medical transcription to window washing. My uncle—her brother—always said my mom had so much *potential.* Too bad about the crazy.

Was my mom really bitter that she hadn't hunted unicorns, or was it just that she was a single mom in a series of dead-end jobs whose biggest hobby was studying a field of cryptozoology that even the biggest Loch Ness Monster nuts wouldn't consider valid?

Extinct, venomous, killer unicorns. As *eccentricities* go, it was rather disappointing. A pathology that she'd—I don't know, dated Elvis—would have been far more bragworthy and less likely to get weird looks at cocktail parties. Not much glory involved in spouting off about great hunts of the past generation or bragging about how you could trace your ancestors back to pre-Christian military overlords. If you're going to imagine that unicorns are real, wouldn't it be better if they were also still around?

One could make the argument that the reason she'd decided her unicorns were extinct was so she wouldn't be saddled with the burden of actually producing one and proving she's right. I know I'm much happier that she believes in extinct unicorns instead of in live ones. As it was, most of our extended family ignored her. As Uncle John says, as long as she doesn't actually *see* unicorns, keeps her job, and never puts her only child in bodily danger, it doesn't count as psychosis. And he would know, since he's a doctor. Well, an orthodontist, but it counts.

I shivered again. All these unicorn thoughts were doing nothing to put me at ease.

A few moments later, Brandt showed up and I shook it off. He ambled up the walk, his arms full of a ratty tartan blanket he'd retrieved from the backseat of his car. "Hey, ya," he called. "I thought we could go sit in the woods."

Sit? I wondered if he'd washed the spread since breaking up with his last girlfriend, with whom, rumor had it, he did things that are illegal in fourteen states. "How about we just hang out on the porch? We shouldn't get too far from the house." I said by way of an excuse, "What if the girls wake up?"

"We won't go far. Besides, you've got that walkie-talkie thing." He slung his arm around my shoulders and steered me toward the backyard, which, like most of the homes in the development, abutted one corner of a state park. The trees flashed white and dark in greeting. "Come on—I'll protect you from the monsters."

I rolled my eyes. Yeah, but who would protect me from Brandt? Tall, with killer blue eyes and sandy blond hair, Brandt Ellison had half the girls in my class swooning. And about a month and a half ago, he'd turned that devastating grin of his in my direction. It would have been social suicide to turn down an opportunity like that. I'd have been forever branded a frigid snob or a lesbian—neither of which was a label I had any strong desire to bear. So I went out with him. Current count held Brandt and me at three trips to Starbucks, fifteen shared cafeteria lunches, a movie, a party, and one pizza and video night.

And now, approaching day forty of the Brandt-and-Astrid Watch, my friends had changed their interrogation script from "Have you done it yet?" to "Aren't you *ever* going to do it?" Kaitlyn told me that I should just get it over with. That my lingering chastity was hampering all kinds of upward mobility. That if I didn't pop my cherry soon, people would start to think I was saving it for something.

Which I wasn't. There was nothing to save it for—not anymore. As previously noted, unicorns are extinct. I wondered if that line would work on my mom, whose discussion of "my virtue" could get downright medieval. Most people are aware of the mystical connection between virgins and unicorns. It's been a popular subject in tapestries and paintings for thousands of years.

My mother, though, refers to these as "historical documents." For all I knew, maybe she had an antique chastity belt hiding in her collection of historical volumes and other doodads. Our itsy-bitsy apartment over Uncle John's garage was filled with her ancient junk.

I didn't necessarily believe Kaitlyn, by the way. My cousin, Philippa, had been one of the most popular girls in our high school, and we'd pinky sworn when we were kids that we'd tell each other every base we passed. Phil graduated last year and headed off to college on her plush athletic scholarship without any kind of horizontal action having taken place. Last I spoke to her, the count still put me at second base, Phil flirting with light third.

Phil never worried that she was weird for not having sex or for laughing at boys who asked her to. Of course, she paddled in the non-batty end of the Llewelyn family gene pool. Phil was also a dentist's daughter and a big volleyball star, so naturally she ranked higher on the popularity scale than an impoverished sophomore whose major accomplishment to date was racking up the most hospital volunteer hours per semester for two years running.

Brandt spread the blanket on a bed of leaves a few tree rows away from the backyard—far enough in to provide decent cover but close enough to the Myersons' that the yellow porch lights filtered in through the limbs. "There." He plopped down and patted the spot beside him. "Still within screaming distance."

I smiled uneasily, hoping he referred to the possibility of Bethany or Brittany having nightmares, and joined him. Within thirty seconds, he was kissing me. Open mouth. With tongue.

Okay, that sounds bad. But it's not like that, really. I wouldn't say Brandt was actively pressuring me. Whenever we were making out and I removed his hand from the inside of the waistband of my panties, he kept it removed for the duration of the session, and he never made any of those *Come on baby, it will feel so good* or *you know you want it* or *but all the other kids are doing it* noises like the guys in those date rape videos they had us watch in Current Issues, which was PC-speak for Sex Ed. However, he always carried condoms in his pocket—another trick from Current Issues—and I knew, I just *knew*, that in about eight minutes he was going to try to undo the buttons on my jeans.

Again, Brandt surprised me, crossing that barrier in under five. "Stop it," I said gently, moving his hand to a safer zone. Usually, if I distract him by letting him get to second base, he forgets all about areas south of my belly button.

But it didn't work this time. He backed off. "No offense," he said, not meeting my eyes, "but exactly how long is this going to take?"

I don't know if it's possible to follow "no offense" with something that doesn't offend. "'How long is *this* going to take?' What do you mean by *this*?" I snapped.

He turned away, not that I could see his face very well in the dark, and ran his hand through his hair in frustration. "That's not what I mean, Astrid. I like you a lot."

"And I like you," I replied, reaching for his hand. "I'm just not ready for that."

"How do you know unless you let me touch you?"

"I mean, I'm not ready for—*that*—even."

He let out a sound halfway between a groan and a snort and fell back against the ground. This was the point in the videos where the boys talked about how much pain they were in because the girls were saying no. This was the point where Kaitlyn says that if a girl doesn't put out, she should at least give the guy a hand job.

But I didn't offer and Brandt wasn't complaining, just lying there playing with the end of my blond braid, which was long enough to brush the blanket when I was propped up on my elbows.

What did I really know about him? I knew he wanted to get a swimming scholarship to college and that he had three older brothers and that his favorite pizza topping was barbecued chicken and that he didn't read books, not even Harry Potter.

(Lilith wouldn't let me read Harry Potter because there was a whole thing in there about drinking unicorn blood that she said was inappropriate. I sneaked Kaitlyn's copy and the unicorn bit is maybe a paragraph or so of the entire novel. Whatever.)

Were these the sort of things that I wanted to base an intimate relationship on? Barbecued chicken pizza and the butterfly stroke? He'd never even asked me why I spent so many hours at the hospital. Never asked me what I wanted to do in college.

On the other hand, the prom was a month from now, and if Brandt took me, I'd be one of the few sophomores at the dance. I could deal with *that* variety of abnormal. Going to prom would be . . . something. Maybe something worth letting him put his hands inside my pants for.

In the woods, the darkness shifted.

"Did you see that?" I asked, sitting up straight. I *knew* there'd been something out there.

The braid popped out of Brandt's fingertips. "No. What?"

"There's something moving in there." I could see it. I could . . . *feel it.* Like earlier, on the porch, only more so. So much more so. "What do you think it is?"

He shrugged. "A deer."

Of course. It was just the size for a deer, too. So then why was I standing up and striding off the blanket and into the trees? I'd seen plenty of deer.

"Astrid! Where are you going?"

If it were a deer, then Brandt's whining and my shuffling through the carpet of fallen leaves would have scared it off. Heck, almost any wild animal would have been leery of all that noise. But there it was, just a few trees over. Standing, frozen, as if waiting. I stepped into the tiny clearing, and the creature emerged from the shadows.

And, no, it was not a deer.

Not a goat, either, though that would be the closest term I could use to describe the way it looked. A goat, or maybe some sort of small antelope. Its fur was white and shaggy and reminded me a bit of the hair on a llama. Its back was about thigh high, and its head and neck hovered somewhere near my waist. Of course, the horn made the creature look much bigger. Protruding in a straight line from the center of its forehead, it was easily half the length of my arm, and twisted like a screw.

Suddenly, I couldn't breathe. My mother's psychosis was not only genetic, it had uniformity of type as well.

I was seeing *unicorns.*

The unicorn looked up at me with eyes as blue as a Siamese cat's, and let out a little bleat that sounded nothing whatsoever like fairy bells. It stepped forward cautiously. This was no hallucination. I prepared to be rammed through the heart, and wondered idly if the poison was very fast acting.

Now I wished I'd paid attention to Lilith all those years. Of course, if I had, I'd simply think that unicorns didn't exist *anymore*, rather than that Mom was nuts and they'd never existed at all.

The unicorn was only a few inches away from me now. I couldn't look away. But then it bent one leg and swept into what looked for all the world like a low, very formal bow. The tip of its horn missed my body by millimeters in its semicircular trip to the ground.

I stood stock-still for several seconds, but the unicorn didn't appear to be preparing for the death blow. Maybe I could just back out of the clearing slowly. But as soon as I lifted my foot from the ground, the unicorn looked up.

"Nice goat," I said softly. "Gooooood goat. Stay . . ." I took a step. The unicorn came forward and pushed its head under my hand like some sort of horned golden retriever waiting to be scratched behind the ears.

Terrified of angering it, I scratched. The unicorn bleated in ecstasy. Lilith had never once mentioned this. Why wasn't I being killed on the spot?

"Astrid? You okay?"

The unicorn stiffened, and the noises it was making turned into menacing growls. Did Brandt see what I saw?

"Fine, Brandt. Just, um, stay where you are, okay?" The unicorn trembled with rage. Its lips curled in a snarl, revealing pointed white teeth.

"Christ, Astrid, what is that thing?" Brandt broke into the clearing.

With the shrieking howl of a bloodthirsty beast, the unicorn charged straight at him.

2

Wherein Astrid Is Called to Duty

I watched in horror as Brandt fell backward. I think I even screamed. The unicorn, ready for a second attack, froze, then promptly reared and took off, cloven hooves scattering the fallen leaves as it went.

Brandt was gulping and squealing, clasping his leg as blood gushed out in a macabre little fountain from the puncture wound the unicorn had left in his thigh. My first aid training told me this meant the unicorn had ruptured Brandt's femoral artery. And it soon became clear that the blood loss was the least of our worries.

Brandt's skin became pallid, and his blood vessels stood out in a violent violet red, protruding so far from his body that they looked almost like the ridges on corduroy. His eyeballs drained of color, and from the sounds he was making as he tried to breathe, I guessed his throat was closing up. I had no idea what these symptoms meant. Not anaphylactic shock, as there was no way he'd come in contact with a unicorn before. Septic shock would reduce the blood flow as his heart shut down, but if anything it seemed as if Brandt was suffering from tachycardia. I could almost hear his pulse pounding from a foot away.

Yep, the horn poison was fast acting, all right. And what could 911 do to counteract alicorn venom?

I called my mom. "Lilith," I said, cradling the phone against my ear as I tied an arm of my sweater in a tourniquet around Brandt's leg and weighed how best to break the news. She hated when I teased her.

"Astrid, we've talked about how you're only supposed to use your phone for emergencies. Our budget's tight." Lilith sounded bored. But I was about to feed her delusion for the first time in ten years. Uncle John would be *so* disappointed in me.

"This guy got gored by a unicorn and he's turning purple."

Brandt let out a muffled moan. His tongue had swelled and his skin was clammy to the touch. I clearly needed to brush up on my diagnostics, because I hadn't the slightest clue what to do next. Keep his airways clear. Stop the bleeding. But cleanse the poison? Way too late.

"What?" Lilith seemed to wake up on the other end. Little wonder. She'd probably been waiting her whole life for this moment.

"A unicorn," I repeated. "Mom, come quick. He might die." As soon as I gave her the directions and hung up, I dialed 911 and told them to get a paramedic over here, stat. And then I sat there and stared at Brandt. I stroked his hand and made soothing noises. I made sure he was comfortable there on the ground and that the tourniquet was tight. I marveled how quickly I'd stopped thinking of him as "boyfriend" and started to picture him only as "patient."

Blood began to soak through my sweater and pool in the

leaves. It was a really nice sweater, too. Angora blend, a gift from Phil. Not that it mattered if it could save his life. But I doubted it would be the blood loss that did him in. I looked at his face and tried not to be sick. I'd kissed that face. I'd seen it across the lunch table for more than a month. But now I barely recognized it. Alicorn venom was clearly some nasty stuff. Either that or my blossoming madness had supplied visions far worse than any I'd found in diagnostics illustrations.

"Hang on, Brandt." I forced myself to stick by his side, though more than anything I wanted to—in order—vomit in the leaves, run for the hills, and dump a whole carton of stain remover on my sweater. Why couldn't I do this? I wanted to be a doctor, for goodness sake! I'd seen much worse as a candy striper at the hospital.

But never someone I knew; never someone I was debating letting get to third base; and, most of all, never a victim of my childhood terror, the unicorn.

Why hadn't it attacked me? And where was it now? I thought about the baby monitor, back on the blanket. Should I run and get it? Could I leave Brandt alone?

"I'll be right back, okay?"

But he grabbed me with a bloody hand, choked out something unintelligible, and stared at me wide-eyed. I sank back to my knees. The kids should be fine. The door was closed. As long as they didn't wander outside . . . Oh, God, please don't let them wander outside!

At long last, I heard my mother calling from the edge of the woods. She strode through the trees, and I saw that she'd brought with her this gorgeous, golden, blown-glass vial that has been sitting in a place of honor in our den for as long as I

15

can remember. She'd always claimed that she got it in the same spot where she met my de facto sperm donor—I mean, my father—and that it contained something very precious.

I'd never wanted to know what exactly she found so precious about a dirty glass she procured during an anonymous one-night stand that had cost her a scholarship and a career. My friends wonder why I'm not sleeping around? Let's just say I *live* with my cautionary tale.

I waved her over, and she took in the scene at once: my tousled hair and swollen lips; the rumpled blanket a few yards away; and most of all, Brandt, who was by this time the color of rotten meat and quaking with odd spasms. She gave me a look that clearly said *we'll talk later*, brushed me aside, knelt, and brandished the vial over him like a magician performing a trick.

Suffice it to say, the stuff in the vial had dried out, but she poured some lukewarm Coke—of all things—inside, swished it around, and dumped most of the contents down Brandt's throat.

As soon as he stopped convulsing, which was relatively quickly, Brandt grabbed Lilith's hand. "What did you give me, you psycho?"

Lilith responded by shaking the rest of the mixture onto his wound, which began to close immediately. Brandt took one look at that and started screaming, which seemed a bit odd to me, given the fact that the danger was over. *Now* he screamed? He must not have gotten a good look at his corduroyed face. I had, and, let me tell you—totally screamworthy. Plus, he was writhing so much that I could barely observe the effects of the Coke on his leg.

"That's it," Lilith said with a shrug. "God help us if it attacks again." She blew her shaggy bangs out of her face and looked at me, completely ignoring Brandt's shrieks and the fact that lights were turning on all over the neighborhood. I could only imagine what Bethany and Brittany were thinking. "Do you know where it is now, Astrid?"

I looked at Lilith, incredulous. "It ran off."

"I know," she said, clearly annoyed. "Where is it *now*?"

As if I would somehow know!

Pretty soon after that, the police and EMT came, and Lilith fed them some story about a rabid goat roaming the woods that had attacked Brandt and me. See? She's usually quite lucid. And, probably thanks to the effect her theories had on her thesis adviser, she liked to keep this unicorn stuff in the family. Otherwise, I'm sure Uncle John would have had her committed long ago.

I backed her up of course (what, you think I'm going to say "unicorn" to cops?), and Brandt seemed a bit foggy on the details. According to the paramedic, the wound looked way too small to have resulted in so much blood loss, but Brandt might need a transfusion, judging by his sluggish pulse and low blood pressure. Considering the way his veins had been looking before my mom showed up—and I think I saw practically every one—I thought that might be a good idea.

The Myersons returned home about that time to discover their driveway overrun with every parent's worst nightmare: cars with flashing lights. Though appalled that all this happened in their backyard, they seemed far more relieved to learn that their children had come through unscathed than upset that I'd left Brittany and Bethany alone in the house while my boyfriend came over.

They were also too distraught by the situation to remember to pay me, but I figured I shouldn't push my luck.

Of course, the fun part of my evening was just beginning. First, I had to wrestle the car keys off my mother, who was entirely too excited to drive. The whole way home, I was treated to a monologue about how this discovery would be the end of all our problems, would make people believe in her research at last; speculation about where in the world this pocket of surviving unicorns could have been hiding for the past hundred years—the Canadian Rockies?—and what could have made this particular unicorn wander out now; and of course, an earful on the merits of *waiting*.

The weekend was more of the same. My mother went back to the forest near the Myersons' house on three separate occasions, twice during the day and once at night, searching for more evidence that Brandt and I had indeed seen a unicorn. Nothing. No spoor, no tracks, no tiny mutilated animals that would have indicated that a poisonous, killer beast had moved into the neighborhood. I stayed indoors and waited for the police to call and tell me they'd found a wandering madwoman in the woods. They never called me, but, then again, neither did Brandt, and the one time I phoned *him*, his mother informed me that he wasn't home. He wasn't at the hospital, either—I checked. Where else would you go the day after you almost died?

In between, I was a captive audience for Lilith's lectures on the history of our illustrious family, starting from when Alexander the Great was nine years old and tamed the fearsome karkadann, Bucephalus. Though the history books teach that Bucephalus was Alexander's trusty warhorse, according to my mom—and several ancient Alexander biographers whose sources were, shall we say, *extremely* suspect—the beast that the great king rode when he conquered half the world was actually a giant, man-eating Persian species of unicorn called a karkadann.

In the accounts my mother read me, the stable keepers in Alexander's father's palace were planning on having the "horse" destroyed because he was *anthrophagos*, which is Greek for "he breakfasted on the stable boy"—or something like that. His name, Bucephalus, was another clue: it meant "ox head"— apparently, they couldn't figure out what a horse was doing with a horn. Alexander, not even a teenager yet, was the only person who could approach the monster, the only one who could tame him. And thus, Bucephalus was spared, and a legendary partnership born.

Between Bucephalus's dietary proclivities, venomous horn, and sharp fangs and Alexander's military strategy and prowess with a sword, the two of them cut quite a swath through the Middle East back in the day, conquering every civilization they came across, taking over half the known world. According to my history teacher, the horse died somewhere in what is now Pakistan, where Alexander named a city after him, then went home for good.

According to my *mother*, Bucephalus vanished into the Himalayas, and Alexander, distraught, found he no longer wielded the power that proximity to the unicorn had given him all his life.

So basically, everything was business as usual in my own personal nuthouse until school on Monday, when Brandt finally put together all of the details of the evening. Or at least enough of them to know that we'd forced him to drink something and that I'd called my mom *before* I dialed 911. His revenge was swift and terrible, and I found myself boyfriendless and humiliated before first period was over.

By lunchtime, even Kaitlyn was giving me a wide berth. "Is it true?" she asked, her voice muffled by the bathroom stall door. I was hiding in the girls' room until I could be sure that my face had gone from utter-mortification magenta to a more reasonable I've-been-dumped mauve.

I sniffled once or twice and availed myself of another square of toilet paper. I still hadn't determined if I was most upset by the public breakup, the fact that I might have inherited mental instability, or the possibility that my mom was actually right.

"It depends on what he's saying." For instance, if he was saying that he'd been attacked and poisoned by a miniature unicorn and then magically cured with the final dregs of a mystical panacea known as the Remedy—and everything else my mom had been blabbing about all weekend—then yeah. Pretty much true.

"Brandt's telling everyone you slipped him drugs and sicced a rabid goat on him, then you and your mom orchestrated a massive cover-up when the police came."

"That's a lie!" I lied. Okay, it was about 80 percent true, though not in that order and definitely not with that intent.

"But then what *did* happen?"

I sighed. Maybe it would have been easier to let him die. Not too Hippocratic oathy of me, but fewer witnesses meant so much less explaining. "Like I told the police, we were in the woods, and this crazy . . . thing came out of nowhere, gored Brandt, then ran off."

"But then what was your mom doing there? And why is there

that weird mark on his leg?"

"What mark?"

Kaitlyn hesitated. I pictured her on the other side of the door, tugging on the hair near her left temple the way she always does when she's upset. "He was showing everyone in PE. There's this weird . . . thing there. He says it's probably a side effect from the drugs you gave him. He's having it removed by a dermatologist next week."

I opened the door and met her face. "What kind of weird thing?"

Kaitlyn backed up a few feet, and now that I could see her eyes, I realized that she was much more freaked out than she'd sounded.

"Kaitlyn? What weird thing?"

She gestured weakly at her leg. "This weird . . . red thing. Like dark red. It wasn't like a cut at all. Looked kind of like a bruise, but shiny. Like a bruise and a boil. Shaped like a figure eight. It was weird. And, Astrid, that's not all."

My throat hitched.

"I didn't want to say anything in the gym, but"—she checked to see if there was anyone else in the stalls—"he was talking about that bottle. The pretty yellow one from your den?"

Busted. And I should work on my poker face, too. Kaitlyn's eyes got very wide. "Oh, God, Astrid, you *did* drug him, didn't you?"

We saved his life is what we did. "Kaitlyn, I'm going to tell you something, and you aren't going to believe me, but—"

She shook her head and backed up until her butt hit the sinks. "No. I don't want to know. I will not be your accomplice."

"*My accomplice?* Kaitlyn—"

But it was too late. And if I couldn't count on my best friend, you can probably figure out how the rest of the student body reacted. Forget about prom, forget about upward social mobility, forget about losing my virginity to anyone, whether he'd passed French or not. I might as well have gone crazy, judging by my new status as a social pariah. And it's not as if the Myersons wanted to hire me again. After all, I was the girl who hung out with rabid goats.

Lilith, on the other hand, was beyond thrilled. She spent every spare second on the computer in the kitchen, e-mailing back and forth with some other nut job she'd found on the Internet while googling for information about what had happened and what it meant for people like us.

Specifically, girls like me. Unicorn hunters.

This is my mom's story: Lilith and I—our whole family—come from a long line of women who can catch and kill unicorns. Well, my mother can't do it anymore. Apparently you have to be a virgin. No one knows how a unicorn can tell. In fact, no one knows anything about what makes us especially equipped to kill unicorns, despite my mom's intense research into the subject. And yet, she believes it. She has ever since she was a grad student and came back from a research trip to Europe knocked up with me, toting that bottle, and raving about killer unicorns and glorious destinies. Everyone thought she'd had a nervous breakdown. But it may actually be true after all. My mother's psychosis has come to life in full, man-eating Technicolor. Who'd have thunk?

"Close call there, wasn't it, honey?" my mother said to me, looking up from her beat-up monitor as I researched "color drained from eyeballs" and "protruding veins" in our copy of

The Merck Manual. I'd already come up blank on "double ring bruises."

"If that zhi hadn't come along—" Lilith began, ecstatic.

"That what?"

"Cornelius says that's the kind of unicorn you saw. A zhi."

Super. Now there was more than one kind. Speaking of . . . "Hey, is there any news from the cops about catching it?"

She shook her head. "Don't be so naïve, Astrid. You think they can *catch* it?" That's one of her favorite tidbits: *Only unicorn hunters can catch a unicorn, blah, blah, blah.* She waved a sheaf of papers in the air. "And what's more, you think it's the only one out there? I have over fifty reports. And that's just in the Americas. They say the problem is much more widespread in Europe and Asia."

They say? I wondered who *they* might be.

"Honey, that thing was not an isolated incident. It's a Reemergence." She leaned over and stirred the pot of canned soup on our tiny, two-burner stove.

"What happened to them being extinct?" I liked that fantasy *so* much better. In fact, I liked it better when unicorns were a fantasy, period.

"We're trying to figure that out." She smiled. "And that's where you come in."

"You want me to research extinction?" I asked hopefully.

"No, baby. I want you to hunt them back into it. Oh wow, we're so lucky this happened when it did."

"We are?"

She gave me a look of rebuke. "Think about it: with you out in the woods . . . with that boy . . . at night . . . and a blanket . . . Who knows? If the zhi hadn't stopped you, you wouldn't have been able to hunt!"

My jaw dropped. "I wasn't going to do—"

"I'm telling Cornelius all about it."

"Mom! Eww, gross! Can you *not* share the non-details of my non-sex life with some weirdo you met on the Internet? I'm pretty sure I read an article about how that's a bad idea."

"Oh, please, honey. He's practically family."

"Yeah, if you go back three thousand years," I muttered, slammed the book shut, and stormed out of the kitchen. *Merck* was so not helpful. In the den, my mom had some dusty, leather-bound antique medical guides that discussed alicorn—the "technical" (ick) name for a unicorn horn after it's been relieved of its unicorn—and the Remedy, but I didn't buy their quackery. I'd read them when I was about twelve, and they said—among other bits of ridiculousness that had gotten me laughed out of sixth-grade science class—that sperm had tiny men living inside them, that cancer was caused by an imbalance of the "humours," and that women got their periods due to demonic possession.

Is it any wonder I tried to stay well away from Lilith's favorite topic? It sounded insane in the twenty-first century. I'm as open to alternative medicine as the next person, but acupuncture and alicorn alchemy aren't even in the same universe. Of course, after the Mad Goat Incident, I could hardly avoid it. Mom was positively giddy about the prospects. Up until now, all she could do was talk about family history. She could be proud of our heritage, but little more. It was a skill set without a practical, real-world application. We were—dare I say it?—normal.

I think I left *normal* back in the woods that night. Now, as far as my mom was concerned, I was a hunter in training. Never mind that I didn't even like squashing bugs.

Maybe I would do some research on animal populations. It was impossible that unicorns could just *reappear*, wasn't it? Even if there had been a few specimens that survived extinction in the wilds of Africa or in Tibet, they couldn't just show up in the woods outside a Seattle suburb. Right? Lilith could never even point to a skeleton of one, despite the claims she made that there were unicorn horns in the treasuries of every monarchy in the world.

There was another huge pile of papers on our coffee table. My mom's knowledge about unicorns had quadrupled in the last few days. Now I knew, thanks to her endless lectures, that there were five species of unicorns—zhi, kirin, re'em, einhorn, and karkadann—though, according to all these reports, only the first three had "reemerged." The zhi was apparently the smallest kind. I couldn't imagine trying to deal with anything bigger. My mother said a karkadann was the size of an elephant.

I stared out the window and across the lawn, to where my aunt and uncle were just sitting down to dinner in the big house. My uncle's family had a breakfast nook and a formal dining room, but our garage apartment couldn't fit more than a card table stuffed into the corner, with two mismatched chairs on the accessible sides.

Apparently, now that they were empty nesters, my aunt and uncle were even eating dinner in the breakfast nook. They looked lonely, and I understood. I missed Phil, too. Before she'd gone off to college, we used to study together in the evenings. Phil's bedroom was almost as big as our whole apartment, and it had matching furniture and an enormous desk that she hardly ever used. Sometimes I wondered what her parents would say if

I asked to study in Phil's room now.

Lilith hadn't told my aunt and uncle about the Mad Goat Incident, which was just as well. I'd hate to see Uncle John start giving me the looks he reserved for his sister. He might even tell Phil that I, too, had gone insane.

Twenty minutes later, Lilith skipped into the room, eyes alight. "Honey, I have amazing news. The Cloisters of Ctesias has been reopened."

"Um, yay? What in the world is a cloister?"

She grabbed my hands and danced me around in a circle. "It's an ancient training ground in Rome for unicorn hunters. You're going to be a hunter, baby!"

"No!" I pulled back and crossed my arms.

Lilith's face turned hard. "What, young lady?"

I backpedaled. "I mean, I can't." *Think*. "I have school. I don't have a passport. I don't speak Italian."

She waved her hand in the air. "Details. We'll get you a passport, and we can arrange for you to take your exams early. You're a smart girl—you'll be fine."

No. She couldn't send me away to some crazy unicorn boot camp. She couldn't enlist me just like that. Didn't I have any rights? I never wanted to see another unicorn again, and here she was trying to turn me into someone who regularly engaged with them. *Killed* them.

She grabbed my arms again, this time with a firmer grip. Her eyes were frighteningly lucid and, even more frighteningly, filled with intensity. "Think of it, Astrid! Rome! The Eternal City!" She spun me around again.

I couldn't think of that. I was too busy trying to decide between fight and flight. Could I run away? But where would that leave me? I was sixteen, without a high school diploma. That was no way to avoid my mother's fate. Could I throw myself on the mercy of Uncle John? He'd never let her send me away like that. He could fight for custody. He'd do that for me, right?

But as soon as the thought sprung into my head, I pushed it away. Tell authorities about my mom? What would they do to her if I did? Tell them about unicorns? Would it do any good? After all, I'd seen one, and Lilith had all those reports. Maybe everyone knew about the Reemergence, too. Maybe they'd side with her.

Perhaps there was another way. "And who's going to pay for it?" I asked, struggling to keep my voice as calm as possible. "Not Uncle John, that's for sure."

"That's the best part. It's all sponsored. It's all free. An opportunity like this—Astrid, it's all I've ever wanted for you."

I stopped her from turning me into a human Maypole. "You *wanted* these monsters to come back?"

She had the decency to look sheepish. "Well, I wanted you to be able to claim your birthright. In a way I never could."

Poor Lilith. She *did* want it. All my life, people had thought she was wrong, crazy—even her own daughter. But now I'd seen the truth with my own eyes. Maybe I owed her for those years of derision. Maybe I owed her because no matter how much I'd resented the way we lived, I'd always loved her. She was my mother.

And she'd parried every argument I'd made, like always. She was a grown-up. No matter what bad decision she made, I had to live with it. The unicorns had eclipsed every aspect of her life—why wouldn't they do so to mine as well?

Besides, it wasn't as if I had some packed social schedule to keep. Or a crazy desire to spend another hour in Current Issues, while my ex-boyfriend and ex–best friend giggled about how I was both crazy and a prude.

Better to hunt the mad goat than to let it attack any more of my boyfriends.

3

Wherein Astrid Is Cloistered

L ILITH DID ALL THE packing, which made sense, as she'd also done the bulk of the shopping. If I'd been in charge of my Rome wardrobe, it would have included more capri pants and kicky dresses, like Audrey Hepburn wore in *Roman Holiday*. Lilith, however, packed utilitarian wear—cargo pants made of space-age microfiber that would move the way I did and featured extra loops and pockets for carrying knives, spare bowstrings, sights, and arrow tips. To judge by Lilith's choices, my duties seemed to involve mostly the skinning of dead animals and setting of traps.

Watching my mother drool at the windows of various gun and sporting-goods stores gave me the creeps, but I didn't really start getting scared until I learned that the unicorn hunting scholarship only provided ticket money for the hunter herself, not for the hunter's mother. I would be leaving the country on my own. Lilith's reaction moved swiftly from devastated to determined. All I could think about was every news story I'd ever heard about kidnappers. Was it possible that these people were using my mom's obsession as a way to get me in their clutches?

I threatened to tell Uncle John about this Roman scheme. "I can't go there alone. We don't know anything about these people!"

"Don't you dare, Astrid," my mom said, folding up another top and placing it in my suitcase. I was perched on the edge of the coffee table and my mom was standing over the pull-out couch where I slept. "I raised you to be independent and self-reliant. You're certainly old enough to get on a plane by yourself."

"And put myself in the hands of total strangers?"

She snapped the lid shut. "What do you take me for? Of course I checked out their stories. I am a researcher, you know. They are who they say they are, and their stories are verifiable. You have nothing to fear. I wouldn't put my daughter in any danger."

"Any danger!" I cried. "What do you call hunting unicorns? Big, sharp horns; fangs . . ." And those were just the goat-sized ones.

"I call it your birthright." Lilith stood tall. "Honey, I know you've been down ever since that stupid boy broke up with you, but this is about more than a prom date. Don't you realize that? You have a destiny. Most people would kill for something like that."

If Lilith and this Cornelius guy had their way with me at this boot camp, I *was* going to kill.

"Six generations ago, our ancestor Clothilde gave her life to protect people from the karkadann. Now you have a chance to—"

"Do the same?" I crossed my arms. "Forgive me if enforced

lifelong celibacy and possible death by dismemberment and poisoning don't exactly get me excited."

"How about being part of something ancient and important, something that belongs only to you?"

And whatever other abnormally unsexed young women they find with the proper bloodlines. "I'm not a hunter, mom. I'm not a killer."

"I know that, sweetie," she said, "but you are a healer." Her eyes practically glowed. "You want to be a doctor, Astrid? Well, think about this: you could help find the secret to the Remedy. You could help cure every disease the world has ever known."

I wanted to shout back that the Remedy was a myth, but how could I? I'd seen what happened to Brandt with my own eyes. Whatever that stuff was, it cured alicorn poisoning at the very least.

Alicorn poisoning was real, too. It was a nightmare come true. "But do I have to hunt to do that? Isn't there, like, a research wing?"

She put her hands on her hips and stared me down. "You have a role to play in this. A vital role. Are you going to shirk it, just because you'd rather have a desk job?"

I swallowed but couldn't think of an answer. Lilith stepped forward and folded me in her arms. I buried my face in her sweater and breathed deeply. She smelled like mothballs and lavender, like the damp that always permeated our apartment, like chicken broth and wool and old books and home. I'd never been away from her for more than a night. And now she wanted me to go halfway across the world.

Her embrace tightened so that I could hardly breathe. "I'm so proud of you, sweetheart. I'm so excited for you," she whispered

31

into my hair. "Go to Rome and train to be a hunter, Astrid. You just might save the world."

Lilith—my mother—believes in magic. She believes in unicorns and panaceas and destiny. She's held that belief despite every bit of ridicule she's had to endure, despite every consequence she's suffered. It's as if she willed these monsters into existence.

But now I'm the one paying the price.

I spent the first of three flights memorizing entries in an Italian phrase book and the second trying to psych myself up about this adventure. Kaitlyn and the others could snub me as much as they wanted; *they* weren't about to go live in Italy! Land of midnight cappuccinos in candlelit piazzas, of gorgeous young Italian guys swooping around on little Vespa motorbikes offering rides and fruity gelatos, of swank beach resorts and sprawling vineyards. I'd put in my hours doing unicorn target practice and dedicate every spare second to living la dolce vita. All this Brandt stuff was just so . . . *high school*. A girl who summers in Rome could hardly be concerned with such minutiae, right?

But my pep talk didn't work, partially because my mother had packed away a little brochure for me to read to help me "acclimate" to life at the Cloisters. On the third flight, bored by language studies and tired of calculating my risk of deep-vein thrombosis from sitting in the cramped plane seats, I decided to take a peek.

"So, you want to be a unicorn hunter," I mumbled, and opened the brochure. The businessman seated beside me gave me an odd look, and I ducked my head as far behind the pages as it could go. He shook out his paper and went back to reading. There was an article on the front page about a mysterious massacre at a campground in the Adirondacks in upstate New York. Twenty deaths. No one could tell whether it was the work of human hands or some sort of wildlife attack. Mysterious toxicology reports showed some sort of heretofore unknown venom.

You saw this kind of thing a lot of late. Word of the Reemergence was spreading, though most reports blamed exploding wolf populations, bioterrorism, or both. But unicorn sightings were becoming more common as well, even in the mainstream media, though they were generally written off as crackpot stories or even hoaxes. No one was connecting the sightings to the attacks, partly because if an attack occurred, there were no survivors to say what they'd seen. Naturally, authorities had yet to catch or kill one of the unicorns, since only a unicorn hunter could do it, and none of us knew the first thing about how.

The brochure covered history, politics, cryptozoology, and a frustratingly minuscule smattering of pharmaceutical biochemistry that left out any relevant information about what they already knew about the Remedy. That was annoying. Instead, I learned that—at last count in the mid-nineteenth century—there were twelve hunter families, all of which could trace their lineage back to Alexander the Great. I also knew all about the five types of unicorns, each larger and more deadly than the last. Finally, I read about the supposed powers we hunters possessed: increased speed and agility—my PE teacher would have something to say about that—immunity to the alicorn poison, better aim and vision, and something called a *potentia illicere* that they didn't deign to translate. Since the only Latin I know comes from an anatomy book, I was clueless.

33

Something "potential," maybe?

No index, of course. I flipped to the back hoping to find a listing for "Virginity, why?" but no dice. In fact, the whole package was surprisingly light on exactly what it meant to be a unicorn hunter, or why they figured that a bunch of teenage girls would be better at the job than a few military snipers or an old-fashioned hand grenade. They didn't understand the immunity the same way they didn't understand the Remedy. And they didn't even explain what that *potentia* thingy was. It was as if I was still back in the nineteenth century. Wasn't anyone interested in the scientific aspects of a lost species or a possible medical breakthrough? Sure, the history bits had plenty of stories about Roman hunters and medieval hunters and hunters who rode bareback, naked, armed only with alicorns, against hordes of invading Visigoths, but nothing that explained what it was they'd done to *obtain* said alicorns. And really, naked horseback riding? What kind of virgins *were* these gals?

Plus reading straight through practically induced a coma.

But the diagrams of three different kinds of bows and five arrowheads rocked. I felt a sort of thrill seeing them, which shocked and repulsed me. Since when had I become all into weaponry? The only bloodletting devices that were supposed to make me happy were sterilized scalpels.

After a good fourteen hours of travel, of which I slept perhaps five, I arrived in Italy. In the terminal, no one waited with a little sign that read UNICORN HUNTER EXPRESS. Since I no longer had the use of my cell phone—for emergencies or otherwise—I had to track down a pay telephone, and a call to the number listed on the back of the brochure gave me a terse, English-accented message about which train and bus to take to get to the place where the boot camp was being held.

Bus? Bogus. So these were the responsible parties my mother had entrusted me to? They left a teenager in a foreign airport to fend for herself? I headed outside and somehow managed to find the train, which deposited me in a seedy-looking area of town a half hour later. The bus was a bit more difficult, but eventually I figured it out. I have a sneaking suspicion that it helped immensely that I was blonde. Aboard, I sailed past the Colosseum as well as buildings that looked every bit as ancient—yet were still inhabited. At last, it deposited me in a tiny depression, a valley between the Oppian and Celian hills, that my guidebook told me was one of the most ancient parts of the city, filled with hidden treasures and bits of enigmatic Roman history.

You think?

The brochure filled in the rest. Built in the fourteenth century, the Cloisters of Ctesias was a convent of sorts dedicated to training and housing scores of unicorn hunters. From the pictures in the glossy brochure, the Cloisters was a Mediterranean palace, replete with colorful frescoes, marble statues of naked gods and toga-clad saints, and towering columns. So it's understandable that after I disembarked from the crowded bus, manhandled my rolly bag up a steep hill paved with uneven cobblestones, and turned down the alleyway leading to the Cloisters, I almost missed the place entirely.

In the brochure, they were very careful not to show the crumbling, poster-plastered wall surrounding the building, the shattered plywood boards covering most of the upstairs windows, the pack of stray dogs sunning themselves on the stoop, and the bum leaning against the wall with a ragged rucksack and a cardboard sign covered in Italian.

Any lingering hopes I might have had of a wild summer spent in Rome, riding Vespas and eating gelato at midnight in picturesque piazzas, promptly disintegrated.

I hefted the bag onto my shoulder and maneuvered my way past the slumbering strays. Here goes nothing.

Beyond the enclosing walls lay a small, oblong courtyard paved in dusty, cracked mosaics and littered with trash. In the center stood a marble fountain featuring a pale stone woman in a flowing stone wrap holding the tip of an alicorn in a small catchment basin. Water cascaded around the horn and spilt over the lip of the basin into the large pool at the woman's feet.

I neared the fountain with care, as if the statue might suddenly spring to life and stab me with the weapon in its hand. I leaned close; the alicorn looked harmless from this vantage point. According to the brochure—which I was beginning not to trust—the horn had been alchemized by some martyred hunter of the past to purify the waters of the fountain. A dollop of bird poop graced one of the twists.

Yeah, some purity.

And yet, attached to a unicorn, a thing like this almost killed a guy in the Myersons' backyard last month.

Shuddering, I turned toward the doors to the Cloisters, which were large and made of bronze oxidized to a pale, sickly green. Decomposing bas-relief squares appeared to be hunting scenes of some sort, but it was hard to make out more than vague shapes—tall, lithe figures in pursuit of longer, bulkier ones.

This place was a dump.

With some difficulty, I yanked open the door with a pop. A wash of cool air enveloped me and with it, a scent that made my nose prickle. In contrast to the sunny city outside, the Cloisters were dark and . . . dank? What was that smell? I closed my eyes and sniffed again.

Fire and flood.

Great, two steps inside and this place was already reminding me of ways I could die. I tightened my grip on my suitcase handle. If I left now, how far would my traveling money take me? How much did a Eurorail pass go for nowadays?

No receptionist greeted me. Instead I entered a large gallery, a rotunda whose ceiling was studded with mosaics of gold leaf and dark-veined marble. Stone statues of Alexander the Great and other historical figures connected to the unicorn-hunting lineage stared out from niches every few yards along the wall. The sound of my footsteps withered on the floor, as if even the soles of my shoes were afraid to disturb the tranquility. Rolling my bag over the threshold, I called into the gloom. "Hello?"

As my eyes adjusted to the dimness, I saw before me the outline of a woman and a beast on a dais in the center of the room. I approached, only to be met with another set of statues— though these looked more like the mannequins and stuffed figures you'd see in a natural history museum diorama than the hunks of marble in a sculpture gallery. A bronze plaque at the base of the dais identified the figures, and I dropped my backpack in surprise. *Clothilde and Bucephalus.*

The woman wore a dress of real purple silk, faded where the sun filtered in from the windows above. Long blonde hair not unlike my own hung beneath an elaborately folded headdress of indigo and brilliant white. Her mannequin face was as white as porcelain, her eyes bright marbles with blank black centers. In her hands she brandished a gleaming sword against the monster before her.

It was as big as an elephant. The hide was a deep chestnut red and in consistency something between a horse's and what I imagined a wooly mammoth's would be like. The nostrils flared on a long, wide snout, and its mouth was open in a snarl, revealing jaws that would make a sabertooth tiger envious. Each cloven hoof was the size of a truck tire, and the beast stood in an aggressive pose, tilting a curved, creamy yellow horn as thick and long as my leg directly back at the hunter.

This was the karkadann, the most dreaded and deadly of all unicorns. This was the creature of nightmares, the thing my family fought for so many generations, the monster that my great-to-the-fifth aunt Clothilde finally defeated, though the battle cost her her life.

Before me stood my enemy. Ancient, unstoppable, unfathomable. The brochure had said that no one knew how old this creature was. It was believed by some—as commemorated on the plaque—that Clothilde had slain the great Bucephalus, the loyal steed of Alexander the Great. All those years I ridiculed my mother for not being able to point to any unicorn remains? Here it was. Every inch of the karkadann's body rippled with power, even in death, even a century and a half after being stuffed.

However, it was the eyes that had me mesmerized. On some level, I understood that these could not be the monster's true eyeballs, and that a taxidermist had replaced them with round black pits that gleamed with red and orange flame. And yet I couldn't look away.

I knew these eyes. In a place beyond memory, I knew them, and I was terrified. I knew every sinew of this beast, how quickly it moved, the shape of its hatred as it turned in my direction, the vibrations that echoed through the earth as it galloped toward me, the sting of poison from its horn.

I stared, and the karkadann stared back.

And then it whinnied.

I shot away from the dais, slid on the slick marble, and wound up sprawled facedown in a mosaic of mermaids about five feet away.

Laughter. Light, bubbling giggles. I stood gingerly, rubbing my butt where I'd smacked it on the stone floor. A girl about my age filled the far doorway, smiling brightly at me. "Forgive me," she said in a crisp British accent. "I simply couldn't resist. You looked so intent there." She stepped forward into the dim light trickling down from a clerestory that ringed the room. "Of course, you've very little to worry about. There hasn't been a single report of a karkadann sighting. And they probably wouldn't be making horse sounds, at any rate—"

"Who are you?" I asked, before I could hear her dissertation on the vocal emissions of various unicorn species.

"Cornelia Bartoli," she said. "You must be Astrid."

"Cornelia?" I asked. "I thought you were a man." So had Lilith. An older, more responsible man.

"No, that's my Uncle Cornelius. But I go by Cory and he by Neil."

"I go by Astrid," I said, and nodded at the dais. "Nice décor."

"You should be proud," Cory said, smiling wistfully at the figures locked in combat. "That's not my ancestor up there." She touched the hem of Clothilde's robe, a look of reverence on

39

her round, freckled face. "You look just like her, don't you?"

I bit my lip to keep from saying that I'd spent my childhood wishing I wasn't related to her, or at least not the daughter of someone so obsessed with our freakazoid lineage.

"I can't believe how well this was preserved," she went on, her short, brown curls bouncing as she spoke. "This place was sealed for a century, and yet this figure looks almost new, doesn't it? Nothing else survived this well. The laboratory is a shambles."

Perhaps that was the smell. Rot and stale air. But no, that wasn't quite right either. "Was there . . . a fire in here?"

Cory frowned. "Probably. Every plague imaginable was visited upon the Cloisters after the unicorns disappeared. Apparently, it was ransacked several times by mobs looking for the secret of the Remedy. I've spent the last month mucking this place out. It was rather disgusting before I got my hands on it. Speaking of which, would you like the tour?"

I reshouldered my backpack and grabbed the handle of my rolly bag. "Yes. But can we start with my room?"

She brightened at this. "Of course. You must be so jet-lagged. This way." And off she bounced toward the door whence she'd come. I did my best to keep up, but the plastic wheels of my suitcase kept catching on ridges in the floor mosaic. Behind me, I could feel the eyes of the karkadann.

As if, even in death, it watched.

The door led to a small hallway and then to narrow, twisting stairs lit by bare yellow bulbs. "The wiring is still a bit spotty," Cory explained, pointing to duct-taped twists of wires running up the walls. Between each bulb was an empty sconce formed with an upturned hock and hoof. All through the stairwell, pieces of bone and horn poked out from the masonry. Even the walls here were made from unicorn. This place was like an elephant graveyard. I shuddered and did my best to keep toward the center of the stairwell.

We reached the next floor amid a tsunami of unicorn history chatter from Cory. She and Lilith would be incredible chums. This girl was every bit as gung ho about hunting as my mother. "So you've been here for a month?" I asked hopefully. "How are you liking Rome? Have you been to the Vatican Museum?" I asked. "Or the Spanish Steps?"

She looked at me, brows knitted. "Why? All the unicorn information is right here."

Um, okay then. This chick was clearly a barrel of fun. Finally we spilled out into a decently sized hallway flanked by a row of doors on one side and open archways overlooking a courtyard on the other. I poked my head over the parapet and looked down into the partially paved courtyard, which currently lay in the shade of the dome we'd just left. Two wide cobblestone walkways intersected in the shape of a cross, forming a small square court in the center, while grassy, untended gardens comprised the rest of the space. The brochure had mentioned that this courtyard and walkways were the cloisters that gave the property its name.

"This is the dormitory," Cory announced, sweeping her arms out. "Our residential hall. Bathroom at the end. The plumbing, thank goodness, is moderately more reliable than the electricity."

She opened a door about halfway down. "And this is our room." She stepped aside for me to peek in, but I simply stared at the hand-stenciled sign that proclaimed CORY AND ASTRID. There were pencil-drawn unicorns rearing up on either side of our names. The horn of one practically punctured the *A*. Great. It was like the Myerson girls' bedroom all over again.

"How many of us will there be?"

"Perhaps nine? My uncle says it's still too early to tell." She flounced into the room. "You're lucky you got here early. I gave us the biggest one."

I checked out the endless hallway. "But aren't there a lot of rooms?"

"Not habitable ones. Not yet. Do come in."

I followed her inside. It was a lovely room, complete with colorful curtains and neatly made beds. Fluffy white pillows and bedspreads in shades of spring green and purple, coral carpets and wooden desks with matching lamps. In contrast to the antique and creepy air that characterized the rest of the building, this room was modern and cheerful, devoid of the weird bones and skulls evident everywhere else.

Cory obviously kept her things neat, and a quick survey of the space revealed that she'd given me the better side of the room, near a window that looked out onto a sea of terra-cotta and stone rooftops. I wheeled my belongings over to the bed clearly meant to be mine and dropped my backpack onto the perfectly smooth coverlet.

"We're going to have so much fun!" Cory assured me, catching on to my lack of enthusiasm. "With all the work I've been doing around here, I know this place like I built it myself. And I'll show you all the really brilliant, secret stuff."

Fun? Killing unicorns? The only thing that excited me about this whole trip was the idea of gelato. I swallowed. Pretty as this room was, it didn't feel right. The walls were too thick, the ceilings too high. The light in the window was brighter than back home. The bedding was totally new, but the place still smelled of ages. Not the comfortable dilapidation of the apartment I shared with Lilith, but ancient blood and ancient danger.

"And it will be good to have another hand to help with the cleaning," she went on. Her bright tone was beginning to sound a tad forced. "I've been on my own for so long."

"What about your uncle?" I said, taking a deep breath. All old houses smelled funny. This one was just older than most.

"Oh." Her voice turned vague. "He's quite busy himself, finding hunters and trying to get the training materials ready. I've been put in charge of the living arrangements."

"It's a very pretty room," I said, hoping to appease her.

"Yes, well enough of that. I expect you'd like to see the rest." Cory looked hopeful, but I had a sudden terror of going on the tour, of heading deeper into this place, back where the skeletons and the scent held more sway. And I didn't want to room with this girl who thought it was funny to pretend I was being attacked by a karkadann. This girl who seemed to like the idea that there were such things as karkadanns. Everything about Cornelia Bartoli was small and round, from her petite, curvy body and apple-cheeked face to her bouncy curls and deep brown eyes. Yet something in the way she carried herself made me realize that this girl was not as soft as she appeared.

I looked longingly at my bed, then back at her, and my protests died on my lips.

There was a unicorn curled up on Cornelia Bartoli's bed.

How did it get there? That bed had been empty a second or two ago.

"Oh no, Cory. Stand still. Don't. Move." I pictured Brandt's face after he was poisoned. My mom wasn't around with her decanter and her can of Coke this time. We were both going to die, right here on the coral carpet.

Cory looked over her shoulder to see what caught my attention and proceeded to go completely berserk.

"Bonegrinder!" she shrieked in a voice I barely recognized as human. "No! Bad!" She picked up her desk chair and flung it wildly in the direction of the bed. It glanced off the stone wall, bounced once near the headboard, and clattered to the floor.

The unicorn barely blinked. And then Cory really went nuts.

"You horrid little beast! You know you're not allowed in the dorm!" Her voice was the shriek of a fire alarm, of an air raid siren, of a harpy. She didn't even seem like the same person who'd showed me to our room. "Get off my bed! Get out! *Get out! GET OUT!*" She flew at it, fists raised.

The unicorn, its blue eyes as wide and limpid as any of the fictional creatures in children's fantasy books, leaped straight into the air in a tangle of cloven hooves and spindly white legs and scrabbled toward the door. It didn't make it.

Cory grabbed it by one leg and its horn and swept it up in her arms. It was bleating now, a pathetic, wheezing sound. In two steps, Cory had it out the door, then she swung it in a wide arc and flung it out over the courtyard.

It flew through the air, legs splayed, then plummeted the two stories to the cobblestoned court. I watched in horror, unable to breathe, as it crashed into the ground with a sound of shattering bones and rending flesh that echoed and bounced along the walls and columns. And then, silence.

Cory stood at the gallery, shivering with rage, staring blindly at the spot where the beast had fallen. Then she turned to me,

44

her face drained of all color except two magenta spots on her cheeks. Tears flowed freely from her eyes.

I was too shocked to cry. *This* was a hunter. This was what Lilith wanted of me. This cruelty, this brutality.

I wanted to ask her what we should do. I wanted to ask her what the hell a unicorn was doing in the Cloisters of Ctesias. But I was afraid to speak. I was afraid to even close my mouth, which hung open, stupid and in shock. I'd never seen anything like that in my life.

And then it got worse, because I spotted movement below. The unicorn was rising, shaking itself off and staring up at us. There was blood smeared along its white coat, but when it moved, it didn't look injured at all.

I gasped, but Cory didn't turn around.

"Trust me," she said. "It's very hard to kill."

4

Wherein Astrid Feels the Rush

Moments later, there were footsteps on the stairs. "Cornelia Sybil Bartoli!" shouted a voice, and then into the hallway stepped an absolutely gorgeous young man in a terra-cotta-colored Oxford cloth shirt and a pair of brown slacks. Black wavy hair curled over his forehead, shadowing deep brown eyes and a tan complexion. "What have I told you about—" He stopped short. "Oh. Hello there."

Cory nodded at me. "Astrid Llewelyn." She crossed her arms and set her jaw. "And if that thing knew what was good for it, it would keep well away from me."

"She can't control herself and you know it," he snapped back. He turned to me and cleared his throat. "I'm Cornelius Bartoli. The, er, don of the Cloisters. You may call me Neil."

Neil couldn't be over twenty-five. This was the crusty dude responsible for the brochure? This was the weirdo who'd been talking to my mother online? This was the guy *in charge*? He shook my hand, and his grip was firm and cool. His sleeves were rolled up, revealing an expensive-looking watch and a ring set with a deep red stone. I'm not usually into rings on guys, but this one looked just as masculine as the rest of him.

"What was that thing?" I blurted.

"Bonegrinder," Neil said. "She's our house zhi." He eyed me strangely. "She didn't try to attack you, did she? I'd understood from your mother that you'd already passed the trial by zhi."

I shook my head in disbelief. Had no one seen what just happened? "We keep unicorns around here? As what, target practice?"

Cory looked thrilled at the idea, but Neil shot her a dirty look. "The zhi are unique to the species," he said. "We've domesticated them. At least, the hunters have. The zhi yields to the true unicorn hunter, but to all others it is a deadly beast. That's how your kind have been tested for centuries."

Tested. Our virginity. "Aren't there easier ways to . . . test us?" I asked. Ways that didn't put our lives in danger?

"No matter what your magazines might say, there's no physiological evidence for virginity, Astrid."

Thanks for the anatomy lesson, mister, but I promise you, I know what hymens are, and the many, many ways that they can be broken that don't involve sex. I'd even read an article talking about how they can be reconstructed with plastic surgery for women in cultures where a lack of hymen can mean a public stoning in a town square. Didn't make them virginal, though.

And a hunter virginity test was, apparently, no less dangerous. "Those things are deadly."

"Like all unicorns, yes. But we do have safeguards." He pulled out a whistle and blew it, one low, warbling note. Cory retreated into her bedroom and shut the door as I heard hoofbeats on the stone steps. I stiffened, but Neil seemed unconcerned.

47

I heard it clattering in the hall and then a large, white bundle skidded to a stop near us. It untangled its limbs and horn and straightened, looking at Neil with enormous blue eyes filled with utter contempt. A growl curled the corner of its jaw, revealing tiny, sharp fangs. Blood was drying in its slightly matted hair, but I saw no injuries at all. It turned to me and, just like the one in the woods, swept into a quick bow.

"She hardly tolerates my presence," Neil said, as Bonegrinder began to nuzzle against my leg with the side of her face. I kept stepping back, but she was persistent, and when she looked up at me, it was with soft, sweet, puppy-dog eyes. Now I could see she was a good deal smaller than the one I'd seen in the woods. A juvenile unicorn was what? A fawn? A colt? "But she won't attack me with this ring on." He waved his hand in front of her and she cuddled even closer to me. "According to the few records we have, all the dons wore it. It's some kind of zhi kryptonite."

"That's impossible," I said.

He smiled. "Doesn't all of this seem impossible to you?"

At last, someone reasonable! "Yes. I don't believe in magic."

"I take it Cornelia hasn't shown you around yet."

Would the rest of this crumbling ruin change my mind? "No, she's been too busy throwing animals off balconies." Wasn't that some sort of sign of a budding sociopath?

Neil set his jaw. "I apologize for that. It was completely unacceptable, and I assure you, it shall not happen again."

Oh, well, as long as he promised, I guess I'd go ahead and room with the lunatic!

I held out my hand to the beast, and she insinuated herself beneath my palm, bleating happily. "I can't believe this is happening." I petted the zhi, and she calmed down.

"It's surprising how quickly it becomes commonplace," he said, his voice weary. "I'd gathered from your mother that you were raised knowing your heritage."

But not believing. Not for years. "Being here is different."

"It is indeed. Six months ago, I was in school, studying to be a barrister. And now I'm . . ." he trailed off. I found it difficult to picture him managing a gaggle of teenage girls. Had he ever even been a babysitter? "I'll take Bonegrinder away." He held his hand out toward the beast, and she growled, baring a mouthful of fangs, then cowered as the ring got closer. "I presume Cory has offered to show you around?"

"I—" Don't leave me with her, I thought. She might throw *me* off something next.

"Or perhaps you'd like to rest from your trip."

I grabbed at that one and nodded. "Yes, thank you."

Neil knocked on our door. "Cory, please come take care of the zhi. Astrid would like to take a short nap before the tour."

A moment later, the door opened. "What would you like me to do to it?" she asked, with a smile that did not quite meet her eyes.

"Wash the blood off would be a start," he said. "Then put her back in her cage for safekeeping. And I think we talked about these displays, did we not? She *can* feel pain, you know."

Cory glared at the unicorn, who pressed her flank against my thigh for protection. "Not enough."

Alone in the bedroom I was supposed to share with Cory, I couldn't fall asleep. What if she returned while I was unconscious? I may have always thought my mother was a few

49

pills short of a full prescription, but I never worried that she'd hurt me. However . . . a girl who threw animals off balconies? She'd seemed so friendly at first, if a bit too focused on unicorns for my taste.

I looked around at the cheerful decor, the bright colors and fluffy pillows, the cobalt-blue vase filled with an artful array of wildflowers, the smattering of photos in chunky glass frames. It looked like a room in a magazine, everything so shiny and new.

I missed the sagging sofa cushions in my apartment back home. They weren't gray, they weren't brown, and they almost always felt just the slightest bit damp, but they fit into our little home perfectly. These mod coverlets and prefab furniture clashed terribly with the carved stone walls, with the bone sconces and stuffed heads, with the smell of mold and ashes that no posies in the world could cover.

I lay back against the bed and flung my arm over my burning eyes. My head ached, and I just wanted to go home.

When Cory returned, I lay very still, hoping she'd think I was asleep.

"That can't be comfortable, with your suitcase taking up half the bed and your shoes still on."

Busted. I sat up and smoothed my hair down.

"My uncle says I'm to apologize to you for my earlier . . . display, but I don't think you need that, do you?"

I remained very quiet and very cautious.

"I know what happened to you in the States. I know that you understand exactly how dangerous these monsters are."

"Yes."

"So don't you agree that we should take every precaution?"

"She wasn't going to attack us. You knew that."

"I also knew I couldn't really hurt it." She turned away from me and faced her desk.

"Don't do that again." The words fell from my lips before I could stop them. After all, what leverage did I have? This girl could take me in a fight, and I was at her mercy here in the Cloisters.

She looked over her shoulder. "I beg your pardon?"

"You did hurt her. Not permanently, maybe, but pain is pain."

"It's not a *pet*, whatever Uncle Neil may want you to believe." She laughed harshly. "What is it you think we're here to do, Astrid? We're *supposed* to kill them. It's our purpose."

"You already said you knew you weren't going to kill it. Hunting is one thing. Torturing an animal is another. Don't do that again."

She stared at me for a long moment, and I waited for an "or what?" that never came. Then she turned back to her desktop and traced the frame of one of the photos. I glanced past her. The girl in the photograph wasn't yet ten, but I could tell it was Cory. It had been taken at Christmastime, and Cory sat in front of a tree, laughing as she and a woman who looked just like a female Neil posed beside a large, spotted spaniel puppy with a wreath of evergreen draped around its neck.

"Is that your dog?" I asked, to break the silence. I wondered if she'd ever thrown it off a balcony. It was too odd—she cuddled puppies; liked pretty, colorful fabrics and flowers; and then went maniacal on me.

She nodded. "His name is Galahad. We had to leave him in England. It's not safe . . . for him here."

51

Because Bonegrinder would eat him. Still, that was no excuse for Cory's behavior. Abuse one pet because it kept her from another?

"Do you know," she said abruptly, "what it takes to kill a unicorn?"

"No."

"Their flesh regenerates. Their bones knit. Their skin closes over wounds."

"Silver bullet?" I suggested, half joking. Unicorns were apparently like starfish on steroids. But I'd seen the Remedy in action. If it were possible to isolate that quality of the unicorn, it would change the world as we knew it. Perhaps Lilith was right; it was worth putting up with the danger.

"Bullets just vanish into their flesh. They need to be torn apart. Decapitation works well, or a wound kept open, like one made with an arrow or a spear." She turned to me now. "That's one of the reasons we make better hunters. We actually stay alive long enough to bring them down, since we're not affected by the poison."

"Being gored through the heart is still the same."

Cory looked down at her hands, squeezing her fingers apart and together several times. "It is, at that. Humans die too easily, hunter or not."

I glanced back at the picture: Cory, the dog, and a woman who was almost certainly her mother. A mother that neither of the Bartolis had mentioned.

"Cory," I said softly. She was rubbing her hands together in earnest now, her movements almost compulsive.

"I won't hurt it anymore, if that's what it takes," she blurted out. "Because I really want you here."

"Why?" I asked. There had to be other hunters coming. Ones who actually knew a little something about killing things.

"You're a Llewelyn. You're from the family that always had the best hunters. The family that got rid of the unicorns last time. I want you to help me get rid of them again."

Over the next few days, I came to the conclusion that Cornelia Bartoli and Lilith would be best friends forever. I didn't know anyone *could* be more obsessed with unicorn trivia than mommy dearest, but this Cory girl had her beat hands down. I'd tried in vain to interest her in any subject that didn't involve unicorns or the killing thereof. I'd asked her what her favorite books were, and she'd responded that the chronicles of Dona Annabelle Leandrus from 1642 were a bit tough to translate, but had all the best battle descriptions. I'd asked about her favorite movies and she said there wasn't yet any video evidence of the Reemergence.

All that, and she screamed in her sleep.

So not an ideal roommate, but she *had* kept her word to me regarding Bonegrinder—no mean feat, considering the penchant the animal showed for following us around. There hadn't been a morning since I'd arrived that we hadn't woken to find the creature curled outside our bedroom door. The first time it happened, I'd been afraid to disturb her. Cory had shown no such concern; she'd calmly walked to the threshold and shoved Bonegrinder across the hall. But I felt it constituted progress. I'm sure, had I not been present, that shove would have been a kick. And yet the zhi proved a veritable glutton for punishment and came back every night until Cory complained to Neil and had Bonegrinder confined to her steel crate at all times.

That worked well for two days, until she gnawed through the locks.

So now we were in pursuit of a more permanent home for the zhi. I trailed Cory through the covered passageways of the cloister, while she tried various doors and dismissed the rooms they opened into out of hand.

"These rooms were made for the public," she explained. "You just don't have the same amount of security."

I could believe that. The central courtyard—or cloister— was the most delicate part of the whole building. And, aside from the residence hall, it was the one most devoid of unicorn bones, instead merely suggesting the building's true purpose. The four barrel-vaulted aisles that bounded the cloister were separated from the open court by rows of arches, each supported by a pair of columns that swirled upward in graceful imitation of alicorns. Small gates topped with arrowheads and guarded by pairs of carved stone lionesses marked the north and south entrances, and the interior walls of the courtyard were ringed with mosaics depicting fair maidens and mythical monsters.

It was almost peaceful—if one avoided the bloodstains in the corner where Bonegrinder had fallen.

Cory told me that in ancient days, pilgrims had entered the cloister through the now-padlocked doors against the far wall on the south end, and waited in the courtyard for the hunters to receive them and distribute the Remedy. Currently, that door led to the church next door, and, as far as its officials were concerned, the Cloisters of Ctesias was the home of a now-defunct nunnery, once known as the Order of the Lioness, whose grounds were being used for storage.

"It's not entirely inaccurate," Cory said.

"Except for the 'defunct' part," I replied. We curved around the northern aisle, which bordered the rotunda, and eventually came to the eastern aisle, where I could hear the sound of pots banging around and the unmistakable odor of oregano. Cory and I poked our head into the refectory, where Lucia, our cook, was already working on the evening's marinara. Neil had found Lucia while doing research for eligible members of hunting families, and the abbess of her convent agreed to lend her out to the Order of the Lioness. I think Lucia was enjoying the change in scenery.

"*Buongiorno*," Cory called. She snarled at Bonegrinder, who was chained to the radiator and happily gnawing away at what looked like a bovine spinal column—tendons attached. "Not giving you any trouble, is it?"

Lucia tucked a bit of gray hair back into her nun's habit. "*Bella bambina?* No, no." She chucked the zhi under the chin and the animal swished her tale back and forth on the floor. "You feed her; she loves you."

No, you're the virgin descendant of Alexander the Great; she loves you. The feeding was just a perk. I watched Lucia hobble over to the counter to lift a huge copper pot, and rushed to offer my help. She shooed me off. Cory unhooked Bonegrinder's chain and hauled the zhi to her feet. Bonegrinder made a feeble attempt to pick up the spine in her mouth, but the end dragged on the floor, and Cory kicked it away. Defeated, the unicorn slumped.

Both Lucia and I shook our heads at her and I retrieved the gory chew toy, holding it gingerly between two fingers.

"We'll just take care of her for you," I said.

"Go, go," Lucia said, waving her hands at us. "The kitchen is my place. The battleground is yours."

"Forty years and one hip-replacement surgery ago, that woman would have made a hell of a hunter," I said to Cory once we were back in the arcade.

"She's a Saint Marie." Cory shrugged, as if that explained all. "They were never the battleground type." Bonegrinder stopped to sniff at the ground, and Cory tugged on the chain, pulling her along.

Cory has this strange idea—one of many—that each of the twelve hunter families has a specific caste. I'm a Llewelyn, therefore I'm automatically an excellent hunter. She's from the Leandrus line, which were supposedly the record keepers. It's all so silly.

Almost as silly as the idea that any of our families have power over unicorns at all.

It was too bad, really. From my few interactions with Lucia, I gathered that she was intrigued by the idea of unicorn hunting. Becoming a nun had been a long-held tradition among the women of her family, but the order she'd chosen was not quite as thrilling as her ancestors' vows to the Order of the Lioness. And yet she was stuck in a kitchen while my "place was on the battlefield"? I wondered if I could concoct some sort of medical discharge, like one did for the army. Break my leg, maybe. Cut off a pinky toe?

Ick. Maybe not.

"I think we'll have to try below in the chapter house," Cory said, and led the way back into the dome, grabbing a pair of lanterns on the way. Behind the tableau of Clothilde and the karkadann was a small door, which Cory unlocked with a slender golden key. I followed her into a narrow hallway that descended beneath the cloister courtyard, and Bonegrinder trotted obediently behind. This was the true heart of the Cloisters of Ctesias; not the dormitories or the refectory or even the grand dome. Beneath the ground lay our crypt, our training rooms, holding pens, and even our burial grounds. Here sat the charred remains of our scriptorium, a sort of combination library and laboratory, where Cory had taken me on my first day. There was little left but ashes now, hundreds of years of records reduced to piles of blackened pages. Chairs and tables overturned, frozen in time to the night mobs had invaded this place in a desperate search for the Remedy.

They'd never found it. Or if they did, the formula was lost to history long ago. No trace remained now. As we passed the burned and broken door to the scriptorium, I glanced in. Tiny bits of glass and brass glittered in the light from my lantern— pieces of the hunters' alchemy sets, fragments of alembics, crucibles, scales, and phials scattered among the ashen remnants of books, maps, and scrolls. I wondered what family was known for its contributions to science. Bonegrinder paused here, too, and gave the threshold an exploratory sniff. According to Cory, unicorns had a highly advanced sense of smell. They could detect gunpowder from nearly a mile away.

Whatever this unicorn sensed in the scriptorium, it was clear she wasn't happy. She shied back against my legs, and even through the denim of my jeans I could feel her shudder.

Cory tested the rotted wood on each door we passed. "Too much of this area has seen damage," she said. "It'll bash through any of these."

We stooped as we traveled deeper beneath the Cloisters. The

stone walls closed in on all sides, and I put my hand out to feel my way along the dark stairs. My fingers trailed over tiny knobs and bumps of bones, here and there punctuated by the sharper ridges of a zhi's screw-shaped alicorn protruding from the masonry. I wondered if the zhi walking beside me recognized these artifacts for what they were. The farther in we got, the less sure the unicorn seemed to be about our path. Her clopping steps turned hesitant, then downright stubborn, and it took both Cory and me to tug her along.

The strange atmosphere of the Cloisters was stronger down here, pressing in around me more thickly than the walls themselves. My head felt stuffed with it, my sinuses suffused with darkness and death.

Presently, the corridor dropped into a steep spiral stair, and Bonegrinder stopped dead. Cory grabbed her by the collar, while I shoved against her haunches until she finally began mincing her way down. Around and around we went, on glossy, worn steps that sloped dangerously downward without the benefit of a banister. The lantern light ricocheted off the walls, careening from alicorn to hoof, from a spinal column that bisected the regular rows of stone to the leering, eyeless glare of a skull.

I reared back and slipped on the stairs, the soles of my feet knocking against Cory's calves. Bonegrinder bleated in complaint.

"Relax," came Cory's crisp voice through the darkness. "It's just a kirin."

And a dead one at that. I shuffled through my comparatively small store of unicorn knowledge. Kirins were the third largest kind of unicorn. They were originally from Asia, but by the time of the "first extinction" they'd spread throughout Europe as well. In ancient China and Japan, the horse-sized monsters had been worshipped as gods by villagers terrified of the alternative. A timely sacrifice here and there was preferable to wholesale destruction. The kirin were wily creatures, who hunted in herds and had even been known to kill for sport. According to Cory, the overpositive portraits of them in much of Eastern lore existed to appease their vindictive tempers—not dissimilar to the characterization of cruel Celtic fairies as "the Good Folk." Treat them well, and maybe they'll leave you alone.

Unlike zhi, kirin had no special affinity for hunters. They'd kill us as easily as any other person.

Cory still hadn't found a decent description of them. They were alternately portrayed as wreathed in mists or flame, or as being covered in ever changing scales that camouflaged them perfectly. I stared up at the all-too solid kirin skull, which laughed at me, at my fright, and at all the secrets I didn't know.

Cory twisted the horn, which opened the door at the base of the stair into a room I'd never entered before. "This is the chapter house," she said. "Brace yourself." She placed the lantern in a small glass cage and hoisted it high, illuminating the cavernous space. Even braced, I hadn't been sure of what to expect.

It was a trophy room. One curving wall was covered top to bottom with skulls, horns, and other bits, some mounted on plaques and marked with tiny cards or engraved nameplates, some affixed to the wall with metal spikes and carved with the name of their killer. Skull after skull ogled me, their dark, empty eye sockets seeming to flicker and wink in the shadowed lamplight.

Bonegrinder was bleating in earnest now, tugging backward against her collar, her hooves sliding and clicking on the stone as she fought for purchase. I held fast to the chain, and her bleats turned into snorts.

"What is it?" I whispered in horror.

"The Wall of First Kills," Cory replied. "For hundreds of years, the hunters marked their passage into the Order by bringing a piece of their kill to hang here. She pointed at one enormous, broken skull. "Look, this is a Llewelyn. Katherine Llewelyn, aged fourteen. Can you imagine if your first kill was a re'em?"

A re'em. The giant unicorn of the Bible, second only in size and ferocity to a karkadann. The oxlike beast had roamed the deserts and plains of the Holy Land for millennia before being subdued by unicorn hunters sometime after the Crusades. In more recent translations of the Bible, they'd downgraded descriptions of the animal to a type of wild ox called an aurochs—a fact that made my mother's blood boil.

Fourteen, and up against something the size of a raving bull.

"No," I said. "I can't imagine."

Cory surveyed the room, a shadowed conglomeration of ancient furniture and large, muslin-draped shapes. "Let's find a good spot to anchor the chain."

I cast a look back at Bonegrinder. Her blue eyes were bulging, and she was practically choking in her eagerness to escape. "We can't leave her here!" I said. "In the dark, alone, with all these . . . *bones.*" The place smelled of death. It was a monument to the prowess of the hunters, a shrine to the destruction of Bonegrinder's species.

Cory snorted. "It likes bones, remember?" She snatched the bloody, gnawed spine from my hand and waved it in front of Bonegrinder. "Nice unicorn. Yummy. See?" She tossed it a few feet away. Bonegrinder paid little attention.

I stared at the wall and dug my hand into the unicorn's coat. With the still-swinging lamplight casting strange shadows over the bones, they seemed to pulsate in place, as if muscles moved just beneath the surface of the stone. I shuddered and put my other hand to my head. It had begun to pound, no doubt my airways and lymph system reacting to the dust and stale air.

"It's only temporary," Cory went on, drawing the chain forward and beginning to wind it around the leg of a table. "Until we can find a more permanent place . . ."

"It's a tomb," I argued. The skulls all laughed at me, laughed at Bonegrinder, who had become almost frantic in her fevered attempts to escape her bonds.

What we were, you are now; what we are, you soon will be . . .

Cory groaned in frustration. "You and my uncle! It doesn't need a bloody palace. It won't die, and it won't be in our way. In a few days, there will be half a dozen girls here. And Bonegrinder will be constantly underfoot, constantly in danger of getting free—do you have any idea what would happen if it got loose and went rampaging through the streets of Rome?" Her voice turned low and dangerous. "Blood, death, destruction . . ."

My eyes remained fixed to the engraved trophies on the wall, which pulsed and echoed back *blood death destruction*.

And then, from impossibly far away, I heard a coppery clang, like the great metal doors of the Cloisters opening, and the zhi leaped to her feet and took off. The chain slid through Cory's hands and whipped past me, disappearing up the stairs.

"Astrid!" I heard Cory call. "Catch it!"

But I was way ahead of her. My eyes zeroed in on the fluffy white behind of the zhi as she vanished up the spiral stair, and it was as if a band snapped tight. The world slowed—the sickly, swinging light, Cory's shrill tones, the strangely vibrating walls—but I did not.

Hunter powers indeed.

I didn't feel the stairs, the weight of time, the depths of the darkness. I felt nothing but pursuit, fresh and free. Have you ever run on a moving walkway or escalator and felt yourself careening forward much faster than you could possibly imagine? I was a tidal wave of feet pounding, a lightning bolt of pumping arms. My blood boiled and my vision dimmed, until all I could see was the outline of the zhi. My prey.

I was almost on top of her as we spilled into the relative brightness of the rotunda. I saw it all in the space of a second: the large doors, slightly ajar, the figure who stood just inside, and the sunny street beyond, populated with the rest of the world, dogs and vendors, nuns and children whose bones would be another addition to our collection if I didn't stop the unicorn.

And then my hands sunk into her fur. "Gotcha!" I cried as we sprawled on the mosaic as one. I closed a hand around her horn and yanked it backward, moving my other arm into a choke hold around her neck. Bonegrinder screamed and snapped her jaws in frustration as I wrestled her into the tiles. She flailed her four legs in the air, and I ducked to keep from being conked in the face by one of her hooves.

A second later, Cory appeared by my side. "Got it?" she asked. I nodded and looked up, blowing stringy strands of my pale hair off my face.

A few feet away stood my cousin, tanned and leggy, with her dirty blond hair pulled into a jaunty ponytail and a huge pair of sunglasses pushing her bangs back from her face.

"Asteroid!" exclaimed Philippa Llewelyn. "Surprise!"

5

WHEREIN ASTRID GAINS AN ALLY

I'D NEVER BEEN HAPPIER to see my cousin. Ignoring the venomous monster I was supposed to be restraining, I catapulted myself into Phil's arms.

"Whoa there," she said, hugging me back. "Miss me much?" She glanced down. "My God, they're real." She drew away and leaned over Bonegrinder, who currently knelt at her feet, horn pressed against the floor. "Real, and adorable . . . and a little smelly. Buddy, who bathes you?"

"One takes one's life in one's hands to try," Cory said, pushing the bronze doors shut.

"Hi," Phil said, and stuck out her hand toward my roommate. "Philippa Llewelyn, reporting for unicorn hunting duty." No attempt whatsoever to keep a straight face.

Cory looked blank. "Another Llewelyn?"

You'd think she'd be happy about the idea. "Phil's my cousin," I said.

Cory shook her head. "I know who she is. Nineteen. A volleyball player at Pomona."

64

"Been stalking me?" asked Phil with a laugh.

"It's just that your mother made no mention of other eligible hunters in your family," Cory said, as if she hadn't heard. "I just assumed . . ."

"That doesn't surprise me," Phil said, "knowing Aunt Lilith. It was like pulling teeth to get her to give up the goods on where you'd scurried off to, Asterisk. And then, as soon as I heard, how could I resist? Free trip to Rome? Count me in! So, where do we go to get reimbursed?"

"Here, I suppose," said a male voice, and I instinctively grabbed hold of Bonegrinder's collar. We turned to see Neil standing in the doorway to his rooms with a distinguished-looking gentleman with white hair and pale blue eyes in an immaculate gray three-piece suit. "Good catch, Astrid."

"Who's the hottie?" Phil whispered. I *hoped* she meant Neil.

"Very impressive, indeed," said Neil's companion. He had a slight accent, but I couldn't identify its origin. "And two Llewelyns. Intriguing." He stepped forward, hand extended, and Bonegrinder began to snarl. "My name is Marten Jaeger. It's a pleasure to meet you both." He came close enough to touch us, but when Bonegrinder lowered her horn, he backed off and ran a hand through his straight white hair, clearly uncomfortable in such close proximity to a man-eating beast. I was surprised that any nonhunter other than Neil was allowed inside.

Neil, armed with the ring, shook Phil's hand and introduced himself, adding, "Mr. Jaeger is sponsoring the renovations and upkeep to the Cloisters."

"And its inhabitants," Cory added under her breath. She tugged Bonegrinder's chain from my hands. "I'll just take care of this."

"So this isn't being run by the Church?" I asked.

"We're working in cooperation with the Church. Donors, if you will," Marten Jaeger explained. "I'm the CEO of Gordian Pharmaceuticals, and we have a vested interest in seeing the lost knowledge of your Order restored."

Of course. The Remedy. I brightened. "So there *is* a scientific wing to this outfit."

"Naturally, Miss Llewelyn. This is the twenty-first century, after all. My staff biologists are fascinated by the return of these marvelous creatures and eager to see if the historical claims are actually fact. So far, they have been holding up, but we've had . . . difficulties keeping a unicorn captive for testing."

"Right." Phil nodded slowly, as the pieces began to fall into place. "Because only a hunter can catch and kill one. Isn't that what your mom says, Astrid?"

I shrugged, distracted. "I'd be really interested to see what kind of data you've collected so far, Mr. Jaeger. I'm very interested in medicine. In fact, the potential for rediscovering the Remedy is the main reason I'm here." Well, other than the obsessed mother.

He smiled. "How fascinating. I would have thought a natural-born hunter like you would be more comfortable with a bow than a beaker."

"I'm not—"

"I'll bring some information for you the next time I drop by." He turned to Neil. "It appears that you will have your hands full. I should leave you to get your newest recruit settled."

I watched Mr. Jaeger retreat to the bright, busy world beyond the bronze doors. Out there, people were doing real work. Out there was real science. But I was apparently a natural-born killer. So I was trapped inside, as thoroughly chained as Bonegrinder.

I brought Phil up to my bedroom while Cory went off to figure out where to put her on a more permanent basis. Over my roommate's protestations, Phil brought the "darling" Bonegrinder along, and proceeded to cuddle it on her lap in the middle of the floor. The unicorn was clearly in heaven.

"Aren't you a puddums?" Phil cooed, rubbing the monster's tummy. Bonegrinder stretched, and her horn screeched along the floor.

I gritted my teeth and decided not to tell my cousin about the raw cow haunch that the "puddums" had devoured for lunch. "But how did you get your father to agree to let you come?" I asked, incredulous. The *U* word was like an A-bomb in Uncle John's house.

"Summer abroad." Phil winked. "I told him that I made a club exhibition team and we'd be traveling across Europe showing off our volleyball skills." Since said skills had earned Phil a college scholarship, I could understand Uncle John's willingness to let her take off. She leaned back against my bed and pillowed her hands behind her head. "We're going to have such a blast here!"

"A blast? You do realize what we do here, right? Kill things like that," I nudged Bonegrinder with my toe. "Bathe in their blood for all I know." Let's see how that sat with her! Phil had been a vegetarian for as long as I could remember.

"That's old-school. Didn't you hear that Jaeger guy? This is the twenty-first century. I'm sure no one here has any interest in the kind of irresponsible hunting practices that caused the last tragedy."

Funny. She called the first extinction of venomous, man-eating monsters a tragedy.

"But I'd be a hypocrite if I didn't endorse responsible culling," Phil went on, like she was reading from her Environmental Studies 101 textbook. "That's all we're dealing with here, I'm sure of it. We've got to do something to stop these attacks Aunt Lilith was telling me about." She leaned in and lowered her voice. "There was a rumor going around campus that the attacks were because our government was testing some kind of bizarre new weapon. I'm relieved that it's just animals doing what they do. So we have to act like responsible custodians of the planet, and I'm pleased to do my part!" She grinned. "Make sure the unicorns aren't a threat to any human populations, keep them in check—then go have fun in Rome. Sounds perfect, right?"

Cory entered, and her eyes narrowed at the site of Bonegrinder on our floor. I had nervous flashbacks to my first day, but she just clenched her fists and paused. Interesting. Perhaps two Llewelyns were better than one.

"I've your room ready," she said in a flat voice. "Didn't have time to make up the bed, but . . ."

"Oh, that's fine," Phil said brightly, standing and brushing bits of white, fluffy hair from her denim skirt onto the coral carpet. Cory's face was a thundercloud. "Astrodome has made plenty of beds in her day, haven't you, squirt? Come on—help me get unpacked."

But Cory blocked the door. "In the future, I'd appreciate it if you remember that the house zhi is not permitted in the residence hall."

"The what in the who now?" Phil said.

"*Bonegrinder,*" Cory spat. "Not allowed up here."

"I'm sorry," I said quickly. "I wasn't thinking. I was just so surprised to see Phil here and I forgot . . ." But the excuse sounded lame to my ears. One did not forget what happened the last time the zhi got into this room, and Cory knew it.

Phil glanced at me and her expression turned contrite. "Man, I'm sorry. Here for five minutes and already screwing up the rules. I'll just take her with me. Thanks so much for understanding, Cory." She brushed through the door. Bonegrinder and I followed, and as I passed, Cory caught my eye. Her expression was impossible to mistake.

She was holding herself in check.

In the privacy of Phil's new room, my cousin turned to me. "Nice girl, but a little intense, huh?"

"You have no idea." I shook the sheets out onto Phil's bed and started tucking as she opened her suitcase. "She's not going to appreciate your 'responsible culling' theory, I'll tell you that much. She wants the unicorns extinct." And she's only tolerating the two of us because she thinks we're genetically predisposed to make it happen.

"We'll talk her out of that." Phil's tone was light as she unpacked yet another adorable little sundress.

I doubted Cory would be swayed by an environmental treatise. The girl was on a mission. I stuffed a pillow in a purple pillowcase and tossed it at the headboard. "It's probably a good idea to keep Bonegrinder out of here, though. Cory hates her."

"Eh, she can't say boo if I've got her in my own room. Right, doll face?" Phil stuck her tongue out at the unicorn. Bonegrinder bleated happily and pounced on the freshly made bed.

Great. My one respite from Cory's unicorn monomania and Phil decided to take a zhi for a roommate. The unicorn pawed at the bedspread and snuggled in. Her horn ripped a long tear in the coverlet.

I sighed, but Phil merely joined the creature. "Astrid, don't worry about it. We're going to have the time of our lives here."

"This isn't a vacation," I said. "Didn't my mom tell you anything? We have a *duty*."

"That too," she replied. "But all work and no play in the city that never sleeps?"

"That's New York. Rome is the Eternal City."

"Whatever. The point is, they may have been nuns around here in the Middle Ages, but we're party girls today."

"How much can we party in a convent?"

Phil rolled her eyes. "And who says we have to *stay* in the convent? I'm sure all that Order of the Lioness stuff is just to keep the rent down. There's no lock on that door, and I'm fully old enough to come and go as I please . . . and squire around my impressionable little cousin. Let's get out of here!"

Finally, someone who showed interest in actually seeing the city. But . . . "I don't know if we're supposed to leave." On the one hand, they did let me come in from the airport on my own. But on the other, Cory balked every time I started talking about taking in some of the tourist sites. "We should ask Neil."

"That adorable British dude from downstairs?" Phil giggled. "Ten euros says as soon as he's tucked you girls into bed, he heads out to the clubs himself. That guy is the most gorgeous chaperone I've ever given the slip to."

Now I laughed for what felt like the first time since Brandt had been attacked.

"Come on, Cuz. It's my first night in Rome, and we're going to see the town. I left you alone for too long back home, and look what happened. You started dating Brandt, of all people. Have I taught you nothing?" She reached over and fluffed my hair. "Not going to let it happen again. First, we get some quality cappuccinos. Then we hang out with some quality guys. You'll see. We're going to have a great time."

Looking at Phil's smiling face, listening to her sunny voice, like a breath from my pre-unicorn past, I could almost believe it.

Then Bonegrinder burped, and I smelled blood.

It took a bit of maneuvering to escape the Cloisters without alerting Cory to our plans. I felt a little bad about leaving her behind—if anyone needed a night off, it was Cornelia Bartoli—but I also wanted some alone time with Phil. We'd barely seen each other since she went off to college, and I was dying for a chance to talk about something other than unicorns.

Phil, however, did not share my desire.

"How crazy was it when you just tackled Bonegrinder like that?" she asked, as we boarded one of the city's orange public buses and slid into our molded plastic seats. "I've never seen you move so fast before. Practically a blur. Did you join the track team or something after I left?"

I shrugged, because the only answer I could think of sounded too bizarre to contemplate. I'd caught Bonegrinder because I had special unicorn hunting powers. But was it any crazier than what I'd already seen? Bones that moved on their own, a unicorn that could shake off a two-story drop to a stone floor, the way Brandt's wound knit together before my eyes?

"I think it's all connected," I said aloud. "I bet you can do it, too." Phil would probably be even better, since she was already a great athlete.

Twenty minutes later, we were making our first circuit around the Piazza Navona, a vast, oblong plaza packed with tourists, Italians, cafés, and gelato stands. From our vantage point at the far end, it was easy to see the piazza's origins as an ancient Roman racetrack. The buildings that had grown around the border maintained the outline of the field, and giant marble fountains were the only break in the flat, cobblestoned court.

"This is gorgeous!" Phil exclaimed, holding her arms out wide. I tried to look inconspicuous, but two teenaged blond girls in Rome were apparently something to stare at. And harass. Every few seconds, a man approached me with a handful of withering roses, trying to make a sale. A few feet ahead, swathed in wraps despite the afternoon sun, a Gypsy woman hobbled along, bent nearly double with osteoporosis. Near the fountain stood a knot of children in dirty T-shirts and shorts with pieces of cardboard in their hands. While Phil brushed off the latest flower guy, I observed the kids, wondering what they were doing out here alone.

It was a mistake. As soon as they noticed me staring, they converged upon me, chattering away in a language that didn't quite sound like Italian, holding their cardboard panels up like serving trays as they pushed against me.

"Stop it!" Phil cried. "Astrid, get away from them!" But I wasn't going to shove a child out of my way. In another second it was over and the kids scurried off.

With my purse.

"No!" Each one was going in a different direction. "No! They're pickpockets!"

"You think?" Phil said drily, but I'd already taken off after the nearest one.

"Stop, thief!" I cried. I sprinted past the fountain, leaped over the legs of a few people sitting on the edge, and kept running. The boy ahead of me dodged and ducked through the crowd with practiced ease, and I started falling behind. Unlike my earlier pursuit of Bonegrinder, here there was no supernatural speed, no strange narrowing of the universe. Here I was just a girl. Not a hunter.

"Stop!" I gasped.

Another figure flew by, shouting in Italian. *"Fermate il ladro!"*

I caught a glimpse of jeans and a faded red shirt rushing past, arms and legs scissoring in perfect runner's form. I puffed and tried my best to keep up as the three of us barreled toward the end of the piazza, where the ancient planes of the racecourse gave way to buildings and shadowed alleyways.

The thief had picked his alley well. So narrow I could touch both sides with my fingertips, it was also blocked by a Dumpster and parked motorbikes. I jumped over a concrete post, banging my shin, and limped on.

I overtook them just as the runner in red grabbed hold of the little boy by the back of his T-shirt. The child squealed and for a second I thought he'd wriggle right out of his clothes. But then the runner closed his hand around the boy's matchstick arm and started issuing orders in a tone I didn't need to know Italian to understand.

Give it back to her.

"What did he take?" The runner asked me. There were traces of sweat on his temple, and his black curls stuck to the dark skin of his forehead. His English held no trace of an accent.

"My purse," I said, still out of breath. I wasn't sure I liked the way my helper's hand completely encircled the child's upper arm, thief or no. "Be careful with him."

The guy looked at the little boy in his grip, then at me. "I hate to break it to you, but this kid doesn't have a purse on him." He let him go, and the kid scampered off almost as quickly as a unicorn.

"No!" I yelled. "He was in a gang. He knows which one of them has it."

"Make up your mind." The guy shook his head. "Besides, your purse is long gone. They're very organized. If you don't have your eye on the actual item being stolen, it'll get passed among them and you'll never find it again."

I growled in frustration and thumped my fist against the lid of the Dumpster. "But we could have made him lead us to it." Maybe.

"No, we couldn't. It's just one of those things. I'm so sorry, but welcome to Rome." He looked me over, and in the dim light of the alley, his eyes were almost black. "You're American, right? Me, too. Giovanni Cole."

I shook his hand. "Astrid Llewelyn. I can't believe it's gone, just like that."

"Astrid. That's an unusual name for an American."

"So's Giovanni," I snapped, but he just raised his eyebrows, so I took a deep breath. After all, he hadn't been the one to steal my purse. "My mom's a little . . . . hard-core. She wanted to give me the name of a warrior."

"My mom's Italian," Giovanni said. "Mine just means *John*." He was silent for a moment, and I still seethed. "Look, I know you don't want to hear it right now, but the next time a bunch of Gypsy kids come at you like that, don't be afraid to just shove them off."

"You can forget that," said a voice behind me. Phil had arrived at the entrance to the alley, along with another young man. "Astrid would cut off her hand before she'd lay a finger on a child."

"So it seems." Giovanni was still looking at me, which made it really hard for me to check him out in return. I took what I could from quick glances in his direction. Slim build, dark, close-cropped hair, high cheekbones, really nice skin.

"I told you we'd find them together," the other guy said.

Phil put her hand on my shoulder. "You didn't have anything valuable in there, did you? Your passport?"

My hand flew to my mouth. "Oh no!"

"It's okay, honey. This happens all the time. The embassy can get you a new one." They'd better! I wanted to be able to leave as soon as I could.

"But what will we tell Neil?" I slumped against the nearest stoop. Maybe this was why Cory refused to leave the Cloisters. "We're not even supposed to be here."

"Who's Neil?" the second boy asked.

"Our chaperone." Phil smoothed my hair. "Come on, Asteroid, buck up. This isn't a big deal." She tugged a few strands entirely harder than necessary and whispered, "Why don't you introduce me to your *new friend*? And *his* friend?"

Oh. I looked up, but I was too late. "His friend" was already doing the honors.

"I'm Seth Gavriel." This one had an accent, though it was a soft, lilting, Southern one. His hair was light brown, his eyes an unusual kelly green. Freckles dotted his nose.

"Phil Llewelyn. So what brings you boys to Rome?" She nudged me again and I stood.

"We're supposed to be in a language immersion program," Seth said. "Don't we look immersed to you?"

"Totally."

"My mom decided it was high time that I embrace my heritage," Giovanni said to me. "And since it meant coming to Rome, I didn't argue."

"That sounds familiar," Phil said. She had taken similar advantage of the situation.

"What are y'all here for?" Seth asked.

"Medicine," I said at the same time Phil came out with "History."

"Wow," said Seth, turning to me for the first time. "Aren't you a bit young for that?"

Translated: *You're not even in college, are you?* "It's a unique program," I said, and Phil stuck her tongue out at me, then whipped it back in as soon as Seth directed those green eyes of his back at her. "But very advanced."

"It's our first night out in Rome," Phil prompted with a pout. "And look what happened! Maybe we should just pack it in, don't you think, Astrid?"

I did indeed, but clearly Phil had other ideas.

"Don't do that!" Seth said, in a tone as tempting as molasses. "I'm sure we can salvage the evening, even if we are down a few euros and a passport."

"And a bus pass," I grumbled.

Seth looked at me. "Tell you what. I'll spot you your first gelato."

"How chivalrous." Phil beamed at him. "Looks like we fell in with a couple of white knights, Cuz."

Knights and maidens. Perfect. And Giovanni was still watching me in silence. As Phil and her new conquest wandered back down the alley, he spoke.

"I *am* sorry about your purse. Maybe I should have let you deal with that pickpocket in your own way."

"Right, the way where I wouldn't have laid a finger on him? Think that would have gotten me any farther?"

"No. You're an unusual warrior."

"You have no idea." If he thought I was fast running after a pickpocket, he should see me chasing unicorns.

Giovanni's lips quirked the tiniest bit, but it was enough to open up his whole face. He wasn't as tall as Seth, nor as broadly built, but I liked the look of him. "You're not really in med school, are you?"

I lowered my head. So much for that. "Try high school. I'm sixteen."

"I just turned eighteen." He pursed his lips and nodded. "That's not too bad."

Now I met his eyes in challenge. "Too bad for what?"

"To do this." He stuck his hands in his pockets and offered me his elbow, and as I took it, thrills radiated out to the ends of my hair and down to my toes. "Come on, Astrid the Warrior."

6

Wherein Astrid Makes the Leap

Seth took us to Testaccio, a neighborhood filled with nightclubs and street performers along the edge of the river. I'd never been much for clubbing, but after the silent darkness of the bone-strewn Cloisters, pounding techno music and flashing lights were a welcome change. The place was packed with young people, they didn't ask for ID at the door, and women in tight tops wandered the place passing out brightly colored shots in test tubes. Seth took an assortment and passed them around. Mine was yellow and lemon flavored, and Phil had both a red and a green. Giovanni took an orange one during the first round, then laughed and passed his purple follow-up tube back to Seth.

We soon got separated from Phil and Seth in the crowd, which didn't surprise me, though it did mean Giovanni had no one to dance with but me. Unfortunate, since Phil is a much better dancer than I am. She does this move where her hair swings in syncopation with her hips that I have never been able to replicate. Giovanni was a good dancer, too, but a few moments after we lost the others, he grabbed my hand and pulled me off the dance floor.

"It's too loud in here," he shouted in my ear. "Want to go someplace more quiet and talk?"

I knew what those code words meant. Talk means *make out*. "I shouldn't leave Phil," I shouted back.

"Good point."

We stood there for a few moments, watching the crowd gyrate. Was I really that bad at dancing that he wouldn't be seen with me out there? I looked at him and he leaned in again.

"I have to leave," he said. "Please come with me. I don't want to leave you here alone. We can just go outside, or I think there's a café next door." He turned and started for the exit, and I followed him, baffled.

As soon as we were beyond the pounding of the music, he stopped and looked at me, his jaw set. "I'm sorry about that."

"It's okay," I said. He didn't look like he wanted to make a move on me at all. "What's wrong?"

"Headache. I hope you don't mind."

I shook my head. "Not at all. Want to get some water or something? Maybe you're dehydrated."

He looked away. "Sure."

We bought a bottled still water and an orange Fanta from a vendor on the corner, then sat on a stone wall near the nightclub, close enough so that Phil and Seth would see us if they looked out.

"Do you want to know why this place is called Testaccio?" he asked me abruptly and pointed at a hill rising in the distance. "That's Monte Testaccio. It means the mountain of potsherds."

"Potsherds?"

"Broken pottery. That hill is made entirely of bits of vases and amphoras from ancient Rome. Traders would bring in shipments up the Tiber River and then dump the empty containers here." He shrugged. "It's like an ancient Tupperware cemetery."

And I was living in the ancient unicorn graveyard. I think I'd prefer broken clay pots. "You know a lot about ancient Rome."

"I was majoring in art history." He took a long drink and stared out at the hill.

"No wonder you were happy about coming to Rome, then." It was official: he really just wanted to talk.

"Yeah."

Though he wasn't talking much.

"I haven't been out much since I got here," I tried, channeling Phil's easy way with boys. "What do you think I shouldn't miss around here—aside from mountains made of pottery?"

"The Colosseum, of course," he said. "They light it up at night. It's amazing."

"That's actually right near where we're staying."

"Really?" He turned back to me. "That's a cool neighborhood." And he began telling me of ancient churches and holy relics, of vast, underground excavations that uncovered a new era of history with every layer they dug beneath the city. He talked of historical popes who threatened to knock down Rome's most famous landmark, the Colosseum, to give themselves straight shots from the Vatican to the Cathedral of Rome, and how the ancient Roman Forum was once half-buried under a cow pasture in the middle of the city. I imagined cattle picking their way among bits of columns and arches that stuck up above the earth, chewing their cuds over the tombs of Caesar and Romulus, dropping steaming patties in the once sacred Temple of Vesta.

His smile came more easily now, and he told me gruesome stories of gladiators and gladiator schools, of how they used to divert the Tiber to flood the Colosseum and hold mock sea battles, of how there hadn't actually been all that many Christians thrown to the lions after all. I wondered if they'd ever held unicorn hunting exhibitions.

"I should take you to the Borghese Gallery," he went on. "There was this Cardinal, Scipio Borghese, back in the Renaissance, and he used his power in the church to bully other patrons of the arts into handing over their stuff. 'Give me your Michelangelo or face the Inquisition.' It's the best collection."

"That sounds fun," I said.

"What sounds fun?" Phil and Seth joined us, holding hands and glistening with sweat.

"Giovanni says there's this great museum—"

"Oh no," Seth groaned. "No more museums, Jo." He turned to Phil. "He's been torturing me with them for weeks."

Giovanni took another drink from his water bottle and didn't respond, but the light had gone out of his face. I looked down at the space between us, at his hand resting on the stone wall, a few inches from my own. I slid my pinky over until it grazed against his.

His eyes met mine.

And there, in the space between heartbeats, I sensed it. Not a sound, not a sight, not a feeling, but some combination of all three. Was it the whisper of a breath or a flash of dark on dark in the shadows under the hill? Was the air tinged with the scent of embers and decay? Was it that feeling of the night in the forest back home, where I knew something was watching me, had ignored it, and had paid the price?

Giovanni frowned. "Astrid?"

I was on my feet, scanning the hill, but the moment had passed. The hair on my arms stood at attention, and adrenaline flooded my system, but there was nothing there. Nothing to chase, either human or monster. Nothing but my paranoia.

"Let's go," I said. "It's getting pretty late, and we're on the far side of town." I practically pushed Phil away from the hill, away from the wall, and powered across the square. Giovanni gathered up our empty bottles and hurried after us, and Seth caught up on Phil's side.

"Well, let's escort you home, at least," he said. "Protect you from all those nasty pickpockets."

"No complaints here," I said, though my goose bumps couldn't possibly be attributed to Gypsy children. As long as we were moving away from Monte Testaccio, I'd be happy.

Even if it meant returning to the Cloisters.

The alley in front of the Cloisters was not lit by streetlamps, and the heavily wooded park across the street provided little in the way of illumination. Phil, who had, perhaps, imbibed a few too many test tubes that evening, practically killed herself by tottering onto the cobblestones in her steeply sloped espadrilles. Seth kept a hand around her waist, making sure she suffered no worse than a twisted ankle; and Giovanni and I brought up the rear.

"You're staying here?" he asked, as we turned past the graffiti-speckled wall and into the entrance courtyard. No lights shone from the few windows facing the enclosure, but the moon, which had been hidden from view in the alleyway, bathed the stones in a pale, silvery glow. "What is this place?"

"It used to be a nunnery," I whispered, which wasn't really a lie.

"It's kind of scary looking."

"You have no idea."

From the dark space under the external wall, we heard Phil giggle. I thought I saw the shadowed form of Seth put his hand on her cheek, and I quickly looked away.

"I had fun tonight," I said. For a few hours, among the crowds of tourists and Romans, none of whom were afraid of suddenly being set upon by monsters, I almost forgot what it was I was doing here. Seth had kept his promise to sweeten the evening for us, though I wasn't sure what had really done the trick—his gelato, Phil's laughter, or my talk with Giovanni.

He was nothing like Brandt, that was for sure. Seth's shortcut route had taken us through a medieval cemetery, overgrown with bougainvillea and clogged by moss-eaten headstones, and Giovanni had been back in his element. He'd even started translating some of the inscriptions on the monuments. I doubted *he* had problems in French class. I wondered if he had problems in French anything. Not that it mattered, what with my new, celibate calling.

"Me, too," he said. He was examining the fountain. "This is very interesting. Do you know who designed it? Maybe Bernini, but I've never heard of this one before. What is the figure holding here? Looks like a magic wand." He peered closer, then stumbled against the lip of the basin. "Ow!" Giovanni shook his hand and stared at it, then up at the fountain. "That thing's sharp."

"What is it? What happened?" I said, rushing forward. I took his hand in mine and examined the wound. A deep scratch ran across the heel of his palm. "What did you touch?"

He shrugged. "I don't know, a rough edge or something. Man, that stings!"

Or maybe the alicorn? Dread set up shop in my stomach. We were a long way away from mom's magic bottle. If it would even work a second time.

"How do you feel? Are you dizzy?" I turned his hand over, searching for signs of poisoning.

"You really are into medicine, aren't you? Don't worry—I've had my tetanus shots. This'll teach me to get too close to art." He pulled his hand out of mine and turned to study the fountain again.

"Tetanus is the least of my worries," I muttered. More giggles and whispers emanated from the corner, but Giovanni seemed preoccupied.

"This is really gorgeous," he said. "I don't know why this isn't in any of the walking tour guides." He kept his distance but squinted to get a closer look at the woman's face.

"Well, they can't cover every piece of sculpture in Rome," I said, wincing every time he clenched his hand. Would a horn still be poisonous this long after being removed from a unicorn? "What was it you were telling me about earlier? Going 'churching'? Wandering from church to church in hopes of stumbling across a forgotten Caravaggio or a random Raphael?" Brandt had reacted much more quickly when he was pierced with an alicorn. This one must have lost its punch.

He didn't answer, and for a moment I wished Seth were here to shame Giovanni into leaving the statue alone. More giggles from the corner. Man, were they making out or having a tickle fight over there? I envied Phil's ability to have fun with boys

84

without ever letting it get to weird, uncomfortable places. She'd never lacked for dates in high school, nor had she fretted about sleeping with someone in order to get invited out. Phil had never put out, and she'd been superpopular.

Why couldn't I be like that? Why couldn't I kiss a guy without worrying where it would go? Was it thanks to Lilith's obsession with my unicorn hunting eligibility? Was it thanks to her insistence that now I *would* be a hunter? That no matter what other ideas I'd had about my life, I'd be shut behind these stone walls and surrounded day and night by the grinning, empty-eye-socketed skulls of my childhood terror?

But Lilith wasn't here, and neither was Neil or Cory. Why couldn't I just kiss this guy right now?

I mean, aside from the fact that he seemed more interested in a block of marble than in me. Maybe it was the universe's way of punishing me for not getting out of this mess by sleeping with Brandt when I'd had the chance.

"Ah, look," he said, kneeling at my feet. "An inscription."

I joined him, and our shoulders brushed as we crouched at the base of the fountain. "Is it Italian?"

"Latin, I think." He leaned away from me and squinted, trying to decipher the lettering in the gloom. "'*In memoriam*' . . . Obviously, 'in memory of . . .' I don't know what this word means. '*Pestilentia*.' 'Pestilence,' you think? Something something 'honor,' I think—and this word, I see it in churches all the time. This one is 'sacrifice.' '*In memory of* something something *pestilence* something *and to honor her sacrifice, a sister of the order* . . .'"

"Lioness," I said dumbly, standing. "To honor the sacrifice of a sister of the Order of the Lioness."

"Is that what the nuns here were called? The Order of the Lioness? That's a kick-ass name."

"They were kick-ass nuns." Nuns who stopped plagues. Nuns who killed monsters. Nuns who had the power to save the world. Or so Lilith would have me believe.

"Are there any left?"

I swallowed. He was talking to one. Or one who was about to be. "They kind of died out, I think. Lost their purpose."

"That's so sad."

"Do you think so?" My eyes felt hot. My throat felt clogged. Maybe *I* was the one who'd brushed against the alicorn. "Don't you think that some things belong in the past? Like closing yourself off from the world, giving up everything you might want just because your parents decided to . . . tithe you to something else?"

He stood, brushing off his hands. "You're right. That would have been rough. But nowadays, people who do things like become nuns or monks or whatever, they do it because they believe in it, because they want that life. It's not what I want, celibacy and stuff"—at that, he ducked his head and looked away—"but I can respect that other people might. A sense of purpose is a powerful thing. Enough of that, and whatever else you give up doesn't feel like much of a sacrifice, does it?"

Oh yeah? Try it.

Another giggle. I closed my eyes against the moonlight and tried to block out the sounds of my cousin and her conquest, the hot anger that banded my chest every time I thought of Lilith, the fear of whatever had been out there in the darkness, the frustration that Giovanni wouldn't even hold my hand on the one night in weeks I could pretend to be *normal* again. . . .

I took a deep breath, and again the sensation came, like hunger at dawn or weariness at dusk. My body clicked into place so naturally I barely had time to fight it. I turned my head toward the entrance to the courtyard and opened my eyes.

Again, the darkness quivered, deepest indigo on black. But then, as I had that night in the forest, I saw it more clearly. I . . . *felt* it. Just beyond the arch it stood, waiting for me, waiting for the boys, waiting to pounce. Far bigger than Bonegrinder. Far bigger than any zhi. Dappled skin, a heavy, dark mane, and a long, evil horn.

"Are you all right?" Giovanni asked, taking my arm and pulling me back toward him. "I've never seen anyone move so fast," he went on. "You looked like you disappeared for a second."

I realized that we were somehow right at the gate. In the blink of an eye, I'd crossed the entire courtyard, flashed forward, just as I had chasing Bonegrinder that afternoon.

The unicorn at the entrance took a few steps forward, then paused, just beyond the reach of the moonlight. It was the color of midnight, of shadows, of nightmares. I'd never seen anything like it. Why was it waiting? We were defenseless. Tipsy and tired and weapon free.

"You should try for a track scholarship when you do get to college if you can sprint like that."

I looked at him, blinking, trying to clear my head, but I only saw blood and death. "There's something out there. . . . Get back. You'll get hurt." I couldn't have another Brandt on my hands.

"What are you talking about?" He asked. He stretched his neck into the darkness, until he was inches from the creature.

Couldn't he feel its breath on his face? Couldn't he see how it taunted me with his death? One snap of its jaws and Giovanni would be gone. Almost two decades of art and nice hands and rare smiles. I pictured the corduroy lines on Brandt's face, remembered his blood pouring into the leaves. We had no golden bottle. We had nothing.

The unicorn's horn arced almost over Giovanni's head. It stood still, flesh and not flesh, hallucination and threat all at once. Perhaps my uncle was right, and those who saw such things were indeed mad. This wasn't Bonegrinder, all fluff and hoof and rabid-puppy attitude. This was a monster. This was magic.

"No," I whispered. *Get away. Get away.*

"Hate to tell you, Astrid the Warrior, but there's nothing out there."

The kirin—for that was what it was—parted its lips above Giovanni's scalp. I saw a flash of teeth. And in that moment, it looked me right in the eyes and dared me to come for it.

I kicked off my heels and sprang.

7

WHEREIN ASTRID DRAWS FIRST BLOOD

THE KIRIN WAS MADE OF night itself. I clung to its back, able to do little more than hang on to its cold, damp coat as it bucked and reared, tossing its head in a vain attempt to snare me with its horn. Up close I could see it wasn't invisible at all, merely brindled in the colors of midnight. And yet, as it spun in silent struggle, its hooves making no sound on the cobblestones, the world around us flickered like a mirage, the figure of Giovanni blurring as we whirled away. Could he see me? Would he hear me if I screamed?

I crawled up the creature's spine, grabbing handfuls of black mane that slid through my fingers like wet weeds. Now I could hear it breathe, hot puffs of air that stank of rot and singed my nostrils as I choked them down. My hand closed around its horn, warm and hard as a baseball bat on a summer day. I squeezed. I pulled. The kirin went berserk, twisting and twirling, leaping and jouncing me. I could hear Phil shouting my name, could make out three blurry figures at the gate, but I couldn't draw breath to yell back. My hands slipped from the horn, down the creature's face; and I dug in desperately, until I felt something squish beneath my thumb. Its eye.

I recoiled in horror, and the kirin bucked once more.

The moon swung in an arc and I crashed against the ground, fire starbursting through my arm. I cradled my hands above my head, certain any second I'd feel hooves crushing my skull into the pavement. Something warm dripped on my face, and then Phil was at my side, pulling me into a sitting position.

"Get up," she hissed. "It's gone."

I rubbed the back of my head where it had bounced painfully against the stone. No cuts, but there would definitely be a lump tomorrow.

"Dude," Seth said. "Are you some kind of acrobat? Lay off the back handsprings without a mat, huh?"

When I pulled my hand away, there was blood running down my arm. I blinked at it, half dazed.

"You're hurt—" Phil said, frowning.

I looked beyond her, to where Giovanni stood, as silent as any kirin.

"Put pressure on it," she went on.

Rivulets of blood were running from my elbow to my wrist from a deep, fiery gash on my inner arm.

"Seriously, though," Seth was saying. "What did you think you were doing out there?"

"What was it?" Phil asked, ignoring her date.

"A kirin," I whispered back. "I'm sure of it."

"On the streets of Rome?"

Unable to get our attention, Seth turned to Giovanni. "What was she doing diving off the wall?"

Giovanni shook his head, but he didn't take his eyes off me.

"I'm not . . . sure. The way she moved . . . she just vanished."

Phil was still talking. "I guess if there can be coyotes at LAX, there can be kirin in downtown Rome. . . ."

I shook her off—the cut wasn't deep anyway—and stood. "I wasn't doing gymnastics. There was something out there."

"Some *thing*?" Seth chuckled. "Like what, a monster? You told this kid too many myths today, Jo. Now she's seeing gorgons and cyclopses."

"Hey," Phil said, her voice turning dangerous. "Watch your mouth." She turned to me. "Come on, Astrid. Let's get you cleaned up."

Giovanni was still staring, but he hadn't moved a step in my direction. Hadn't even asked if I was okay.

"We can't leave them alone out here," I said. "What if it's nearby?"

Phil closed her eyes like some whacked-out psychic. "It's not. Can't you tell?"

No. I felt covered in kirin. Filled with it. Kirin caked my body like oil, burned within my blood. I hugged my arms to my chest and shuddered.

"Uh, ladies?" Seth said. "We're going to take off." He tugged on his friend's arm. Giovanni backed up a few steps but didn't turn around.

I wanted to say we weren't freaks, that whatever he saw, there was a rational, non-invisible-unicorn explanation. But what was the point? Brandt hadn't believed the mad goat story. Not even Phil's charm was having much of an effect on them. "Be safe," was all I could manage.

Giovanni looked like he would speak then, but Seth strode off, and he only hesitated for a second before following.

"Jerks!" Phil stamped her foot. "I hate boys. One second they have their tongues down your throat, the next second they bail. I hope they *do* get eaten by unicorns. It would serve Seth right for making fun of you."

I watched their figures recede into the darkness and held my breath, but if a unicorn was stalking them, I couldn't tell.

"Well, that sucked. What a downer to end a great evening, huh?" Phil said.

"A great evening that started with me getting my purse stolen?"

Phil pursed her lips. "Oh yeah. Well, nothing we can do now. Come on, let's take care of your arm. I can't believe you went after it like that! What do you know about killing unicorns yet?"

I tucked my chin into my chest. "I don't know why I did it—it was stupid. I didn't even have a weapon. But it just . . . looked at me. It was going to *eat* Giovanni."

"So you thought you'd let it get you instead?" Phil sighed, looped her hand through my uninjured arm, and guided me back into the courtyard toward the doors of the Cloisters. "Your mom would kill me if she knew I was letting you jump on unicorns your first week here."

"Lilith would kill you if she knew you were taking me on dates."

"That's true." Phil grinned. "I think it's the curse of single moms. They're afraid of their kid falling into the same trap."

No, Lilith wanted to ensure my hunter eligibility. I glanced down at my arm. Dried blood crusted on my skin, but the wound looked like little more than a scratch. Phil pulled open the giant doors, and we tiptoed into the rotunda. It was even creepier by night. No lights glistened off the gilt mosaics, and all I could make out of "Bucephalus" was an amorphous, menacing bulk; the hint of the horn; and those two, glowing, pit-like eyes.

"Have fun?"

We both jumped. A light flicked on, and I blinked at Cory, who pointed a large flashlight at us like an interrogation lamp. Neil stood next to her, his arms crossed over his chest.

"Where have you two been?" he asked.

Phil straightened. "We went out."

Cory directed the beam of her light at my arm. "Must have been a wild night."

"There was a kirin—" I began, but Neil cut me off.

"You are not to leave the grounds without permission. Imagine my shock when I was trying to introduce a new hunter and her parents this evening, only to discover that I'd lost a minor under my supervision."

"What's the big deal?" Phil asked. "I took her out for dinner. I'm her cousin. I can do that."

"Astrid's mother put her in our care, not yours. Though you're not a minor, I don't entirely approve of the fact that you're here without the knowledge of your parents. But what I do know is that you arrived without invitation or announcement and the next thing I know, you're vanishing with my hunters."

"*Your* hunters?" Phil replied. "What is it that makes you qualified to be in charge?"

Neil ignored that. "Astrid, you will wash up and go to your room. Philippa, you will come to my office at once."

I stepped forward. "Not without me, she won't." She'd defended me to Seth, now I could do the same. "Phil didn't force me to go anywhere. If we're going to get in trouble, we're going to do it together." What was the worst he could do—kick me out? Bring it on!

Neil frowned. "Fine." He turned and stalked off to his office. We followed, and Cory trailed behind until Neil practically slammed the door in her face.

"Pardon the mess," he said in a tone lacking any trace of apology. Neil's office was crowded with books and papers, computer printouts of satellite photos, and yellowed sketches of unicorns. The walls, however, were painted a smooth cream, and there was no sign anywhere of unicorn bones.

He shifted a pile of folders from a bench to the floor, and gestured for us to sit. We did, and then he took his sweet time parading around the corner of the desk and sinking into his own chair. His shirt was rumpled, his hair more so, and I thought I detected bags under his eyes. I felt a stab of guilt that he'd been worrying all evening. I'd done enough babysitting to know how tough it was to have parents show up when you didn't have everything perfectly under control.

"I'll hear your explanation."

"That's it," Phil said. "There is none. We went out. We had fun. Last I checked, those things were not illegal."

"If you believe that, then why didn't you inform me?" Ooh, score a point for Neil.

Phil was smooth, though. "If we'd asked, why would you have said no?"

He pointed at my arm. "Is that not reason enough for you? Your cousin was attacked by a unicorn tonight. An untrained hunter is in danger any time she's not inside. Don't you get it? The *potentia illicere*—the unicorn is drawn to the hunter, always. And tonight, it came for *her*."

94

"I beg to differ," Phil replied. "From what I heard, *she* attacked *it*."

I nodded in support. And perhaps now wouldn't be the best time to bring up my lost passport.

"What you heard from whom?"

"Her date."

Now Neil stood up. "You must be joking. Not only did you remove my charge from the Cloisters without permission but you set her up on a date?" He shook his head in disbelief. "Have you no respect for what we're doing here?"

"I don't see how we've jeopardized anything." Phil rose in turn.

"There's no dating allowed. That goes against every rule of the Order."

Phil laughed. "Please. I've been dating for years and I'm still an eligible unicorn hunter. What do you take us for? We just met these guys!"

"So *you're* dating, too, then." He crossed his arms. "These points aren't negotiable."

She shrugged. "You're the one desperate for unicorn hunters. How many is it you have coming now, six? Nine? Against how many unicorns?" She smiled. "*Everything* here is negotiable."

He leaned forward and smiled every bit as charmingly. "Not that. I assume you know *those* rules."

I groaned. "Don't you get it yet, Phil? This isn't a summer program. It's a lifestyle choice. If we're going to be hunters, then that's it. That's all we're going to be. Not girlfriends, not wives, not mothers . . ."

Phil looked at me, appalled. "So that's what Aunt Lilith meant. And you agreed to this?"

What were my options? Maybe I would have fought harder if I felt like I was giving up anything. But after Brandt, it wasn't like I had much of a chance with any of the boys back home. And things with Giovanni hadn't been going anywhere even before the kirin showed up. Maybe I wasn't cut out for romance, unicorn hunting or no.

"Well, that's just ridiculous!" she cried. "How do you expect anyone to submit to that?"

"Now you see why we're having such a hard time," Neil said. "The historical stigma is a tough mantle to shed. Half the extant family lines are descended from the female side—a population who rarely had descendants before the unicorns became extinct. Even if they're aware of their heritage, few are in support of it. Resistance was expected."

"Then why follow the old rules?" I asked. "You're saying you're willing to lose Philippa because she doesn't want to give up every aspect of her life to be a hunter. That you're willing to give up all of us. I'm here because my mom is making me, and because, as you say, I'm a minor. You're trying to recruit more hunters and you're just making it harder on yourself. Wouldn't it be better to change the rules to suit the fact that nowadays women are more independent?"

"To what end?" Neil asked. "Spend time training girls who ditch us the moment they decide to take their relationships to the next level?"

I didn't have an answer for that.

"I understand your points, believe me," Neil said, sitting back down. "I deeply resent being forced into the position of caring about your personal affairs. It's none of my business. But there was a reason that the Order of the Lioness was formed in the guise of a convent, and it had nothing to do with Catholicism. By taking the hunters out of the secular world, the Order removed any possibility that they would lose them to it." He gestured to Phil. "You're nineteen; you say you've been dating for several years; and yet, you're still . . . *eligible*. Do you have any idea how rare that is in this age?"

"Call me a loser to my face, why don't you?" Phil said.

But Neil was not to be sidetracked. "Especially someone as attractive and vibrant as you are. To be perfectly frank, if I hadn't seen you pass the trial by zhi with my own eyes, I'd be hard-pressed to believe it."

The look of surprise on both of our faces made him blush, and he backtracked. "You're the oldest girl here by several years."

"How does her age have anything to do with it!" I exclaimed. "You think because she's pretty and nice and fun that she should be having sex?"

"No!" Neil ran his hand through his hair. "Don't you see? *I* don't care. I didn't make the rules. But I have to follow them. The old way *worked*."

"The old way," I said, "was developed in a society where women were nothing more than chattel."

"Nothing more than what?" Phil's brow furrowed.

"Possessions." Neil explained, and slumped in his seat. "I know. And, to some extent, I agree. I see the problems inherent in asking teenagers to make a lifelong commitment. But we don't know how long it will take to have any hunters ready to fulfill their duty. In the old days, you would have been trained from childhood and you would hunt well into old age. So what do we set the terms at? Four years, like military service? Thirty, like the vestal virgins of ancient Rome?"

"Thirty!" Phil choked. "Might as well be a lifetime."

Or we got killed in action on our first hunt. There was always that option. I checked out the scratch on my arm, which had scabbed over completely. What had I been thinking, to leap at the kirin like that? I could have been killed tonight.

"Why do you get to be the one to set the terms?" I asked. "Who appoints the don? How does that work?"

Neil looked beaten. "Usually, the old don or a quorum of experienced hunters. In this situation, we had none, and so I just stepped into the role."

Good thing Lilith hadn't known Neil's position was self-appointed, or I had no doubt she'd have tried to usurp it.

"But maybe that was a mistake. Before, when it was just Marten, Cornelia, and me, it all seemed cut-and-dry. But in practice . . . maybe you're right. The old system won't work anymore. And maybe this is something we all need to discuss, as an Order, together. Nobody owns you; no one can force you to do this. And I'll admit to you: I've been hating every minute of it."

No one can force me to do this? Neil *had* been talking to my mother, right?

Phil shook her head. "If you hate it, then why are you here? No one's forcing you, either."

"Depends upon how you look at it." He put his head in his hands and was silent for several long moments. "I shouldn't be telling you this. None of it. But you're right. What makes me any more qualified to be in charge here than Philippa? At least she's a hunter. The dons never were before, but this is now."

I saw Phil lift her chin, but I was still watching Neil. He sounded nothing like the crusty Cornelius Bartoli who'd been so eagerly e-mailing back and forth with my mother.

"My sister," he began, still crumpled on the desk, "was a genealogist. It is from her records that we have been able to track most of the families. She thought the unicorns were an interesting family story, helpful only as far as they gave an intricate portrait and a series of records she could use to trace our line. She never believed it." He straightened and met our eyes. "One day about six months ago, she was out in the woods with her daughter, and they were set upon by a herd of zhi. She was killed."

"Oh my God," Phil whispered. "Neil, I'm so sorry." But I was shaking so hard I couldn't speak. *Just like Brandt.* Just like Brandt, only no one was there to save her.

"When I found them," he said, "the zhi were dead. Cornelia had bludgeoned them to death. All but one. She'd passed out, covered in cuts. The only one left was fast asleep on her lap."

I swallowed hard. "Bonegrinder." No wonder she'd wanted it dead. And I'd protected it. And Phil had . . . *cuddled* it.

He nodded, miserable. "The unicorn is drawn to the hunter, always." After a moment, he went on. "Cory knew nothing about this, nothing about her abilities. You wouldn't have recognized her then. She's changed so much. When she went through her mother's things, she discovered the existence of hunters, of the Cloisters, of the Order. Became obsessed, really. It was Cory who contacted Marten Jaeger, who contacted Lilith Llewelyn."

So it had never been Neil writing as Cornelius. Always Cory. No wonder he sounded so different in person than in Lilith's e-mails.

"We needed an adult to become don, to keep looking for new hunters, so I came aboard. What else could I do? Sybil was my sister, and now I'm all her daughter has left."

Phil reached out and laid her hand on his shoulder. "Neil," she said softly.

"You're a fraud," I said. "You and Cory brought us here under false pretenses. You haven't the first clue how to turn us into hunters."

Neil set his jaw. "We have whatever records remain, and we've been working night and day to form a program. I've got an expert bowman coming in to teach you archery; we've got Gordian Pharmaceuticals for any other resources we might need. No, we have no experience—no one does, anymore—but we know more about the unicorns than anyone alive."

"And," Phil said in encouragement, "I'm sure that the new hunters might have family records that could come in handy." She smiled at him and I felt the urge to scream.

I stood up. "Yeah, you people are just *steeped* in expertise. I'm going to call my mother and tell her exactly what's going on here."

Now Phil did turn on me. "Think it will make a difference to her, Astrid? 'Oh, sure, sweetie. Forget that whole unicorn hunter business and come on home.' Yeah, right." She looked back at Neil. "I want to help you. You've been through way too much on your own. But it has to be on equal footing. I'm a hunter, yes, but I'm not going to sit back and be anyone's . . . chattel, or whatever. I'm a grown woman and I get to make my own decisions."

"Agreed," Neil said, and he sounded relieved.

She glanced at me. "And we should take into account the desires of the underage hunters as well. Not just Cory but all of them. I'm not saying chaos, but it's unfair to enforce centuries-old rules where they no longer apply. I know we can work something out."

I made a sound of protest, but she ignored me, continuing to outline her little coup to Neil. That was it. I'd been bossed onto a plane by Lilith, bossed around since I arrived by Cory. I would not be bossed around by my three-years-older cousin. I whirled on my heel and stormed out of the office.

Phil caught up to me before I was halfway across the rotunda. "Astrid, wait."

"No!" I hugged my arm to my chest and kept on going. "You were supposed to make all this better. Bearable! And now you're buying into it. I wish you belonged to Mom and I belonged to Uncle John! Then I'd never have to be here."

She tugged me in close. "Astroturf, come on. Don't be like that." Inside her arms, she felt like Lilith. Taller than me. Stronger than me. I tried to push away, but Phil had spent hours in the gym and could spike a volleyball so hard into the court it left a mark. "Don't you see how much better this is going to be?"

"No. I'm trapped here either way."

"But not forever. And not the way they want. Think about it. You said Cory wants to hunt the unicorns into extinction. And if your mom had her way, she'd lock you up in here and throw away the key. I may not know all your fancy words, I may not know anything about hunting at all, but I can read Neil. He can't do this alone. He needs us, as hunters and as helpers. And we need him on our side. Don't you see? *Work* the system. Don't fight it."

"Fight the unicorns?" I scoffed, pushing away and holding out my injured arm. "So that next time they can hit me someplace much more delicate? We may be immune to the

101

poison, but no one is immune to a big sharp horn through the gut. A foot to the right, and I could have died tonight. Brandt could have died in the woods back home. Sybil Bartoli? *Dead.* And nobody here has the slightest clue about how to train us, how to make us safe."

Phil had no answer to that.

I pointed at the figure of Clothilde behind us. "She trained all her life, and she was still killed by the karkadann. Unicorn hunters *die*, Phil. This isn't a game. You can make all the pacts you want so that we can go on dates, go to college, leave after however many years in service, but it doesn't change the fact that my life is in danger here. I don't want this. I'm *not* a warrior."

"But tonight—"

"Tonight I was crazy. It won't happen again." I stopped talking, suddenly feeling very out of breath.

Phil bit her lip and studied me. "Astrid, I love you so much. And I swear—I swear—that I want you to be safe, and I want you to be happy. And I'm going to do what it takes to make that happen."

"You're going to get me out of here?"

She didn't respond.

"Didn't think so. Good night."

I took the stairs, wincing when I reached for the banister and stretched the scab on my arm. I wanted to rip the bone sconces from the walls. I wanted to smash the bones that jutted from the masonry. On the dormitory floor, I saw a light on beneath the door of another room that must belong to the new hunter. I glanced at the names on the door as I passed by on my way to the bathroom at the end of the hall. DORCAS AND URSULA.

You've got to be kidding me.

I washed and disinfected the nearly healed cut as best as I could. I may be immune to alicorn venom, but who knew what kind of germs unicorns carried? On the plus side, I got to use some of the first-aid supplies Lilith had packed for me. I applied both a liquid bandage and a surprisingly neat row of butterfly stitches—considering I was putting them on one-handed.

The light was off in the room I shared with Cory, and the lump on her bed clearly had nothing to say to me. Moonlight glinted off the glass frames on her shelf, the pictures of her mother, of her dog, of a time when she, too, was normal.

I tried to be as silent as possible as I tiptoed in, changed into pajamas, and climbed into bed. I lay still and breathed deep but remained awake. Phil had joined me at the Cloisters, but she wasn't on my side. My passport was gone, so I couldn't even run away. And I'd never see Giovanni again. Minutes passed, maybe even hours, but my head was too full for sleep. My eyes burned, my head ached, and my arm itched, but I didn't cry.

Instead, I thought of the kirin.

8

Wherein Astrid Welcomes the Hunters

W HEN I WOKE THE NEXT morning, Cory had already dressed and vamoosed, which, to be honest, was a relief. I still didn't know what to say to her. I made my bed, then padded off down the hall to the bathroom, rubbing my thumb against my palm. I'd washed it thoroughly last night, but it hadn't made a difference. My dreams had been filled with kirin, and my skin smelled of fire and flood. When I emerged from the shower, seven lukewarm and trickly minutes later, I saw a tiny, pale-skinned girl with a mousy brown shag standing over the sink, dabbing at her red-rimmed eyes.

"Hi," I said. This must be Dorcas. Or maybe Ursula.

She burst into tears and ran from the room. At last, someone who wanted to be a hunter even less than I did. I hurried after her, tying a knot in my robe belt as I went. I saw her brush past Cory in the hallway and disappear into her room, slamming the door behind her.

Cory shifted the bundle of linen in her arms and snorted. Then, without acknowledging me, she walked into yet another of the rooms. I followed.

"Is she okay?" I asked.

Cory turned her back on me and heaved the linens onto one of the beds. "Dorcas Bourg, of the family Bourg. Belgian by birth and spoiled princess by trade. You should have seen her complaining about the rooms yesterday." She ducked her head into the wardrobe and began rummaging around.

"Is there anything I can do to help you?"

The sounds stopped, but Cory stayed behind the door. "Aren't you going home soon? With your cousin?"

"No. We had a long talk with Neil and—"

Cory slammed the wardrobe closed and glared at me. "He told you."

I met her gaze. "Yes. Cory, I'm so sorry."

She clenched her fists, then stretched out her fingers several times, breathing hard. I thought she might throw something again. I thought she might throw *me*.

"I can't imagine what you've been going through," I managed.

She crossed to the bed and starting snapping out the sheets, whipping them across the mattress and tucking them in so tightly I was surprised the bed didn't buckle under the onslaught. I fell silent. My wet hair dripped onto the carpet.

At last, she said, "We've two more hunters arriving soon, so there's plenty of work to be done."

And that was that. She didn't speak again, and she avoided me for the rest of the day. Even when our chores brought us together, she wouldn't look me in the face, and she refused to join any conversation Phil and I had. Even the ones about unicorns. Now that Phil had decided to take on a more active role at the Cloisters, she was filled with curiosity. There was no escape.

I caught myself thinking about the kirin quite a bit, remembering its greasy mane, the fire in my blood when its horn punctured my skin. The scab on my arm was almost completely healed, thanks to my careful ministrations. But I could still feel kirin eyeball against the pad of my thumb.

Dorcas's parents returned to the Cloisters to take their leave. They swept by us—the husband in a business suit, the wife bejeweled and smelling of expensive perfume—with nary a backward glance, and disappeared into Dorcas's room. I noted that Ursula's name was crossed off the sign on her door.

"Apparently," Phil whispered to me, "she can't have a roommate."

"What, like she's allergic?" Maybe I should have tried that excuse myself.

"No, she *can't* have one or she won't stay, according to Neil." Phil shrugged. "See what I mean about negotiable?"

To judge from Dorcas's behavior in the days that followed, it was also negotiable whether or not she would come out of her room to join us. Neil, Cory, Phil, and I worked night and day to get the Cloisters ready for real training. I mucked out ancient, dusty stalls filled with the bones of rats—better than unicorns—and dusted off targets galore. We hauled mattresses and swept closets and helped Cory organize stacks of yellowed diaries and other records.

Cory began to speak to me again, and I studiously avoided any conversation that might touch upon her mother. I worried every time I mentioned my own in her presence. How could I talk about how much I resented Lilith when I knew that every moment Cory would kill to have her mom bossing her around? *Had* killed.

The next hunters to arrive were Rosamund Belanger, a budding pianist from Vienna, and Zelda Deschamps, a Parisian model Phil swore she recognized from last fall's *Vogue*. Zelda was about six feet tall and had the most gorgeous skin I've ever seen—smooth and so black it almost looked blue in the half-light of the entrance hall.

Both Rosamund and Zelda seemed skeptical about the displays in the front hall, as well as the existence of Bonegrinder—who acted just as happy to see them as she was to make the acquaintance of all the hunters. Phil had been keeping the zhi in her room, which kept me well out of it. I'd been creeped out by the unicorn before, but now, knowing what it had done, I wanted to be nowhere near the animal.

Cory had said nothing about the new sleeping arrangements. I think she worried that broaching the topic of Bonegrinder with Phil would no doubt lead back to the reason the zhi lived here in the first place.

But I was dying to ask her who had named it.

"You must understand," Rosamund said in accented English, stroking Bonegrinder's soft fur with long, slender fingers. "My family knows nothing of our heritage. Cornelius Bartoli told us that we are of the"—she looked at Cory as if for confirmation—"Temerin line."

"Female descent," Cory clarified happily, and I wondered if it had been she or Neil who'd been acting as "Cornelius" when talking to Rosamund's family. "But for all we know, that could make you even stronger. I'm from a bastard line myself—several generations back of course. Great-great-great-grandmother was a governess in a Leandrus household."

"When did you guys strike it rich?" Phil asked. I frowned.

The Bartolis were rich? And Phil knew it?

Cory grinned. "When her hunter daughter saved a son of the noble line of Bartoli from a particularly nasty re'em. Apparently, it was love at first sight."

"Wait," I said. "She was a hunter who left the Order to get married? I thought that was verboten."

"No," said Cory. "This was around the time of Clothilde and the Last Hunt. She was out of a job."

Good for her.

Zelda had kept her distance from the zhi during this exchange. "I don't do animals," she said.

"That's going to make this mission of ours a little tough," said Phil, ruffling Bonegrinder's floppy ears.

"Not if all I have to do is kill them."

I heard Cory mutter under her breath, "I like this one."

Both Rosamund and Zelda were seventeen, and Cory had assigned them to the same room. Early the following morning, though, Zelda was still in bed while Rosamund stood dressed and ready at our door, asking where the music room could be found.

Cory had blinked. "I think there's a piano or something downstairs in the chapter house. But I would be shocked to discover that it worked after all this time."

Phil joined us, with Bonegrinder clopping along at her heels. Zelda emerged, sleepy eyed and wearing a silk robe, and even Dorcas deigned to trail along, curiosity clearly getting the better of her determined isolation.

Back into the bowels of the Cloisters, down to the chapter house, with its Wall of First Kills, its darkness and its grimacing skulls. Even if the piano worked, I didn't know how Rosamund planned to play it in the dark, with all those dead things watching her.

We all took lanterns this time, so at least there was a little more light. In fact, well lit, and facing away from the Wall of First Kills, the room was almost cozy. Perhaps the horror factor was entirely due to the decor. Walls of bones might have been the height of interior design fashion in the sixteenth century, but I'd take a chair rail and a still life with fruit over that any day.

The vaulted ceiling was high and practically airy, like a giant cavern or even a cathedral. Phil pulled the muslin covers from the furniture, revealing chairs, tables, even couches. She moved across the vast space, shoving aside dustcovers and lighting sconces as she went, and I realized that not all the room looked like a student lounge.

On the far side of the chapter house, another wall was hung with rows upon rows of weaponry. Axes, spears, bayonets, long bows and crossbows, a katana engraved with golden lions, and small round copper shields showing dents and puncture marks all through their colorful emblems and embellishments. Arrow tips of alicorn and swords whose grips and pommels were set with shavings of the same. There was indeed a piano, with legs that swirled upward like mahogany alicorn and keys not made of ivory, but of bone; as well as a harp that seemed constructed of a giant, curved horn like an elephant tusk, carved with fanciful beasts and resting on a base of golden lions.

Was everything in this room made of unicorn?

"Wow, look at this." Phil pulled off another cover. Smack-dab in the center of the room sat the largest relic of all, an enormous throne, resting against the base of the composite column that supported the vault of the ceiling. Every inch of this throne was constructed of alicorn, from the enormous arcing horns that made up the frame, to the twisting maze of many-sized alicorns that crossed and recrossed the back, sides, seat, and base. From a distance, the horns seemed to twist around one another like snakes, endlessly writhing within the prison of the throne, patterns forming and dissolving in each flicker of lamplight. Every time I blinked, I saw something different—a crescent moon, a lion digging its claws into a unicorn's back, a vast field of battle, a temple afire.

I hated it. It made the hair on the back of my neck, my arms, everything, stand on end. I swayed on my feet, fighting back waves of nausea, dizziness that had erupted the moment Phil had uncovered the throne. I stayed back, choosing to hug the formerly terrifying Wall of First Kills.

Cory stared at it, agog. "Unreal," she said. "There's no mention of an artifact this intricate in the records I've seen."

"Maybe they wanted to keep it a secret," Phil said, "if horns are as valuable as you say."

Cory looked at Zelda. "You're from the Hornafius line—the craftsmen. Could they have made this?"

Why was she so insistent that we carried on the same specializations as our distant ancestors? Despite the trials by zhi, I still wasn't sure there was anything to the claims of Alexander the Great's DNA being responsible for our abilities. I certainly didn't feel like I had anything in common with a Macedonian warlord. Genetics didn't work like that, anyway.

But my roommate never let a little thing like science get in the way of her quest to eradicate an entire species of mammal.

She confronted Zelda. "Does your family have anything—"

Zelda threw back her head and laughed. "My grandparents disowned my mother when she took up with my father. I'm afraid I won't be much assistance on the family history front."

"But," Cory argued, "now that you have adopted your family birthright . . ."

"They're racist pigs, more interested in the purity of their family legacy than the reality of their actual family." She shook her head. "I want nothing to do with the Hornafii."

Rosamund wandered toward the wall, then stopped short. "Do you hear that?" she said.

We all glanced at each other. "What?"

"The wall. It hums." She leaned in. "This note." She sang a single note, high and clear.

Cory shook her head. "I hear nothing." Philippa, Zelda, and Dorcas concurred, but I stood there, frozen.

I didn't hear anything . . . not exactly, but when she'd sung, I felt . . . I don't know. I felt the same sharp pain the wall always caused. "Sounds are vibrations, right?" I asked. "I feel . . . vibrations, near these bones."

The other four looked at me in shock, and then, one by one, came closer to the wall and placed their palms against it. I gritted my teeth and joined them, and Rosamund did the same.

And then, at once, we heard it. A chord, wild and triumphant, stark and cold. And then, again, stronger than ever, I tasted the same scent I had encountered the first time I'd entered the Cloisters. Fire and fungus, oldness and ozone.

We took our hands away and the chord stopped. Rosamund crossed to the piano and sat down on a small stool, brushing her red hair away from her face as she placed her hands on the

111

yellowed keys. "This chord . . . it was this chord." She played something, and the strings vibrated that same wild sound.

Zelda shook her head. "I know little of music. What does that mean?"

Cory watched Rosamund intently. "I can't believe it . . . I've been here for weeks, and I never heard."

I lifted my hands. "Okay, while we're talking about weird things we're sensing around here, does anyone else notice that smell?"

Zelda looked at me. "I thought it was mold."

Dorcas shook her head and spoke for the first time. "No, it smells like wood burn. That's what I thought it was."

Cory looked clueless and bit her lip as all the other hunters concurred. "I smelled it," she protested finally. "At first. I just . . . haven't in a while. I've been here so long, I guess I just got used to it. I'm going to do more research into these vibrations," she added quickly, then turned away from the wall.

"Great!" Phil said, plopping down on the throne. "Now maybe we can hear Rosamund play—" Her words dissolved into a scream and she leaped up as if burnt.

"What's wrong?" I asked, rushing forward. Phil's arms shook, and she seemed to have trouble standing.

"It . . . shocked me," she whispered, then choked, as if retching. Everyone backed away from the throne, and I helped Phil to another chair. "It hurts."

Phil felt better after a minute or two, and in the end, Cory and Neil roped off the chair until we'd looked into the situation. According to the records we found later, the throne had been a gift to the Order from the people of Denmark, following a particularly bloody battle in the fourteenth century. Phil went around touching every bit of bone in the building, but she said nothing shocked her the way that throne did. I suggested that maybe it had been a fluke of static electricity, but then Dorcas dared me to go near it, and I'd hardly gotten my hand on the armrest before I felt arrows of pain shooting up to my elbow.

Between the alicorn throne and the hum from the Wall of First Kills, Rosamund was the only one who was willing to spend any amount of time down in the chapter house, banging away at the piano, which, miraculously, had lost neither strings nor tune in the centuries since it had last been played.

I wondered if the instrument employed unicorn gut instead of cat.

Phil and I were the only representatives at the Cloisters from our family line. The next to arrive, sixteen-year-old Melissende Holtz, was, like Rosamund, another descendant of the Temerins. They were a family, Cory informed me in hushed tones, that accounted for some of the most ferocious and bloodthirsty hunters in all of her records. Personally, I wondered how far back their common ancestor was located, for I'd never seen two more dissimilar girls. Rosamund was a tall, elegant redhead who'd bonded instantly with Zelda and Phil and whose clear, well-trained soprano had been echoing through the stone residence halls since her arrival. Melissende had black hair, gray eyes, and a permanently sullen expression on her face. She seemed to like it here as little as I did, but, if asked, would only say in her gruff smoker's voice how thrilled she was to get out of Bavaria. Her parents had been aware of their unicorn hunting heritage, and when reports started to leak into the media about the Reemergence, they contacted us.

Melissende also completely ignored her kid sister, Ursula, to the point that the younger girl had been in the Cloisters for almost a full day before I realized they were related. Ursula, twelve, had been intended as fourteen-year-old Dorcas's roommate, and at first Cory was worried that Ursula would feel isolated without someone closer to her age around. Luckily, around that time, Neil received reports of a twelve-year-old outside Delhi who had been keeping a zhi as a pet, and we added Ilesha Araki to our roster and to Ursula's room.

We did not, however, add her zhi, as Bonegrinder more than kept our hands full. Ilesha was reportedly heartbroken at leaving him behind. Cory wondered why they hadn't put the beast out of its misery then and there.

"We're supposed to kill the bastards, not feed them," she argued, knee-deep in a vain search to trace Ilesha's ancestry. "Am I the only one around here to remember that?"

"Neil says she's got a little sister who promised to take care of it." I was helping Cory, mostly because Neil's office was one of the few places in the Cloisters that didn't make the hairs on the back of my neck stand up. I found the hum of his computer rather soothing, but it was the complete lack of unicorn carcasses that really pulled the room together.

Cory switched to her Latin dictionary. "That little sister would be far better served coming here and learning how to kill unicorns than staying home and caring for one. Ten is more than old enough to be away from home, in my opinion. What was my uncle thinking?"

Perhaps that he didn't want to pay for two tickets from Delhi if the kid would wimp out within the week.

Then came Grace and Mika Bo, of the Singaporean family

Bo. According to Neil, the Bos had been highly discriminated against in the previous incarnation of the Order of the Lioness because, back then, the European families considered them "Oriental savages." It had apparently taken a Herculean effort by Neil and the influence of Marten Jaeger to get the family to agree to come to Rome at all.

The hunters had taken to gathering in the rotunda to witness the trial by zhi, and as we formed our customary shield around Mr. and Mrs. Bo, all I could think was that the father seemed quite happy with the proceedings, while the mother looked ready to cry.

"There's nothing to fear, ma," the older girl, Grace, said over her shoulder as she brushed past our shield. "Ugh, what is that smell?"

The younger girl sniffed at the air. "What? I can't smell anything."

"Because you're a snot nose." Grace yanked her younger sister by the hand. "Come, Mika."

Her father glared at her. "Gentle with your sister." Grace rolled her eyes.

Phil was standing across the rotunda, restraining the zhi with a hand on the bright blue bandanna she'd foolishly tied around the monster's neck, and Bonegrinder practically hanged herself on it in her eagerness to get at the newcomers. The Bo girls took their place before the shield, hands joined, and Bonegrinder began to yip in short, breathy gasps.

"Oh, do strangle yourself," Cory whispered.

Behind me, Mrs. Bo sobbed softly. On either side of me, Cory and Rosamund were exchanging glances of uncertainty. But I felt it, too. Something was wrong. Together, we glanced back at

Bonegrinder as Phil released her hold on the bandanna.

There was bloodlust in the zhi's eyes.

"No!" Mrs. Bo cried, breaking out from between Cory and me. "Take me!" She slid to her knees in front of the body of her youngest as Bonegrinder barreled toward them, her horn aimed directly at the woman's heart.

9

Wherein Astrid Offers a Challenge

Not *again*. I stood, frozen, as the unicorn galloped toward the girls. In my mind's eye, I saw Brandt's face, purple and poisoned, but I could not will my feet to move. The scent of death filled my nostrils, blood roared in my ears. And yet, even through my fear, I could feel myself—my innate hunter instinct—gauging the distance between my body and the unicorn's. The world slowed, just like the last time I'd chased her, just like the time I'd gone after the kirin. My thigh muscles tensed as if to spring. And yet I didn't move. I couldn't make it in time. It was too late.

Grace Bo put out her hand and grabbed Bonegrinder by the horn as she flew by. She swung the beast roughly around, and Bonegrinder's hooves knocked Mrs. Bo to the floor. Mika Bo cried. Everyone screamed.

The other hunters hastened to re-form the shield around Mika and her mother, as Grace, with Phil's help, wrestled the unicorn to the ground.

Mr. Bo's face had turned purple. "What is the meaning of this?"

Mrs. Bo lowered her head and clutched her daughter to her chest, but did not respond.

Grace pushed her long black hair out of her face and stood, leaving Phil to wrangle Bonegrinder. "Ba ba," she said to her father, bouncing on her toes. "Did you see me? Did you see me take the unicorn?"

He brushed her aside, pushed into the shield, grabbed his wife roughly by the elbow, and pulled her to her feet. "Who has been messing with my daughter?" he seethed.

Tears fell freely down Mrs. Bo's face, and she shook her head. He moved on to Mika. "Tell me, light of my life. I shall ruin him. Tell me."

"I swear, Ba ba, I swear . . ." Mika began.

"Don't you see, Ba ba?" Grace said. "She's not hurt. She's just not yours." The words echoed around the stone enclosure, and the girl once more circled until she faced her father. "*I'm* your daughter, Ba ba. *I* am."

Mr. Bo just looked at his wife and blinked.

"Phil," Neil warned, and my cousin sprang into action. She herded the rest of the hunters out of the rotunda, keeping tight hold of Bonegrinder's bandana collar.

Dorcas shook her head as we were hustled away. "I don't get it. What was wrong with that girl?"

"Have you ever seen that before?" Ursula asked Cory. We had retreated to Rosamund and Zelda's room, a spot that had quickly become the social center of the dormitory floor. Zelda lay sprawled on her bed, flipping through a magazine thick with glossy photos of bony models. Rosamund was painting her nails. Phil was brushing Bonegrinder, and Cory was looking green around the gills.

"Not that particular issue, no," Cory said. "I've seen a few who failed the trial by zhi, which was awkward in the extreme. But in most cases, it's a self-selecting process. If the girl understands the danger Bonegrinder poses, she will admit if she's ineligible, no matter what the consequences might be at home. We've even fudged the facts for the parents if the girl comes to us privately."

"What I don't understand," Phil said, "is why you don't just give every girl being tested the ring Neil wears. That way, if she doesn't pass on her own merit, at least she isn't hurt."

"Then what would Uncle Neil do for protection?" Cory asked.

"What does Neil need to be there for?" Phil said. "Make a hunter administer the trials."

"But now that we're all here," Cory said, "we hunters will be preoccupied with training."

Phil shrugged. "I don't know. It just seems barbaric, the way we do it now. In the old days, I bet they used to let the girls who failed the test be killed by the zhi."

I shuddered.

"They used to do all kinds of horrific things in the past," said Melissende. "One of my ancestors was a donna of the Cloisters, and every year she tested the girls by piercing their chests with the tip of an alicorn. If they healed, they could stay."

Gross.

"And if they didn't, they were dead anyway," Cory said. "Immunity to the poison is contingent on virginity."

"There are many bad ways to die," said Rosamund. "A vestal virgin who was guilty of breaking her vows was buried alive."

Yeah, but suffocation was supposed to be like going to sleep. Alicorn poisoning was gruesome. Then again, at least it was quick.

Dorcas looked up from where she was biting her nails. "Were the vestal virgins unicorn hunters, too?"

"*Wirklich?*" Rosamund exclaimed. "Then they would have something more to do than tend a hearth all day. I always think that job is too easy."

"There's some evidence for it," Cory said. "Especially since the cult of the goddess Diana was based outside Rome—in Aricia—in ancient times."

Phil leaned over and whispered in my ear. "Who were the vestal virgins again?"

Cory looked over, smirked, and broke into lecture mode. "Vesta was the Roman goddess of the hearth. The vestal virgins were her priestesses. Their job was to make sure that the sacred fire in her temple in the Roman Forum never went out. According to legend, as long as it was lit, Rome would not fall."

"Got it. Thanks," Phil said brightly. "So what—"

But Cory wasn't finished. "They also were in charge of various and sundry items that were sacred to the Roman people. They performed certain rites, presided over the court system, and had rights and privileges that no other Roman woman possessed."

"Interesting," Phil said, in a tone that meant *enough*.

"Like what?" Ursula asked.

"They could own property, for one." Cory began counting off on her fingers.

"So not just *chattel*," Phil whispered.

"And they could be carried around the streets on a litter. And if they met a condemned prisoner on his way to execution, he was pardoned."

Zelda flipped a page in her magazine. "What does any of that have to do with unicorn hunting? So far, they're just other virgins. Like Catholic nuns. Isn't that what the Order of the Lioness pretended to be?"

"Right, but all the vestal virgins' responsibilities were associated with purification," Cory said. "They performed ceremonies that supposedly kept the granaries free from poison, and for the festival of Lupercal, they made these special cakes that supposedly induced fertility and health in anyone who ate them."

"The Remedy," I said softly. "They were the hunters in charge of the Remedy."

Cory nodded. "Exactly. The priestesses of Diana in the temple in the Arician countryside south of Rome were the hunters. But the priestesses of Vesta, here in the city's center . . ."

"Were the healers," I finished. So ancient Rome divided up the hunter responsibilities between those who killed the unicorns and those who healed the people. I liked that idea. It must not have been combined until the medieval period, when priestesses of pagan gods gave way to Catholic nuns.

Dorcas piped up again. "My father always said our gifts are a heritage from Alexander the Great."

"The lineage of Alexander the Great determines who gets hunter powers," Phil said, clearly happy she knew something about it. "If you're his descendant and a female and a virgin . . ."

"Very stupid," Rosamund said. "He was not a woman or a virgin!"

"Had to be a virgin at some point," Melissende grumbled. Phil laughed.

"But do you know why that is?" Cory asked Phil. "Do you even know why we're here in the first place?"

"I'm sure *you* do," Phil said, and seemed very interested in a knot of hair under Bonegrinder's chin. She tugged, and the animal nipped at her fingers with razor-sharp little teeth.

Cory did indeed know. "In 356 B.C.," she began, as if narrating the prologue from an epic blockbuster, "on a hot summer night, a fire broke out in the Temple of Diana at Ephesus—in modern-day Turkey—one of the Seven Wonders of the Ancient World."

Zelda stopped flipping pages. Rosamund paused, her polish brush hovering over her thumbnail.

"They say it was set by a man named Herostratus, who wanted to be remembered for some action of his."

"Arson?" Phil twirled her finger in the air. "Whoop-de-do."

I shrugged. Clearly, it worked. Now *I* knew his name.

"The temple was the home of many priestesses of Diana. In one of her incarnations, she was the Mistress of the Animals and held sway over all the creatures of the forest, the mountains, and the desert. Like her, many of her priestesses were virgin hunters charged with tracking and culling the beasts of the land." Cory paused. "The most fearsome of which was the unicorn."

Bonegrinder started licking her own belly.

"On the night of the fire, these priestesses were trapped within the temple and burned alive."

A chill passed through my body.

"The goddess was not present to save her priestesses, because, in her incarnation as the goddess of childbirth, she was in Macedonia, watching over the wife of King Philip as she gave birth to his son, Alexander. So the story goes that in memory of the priestesses she lost, the goddess Diana bestowed upon Alexander the Great and his female descendants the powers of the virgin huntress." Cory smiled beatifically, and everyone was silent.

I snorted. "Are you serious? *That's* the explanation?"

Cory looked offended. "Of course."

"That's idiotic," I said. "First of all, we don't have any special hunting powers for bears or boar or mallard ducks. Just unicorns. Diana must have been a little stingy, huh?"

"It was unicorns because they are the most deadly of all the animals!" Cory argued.

"Okay," I said. "Here's another thing. Why does Alexander get to be the only guy with special unicorn powers, and after that it's just the female descendants?"

"Because it was Alexander's birth that prevented her from stopping the fire."

"So all of a sudden the goddess Diana, who isn't exactly man friendly, decides to sacrifice all of her priestesses, her entire virgin huntress entourage, for the sake of one baby boy who is more interested in conquering cities and doing stuff that virgins *certainly* aren't doing—otherwise we descendants wouldn't be here in the first place—than doing the whole virgin hunting thing?"

Rosamund looked thoughtful. "Even more, Alexander the Great didn't hunt unicorns. He tamed them. His warhorse Bucephalus, the one he tamed as a child, he was a karkadann, yes?"

Melissende nodded. "In my family, they say that Alexander's military power was due to Bucephalus. That he planned his strategy with the unicorn, carried on conversations with it. That's why he couldn't conquer anymore after Bucephalus was gone."

"A talking unicorn?" Cory said skeptically. "I think that's a tad unrealistic."

I let out a bark of laughter. *That* was the unrealistic part? "This whole story is nothing more than a myth! Who were the hunters before the birth of Alexander? Just those priestesses? Are you saying no one had any defense against unicorns outside this one Turkish temple—no one in the Far East or in Western Europe—because they didn't worship the goddess Diana?"

Cory crossed her arms. "Okay, Astrid. What's your oh-so-rational explanation?"

"I have no idea," I said. "I think the whole thing is nonsense, frankly."

"How can you say that after everything you've seen?" Cory asked. "After what we all just witnessed with the Bos? One a descendant of Alexander, one not. And look what happened."

"Just because I don't know doesn't mean there isn't a good explanation," I said.

"You work on that," Cory said, "and I'll use the explanation we've got."

Phil looked back and forth between us. "Come on, girls. Don't tell me we're going to have to separate you two. Sock one of you in the Temple of Vesta and the other in . . . Where was the Roman Diana place again?"

"The Temple of Diana in Aricia," Cory said. "But it doesn't work anyway, because I'm a Leandrus, and she's a Llewelyn, and the Llewelyns are supposed to be the best hunters—"

I groaned. "Oh for the love of—"

Bonegrinder jerked almost out of Phil's grasp. In the hall, we heard voices, and I stopped talking.

"You aren't leaving already?" It was Grace Bo.

"I'm afraid we must," said her father. "It's a long trip home."

"But, Ba ba—"

"Do not shame our family." Footsteps in the hall. A door closed.

Bonegrinder pulled to her feet and Phil led her out of the room. She crossed the hall to the door marked MELISSENDE AND GRACE and knelt on the floor.

Cory glared at me. "Explain that."

Now that we had gathered a good group of hunters, Neil wisely decided it would be best if we were actually trained to, you know, *hunt*. He and Marten brought in an archery and bowhunting expert from the countryside to teach us the basics. His name was Lino, and they found him after a news story on the rise of wild animal attacks profiled him as one of the top game hunters in the country who, despite his prowess, had been unable even to hit one of the strange animals who were depleting livestock in his area.

The poor guy was despairing of our abilities before we'd finished setting up the targets in the courtyard. Lino watched us struggle to anchor the legs of the target in the ground, shaking his head and casting worried glances back at Neil, who sat with Marten Jaeger on the edge of the wall separating the aisles from the courtyard. At the far end of the courtyard, Phil was fastening Bonegrinder's chain to a metal ring set in the stone walls. The presence of the three men agitated the beast more than a little. She'd been drooling all morning.

The overcast sky had been threatening rain for the past hour, and I secretly wished the barometer would drop a bit more. Perhaps a storm would send us all inside. Then again, Cory hadn't spoken to me since our argument about Alexander the Great, so maybe being trapped in our shared room was a fate worse than archery.

Last night at dinner—which Grace Bo had not attended— Cory had taken one look at our table, which featured a full-throttle Phil regaling Neil and the other hunters with a story about last semester's state volleyball competition, and remembered some very important research she'd had to do in Neil's office. I almost wanted to join her. Post–Mad Goat Incident, I knew exactly what it was like to feel left out.

Yet I remained where I was at Phil's side.

Lino had unpacked half a dozen bows of different sizes and shapes, some featuring gears and levers and struts that made the contraptions look more like camouflage-pattern torture devices than the graceful—if gruesome—ancient bows on the wall downstairs.

"Who is the first?" Lino asked. "We must test your draw." He pointed at Dorcas and held out a bow that looked like a picture frame made of carbon alloy with metal strings. She took the weapon gingerly in her hand and began to ape his positions and movements.

But she couldn't draw the string back at all. He fiddled and adjusted, encouraging her all the way, until she managed to pull it about halfway back. After that, it seemed to be a bit easier, but she could hardly hold it for more than a second before setting the whole thing down and shaking out her arms.

"Ten kilos only," Lino said sadly.

Jaeger and Neil exchanged looks.

As Lino repeated the process with the next hunter, I joined Cory and a few of the other girls by the table of weaponry. Along with a variety of bows, he'd laid out hunting knives of all shapes and sizes, as well as arrowheads barbed with movable bits of metal and wood and fiberglass arrows, fletched with different kinds of feathers or even tiny, paper-thin flecks of plastic. At one end of the table, nestled within protective foam cases as if made of fine china, lay several guns.

"What I don't understand," Melissende was saying, flipping an unlit cigarette around and around in her fingers, "is why we're wasting time with bows and arrows. This isn't ancient Rome. Can't we just shoot unicorns with sniper rifles?"

"No," Cory said. "They can't be killed by bullets."

Oh, here she went again. I'd personally gouged out a unicorn's eye with my thumb. They weren't made of titanium.

"Why not?" Melissende asked. She lit the cigarette, and Lino stiffened, marched over, whipped it out of her mouth, and stamped it out in the grass.

"You will stop that. The animal can smell it. And all of you, no more perfume, okay?"

We nodded, our eyes on the giant bow in his hands.

"We are very far from even using arrows, today," Lino said. "You all must do many exercises to improve your arms." He marched Ilesha off to test her draw.

The other hunters started playing with the various articles of camouflage and scent masks the instructor had brought along. Not that they'd be much use, considering how unicorns were drawn to us, no matter what we wore.

Cory began playing with one of the guns, picking it up and

screwing things on and off. "You really want to know why not?" she asked Melissende, who shrugged and moved on.

"I'm more interested in why we can't use crossbows. They're cooler than either guns or longbows."

"It's all the same reason," Cory went on, but Melissende had lost all interest. "It's because the bolt's too short." Melissende took out another cigarette and turned away. "I'll show you!" Cory said in a rush.

"What do you know about guns?" I asked Cory, terrified that any second the thing would explode.

"A bit," she said. "More rifles than handguns, though. My grandfather used to hunt quail and pheasant and other fowl on our estate. He took me out to shoot skeet with him when I was young."

"So you have some hunting experience, then."

She shrugged and collapsed the base of the handgun. It made a strange, echoing click.

"Though birds aren't exactly unicorns," I added, as she pulled a lever on the barrel.

She looked at me, gun pointed down at the ground. "I've killed more unicorns than you." Then she lifted the gun and aimed it at Bonegrinder. I heard a pop, and the zhi staggered against the column.

Phil screamed.

Bonegrinder dropped to one knee, wheezing, as blood poured from her body in twin streams.

10

WHEREIN ASTRID SHOOTS AND SCORES

PHIL RUSHED ACROSS THE courtyard toward the unicorn.
Lino had Cory's gun in one hand, and Cory's arms pinned behind her back with the other. He was shouting at her in Italian.

"Astrid!" Phil called to me. "Help me! She's bleeding!"

I ran over to my cousin and the animal. Blood gushed from opposite sides of Bonegrinder's torso. Phil placed her hands over the wounds, and blood spurted from between her fingers, dark and so hot it practically burned.

"Help me, oh, God, help me," she begged. Bonegrinder calmly lifted her head and licked Phil's face. Blood began to pool around the zhi's white fur. So much blood. I pictured collapsed lungs, organs shredded within her body. The little unicorn didn't have a chance.

From a distance, I heard Neil yelling at Cory.

"A towel!" I cried. "Someone get us a towel!"

A shadow fell across us. "She will be fine." I looked up. Marten Jaeger stood over us, making sure his shiny leather shoes were well away from the creeping pool of blood. "Take your hands away—you will see."

"Don't," I said to Phil. "Keep the pressure on."

But Phil lifted her soaked, red hands and peered down at one wound through blood-matted fur. "It's closed up."

Marten nodded, a soft smile on his face. "Cornelia is correct. Bullets will not harm a unicorn. Why do you think Clothilde used a sword even in the eighteen hundreds?"

Ilesha cleared her throat. "May I let go now?" she asked. Her arm shook, but she still held the string back at full draw. Lino's jaw dropped and he released Cory.

Bonegrinder began to lick at the spot where the bullet had gone in. Rosamund joined us, her arms full of both wet and dry towels. She began mopping up the blood as Phil scrubbed at Bonegrinder's fur.

"It's healed," Phil said, half in exultation, half in wonder. "It's all healed. How is that?"

Marten shook his head. "I wish we knew. This is what my research is all about. Somehow, the regenerative power of the unicorn is embodied in the Remedy. Unless the wound is kept open, it heals almost instantaneously. But despite all the tests we have run on this particular animal, we cannot isolate this property."

"You tested her?" Phil said angrily. No wonder Bonegrinder had been scared of the scriptorium.

"Of course. We had the zhi under our care until the Bartolis departed our facility to work on the Cloisters. We couldn't keep the zhi without young Cory's supervision, you see, and she was very eager to . . . look into the potential of reconstituting the Order. A shame, really."

"Really," Phil mocked.

"See that mark on her horn, on the right? We shaved off a bit for testing." I looked and saw that one of Bonegrinder's screw-shaped twists was a tad lopsided. "We took blood, urine, and stool samples. We tried various and sundry operations and poisons. Nothing had any effect." He gestured at the zhi. "You can't even see the scars from the vivisection."

Phil was speechless with rage, and I was sure she was about to sic Bonegrinder on Marten. The zhi looked like she might enjoy it, too. Clearly, the smell of blood—even if it was her own—had whetted her hunger for flesh. And maybe I understood Bonegrinder's angst, but at the same time, how many humans would Gordian Pharmaceuticals save if they discovered the key to the Remedy? Wasn't that the whole point of hunting unicorns? Saving people?

"Sir," I said quickly, "you promised to show me some of the papers you'd been working on."

"Certainly," Marten replied, but then he was distracted by a commotion in the courtyard. Neil and Cory were locked in a full-fledged screaming match.

"—discharge a firearm at such close range, with so many people around!"

"Look!" Cory pointed at Bonegrinder. "She's fine. It was just a .22—"

"And what if you missed?"

"Grandfather trained us both, and I was always a far better shot than you!"

"Cornelia, this is unacceptable. We talked about this. We talked and talked—"

"Yes," she said. "We talked plenty, *then*, didn't we?"

Neil stiffened. "What do you mean by that?"

Cory crossed her arms.

Neil took a deep breath. "Go upstairs to your room. I shall speak to you at the end of the lesson."

She lifted her chin. "So now we play you're the don and I'm the hunter? How droll."

Neil stared her down. "I *am* the don, Cornelia. And you *are* the hunter. Go. To. Your. Room."

Everyone else became very concerned with the state of his or her shoes, and all was silent for a moment. Then Cory turned and walked off, as stately as a queen.

"An unfortunate spectacle," Marten said with a little shake of his head, as Lino locked up the guns and moved back to the bows. Phil was cosseting Bonegrinder, who seemed no worse for wear. "Would you like to go next, Astrid? I am very curious to see your archery skills."

"I have none," I said. "I'm not much of a jock."

"But you are a Llewelyn."

I resisted the urge to roll my eyes. Were even the unicorn scientists nuts?

"And, what's more, I heard that you single-handedly took on a kirin the other day."

I didn't know if that was something Neil should be bragging about. If anything, it showed how unprepared we really were. I tried to get back on topic. "Actually, I heard something very interesting yesterday about historical hunters." Maybe Cory's information could do some good after all. "Apparently some of them were experts in the Remedy rather than in hunting—"

"Yes, but not from your family."

I was pretty sure there was no one named Llewelyn in ancient

Rome, so how would he know what family the vestal virgins were from?

"Look," I said, hating the note of desperation in my voice, "I've been studying biology and chemistry my whole life. I've never wanted to be anything but a doctor."

"That's nice," he said, watching the hunters struggle to draw their bows. Grace was doing pretty well, actually. Lino moved her on to nocking her bow with one of the arrows he'd brought, but her first shot went way wide, soaring over the roof of the aisle and clattering against the wall of the dormitory.

Of course Marten wasn't impressed by me. He probably had a fleet of biochemistry Ph.D.s on his payroll. High school chemistry didn't mean he was going to toss me a lab coat and tell me to have at it. My powers were only for hunting, not for wielding beakers and microscopes.

Now Zelda couldn't even hold her bow up. So how much were these hunter powers of ours good for?

"So anyway," I tried again, "I would love to see what you're working on. If there's anything I can do from here to help you with your research, just let me know."

Now he looked at me sideways. "And what would that be?"

"Whatever you need. Any observations I notice when I'm . . . out in the field. Any kind of information I can give you." Like what it felt like to squish a unicorn eyeball. "I just regret that we don't have that sample of the Remedy from home. This whole process could have been so much simpler—"

He narrowed his eyes. "You were in possession of the Remedy?"

"A few traces, yes. My mom had this antique bottle with some residue inside. But we used the remainder on a . . . friend of mine after he got gored by a zhi."

"And it worked?" he pressed.

"I don't know what it's supposed to do, but he didn't die." Come on, Astrid, you can do better than that. You just finished telling him what a great scientist you are! "In fact, the symptoms of alicorn poisoning stopped almost immediately, and the wound closed like . . ." Like magic.

"Was it administered orally?"

"Mostly, but we also poured some directly onto the wound. My mother tried both, since she wasn't sure how it was supposed to be used."

"Did your friend give any description of the experience?"

"No. The next time we spoke, he broke up with me."

"Ah," Marten smiled knowingly. "Not a very good friend, then." He regarded me. "A very foolish one, in fact. You saved his life. And you're a hunter. Both are very admirable qualities."

Ha. The quality Brandt had looked for most in me was not compatible with unicorn hunting. "Yeah, well . . ."

"What was this young fool's name?"

"Why?" I asked. "Gonna track him down and beat him up?"

"No, but I would like to look into his recovery. He was cured by the Remedy. Who knows what sort of properties his immune system might now possess?"

Of course. How stupid of me. "Brandt. Brandt Ellison."

"Excellent." Marten folded his hands before him. "You may be a big help to my search after all, Astrid."

I beamed.

"Look; it's your cousin's turn." He turned back toward the courtyard. Phil was taking her place beside the table of bows. She'd wiped off most of Bonegrinder's blood, but her clothes were stained red, and bits of hair and gore stuck in the fleshy bits between her fingers and on the insides of her elbows. The sun had begun to burn through the clouds, and her hair shone golden in its light.

She picked up a bow and arrow, nocked it, drew back, and let go. The arrow pinged straight into the heart of the deer-shaped target.

"Lucky shot," Grace whispered to Melissende.

But I knew it wasn't. I'd been watching Phil play volleyball for years. Her serves were deadly. Phil proceeded to shoot three more arrows, each plunking into the target within inches of one another.

Marten Jaeger's eyes practically sparkled. "Now *there's* a hunter."

Suffice it to say, I was not as good a shot as Philippa, but even I was surprised when I hit the target—in the knee, but at least I was close—twice in a row.

"The Llewelyn girls are by far the best of the group," Lino reported to Neil and Marten.

"That surprises no one," Marten said, peering at us. "How soon do you think they'll be able to hold their own?"

"Against a stag or even a boar, like I hunt?" Lino asked. "I wouldn't want them with me now—they'd take all the game; they are that good. But against an animal like the one here today, or the bigger ones"—he shook his head—"I don't know. An animal that will hunt you even as you hunt it. . . . It is different."

"But how soon?" Marten said, a note of anxiousness in his cultured tones. "In your opinion."

"They will train very quickly," Lino said. "They are natural born."

I groaned. So much for my new scientific calling.

"And the others?"

"The red-haired girl is promising," Lino said, "if she weren't so concerned with hurting her hand."

"My piano is my life," Rosamund exclaimed in defense.

"The Indian girl as well."

"Don't we have names?" Phil hissed to me.

"And Grace has excellent form. The rest will need some work."

"There," I whispered back. "A name."

Lino lowered his voice and whispered something to Neil, whose face turned grim.

"Yes, well, we know that about her," he said, his jaw tight.

I bet they were talking about Cory and her fabulous aim.

I found the hunter in question lying on her bed in our room, reading yet another of her ancient diaries. I stripped off my blood-spattered clothes and gathered my shower things without speaking to her, and she didn't look up. Then it was more of the same when I returned, dressed, and combed my hair.

So this was how it was. Just like after Neil had first told us about her mother. Last time, I hadn't pressed. This time, I figured enough was enough.

"Cory," I said. "What you did today—"

"Don't you lecture me, Astrid Llewelyn. Don't you *dare* lecture me."

"I'm not."

"Then what are you here to say?" She looked up from her pages. "That you're leaving because I broke my promise? Fine!"

"What promise?" I was confused.

"That I wouldn't hurt that—*thing*! That horrible, awful, wretched, bloodthirsty monster! That I wouldn't do anything to your precious little man-eating beast. And you and your stupid cousin could pet it and snuggle with it and tie little pink bows around its neck, and all the while, it's sizing up the people you love for lunch."

I'd forgotten about our bargain. It seemed so long ago—before Phil, before the other hunters, before I knew the truth about Bonegrinder.

"And I promised I'd sit here and pretend that wasn't so, pretend that every time I look at it, I'm not seeing . . ." She broke off.

I dropped to my knees by the side of her bed. She was clenching the sheets reflexively. "No," I said. "I don't care about the promise. I understand."

"It's all I see. It's all I feel, the blood on my hands. Sometimes it's like it's still there. Little bits of blood and hair and skin and meat. Under my fingernails, all over my body."

I put my hands over hers, held on tight until she stopped moving. "I know." I could still feel the kirin, days later. And I hadn't even killed it.

"There were three of them," she said. "A family. A sow and a bull and then . . . her."

It was the first time I'd ever heard Cory refer to Bonegrinder's gender.

"And Neil said she was just a baby, like it *mattered*." She dropped her face into the coverlet. "And he made us keep her. And feed her. And *name* her." Her voice broke. "Actually, he was the one who named her. I was busy trying to find someone who would take her off my hands."

How it must have rankled to see Phil caring for Bonegrinder all this time. I should have considered it. We both should have.

"And so I found Marten Jaeger, and Gordian. It's terrible to say, but I liked the idea of her spending the rest of her miserable life in a cage, the subject of horrible medical tests. I used to fantasize about her all covered in little electrodes—oh Lord, I sound mad, don't I?" She lifted her head, and her eyes were red and swollen with tears.

"A little," I admitted. I hadn't minded the thought of using Bonegrinder for medical testing, though even I had been appalled at the idea of vivisecting her and then—what, tossing her in the corner and seeing if she healed? But at the same time, I didn't want to dwell on it.

But the unicorn hadn't killed *my* mother.

"However, it was much worse than I imagined. And I couldn't leave. If I wasn't present, she escaped. No matter how many cages, no matter how many restraints. And I couldn't watch them do those things to her. Even after what she did." She swallowed thickly, then said, "I know you don't believe me."

It was, in fact, very hard to imagine Cory doing anything other than relishing the experience of watching Bonegrinder suffer. She'd thrown the zhi off a balcony just to watch her squish. She'd shot her in the gut today with nary a thought.

"So I left. And she came with us, our 'house zhi.'" She let out a little sob. "And I hate myself for not killing her, for not being strong enough to do it myself, strong enough to let *them* do it by inches. And I hate *her* because she couldn't figure it out. She didn't know I wished her dead every second. She loved me, and I hated her, and I hurt her, and she *still* loved me. She wouldn't go away!"

138

And now the tears did flow. "But you know what I hate most of all? That it's not true. She *doesn't* love me. She loves *hunters*—it could be you or Phil or anyone. A hunter. And if not a hunter, then meat. They can't help it. She didn't *murder* my mother. None of them did. It was just meat, like wolves after a hare. Like my grandfather and a pheasant."

Part of me wanted to agree with her, but the other part remembered how the kirin had taunted me, shown me a vision of Giovanni's gory death. Giovanni wasn't "just meat" to that unicorn. He was something that belonged to a hunter. But that was a kirin. Maybe the zhi were simpler, as well as tame.

And I didn't know what to say to comfort Cory, either. In the end, did it make a difference whether her mother was killed by simple wild animals or by magical monsters that knew they were attacking something important to their only known predator? Either way, Sybil Bartoli was dead. Either way, Cory was stuck caring for her killers' colt.

"So now she doesn't even love me anymore. I guess I drove her away after all. And she's not the only one."

There was a knock on the door. I answered it, and Neil brushed in. He went straight to Cory and enfolded her in his arms, saying nothing at all.

I left the room and closed the door behind me.

We all sat together for dinner that evening. Marten Jaeger had left, citing urgent business, and Lino had packed up his bows and departed. Bonegrinder had completely recovered and was lying at the foot of Phil's chair, her forelegs curled protectively around what looked like an elephant vertebrae. Cory and Neil had arrived late to the table, both mildly red-eyed but with pasted-on smiles and hearty appetites. Neil joined the discussion about the afternoon's archery lesson and Cory remained quiet, though I caught her looking at me enough that I wondered if I should propose a joint trip to the ladies' room to finish our conversation. In fact, I'd opened my mouth to do so when there was a huge slamming sound against the bronze doors of the rotunda.

"Bloody hell," Neil grumbled, ripping the napkin off of his lap. "We need to get a lock on that door. Someone grab the beast, then."

Bonegrinder was already on her feet and shivering. Phil looped a rope around the zhi's neck, and we all rushed out toward the rotunda.

"Wait!" Dorcas cried as we went. "That's a big sound. You don't think a unicorn would actually try to come inside, do you?"

By this time, Phil and Bonegrinder had made it into the rotunda. I was right behind them, and practically tripped over Phil, who had stopped dead.

Just inside the door stood a grungy-looking girl. There were dark, baggy circles under her eyes, her hair was chopped in rough chunks colored a variety of faded-out shades (but mostly black), there were few spots on her face that didn't sport piercings, and the leather cuffs at her neck, wrists, and waist all had metal spikes sticking out. She was wearing about fourteen layers, torn fishnet stockings, and combat boots. She stood there, pigeon-toed, face downturned, dragging a rucksack with one hand and a half-filled military-issue duffel with the other.

"*Prego*?" Neil asked.

She looked up from between her rough bangs at the gaggle

of figures in front of her and smirked. "They said you feed me." Her eyes were bloodshot and her pupils were dilated so much you almost couldn't tell the color of her irises.

"Oh dear," Cory said, stepping forward. She still held her fork. "You must be mistaken. We're not that kind of nunnery. There's a soup kitchen a few blocks from—"

"No!" the girl shouted. "They said *you* feed me!"

I held out my hands, palms up, and moved toward her. "Hi," I said gently. "What's your name? I'm Astrid."

"Val. Valerija Raz." She glared at me. "I'm hungry."

"Who, ah—" Neil searched for the right tone. "Who told you to come here?"

She shrugged. "Dunno."

Cory tried again. "We'd like to help you, but really, there's some sort of error. We don't deal with . . ." she trailed off. I saw her mouth move in question at Neil. *Urchins?*

Whatever. Surely we could spare the girl some pasta. I took another tentative step in her direction. "Hey, Valerija," I began.

She jumped back. "They said come here!" She reached into her duffel. "They see what I did to *this*."

She held it aloft by its horn and we all gasped. The midnight dark skin, the brindled coat, the gaping maw, and most of all, the blood that oozed freely from the jagged edge where head had once met neck. A kirin's head.

Phil grabbed my arm, hard. The kirin was missing one of its yellow eyes. Apparently, not everything regenerated.

Valerija Raz lifted her chin. "They said here is where I belong."

11

Wherein Astrid Devises a Strategy

It wasn't until I saw Valerija unpacking her meager and questionable supply of belongings in Philippa's room that I began to truly appreciate sharing with Cory. At least I never worried that I'd be garroted in my sleep.

Valerija had brought with her a change of clothes, a hubcap, seventeen watches, three knives (one regular, one switchblade, and one Swiss army), a plastic retainer case that rattled like it was filled with pills, a bowl and spoon encrusted with gunk, three paperback books in an alphabet I didn't recognize, a bottle of perfume, a coat, and a plastic bag filled with snapshots.

Even Phil looked nervous. "How did she kill that thing?" she whispered to me from the door. "Not with a switchblade, that's for sure."

"Ask her," I whispered back, and gave Phil a little push.

Valerija whipped around, eyeing Phil ferociously.

We all backed away. "Maybe I'll just let you settle in," Phil said, retreating.

The hunters convened in Zelda and Rosamund's room. "I'm locking my door," Rosamund said. "Did you see her knives?"

"Did you see that kirin?" Phil insisted. "How did she kill it with a knife?"

I nodded. "Even if she slit its throat—unlikely, given what we know about Bonegrinder's rejuvenation capabilities—she'd need something much stronger to saw through the spinal column."

Cory arrived. "Neil's still trying to get in touch with Marten. This is so exciting! A completely unknown hunter, coming to us on her own! Has anyone been able to figure out who sent her here?" She looked at Phil.

"And get shivved for our efforts?" Phil asked. "No thanks." I bit my lip. Truth was, Phil had spent the last ten minutes trying to strike up a conversation with her new roommate and had gotten precisely nowhere.

Cory made a sound of frustration in the back of her throat. "Fine. I'll do it." She set her shoulders and marched out.

I stared after her. "Maybe someone should go along, just to make sure . . ."

"She can look after herself," Phil said. "Besides, Cory's the only one who cares where she's from or what *family* she belongs to. As far as I'm concerned, if she killed a unicorn, that puts her far ahead of most of us."

"She's clearly homeless," said Zelda, "whatever else she might be. I'm curious, though. It's uncommon that someone in her situation would be also . . ."

"*Eligible*?" Phil said. "Well, don't judge a book by its cover. We have no idea what her story is."

"True," Zelda admitted. "After all, most of the girls I know from work aren't virgins anymore. They are always surprised when they learn I am." She looked at Phil. "Why are you?"

Phil shrugged. "I've got high standards. There's no real reason. I'm not saving it for anything special, like my one true love or the person I marry. I just don't want to sleep with every guy who comes along."

"I'm Catholic," Rosamund said. "I don't want to sleep with anyone but my husband. That's very difficult for my friends to believe." She looked at Zelda. "Are you religious, too?"

Zelda ducked her head and walked over to her desk. "No. But everyone thinks that's the only good reason."

"True!" Dorcas said. "Whenever someone finds out I'm a virgin, they say it's only for religious people. And then they try to talk me out of it."

"My friends say that, too," I said. "My last boyfriend—I was supposed to sleep with him."

"*Supposed* to?" Zelda said. "Why?"

Oh, this sounded so idiotic now. "Because he was going to take me to the prom."

Everyone groaned.

"I know, I know," I admitted sheepishly. "But it didn't matter. He got attacked by a zhi."

"Really!" Rosamund exclaimed. "What happened?"

I explained to them about the Remedy, and how he'd broken up with me after I'd cured him.

"Be glad you didn't sleep with him!" Phil exclaimed. "Brandt Ellison is bad news. You should have let the zhi finish him off." She shook her head. "I still haven't forgiven you for dating him."

"I broke up with a boy to come here," Dorcas said. "That's why I was so sad at first. I loved him, but he wouldn't sleep with me. He kept telling me he didn't want to be *The One*. We could do everything but have sex." She lowered her voice. "He even wanted to . . ." She gestured vaguely behind her.

"Gross!" Phil exclaimed. "He'd do that but not the regular kind? What is with guys, seriously?"

"Well, he said that way I couldn't get pregnant."

I shuddered. Maybe not pregnant, but all other manner of terrible things.

"Can't get pregnant with a condom, either." Melissende said with a snicker. "I hate men. There's my answer."

Grace watched us all from her corner. "My father wouldn't let me see boys. I went to an all-girl school and he was very strict about dating."

Dorcas sighed. "Well, when you finally do get to meet one, they'll decide you're a freak for waiting."

"I get that a lot, too," Phil said. "It's worse since going to college. Apparently, if you haven't slept with anyone in high school, there's something wrong with you—you must be saving it for *something*. And no one wants the responsibility." She laughed. "I couldn't care less, though. To me, it just proves that if a guy doesn't want the 'responsibility' of being first, he isn't worthy of being any number at all."

"That's easy for you to say." The words escaped my mouth unbidden.

Phil looked at me, hurt twisting her mouth into a frown. "What do you mean, Asteroid?"

"You were always so pretty and popular in school. If you didn't sleep with one guy, there were plenty lined up. We don't all have that."

Phil blinked. "You're telling me you dated that slimeball, Brandt—that you would have *slept* with him—because he was the only one who wanted to?"

Everyone was looking at me. I said nothing.

"Because that's the worst idea I've ever heard of. Screw those idiots at our high school, Astrid. There are a lot better guys out there. What about those cute boys we met the other day?"

Giovanni and Seth? "The ones who thought we were freaks and ran—*ran*—away from us? Yeah, they're prime dating material."

"Well, they were both about ten times cuter than any boy we went to high school with. So don't judge the entire male species by whatever losers we happened to date back in our hick hometown."

"What does it matter?" I cried. "We're not dating anyone anymore. We're hunters. We're chaste. It doesn't matter who we would have slept with or why. If I'd gone ahead and slept with Brandt, I wouldn't even be here!"

"An Actaeon," Melissende said. "That's called an Actaeon."

"What is?" Dorcas asked.

"The man a hunter has sex with in order to be released from duty." She pulled another cigarette out of her shirt pocket, looked at it fondly, and sighed. "It was a relatively common situation. Not everyone who *could* be a hunter wanted to be. It was one way to get out of it."

No surprise there.

Rosamund said, "Actaeon . . . from the myth? He was the man who surprised the goddess Diana in her bath."

Melissende nodded.

"But he was killed! Turned into a stag and torn to pieces by his own dogs."

"The hunters had a different punishment," Melissende said with a cold smile, "because we had different pets."

I shivered. "Did they punish the woman, too? Bury her alive like a vestal virgin? Set the zhis on her?"

"What do you think?" Melissende hissed, then lit her cigarette.

Phil held up her hands. "Okay, enough of this talk. People did all kinds of bloodthirsty things in the old days. Inquisitions and torture and throwing folks to lions for sport. But that was then. No one is burying anyone alive around here. Or letting Bonegrinder loose. Understood?"

Dorcas and Rosamund nodded. Zelda rolled her eyes and turned a page in her magazine. Melissende blew out a cloud of smoke and exchanged glances with Grace. "Of course," she said.

Cory came running in, eyes alight. "She's a Vasilunas!" She smiled and bounced. "Can you believe it? A Vasilunas. They were supposed to have died out."

"How does she know?" Phil asked.

"She traced it herself," Cory said. "The Vasilunases were known for their tracking ability. They were beyond compare when it came to finding unicorns."

"Oh," said Melissende. "Like dogs."

And for the first time, Cory, Phil, and I were in perfect agreement. We all gave Melissende a dirty look.

"Where are you taking me?" I asked Phil for the seventh time.

And for the seventh time, she deferred. "What part of 'it's a surprise' are you having difficulty with?"

"The part where I don't like surprises. Does Neil know you're 'removing one of his hunters from the Cloisters?'" It had been a week and a half since I'd last left the grounds—the night I'd met Giovanni and attacked the kirin.

She tossed her head and walked on. "Neil and I have an arrangement." We were in a stunning wooded park in the north of Rome. The afternoon sun slanted through the leaves; birds sang overhead; people walked to and fro with their pet puppies; and all along the path, vendors sold gelato and pastries from carts and stands.

"Really," I said in disbelief. "And what is that?"

"We both understand that what he doesn't know can't hurt him."

"Phil!"

She sighed. "Such a goody-goody. Fine. I told him I needed a more hunting-appropriate wardrobe and that I was taking you shopping with me." She grabbed my hand and pulled me along. "Come on, we're going to be late."

We went over another rise and into a sunny clearing dominated by a large palace in creamy stone and marble. Knots of people milled around the fountains and steps outside. At the end of the path stood Seth and Giovanni. Seth smiled and waved as soon as we came into view.

I stopped dead.

"Surprise!" Phil said, and tugged harder. "Come on."

"But—" I trotted at her side. "I thought we were angry at them. They ditched us."

"Seth called my cell the other day and apologized," Phil said lightly. "Said he couldn't stop thinking about me. That Giovanni couldn't stop talking about *you*. And that they wanted to make it up to us." She cast a glance at me over her shoulder. "See, there are some very cute, very nice guys who *do* like us. Let's not go slumming with jerks like Brandt, hmmmm?"

By now, we'd reached the boys, so Phil was spared my response.

"Hey!" Seth said. "We were beginning to think you wouldn't show. They're really strict with entrance times around here." He started handing out paper tickets.

"Where's here?" I asked, looking up at the building.

Seth cocked his head toward Giovanni. "Blame the professor and his art fixation. He pulled all kinds of strings to get us these tickets."

"Did not," said Giovanni, who had materialized at my side. "I just bothered to call in advance."

"I like Seth's story better," said Phil.

Giovanni turned to me. "It's the Borghese Gallery, like I told you about last time. There are some amazing pieces inside. Raphael and Bernini. All kinds of stuff. I thought you'd enjoy it."

I smiled at him, but all I could think of was the look he'd given me after I'd attacked the kirin. The curators opened the doors, and guests with the correct entrance times on their tickets began moving inside. We followed the herd, listening to Phil and Seth chattering away.

"Let's go upstairs first," Giovanni said. "Everyone does the ground floor first and it gets crowded." He led us up a wide spiral staircase done in gilt and marble, different in almost every way from the steep, dark, narrow stairs in the Cloisters.

The first few galleries featured oil paintings of the Virgin Mary holding baby Jesus on her lap, as well as portraits of famous Italian noblemen and church officials. There was even a set of busts showing Cardinal Scipio Borghese, the famous patron of the arts himself. He was a burly man, with round cheeks, intelligent eyes, and a very presumptuous air.

"He was pretty ruthless in getting the artwork he wanted," Giovanni explained. "And because he was a cardinal, he had a lot of power. There was one time that another nobleman had commissioned a painting, and when Borghese saw the artist working on it in his studio, he insisted on being the one to receive it. When the nobleman refused, Borghese set the Inquisition after him until he agreed to give it up."

I looked at the sculpture before me. The face in the stone seemed almost smug now.

"That's cool," Seth said. "I'd like to have that kind of pull." He took hold of Phil's hand. "Come with me if you want to live!"

Phil yanked her hand from his and wagged her finger at him. "He was a priest. No girls."

"Eh, they were all corrupt back then, anyway." Seth threw his arm around her shoulder and led her across the gallery.

As soon as we were alone, Giovanni fell silent. I waited for him to show me the next piece of art, but he said nothing, just moved forward and started studying the bust from another angle.

Great. He didn't really want to be here with me. He was just babysitting so Seth could hang out with the girl who *didn't* chase invisible unicorns.

Seth and Phil wandered out of the room, and I trailed after them, but at the door, I couldn't tell which of the many rooms jutting off the foyer they'd gone to next. I turned to the right and found myself in the biggest gallery of all. Over a massive fireplace hung an enormous oil painting of the goddess Diana, a crescent moon on her brow, surrounded by a bevy of half-naked girls with bows and arrows. Some were shooting at targets, others splashed with their hounds in a clear pool, and still others carried in their prey, tied to sticks slung over their shoulders. I stopped dead and just stared.

"It's Diana and the Hunters," Giovanni said from behind me. "By Domenichino. Another artist Borghese had thrown into jail until he gave him the painting." He pointed at a figure hiding behind bushes near the right-hand edge. "See that guy watching them? It was supposed to be a terrible crime to catch sight of the virgin goddess bathing."

So I'd been told. "Like Actaeon," I said.

Giovanni nodded. "Exactly. You know your mythology. Here, he's only watching one of the hunters in her entourage, though. He may survive that."

"She may even like it." I pointed to the naked, swimming hunter. "See, she's looking out of the picture at us and smiling. She knows we can see her, and she doesn't mind." Maybe she even thought this Actaeon could get her out of the hunting gig altogether.

Giovanni grinned at me. "You're a pretty good art critic."

"Thanks." I looked down.

"Sorry—Does this bother you?"

"What?"

"Me making fun of the cardinal and stuff."

"No!" I shook my head. "Why would it?"

"Because you're going to be a nun."

My mouth dropped open. "I'm not going to be a nun!"

His expression turned confused. "But . . . I heard you were. And you're staying at that convent . . ."

Exactly how much had Phil told Seth about our little "convent?" "I'm not going to be a nun," I repeated. "It's . . . kind of complicated. There's a family tradition, but I don't want any part of it. I'm only here because my mom is making me. I'm going to leave as soon as I can."

"Oh," he said, sounding relieved. Perhaps that's why he'd been acting so weird. How awkward would it be to go on a date with someone you thought was about to take holy orders? "I thought you were a little young to be making that kind of decision. But when he told me, with the way you were acting the other day . . . it made some sense."

"The way I was acting?"

"Yeah." Now he looked away. "You kept running away from me, and then—"

"I can explain about that," I said quickly. But how could I even start? I wasn't running away from him. I was protecting him!

"Yeah, I can, too." He frowned. "I just don't like the explanation." He started moving to the next painting. "Come see this one. It's a Raphael." He led me toward a smaller painting, hung on a side wall, off from the others. Giovanni stopped before it and looked back at me. "What do you think?"

I gaped. The portrait showed a young woman sitting by a window, cuddling a zhi in her lap.

"It's called *La Dama con Liocorno*," Giovanni said, studying me. "The Lady with the Unicorn."

My heart pounded, but I pulled myself together. "Nice." Phil would probably love it. "Was it any lady in particular?" Heck, Cory probably knew the family lineage off the top of her head.

"Not sure," Giovanni said. "But apparently it was common to paint portraits of brides posed with unicorns before their weddings as gifts to their grooms. It was a symbol of innocence and purity. That's probably what this painting was."

"Probably," I said, staring at the portrait. Around her neck, the girl wore a necklace with a red stone not unlike the carbuncle in Neil's ring. Maybe she wasn't a hunter at all. Maybe she just wore the stone for protection while she posed. Still, would a zhi be so well behaved in the arms of any non-hunter?

"I bet they painted her with a lamb in her lap and added the horn later," Giovanni was saying.

"Probably," I echoed. But I knew a zhi when I saw one. This one was even tinier than Bonegrinder, a real baby unicorn. I couldn't imagine how scared Raphael must have been to have this monster in his studio. I finally tore my eyes away, and Giovanni was still staring at me. "What?" I asked at last. "You're creeping me out."

"Nothing." He shook his head and forced a laugh. "No, actually, it is something, but it's crazy, and I probably shouldn't even tell you. I'd never see you again."

"Try me," I said. Maybe he knew. He brought me to this picture for a reason. Maybe he'd seen the kirin after all and couldn't believe his eyes. Maybe it wasn't me who'd scared him off the other night, but the monster. *Just say the word "unicorn" out loud and I know you won't think I'm a freak if I tell you everything.*

A few steps away was a wide bench upholstered in black leather. We sat down, knees grazing, and Giovanni rested his elbows on his thighs and folded his hands. "Here's the thing," he said, eyes focused on the floor between his feet. "I'm not just here to learn more about my mom's side of the family."

"I know. You wanted to see Rome, too."

"I got kicked out of school."

153

"What?"

He sighed and was quiet for a long time. "Last semester. I was way into partying, I was rushing a frat, I lost track of everything. One night . . . I was incredibly drunk, and a little high, and there was a huge fight. People got hurt—the whole pledge class was brought up before the school's disciplinary committee and we got expelled. I lost my scholarship."

"Oh." I clasped my hands in my lap, unsure of what to say. What did this have to do with the other night, with that chick over there with the unicorn in her lap?

"My mom and dad—they didn't want to deal with me. They sent me away to stay with my relatives here and 'think things over.' But mom's family is really strict and religious and it was driving me crazy. So I applied to this program, and by some miracle got in, and I'm hoping that I can parlay it into getting back into college."

"I bet you can," I said. "Any art history program would be thrilled to have you. You're really smart."

"No, I'm really stupid. When we went out the other day, I had that drink. It was just that one drink, but I wanted more. That's why I left the club. I knew I could stay and party, but if I got in trouble again . . . this is my last chance."

"I understand," I said. In a way, he was trapped here, too. "So . . . about the unicorn?"

"What unicorn?"

All the blood drained from my face. "The one in . . . the picture," I said lamely. "Didn't you—weren't you—trying to make a point?"

He cast me a sidelong glance. "Why would you think that?"

I had no words. Where was Phil to help me pull my foot out of my mouth? What would Giovanni say if I confessed everything? All I could picture was that moment back home, when Kaitlyn looked at me like I was a freak. When Brandt had laughed at me in front of the whole school.

Giovanni was silent for a moment, then almost groaned. "Okay, here's the thing. I thought I saw a unicorn, the other night, when I was with you. Crazy, huh? That's why I split. I thought maybe there'd been something weird in that drink back at the club—some drug—and I'd screwed up again, without even knowing it. I didn't want to go berserk in front of you."

"I think there was something in our drinks," I said softly, hiding my disappointment. Crazy, indeed. "I saw a unicorn, too."

"Weird that we had the same vision. Must have been after seeing that fountain in your courtyard."

"Or maybe it was real," I suggested, but he must have thought I was joking, since he laughed.

"I'm really sorry you got hurt," he said. "I felt like a jerk afterward. I was scared of what I'd done. After all my work to fix my life, just one little drink, and things slipped right out of my control. I don't want to be that guy anymore. The one who parties, who fights. But I should have stayed and helped."

"I had Phil," I said. "Besides, it will teach me not to chase unicorns."

He chuckled, which was totally the wrong answer. "I don't think it's a good idea for you and your cousin to hang out with us. We're bad influences. You're too nice."

Nice meaning *innocent.* I could translate Giovanni's English just fine. "So you see me and you what—think of that girl up there?" I nodded to the portrait.

"Hardly." He took my hand. "You're way prettier than she is."

I rolled my eyes at the flattery.

"Plus, she probably couldn't even read and I'm betting you can. A major plus in a girl, as far as I'm concerned."

"A bit better," I said.

"And I really like the way you dance. I was sorry we left the club the other night." He was looking at me again. Though there was no smile on his face, now that we were so close, I realized that his big, dark eyes did all the smiling for him.

Above our heads, the portrait of the lady with the unicorn sat still, as she had for centuries. The hunter in the picture clutched the little zhi in her lap. She stared out at us, a cross expression on her frozen face. Was she angry that she was getting married and giving up her hunting? Was she angry that the painting was taking so long to finish? Or was she pissed that I was the one here with a boy who knew everything about art and liked the way I danced?

A boy who'd told me all his big secrets. A boy stroking the back of my hand with the pad of his thumb in a way that sent shivers through every bone in my body, that made me forget the feel of kirin, the rush of hunting, the stench of fire and flood.

To my right, the naked huntress in the water stared out boldly from her painting, inviting the gaze of the hidden men, heedless of the cold-hearted goddess Diana holding a bow only a few feet away. She was looking for her Actaeon. Raphael's hunter with the unicorn on her lap was on her way to hers.

There *was* a way out. *Actaeon.* I smiled at Giovanni.

"You know," he was saying, his head tilted so close that our foreheads almost touched. "Just hanging out with you could get me into trouble. We're in a language immersion program. We sign a contract that we're only supposed to be speaking Italian."

"Then maybe you should stop talking," I whispered, and pressed my mouth to his.

12

WHEREIN ASTRID TAKES ACTION

GIOVANNI HAD FULL LIPS, and he squeezed my hands in his as we kissed, and then our mouths parted, and our tongues touched, and the blood rushed through my body faster than any unicorn had ever made it go.

When he pulled away and looked at me, his eyes were smiling so much I wanted to laugh out loud. "Wow," he said.

"See?" I flicked my hair back. "Not quite as innocent as you think."

I hardly remember the rest of the museum. We saw heaps of gorgeous art, and Giovanni seemed to know a little something about all of it, but how could I spend time thinking about the marble sculpture he was showing me when I was much more interested in the lines of his body? He kept my hand in his for the rest of the tour, and I noticed the way the muscles moved under his shirt, how his collarbones peeked out of his collar and his shoulder blades pressed against the fabric. He had wide hands, like Bernini's statue of David that we saw on the ground floor, but he was thinner, more like a runner than a wrestler. His skin was a shade or two darker than the last time I'd seen him, and his hair curled tightly over his brow and the crown of his head. I ignored most of the marble statues of Italians he showed me, choosing instead to focus on the contours of Giovanni's face—his broad nose, lifted cheekbones, and wide-set dark eyes with their thick black lashes.

I memorized every feature. This was the man I'd sleep with. Giovanni would be my Actaeon.

Once he pulled me into a corner and kissed me until a security guard cleared his throat and gestured for us to move along. Another time he moved his hand from mine to the small of my back and let it rest there, warm and heavy, until my spine almost went numb with the sensation.

The decision was so easy. Why had I been freaking out so much about this? When it came to Brandt, when it came to every boy I'd ever dated, I'd felt so pressured to move along, I hadn't just stopped to enjoy every step along the path. But now that I knew where I was going, knew I wanted to get there, it felt delicious. This hot, thrilling jolt of power through my system was heady, intoxicating. I flirted like never before. Wouldn't Giovanni be surprised? No coaxing, no slow, steady seduction waiting for me to give it up. I was ready to go.

The only question was where to do the deed.

Obviously, the Cloisters was out. Where were the boys staying? Would his dorm allow us enough privacy? Would it be possible to get a hotel room? I wasn't crazy about losing my virginity on a blanket in a quiet corner of the park, but beggars couldn't be choosers.

Eventually, our time limit in the museum was up, and the security guards herded the patrons out the door. We found Phil

159

and Seth making out by a fountain in the yard.

"There you guys are!" Phil tore herself away and bounded over to me. "That took forever! I'm starving. Let's go eat."

The sun was setting now, but most of the Italians wouldn't be eating for hours. "Actually," I said. "I'm not really hungry. Maybe you and Seth should go ahead." I made goo-goo eyes at Giovanni.

"Really?" he said. "To tell the truth, I could eat. I skipped lunch today."

I bit my lip. This was going to be tricky. I leaned in and whispered in his ear. "I thought maybe . . . we could be alone."

Giovanni raised both eyebrows. "Okay." He glanced at Seth. "Astrid and I are going to take off."

Phil eyed me, a strange expression on her face. "Astroturf? You okay?"

"Yeah," I said. Did she have to use the dumb nicknames right now? "I'll meet you back at the Cloisters."

"What time?" she asked. "We're supposed to be together. What if you get lost?"

"I'm not going to get lost." I looked at my watch. "How about ten?" Would that be enough time? I'd tell Phil in advance about what I'd done, and then we'd go straight to Neil and start arranging my trip home. I just hoped she didn't get in trouble. She was supposed to be chaperoning me.

Which she suddenly started doing, much to my consternation. "I don't know," she said. "We should stick together. For safety if nothing else." She made a face at me, and the face said, *Remember the kirin?*

"Jo can take care of her," Seth said. "Come on, Phil."

They left, but Phil threw curious glances at me over her

shoulder until they were out of sight.

"So," Giovanni said when they were gone. "What do you want to do?"

"Why don't you show me where you're staying?" I asked. Let's get this show on the road.

He looked skeptical. "It's just a boarding school in Trastevere. Nothing very noteworthy, and a bit of a trek from here, anyway."

I kissed him, hard and long, and pressed my body against his. "I want to see it."

So we got on the bus and went to Trastevere. It was a fashionable little suburb, filled with narrow streets packed with boutiques and restaurants, ancient mansions, and big parks.

"What I like so much about the city here," Giovanni said as we strolled hand in hand down one of the streets, "is that it's so green. It's not like New York. There, if it's not the park, it's all skyscrapers everywhere. These old buildings aren't like that."

All the better to hide unicorns. "You're from New York?" I asked.

"Born and raised. My dad, too, though he's from way up in Harlem. I was born downtown, in the Village. But we live in Brooklyn now."

"The only time I was ever in New York, I didn't leave the airport," I said.

"Well, I've never been to Seattle at all," he said. "Is it nice?"

I shrugged. "I don't go there much either. You really need a car to get into the city, and my mom works a lot of nights, so she needs ours."

"Your dad in the picture?"

"Never was."

161

He squeezed my hand, and after a moment, spoke again. "You and Phil are funny. More like sisters than cousins. You remind me a lot of the way my Italian cousins act with each other."

"We grew up next door," I said. "Pretty much. My mother and I live over her dad's garage."

Apparently, that gave away too much, for he got very quiet, and I wondered if he was thinking about my lost purse. He stopped outside a small trattoria. "How hungry are you now? This place is really good and pretty cheap. Do you like seafood?"

"I'd better!" I said. "Living in Washington!"

"Well, they have great spaghetti and shellfish. You're going to love it."

I checked my watch. We still had time to eat, have sex, and get me back to my side of town by ten. "Okay."

Except Italians don't understand the meaning of the word *hurry* when it comes to eating, and the jolly old woman running the place was apparently a huge fan of my hair—almost as much as she was charmed by Giovanni's knowledge of the language. I made out one in five words, including the times she kept touching my head and saying "*Bella*."

"*Sí*," Giovanni agreed, and winked at me. "It's the color," he explained. "Don't you know Italians are suckers for blondes?"

Dinner took hours. By the time we rolled out, stuffed full of artichokes and tomatoes, shellfish and pasta, some sort of veal stuffed with bits of cured meat and cheese, and a tower of multicolored gelato that the chef wouldn't let us leave without finishing, I'd started seriously getting concerned about the time. I knew that you could do it really quickly if you wanted, but I wasn't sure I wanted it to be that way.

Even to get out of hunting, I wanted my first time to mean something.

But for all my annoyance at the length of our meal, I had to admit that the experience had been a blast. We were shoved into a minuscule table in the basement restaurant, under a yellow-painted barrel vault lined with black-and-white photographs of the chef's family. The place smelled of smoke and cheese and wine, and all the other diners were young, fashionable-looking Italian couples or big families who let the kids run around the restaurant while they ordered bottle after bottle of wine. My knees touched Giovanni's under the table, and he kept nudging my foot as we talked. The candles made his eyes seem almost black, and when he talked about art, his face glowed.

"I should be extra careful around here, though," he said. "Someone from the program could catch us." He kept his voice low when he spoke to me, and occasionally broke into Italian when the door to the restaurant opened.

"Ferrari, espresso, Dolce e Gabbana, biscotti, fettuccini," I said one time in response.

He burst out laughing. "Don't you want to learn a little Italian, since you're living here?"

I'd been too busy learning archery. "You can teach me." Of course, he couldn't. If things went as planned, I'd never see Giovanni again after tonight.

I wasn't sure how I felt about that.

"So here we are," Giovanni said, when we finally arrived at his school. "See? Nothing special."

It wasn't. A plain brick structure, like any seventies-era school building you could find in America. There were sporting fields and a big open courtyard dotted with picnic tables where the students could eat or study. Around the side was a neglected swimming pool with a few lawn chairs and sun loungers.

"I wish I could invite you in, but they're pretty strict about visitors, especially of the opposite sex."

Darn. "That's nothing compared to where I'm staying."

"The convent?" he asked. "No, I suppose not." He led me around the corner, toward the dark pool area. At last, someplace private. I checked out the sun loungers. They'd do.

We sat on one and started kissing again. Giovanni tasted spicy, like our pasta, and a bit sweet from the gelato. The evening breeze had picked up and I snuggled in closer to him, glad when he wrapped his arms around me.

In the past, I'd waited for boys to make the first move, to put their hands under my shirt or down my pants. Did girls even put their hands down boys' pants? Should it be the front or the back? Sometimes boys grabbed my butt. Giovanni had a nice butt. Should I grab it?

"Hey," he pulled away and put his hand on my face. "What are you thinking about?"

"Your butt," I admitted.

He laughed. "I've never heard a girl say something like that before."

"First time for everything," I hinted.

He kissed me again, splaying his fingers over my jaw and throat. Warmth seemed to radiate from that point, and a flush spread over my face and neck and down my chest. I let my hands slip down over his torso, hoping he'd do the same. His kisses moved from my lips to my throat, and his hand migrated south, following the spreading heat. He found a pulse point above my collarbone and when I felt his tongue against it, I moaned.

He paused. "You okay?"

"Yeah," I gasped. "Keep going."

He laughed again, a soft little whoosh of colder breath against my skin, and I shivered, though I was so hot I was sweating. His hands were under my shirt now, one cupping my breast through my bra, the other flat against my back. I had my hands under his shirt, too, tracing little circles on his skin, imagining what it would feel like when there were fewer clothes between us.

What was next? Something was next, but I was having a hard time keeping my thoughts straight. What he was doing to my neck felt so good. The way his thumb was tripping along the lace edge of my bra felt so good. It all felt so good and I wanted more.

I leaned back on the lounger and he slid on top of me, one leg in between mine, our belts rubbing together. The slats of the sun lounger bent beneath our weight. I could feel the metal tubes on the sides, gritty beneath my fingers as the paint flaked off in bits.

"Astrid," he whispered into my skin, and I knew he meant it—meant *Astrid*, not *girl beneath me*.

I opened my mouth, but the only word that came to my lips was *Actaeon*.

I was saved from speaking as he moved his mouth up to mine again. His kisses were harder now and more urgent than ever before. He was shifting on top of me and I could feel he was hard, could feel it pressing against my leg. I slid my hands between us and started tugging on his belt.

He pulled away. "What are you doing?"

I yanked the belt out through the buckle and started unfastening his jeans. "Guess."

"Stop."

My hands stilled instantly. "What's wrong?" I said.

"Nothing." It was too dark to read his eyes, so I couldn't tell if he was smiling or not. "But I'm not getting naked on a rusty pool chair." And he started kissing my neck again.

Rusty or no, I was running out of time. "Come on," I coaxed, in the most coquettish tone I could muster. "I really want to."

He raised his head and stared at me until I looked away. And then he said it.

"You're a virgin, aren't you?"

I squeezed my eyes shut, and all the heat escaped my body.

"Astrid. Look at me."

I opened my eyes, and he was still staring at me, but I could read his expression just fine now. Pity.

"Yes." I could have lied, but I doubted he'd believe it anyway. He could probably smell it on me, like a unicorn could.

"I see." I felt his weight shift, and then he was sitting beside me. I wanted to curl up in a ball. "Don't take this the wrong way—"

Oh, God. It was "no offense" all over again!

"But I don't want to sleep with you."

I shot up. "Why not?!" All the boys in Rome, and I had to pick the one who *didn't* want to have sex? "Because I'm a virgin?"

"Yes. No. A little of both."

"And you don't want the *responsibility*?" I hissed. "I don't care, I promise. I'm not expecting anything from you if we do it."

He blinked at me. "That's . . . disappointing."

"Why?" My eyes were burning, and I hoped he hadn't noticed. "Isn't that the dream come true? A girl who will sleep with you

166

and then never see you again?"

"No," he said. "I like you, Astrid."

"Then why won't you?" I tried in vain to keep the hitch out of my voice.

He curved his arms around me and held me close. "Well, I make it a point never to have sex with crying women, for one."

"Stop it!" I shoved out of his embrace. "Don't condescend to me on top of everything."

"Fine," he said, a note of anger finally entering his voice. "Don't treat me like a piece of meat. 'Sleep with me and then never see me again.' What the hell is that?"

My only chance, is what. "I didn't mean to put it like that," I said. Maybe I could fix this. "I really like you, too. I want to sleep with you."

"You just met me. I'm having a great time, but—"

"But what?" I said. "Since I'm a virgin it has to be some big deal? I'm so sick of guys saying that!" Actually, none had said it to me, but I'd heard enough from Dorcas and Phil to know the score.

"So you try to seduce a lot of guys and fail?" Giovanni's tone was cruel.

I stood up and walked toward the pool. I *had* been crying, I realized, as the evening air cooled the tears on my face.

I felt him behind me before he spoke. "Astrid," he said. "Please. I don't want to ruin anything."

I did. I wanted him to ruin me. Ruin me for hunting forever.

"But I don't feel comfortable. Not just because you're a virgin, but because we don't know each other all that well. Don't you want to wait a bit and see where this goes?"

"No," I snapped. "If we wait, it'll go nowhere at all." How many times would I be able to sneak out again before Giovanni went home to Brooklyn and I was stuck being a hunter for good?

"That's not true. Come on." He tried to put his hand on my waist, but I shook him off.

"The girls you sleep with," I said. "Do you love them all?"

"There was only one," he said. "And, yes, I did love her."

I felt a rush of hate and jealousy for this unknown girl Giovanni had loved and lost his virginity to. I was jealous of Giovanni, too, for not being a virgin, for not being a woman, for not being a descendant of Alexander the Great. For not having this weighing on him at all.

"Forget it," I said, and started walking back to the road. Maybe I could still catch a bus back to the Colosseum in time to get home by ten. And maybe tomorrow I'd wake up in my bed back home and unicorns would still be imaginary.

He grabbed my arm. "Forget it? Forget me? Hey, don't run off like that—we aren't done!"

I whirled on him. "We're done," I said, "because I'm going into that convent of mine and I'm not coming out. You were my only chance."

"That's not true," he said. "You have a choice. You don't have to do anything you don't want to."

"You have no idea what I'm dealing with."

"Really," he said. "Well, I certainly know what it's like to feel pressured, don't I? It sucks, to be honest." He cocked his head back at the lounge. "Fine. If it makes you happy, let's go back to that chair and I'll have sex with you."

I jerked out of his grip. "No."

"See? You don't want to." His voice grew soft. "Astrid, you don't."

And then I was in his arms, and my face was pressed against his chest, and there was nothing sexual about it. It was just the two of us in the dark courtyard, wrapped around each other so tightly I could hardly even feel the breeze.

"I'm sorry," he said. "Maybe when—"

"It's okay." I kissed him before he could finish that thought. I didn't want a rule, or a guideline, or a timetable. I didn't want anything to make me forget that the guy in my arms wasn't Actaeon at all. He was Giovanni Cole.

He rode the bus back into the city with me. We were mostly silent, but Giovanni held my hand and rubbed his thumb against my knuckles the whole way home.

He walked me to the Cloisters entrance and pointed at a spot on the cobblestones. "There," he said. "That's where I thought I saw the unicorn."

I nodded. "Well, there are no unicorns out tonight." It was true. I could tell.

I could still tell.

We kissed again, and then he left, and I entered the courtyard alone. It was well after ten. I hoped that Phil hadn't gotten in trouble for coming home without me.

A low, oblique light shone from the stair into the rotunda, illuminating Clothilde and Bucephalus, as well as the three smaller figures seated at the base of the tableau. Cory and Phil sat with Bonegrinder between them, their hands firmly clenched around her collar.

"Am I in trouble?" I said.

"Hush," Cory replied. "Don't wake Neil."

Phil stood and Bonegrinder trotted along beside her. When they came close, the zhi turned to me and sniffed. Her tail wagged, and she swept into a bow.

"Thank heavens," said Phil. "I was so worried."

13

WHEREIN ASTRID DRAWS A BOW
AND A CONCLUSION

PHIL AND LINO WERE arguing. Again.

It's not that I minded these almost daily debates about environmental issues and animal rights. I just preferred that they didn't happen at dawn while I was shackled to a tree stand twenty feet off the ground.

It had been two weeks since I'd utterly failed to seduce Giovanni. We'd never talked about that night again, but every time he touched me, or even looked at me for a second too long, all I could think of was how I'd offered him my body and he'd turned me down.

Not that I'd seen him much. My days had been filled with lessons in bow stringing, arrow cutting, and hours of archery practice that left my back, chest, and shoulders in so much agony that I wanted nothing more than to sink into oblivion in my bed every night.

Those were the days. Four nights in a tree stand had made me nostalgic for even the Cloisters.

Below me, Valerija was sitting cross-legged on the ground

with her back against the trunk. Her eyes were closed, but she wasn't sleeping. Twin white wires ran from her ears into the pocket of her jacket, the only detail that stood out from her dark hair and clothing. I couldn't believe she was listening to music while on the hunt!

I looked up and met Cory's eyes. Another stringer, she was also cooling her heels in a nearby tree. The theory, as far as I could tell, was that Valerija was supposed to be the decoy, our traditional virgin bait that would lure the unicorns in. Apparently, this was a common role for a member of the Vasilunas family. Because she had experience in on-the-ground knife fights but had sucked at every archery trial, Valerija was given blade duty while the rest of us were sent up into the trees so we could launch a surprise attack on the unicorns when they showed.

If they showed.

But I'd been here for five hours and I hadn't sensed them once.

This, it seemed, formed the bulk of the current debate.

"You be quiet," Lino said, "or they won't come."

"Talking or not," Phil snapped back, "they know we're here. That's the whole point. That's not some sow unicorn in heat down there"—Phil was, perhaps, lucky that Valerija had headphones on—"it's a hunter. If they're drawn to us like the legends say, a little talking isn't going to make a difference."

Poor Lino. He'd had his hands full dealing with us. Problem was, everything he knew about bowhunting—which was quite a lot—paled in the face of the magic. I'd listened to his lessons on scent marking and stalking and tree standing and string jumping and ten thousand other things that were important to the average game hunter. But most of the rules didn't apply when it came to trapping and killing unicorns. Lino spent half an hour one day explaining to us how to shoot, wait, then follow a blood trail to our carcass before he understood how useless such advice would be to unicorn hunters. You couldn't wait for a wounded unicorn to die. First of all, most unicorns would charge, not flee, before you could get in a second shot. Additionally, if the arrow passed through the animal, or was torn out, the wound would heal. That meant that once you drew blood, you needed to press your advantage and take the monster down.

Thus, backups in the trees. And thus, the rather large knife strapped to Valerija's thigh. Lino was also in a tree, safely away from horns' reach, to offer coaching, moral support, and an extra pair of eyes. Cory insisted that the last bit wasn't needed. That if a unicorn came into range, we hunters would be able to sense it long before Lino could see it, night-vision binoculars or no. It was true. Nowadays, I knew Bonegrinder was at the door before she even started head-butting it.

Still, I found it refreshing to work with someone who talked in scientific terms: the ratio of draw poundage to kinetic energy and how it affected arrow velocity; where to aim to do the quickest and most damage (behind the animal's shoulder, where the arrow would be more likely to pierce both lungs and heart); and why the chances of a nonfatal shot increased unless the animal was broadside to the bow instead of facing us or quartering away. For all that Marten Jaeger ran a pharmaceutical company, he seemed just as fascinated with the magical potential of unicorns and the hunters as the Bartolis did. Though he had given me some papers about the tests they were running at Gordian, it was obvious that unless I had a bow in my hands, he wasn't interested.

I heard night creatures skittering in the branches above me and shuddered. Tonight, we were stationed in a grove that bordered a farm. The farmers were friends of Lino and in the past month, they'd lost a bunch of sheep, a horse, and three herding dogs. Though there were known to be wolves in the area, the remains showed distinct signs of alicorn poisoning. Lino wanted us to do our first official hunt before the monsters got their horns through a rancher. He tapped Phil, Cory, Valerija, Ilesha, Grace, and me based on our experience and performances during archery training. His pride had been wounded by his inability to catch one of the animals himself. To judge from his behavior the last few days, it was bag-this-unicorn-or-bust time.

We were nearing our fourth day in Tuscany—my fourth night spent in a tree—and the wonder of the Italian countryside was beginning to wear thin. Phil was frustrated by the lack of phone reception and the fact that a week spent without sneaking out to see Seth was a week that he could be finding new companionship. Phil was a big believer in the "out of sight, out of mind" philosophy when it came to boys.

But Giovanni was never very far from my mind. I remembered every kiss, every conversation . . . and every humiliation. Phil had correctly assumed the worst when Giovanni and I had broken off from her and Seth after the museum trip, but she seemed to think that he was trying to take advantage of *me*. She'd kept a careful eye on the two of us ever since, and I was too embarrassed to explain that her attempts at playing chaperone were unnecessary. I have no idea what she'd told Cory to keep her from tattling to Neil about our extracurricular activities, but the two of them had almost become friends after that night.

At least Cory had stopped making snide remarks about my cousin in my presence.

Part of the change may have been due to the fact that the newcomers to the Cloisters proved far more aggravating to my roommate than Phil ever had. Cory's boasting rights had centered on her two zhi kills and her vast store of unicorn hunting lore. But Valerija's splashy kirin decapitation had quickly usurped Cory's spot as a hunter of note, and Melissende's arrival had introduced an entirely new perspective on the history of the Order of the Lioness.

It was a perspective, I must admit, that scared the daylights out of me. Melissende's Cloisters histories sounded more like the Inquisition. I understood now what Cory meant when she described the Temerins as bloodthirsty and sadistic. Wasn't it enough that I spent half my days listening to Lino describe the best way to garrote a carnivorous bovid? Did I really have to relax in the evening to arguments between Cory and Melissende about which Cloisters don or donna had best protected the virtue of his or her charges—regardless of whether or not said charges survived the protection?

Still, at least I had a soft bed back in Rome. Here I had little more than a square meter of sitting space and the spiderwebby tree trunk to lean on.

The arguments continued.

"Signorina," Lino said wearily, "this is to be talked about with Signors Bartoli and Jaeger, yes? I do not choose."

"No, no, Lino," Phil said. "I understand that. But we're here now. With you. So you could say that we are currently under your direction. Neil doesn't have the same knowledge of animal husbandry as you do. And Mr. Jaeger has his own . . . agenda."

"Signorina, if there is anything I learn after these weeks it is I do not know many things about *liocornos*."

"But they are endangered. Yes, I don't think they should be eating these poor guys' livestock. But killing an endangered species? Shouldn't that be illegal? Why can't we work on trapping them and relocating them to a more wilderness-oriented environment? That's what they do with endangered animals back in the States."

"As far as I know," Cory muttered, "there's no official ruling on whether or not unicorns are endangered. They are not protected under the law of any nation or any international treaty." I'm sure Cory liked it that way.

"That's a problem!" Phil exclaimed. From the corner of my eye, I saw Valerija look up at them, shake her head, then stick her hand in the pocket of her jacket, no doubt dialing up her volume control. "We should be educating the public about these creatures. We should be fighting to get these laws on the books."

"We're supposedly the only ones who can kill them," I said. "If that's true, then I'd say with our current track record, they have no fear of being wiped out again."

"All I'm saying—" Phil began.

"All she's been saying for *hours*," Cory grumbled.

"Is that we've spent ages training to hunt and kill, but no time at all studying the behavior of these creatures, trying to understand why they've Reemerged now; where the population is coming from and how it is breeding; and how it might be feasible, in this day and age, to capture them, reintroduce them into wilderness areas where they will be no threat to humans, do whatever we can *other* than kill them."

It's not that I didn't agree with Phil's points. I did. But she'd been arguing them for weeks now, and nothing had changed. No one seemed to have any information on unicorn behavior, other than the ever-increasing stream of stories we'd found outlining attacks on livestock and occasionally people. Cory's books had a scant few mentions of how zhis lived in family groups, kirins hunted in herds, and karkadanns were solitary creatures; but other than that, we knew nothing about the life cycle of any unicorn. How long was the life span of each species? How long was gestation? Apparently, there was no hunter family whose specialty was zoology. Stupid nineteenth century. Hadn't they ever heard of Darwin?

So for all Phil's posturing and debating, we were still tasked with killing the unicorns, not subduing them until such time that they could be relocated to the Black Forest or the Kenyan savannah or the farthest reaches of Tibet. That we remained in line with a centuries-old policy that had previously resulted in what we thought of as the extinction of these animals did not seem to bother the good people of Gordian, and the Bartolis tended to do as instructed by either the history books or Marten Jaeger.

What Phil didn't seem to understand, despite strong hints from both Neil and now Lino, was that the person paying the bills called the shots. Right now, that was Marten and Gordian. They wanted specimens, and we weren't going to be allowed to go home until we'd handed them a unicorn. I comprehended that much. If I was forced to go to Rome to train to be a hunter, why couldn't I also be forced to actually kill unicorns in Tuscany? It was all part of the same gig. Phil, who had chosen to come here of her own free will, didn't see it that way. She wanted to influence *policy*.

Purplish, predawn light had started to filter through the tree branches. Another night wasted. Mist lay heavy on the field beyond the grove, glimmering in a soft, silvery lavender, punctuated here and there by the larger, lumpy shapes of sleeping sheep.

Even the livestock had better living arrangements. Below me, Valerija's head was nodding forward. Cory's bow rested across her knees. Phil had scooted until she faced away from Lino, and had her arms crossed and her chin held high. Ilesha was picking at her split ends. Grace was meditating in full lotus.

At once, we all snapped to attention. A unicorn.

"What?" Lino hissed. He looked through his binoculars, but it was too light now for the night vision setting to work well.

Phil motioned him to silence with her hand. The creature wasn't visible yet, but we could all feel it. I realized now that I had probably felt the zhi that night when I was babysitting, too—I just hadn't known what the sensation meant at the time. My senses aflame, I forced my limbs to stay still, forced myself to keep from leaping off my perch and stalking the animal down. Phil could argue against the morality of the hunt until her voice was hoarse, but this fire didn't burn only in my veins. The treetops shivered as their occupants narrowed their focus on the presence in the woods beyond.

Minutes passed. If we could all feel it, could it feel us? Could it feel how many of us there were? Would that spook the unicorn or draw it in?

With aching slowness, I crept into a crouch and lifted my bow. The unicorn was coming from the north, from behind the trees where Phil, Lino, and Grace sat. It was still too dark to see much farther than the next tree over. I strained to peer through the branches. Even if it was closer to them, they wouldn't get a good shot from their side. Then again, the angle would be bad for me as well. The unicorn would approach me from below. Its head and neck might block a clean shot into its torso.

The sensation was stronger than ever now, but I still saw nothing, not even the telltale shifting of shadow that had tipped me off to the presence of a kirin that first night with Giovanni. As my companions silently scanned the forest floor, I closed my eyes and listened. Last time, I could hear it breathe. Last time, I could smell it. If it *was* a kirin, in the dappled forest night, we'd never be able to see it. Perhaps it had already passed.

And as soon as I thought it, I knew it was true. It *had* passed. It was probably even now in the pasture, picking out its prey. I unhooked my harness from the trunk restraint and half-climbed, half dropped to the ground.

Valerija, earphones still in place, jumped as I landed in the moss at her side.

"It's in the field," I whispered in a voice little more than a breath. It had ignored the hunters entirely in search of more sheep. Perhaps it knew the sheep wouldn't fight back if it decided on mutton for breakfast.

I motioned to the hunters still in the trees, who were peeking over their platforms in confusion. A moment later, we all heard it, the muffled, bleating cry.

Valerija and I broke into a sprint. When we reached the edge of the field, I hopped the low wooden fence and kept running, hoping the others were behind me, compelled by the lingering vision in my mind's eye of the unicorn sneaking up behind the slumbering sheep. Lack of sleep had apparently given me a particularly vivid imagination.

Ahead, I saw movement, a mass of sheep swarming in no particular direction, pressing against one another in their terror. Beyond them, moving shadow, a flash of blood. I was right!

I slowed, sliding in the dew. The kirin had an animal impaled on his horn and was tossing it around. Blood spattered over the backs of the stampeding sheep, and they came right toward us.

"Get out of the way!" I heard Phil scream from far away and I jumped aside, shoving into Valerija as the sheep swept past. The ground rumbled beneath us and for a moment, everything was wool and noise and sliding in the muck. We scrambled to our feet once more.

The kirin had disgorged the sheep from its horn by this point. I hoped the animal was dead. I saw it twitch for a moment on the ground, then go still, a fuzzy red lump of flesh.

Valerija made a sound like a curse as the kirin turned in our direction and lowered its head to charge. It was smaller than the one I'd seen before, barely more than a yearling, yet every bit as deadly. I froze, forgetting all Lino's archery lessons as the monster stared me down with its glowing, golden eyes.

"Back up!" Phil was shouting now. "Get back!"

"What is it?" I heard Lino's voice. "I see nothing."

Valerija grabbed my arm and started to pull, and I retreated toward the fence, scattering sheep in my path. Grace flew by as I reached the other hunters, her black hair streaming behind her. I looked over my shoulder and saw her stop dead at less than twenty yards, nock her arrow, draw, and release.

There was an empty, hollow thunk, and the unicorn roared.

Grace shouted in delight and pumped her bow in the air. The unicorn was on two legs now, cloven hooves flying, dark blood spurting from the arrow that lay lodged in its shoulder.

"She hit it!" Lino cried, incredulous, but then recovered. "*Dai!* Quick! Another shot! You must make the fatal wound!"

But Grace was having trouble drawing her bow—from fear or adrenaline, I couldn't tell. Her hands shook as she nocked her next arrow, and she twice tried to draw the string back and failed. A moment later, she knelt and rested the bow against the ground. The unicorn was tearing at the arrow with its teeth now, now lowering its head and charging.

I ran forward and dragged Grace to her feet. "Run. Now!" But it was like her legs were rubber and she collapsed against me. The kirin moved closer, swinging its head from side to side like its horn was a scimitar. The smell of flames and rot burned in my throat.

Another snap of string on my right and an arrow glanced off the unicorn's flanks. Ilesha. She drew again, then checked the distance between the unicorn and us and paused. "Get down!" she cried. But it was too late. The kirin was upon us.

Again, time slowed. The kirin's head, at the far side of its swing, faced us broadside, ready to slice us both down with one giant sweep. I grabbed Grace's abandoned arrow from the ground and plunged it into the animal's neck, right under its jawbone. The aluminum bent and broke beneath my hand as the kirin wrenched away, almost ripping my arm from its socket.

We ducked as it reared again, falling hard against the wet ground. Grace regained her faculties and skittered out from beneath the flailing hooves as the unicorn turned tail and galloped away across the field.

"Where is it?" Lino asked. He was looking around wildly. He had his bow out, but he didn't even seem to know which way to aim.

"Um, across the field?" Phil said. "Didn't you see it turn around and run?"

His mouth dropped and he shook his head. "No. It . . . go away." He looked so confused. "You all see it? Go get it!"

Not one of us moved. Grace and I were covered in blood, mud, and wet grass. Ilesha had curled into a ball on the ground, head tucked between knees, shoulders shaking as she wept. Phil was staring at us in revulsion, and Cory stood by Lino on the other side of the fence, her face as gray as the dawn while the unicorn's screams echoed across the field.

"Go!" Lino shouted again.

"No!" Phil said. "Not without a plan."

I bent down to check out a deep scrape on Grace's brow, but she pushed me away.

"It heals as we stand here!" Valerija said, gesturing into the field with her knife. "And now it is angry."

Ilesha sniffled and shook her head.

"Another rogue kirin," Cory said in wonderment. "They are supposed to travel in herds."

"*Packs*, you mean." I rubbed my shoulder. "They aren't deer. They're wolves." And wolves had loners, too. Usually adolescent males who hadn't become dominant enough to form their own pack. That's what this was, I realized. A young lone unicorn with no pack to teach him to stay the hell away from hunters like us.

181

In the distance, the unicorn bellowed.

Lino clearly heard that. "Go now!" Lino said again. "This is an order."

"Shut up!" Phil screamed at him. "You want this unicorn, *you* go kill it."

Lino stared at her for a moment, fury raging in his eyes, but said nothing. Phil seemed to grow an inch or two as we stood there, all of us shivering from fear and cold and weariness. She was right; he couldn't hunt it down. Both Lino and the unicorn, and all the sheep in the field, were at our mercy. If we didn't obey, there'd be no dead unicorn for Gordian to play with tonight.

Lino turned away from the group for a moment and stared out at the breaking dawn. I wondered what he saw when he looked at the kirin. Giovanni had barely been able to glimpse it in the alley that night. What did non-hunters see? What had Lino witnessed just now? A bunch of girls and sheep sliding around in the muck while a deadly shadow flitted among us?

Grace stood and brushed off the worst of the grass. "I will follow it." She hefted her bow and checked her quiver. "I drew first blood. This kill is mine."

She stalked off into the mist, blood still seeping from the cut on her forehead.

"She cannot go alone," Valerija said.

"Why not?" asked Cory. "*You* killed a kirin alone." But the other girl had already followed Grace.

I looked at Phil. "Please," I said. "She's hurt, and it almost killed us with one swipe. This isn't some rite of passage."

Phil gave a big sigh and shouldered her bow. "Fine. Let's go. But I'm only going to protect Grace. I don't believe in this." She looked at Lino. "You stay here, where it's safe, and bark more orders. You were so *helpful* last time."

"Stop it," I said. "He's trying to train us as best he knows how."

Phil bit her lip and cast him a long look. Then she crawled over the fence and joined me. "Don't get me started on you. For the love of God, Astrid, stop chasing unicorns. For someone who doesn't want to be here, you're certainly acting like an obedient little huntress."

I flicked mud from my pants leg.

"What about Ilesha and me?" Cory called from the fence line.

"Come or don't," Phil called back without turning around. She lowered her voice again. "Nothing to say?"

"I'm sorry. I heard the sheep and—" And what? Had a vision of death? That sounded nice and crazy.

"I'm not talking about that. I'm talking about earlier. Why don't you ever take my side? You say you want things to change, but then you just stand there with a bow and keep your mouth shut whenever I try to make it happen."

"Tell me what to do to make a difference and I'll do it," I said. Cory and Ilesha had clearly opted against following us to the kirin. "So far all I've seen is that you argue and they ignore you."

"Because I'm the only one. But, come on. You've seen what emphasis they place on the fact that we're Llewelyns. If both of us rebelled against the status quo—"

The sound of barking dogs stopped us short, accompanied by bellowing, and then a girl's scream. We broke into a run.

A hundred yards on, we saw them. Valerija lay facedown

in the grass, motionless. I saw two sheepdogs keeping their distance and barking their heads off, while a third limped around, holding one leg in the air and whimpering. Whatever had happened to the poor thing, it didn't look like alicorn venom.

Grace and the kirin were facing off. She had her bow raised but not drawn, and he pointed his horn at her chest, pawing the ground and snorting hard. Blood still dripped down the broken arrow protruding from his jaw, dark black blood that blended with his midnight-brindled coat.

"Grace," Phil called. "Move away. We've got your back."

"Don't you dare," she replied, her voice almost toneless. "This is my kill." Her hands shook as she attempted to draw back the string again.

I sidestepped over to Valerija, and knelt in the grass. "Are you okay?" I rolled her over. There was a puncture wound near her shoulder, perhaps an inch or two deep, from the look of it. I pulled down the edge of the hoodie to see the skin.

"Burns," she gasped. I remembered that part. But it bled little, and as I watched, the wound seemed to knit together, growing shallower and narrower by the second. Valerija writhed in pain on the ground, but she'd live. Was this what had happened to my arm after I'd been thrown off the kirin? It looked like Brandt's leg after we'd treated it with the Remedy.

I glanced up at Phil, who held her own bow, nocked arrow at full draw. The unicorn glared at her. Phil had a far better shot. "Grace," she said again, not taking her eyes off the kirin. "Back off."

"You back off," the other girl hissed. "This one is mine." And then she released.

The unicorn leaped, but not quickly enough, and Grace's arrow pierced its gut. He screamed again, a horrid, desperate sound, and landed hard on both hooves. Then he charged his attacker.

I barely had time to flinch before I saw Grace's body tossed in the air. She flew several feet, then landed in a heap as the unicorn charged again, horn lowered, teeth bared, at the crumpled figure on the ground.

Phil let her arrow fly as the animal quartered away. Another hollow thunk into the unicorn, just behind the left shoulder. But did it go far enough in to pierce the lungs? The beast turned and galloped back toward Phil, who dove out of the way as he careened by.

After it passed, the unicorn turned once more, then dropped to his knees. Grace still wasn't moving. I grabbed Valerija's knife and slid it across the wet grass toward my cousin. She grasped it by the handle and stood.

The kirin was grunting now, prostrate on the grass, each labored breath punctuated by wheezing shrieks I'd remember for the rest of my life. His eyes were wide with terror, rolling in his head like yellow pinballs, as Phil slowly approached. He barely moved as she stood above his broken body, breathing every bit as hard as the dying animal. She raised the knife high.

Do it. Oh, God, just do it. I squeezed my eyes shut.

Squish. Squish. Squish.

When I looked again, it was over, and Philippa Llewelyn was drenched in unicorn blood.

14

WHEREIN ASTRID RECOVERS

"Hello, Mom?"

"Astrid! It's two in the morning."

"I know, I'm sorry. I just . . . had to call."

"Are you all right?"

"No." I was covered in mud and blood, and Grace was getting stitches in her forehead by Gordian technicians in the room next door. "I want to come home."

There was a long silence on the line.

"Mom, are you there?"

"I'm here, Astrid. I'm just trying to understand. You're not fighting with the other girls, are you?"

"No."

"And they are treating you well?"

"Yes." They weren't beating me, or anything.

"Then what's bringing this little episode on?"

"It's the *hunting*, Mom. I don't like it."

"Have you been hurt?"

"No. I'm maybe the only one who wasn't."

"Good for you! I'm so proud!"

"No, don't be proud! I hate it."

Her voice turned cold. "What do you mean, 'you hate it'?"

"Well, the blood . . ."

"Blood?" Lilith scoffed. "This is the girl who says she wants to be a doctor, and she's scared of some blood? Astrid, I'm surprised at you."

I tried to remember how Phil had put it. "I'm just not sure it's ethical. They're endangered. There has to be a more humane way to deal with the threat."

"Humane? Oh, I get it. You'll get better, honey. You'll get better at shooting them so they go down quick and don't suffer so much."

"That's not what I mean—"

"Did you kill one today?"

"No. Phil did."

"Phil. I see." My mother was quiet for a long moment. "Well, you're just going to have to tough it out, Astrid. I know you can do it."

"I don't *want* to do it, though, Mom! I tried. I put in a real effort, just like you said, but I hate it." The training, the tree sitting, the death, the magic . . . "I want to come home." I waited, but there was no response to my plea. "Mom?"

"Maybe it's just too early over here, but I really don't understand where this is coming from. You're doing well, you're healthy, you're getting along with the other hunters. . . . What's the real problem here? Is it because Phil's a better hunter than you are?"

"No! I don't care about that. Phil doesn't, either. She doesn't want to kill anything."

"And yet she's out there doing it and you aren't. Maybe you could learn something from your cousin's dedication."

"No! Mom, it's not about that at all! You don't understand."

"Maybe I don't, but I do understand that you made a commitment, and the second it starts getting hard, you're calling me to complain."

"That's not true." I took a deep breath. "School's starting again soon."

"Oh, right." My mother sounded distracted. "I meant to discuss that with Cornelius. I'm thinking maybe a tutor, or enrolling you in an American school in Rome. We'd have to see about the cost, though. What are the other girls doing?"

I didn't know, but I knew that a few of them weren't in school anymore, and that others—like Dorcas, Cory, and Grace—probably weren't factoring cost into the decision.

"And it would give you a chance to learn Italian. Have you been picking up much of the language, what with all your training?"

Only what Giovanni had been teaching me. But I could hardly tell my mother about *him*.

"Think of how great studying in Italy is going to look on your college applications, Astrid."

I tried to imagine a college application essay about what it was like to crouch in a field at dawn and watch my cousin stab a man-eating monster to death. That probably would make quite the impression on an admissions committee.

It certainly had on my mother's academic counselors.

"Besides, what is there for you back here? Those silly little friends of yours? You remember that boy, Brandt? He ran away from home! What kind of associations are those for you?"

Brandt had left home? Weird. Then again, I understood the urge to escape your parents. I tried to push my hair back, but the matted strands were crusted to my face. "Mommy," I whispered. "Please."

I don't think she even heard me.

"What you should be focusing on, Astrid, is training even harder. Killing more quickly, more humanely. I know you probably think Phil's a natural at this, because of all her athletic experience, but think about who your ancestors were. You have the same abilities. You even have more. You should be doing better than your cousin."

"How do I have more abilities than Phil?" I asked.

"I know you can do it! I'm so proud of you, honey. It's a dream come true, knowing that you're over there fulfilling the family destiny. I should let you go now. I love you, Astrid."

"I love you, too, Mom."

I hung up the phone and bit my lip. The glaring fluorescent light in the empty Gordian office made my hunting clothes look even more stained and dingy. I'd probably contaminated the plastic chair just by sitting on it. I'd washed my hands twice, practically scoured off the skin the second time, but the sticky feeling of dark kirin blood lingered. I couldn't sit. My blood seemed to buzz in my veins, a thousand times harder than caffeine or even adrenaline. I hugged my arms to my chest and bounced on my heels. The others didn't seem to feel this. Maybe it was because they'd been injured. Their energy was focused on healing their wounds. Mine just brimmed inside me with no outlet.

I stood at the doorway to the next room, a lounge where the other hunters were resting, icing sore body parts or flicking bits of mud off their clothes. A television was bolted to the ceiling, showing a boisterous Italian game show. Grace sat on a long bench, a row of neat stitches glistening on her forehead. She held an ice bag to the back of her head and refused to look anyone in the eye. They'd said she had a concussion and a sprained ankle on top of her cuts and bruises, but miraculously, no skull fractures or other broken bones.

Still, it was like staring into the waiting room at my old hospital.

Ilesha was curled up in an armchair, sleeping. Poor girl. She'd apparently spent the entire time we were chasing the kirin being sick in the field. She was a decent shot, but if she fainted at the first sign of violence, she wouldn't be much good to the Order.

Valerija took a small case out of her coat pocket and removed a pill. She offered the case to Cory, who reeled back, disgusted. Valerija shrugged, popped the pill, then readjusted her headphones and closed her eyes. She'd refused to let any of the doctors touch her, but I could imagine the kind of pain she was feeling, even if the puncture wound had mostly healed by the time we'd gotten to Gordian. She wasn't even wearing a bandage now. Valerija had also been limping pretty badly when we walked off that field. I'd have offered to help, but Phil and I had been carrying an unconscious Grace.

Maybe whatever she'd taken now was an attempt at self-medication. Maybe I should find out what it was. Perhaps it stopped this feeling, like I was speeding out of control, even when I was standing still.

Cory shook her head and came over to me. "We really need to do something about her."

"Do your books talk about an official Cloisters drug policy?" I snapped. "By my count, she did more damage today than you did." As soon as the words were out of my mouth, I regretted them.

Something flashed across Cory's face, but she recovered quickly. "And she almost died, too, didn't she? A few inches down and that kirin would have pierced her heart."

True. I didn't want to know how many of us had been close to death today.

Cory sighed. "Let's not bicker over this."

"Agreed. I'm . . . sorry for what I said."

"I don't blame you. You were out there and I was not." She nodded at Phil. "Is she all right?"

Phil sat splayed on a chair in the corner, watching the incomprehensible television show, looking as strung out as if she'd taken one of Valerija's pills. She hadn't spoken to me since we'd left that field. I sat down by her now.

"Hey."

She nodded but kept her eyes on the screen. If she was buzzing like me, there was no sign of it.

"Just got off the phone with my mom."

"Yeah?"

"I told her about your kill."

Phil said nothing for a moment. Then, "Wasn't mine. A mercy kill by that point. If Grace wants the honor, she can have it."

Grace sniffed from the corner. "No, thank you. When I get my first kill, I'll do it without anyone's help."

Phil didn't respond. I tried again.

"I asked her if I could come home."

"Are you going?"

"No."

Phil pursed her lips and nodded, but said nothing more. I was too afraid to ask if she was planning to leave herself. What would I do if Phil left me here alone? I imagined Lilith would be thrilled. No other Llewelyn to steal my thunder. But I dreaded the very idea.

"We'll be heading back to Rome now," I said in as bright a tone as I could muster. "Maybe you should call Seth and see if we can get together with the boys tonight." Nothing. "Or tomorrow. Give the bruises a chance to fade."

Still nothing. Not even a chuckle. From *Phil*. I bit my lip, wanting more than anything for both of us to be back in Uncle John's yard, where we were more in danger of getting bitten by mosquitoes than being gored by unicorns.

Giving up, I rested my head against the back of my chair and tried not to think about all the parasites and other nasties on my mud-soaked pants. At least, I hoped it was mud. There were a lot of sheep in that field. *Calm down*. My feet started tapping against the floor.

"I'm going for a walk," I said. I couldn't bear it another moment, sitting in there among the injured hunters, wondering how long it was going to take until Phil started acting like herself again. I wanted to sprint a marathon. I wanted to run and run until I left this all behind. My feet began to pound against the linoleum.

But the hall dead-ended in a room furnished with a slab. And on the slab lay the corpse of the kirin.

Technicians in white lab coats clustered around the body, drawing blood here, taking skin and hair samples there. I wondered when they'd start the autopsy and how they'd manage it if they couldn't keep cuts open.

I watched in silence as they clamped sensors from various machines to the corpse, finished collecting their specimens, and bustled out a side door. The machines whirred and beeped. From the door, I could see that one was measuring body temperature and another, horn temperature, which seemed to still be in the low forties. Celsius. That was awfully hot, for a corpse.

I tiptoed into the room to get a closer look at the sensors. Funny, the kirin didn't look as big now, draped and still like that, its mouth slack and tongue lolling out from between its fanged jaws. Its wounds, fatal and otherwise, had all but vanished now, leaving dark, shiny striations of scar tissue on its hide. Strange—unicorn flesh regenerated even after death. I reached two tentative fingers out to touch the skin.

"Astrid?" I jumped and knocked the unicorn's hoof off the slab, and it clunked hard against the side. Marten Jaeger stood at the door, watching me. "You don't belong here."

"I—"

He seemed to catch himself. "I mean, I would have thought you'd want to be with the other hunters, relaxing." He beckoned to me.

"I can't seem to chill out," I admitted.

He nodded, though there was a confused look on his face. "Is it too warm for you?"

"No. Sorry, it's just a saying. I can't relax."

"Oh. I see. That is very common, after something so exciting." He closed the distance and stepped between me and the display screens. "Did you . . . enjoy the hunt?"

"No," I said, too frazzled to lie. "I hated it."

"I see."

"Maybe, since Cory doesn't want to be here anymore, I can stay here, help you out in the lab—"

"No," Marten said. "That wouldn't work, I'm afraid."

"But you need a hunter around if you're going to keep specimens from—"

"I don't think so, Astrid." He shook his head. "I'm very sorry. It seems like you have a natural curiosity for the type of work we do here. I find it quite unusual, in fact. If I had your abilities, I'd be far more interested in those."

"Want to trade?"

He said nothing, just watched me with his strange, pale eyes.

"Maybe," I said at last, "we could renovate the scriptorium. I could make a little lab right in the Cloisters. It wouldn't interfere with my hunting, I swear!"

He raised his eyebrows. "No, the scriptorium has . . . structural problems. I don't want any of the hunters going in there. It's too dangerous. Perhaps later, we'll be able to look into restoring that part of the building, along with the other wing . . ."

He kept talking about future plans, but it all blended into the rush of blood in my ears. The dead kirin stared up at me with glassy yellow eyes. To Marten, to my mother, to all of them I was just a girl with a bow. An assassin, good only for what she could kill.

And I wasn't even particularly good at that.

"I hate to discourage you, Astrid. Really I do. After all, your most recent theory about the connection between the Remedy and the hunter's own immunity was one my own lab saw fit to test . . . several months ago."

Test and dismiss. Boy, had I felt sheepish when I shared my

194

observation about the way Valerija's alicorn wound had healed with the people from Gordian. They'd merely grunted, and then ignored me. Later, Cory had explained that everyone was well aware that hunters healed from alicorn puncture wounds with supernatural quickness. They'd even tested her once by making a regular incision then dripping alicorn venom into the wound. Nothing happened, and the wound healed normally.

Marten had filled in the rest. Apparently, they'd done extensive testing on whether or not hunter blood was a possible ingredient in creating the Remedy. No luck yet. However if I wanted to donate some blood to keep testing with, they'd be happy to accept it. Then all the hunters had given blood samples.

I was nothing more than a tool, like this unicorn on the slab.

Someone cleared his throat. I turned to see Lino, looking as battle weary as the rest of us. He began speaking to Marten in Italian. I made out little more than our names before the conversation turned to an argument too fast and furious for me to follow. Marten's tone made it clear he was issuing orders, though.

"Why?" Lino asked in English. "She does not understand me. Do you, Astrid?"

I shook my head. What was I supposed to be understanding that Marten didn't want me to? Why wasn't Cory standing here to translate?

"Astrid, don't listen to him," Marten said. "He's a foolish peasant."

Lino made a rude gesture at Marten. Marten shrugged, crossed to the wall, and picked up a phone. Lino shook his head, then spat on the floor.

"Astrid," he said to me, as if we were alone in the room. "I have taught you to be a hunter. It was wrong. You are not a hunter here. They are not animals. Even a bear, even a lion, would run. These attack. You are not a hunter."

"What?" I said.

"You are a soldier." The words slammed into me like a punch.

Marten looked as if he might throw the phone at Lino, but the archer kept talking to me. "I am leaving now. But I say to you . . . if you can go home, do it. Go home. This is no place for any of you."

Two men in security uniforms showed up on either side of Lino. He sneered at them, then turned and walked away as they followed him out.

Marten studied me. "Well, Astrid, I'm sorry you had to witness such a scene. It was apparently a mistake to let someone so irresponsible watch over you girls. I shall not let it happen again."

I hardly knew what to think. "What was that all about?"

Marten sighed. "I was taking him to task for allowing so many of you to be injured. He did not want to accept any of that responsibility, as you can see. It was very . . . uncouth of him to be so cruel and unfeeling in your presence."

"Oh," I said, still unsure. When even my trainer was telling me that my fears were justified, I didn't know what to think.

"Of course, he is right about one thing. It is a very dangerous path you have embarked upon. Perhaps you would wish to return to the United States, if you could."

"If I could," I said. "I'd be on the next plane. But my mom won't let me."

Marten nodded thoughtfully. "Ever thought about *not* going home? About going someplace else?"

Run away? Like Brandt apparently had? A tiny spark of hope flared to life in my chest. "Yes," I said softly. "But what difference would it make in the end? I'm still a hunter, aren't I? Anywhere I go, unicorns will be drawn to me."

"And you would kill them if you had to?" Marten asked.

I bit my lip. I hadn't finished the yearling today, but I had attacked it. Stabbed it. And the kirin who'd threatened Giovanni. I almost couldn't help myself. If I was in a situation where it was kill a unicorn or let it kill me or someone else—"What choice do I have?"

Marten looked down at the dead kirin on the slab. "What choice indeed?"

Later, Neil reported that Marten had been dissatisfied with our progress under Lino's tutelage. He promised us that a new archery trainer would arrive soon to replace him, but that Marten wanted to be sure this time that he hired only the best. Cory wondered if he'd taken Lino's advice about combat training to heart. I decided I'd believe that the day a Green Beret arrived on the doorstep of the Cloisters.

Meanwhile, we were reduced to training with two practice bows and a half-full quiver that Lino had left behind, which made for a lot of sitting around and twiddling our thumbs while we waited for our turn at the targets.

It was three days after the hunt before I started seeing glimpses of the old Phil again. She hadn't even bugged me about getting together with the boys since we'd gotten back to Rome, and despite her dutiful practice whenever it was her turn with the practice bow, I began to wonder if she was having second thoughts about being a unicorn hunter. Maybe she wanted to pack up and go home.

Then one morning I was walking the dormitory hall when I heard her laughing in the courtyard. I looked out to see Phil showing off the new trick she'd taught Bonegrinder to Neil and Lucia. She made the unicorn stand very still while she balanced meatballs on the zhi's nose. I'd seen Bonegrinder perform obediently before, but today she was being truculent, growling and snapping at Phil as punishment for putting her through the indignity of behaving in front of anyone who wasn't a hunter.

"That's enough, Pippa," Neil said after the fifth meatball went rolling in the grass. "Lucia won't have any left for tonight."

"Come on, *Celius*," Phil trilled and tossed a meatball to Bonegrinder. The zhi caught it in midair, then went snuffling about for the ones she'd dropped. "Pippa's a dumb nickname. It sounds like a baby bird."

"Well, *Phil* sounds like a lorry driver."

"Preferable." She threw a meatball at him, and he ran when Bonegrinder lunged.

Lucia shook her head at the both of them, wiped her hands on her apron, and headed back into the kitchen. I pulled away from the parapet, suddenly embarrassed to be spying. But when I'd seen Phil later on, it was as if the kirin hunt had never happened.

"Hey, Astronomy," she said, and plopped down beside me. "Want to go out tonight?"

I was checking the fletching on one of our shafts. The constant use was beginning to show on the arrows. If we didn't get a new trainer in the next few days, we should at least get Neil to buy us some supplies to tide us over.

"Giovanni said he had a test tomorrow." I screwed the point back into place and set the arrow down beside the others.

"I'm sure you can persuade him to blow off studying *one* evening. You two are peas in a pod with the schoolwork, huh?"

Well, neither of us was currently enrolled in degree-granting educational institutions, so yes, she was right there. "You know they're breaking the rules of their program every time they hang out with us?"

"Another thing you two have in common!" She was grinning now, and I was so glad to see it, I relented at once.

"Okay, call. But make sure Giovanni knows this was *not* my idea."

Phil and Seth were in rare form that evening, each seemingly determined to top the other in enthusiasm and daring. They conned a dozen roses out of a street vendor, joined a troop of buskers in a dance show, and sweet-talked their way into a nightclub with a line that stretched around the block. I half expected the evening to cap off with either breaking into the Colosseum or taking a midnight dip in the Trevi Fountain. Giovanni watched their antics, amused, but didn't join in, and I started to wonder if he regretted coming along. He'd been quieter than ever this evening, and I worried he was angry we'd dragged him away from his books. I knew how important it was that he got good grades in his program. His reacceptance to college depended on it.

We ended the evening with desserts at a restaurant on top of

Monte Mario, overlooking the northwest end of the city. Phil and Seth soon wandered off into the darkness, leaving Giovanni and me alone together for the first time since that night in Trastevere. Apparently Phil had decided I could be trusted on my own again. Or she forgot. Or she wanted us both out of the unicorn hunting gig.

Looking at Giovanni, seated in silence all the way across the bench, I doubted that was going to come close to happening.

"This place is nice," I said, feeling more stupid by the second.

"Do you know what they call it?" His voice floated out of the gathering darkness. "*Collina degli innamorati.* Lover's Hill."

"Oh." He didn't say anything else, though, and the awkwardness spread faster than the night.

At last he spoke. "I'm probably going to regret asking this, but what have you been up to for the last week?"

"I was sent on a trip. Out of town."

"Really."

"Yeah."

"No more detail than that?"

I spent most nights in a tree, I was stampeded by a herd of sheep, I stabbed a unicorn in the neck, I hated the whole thing, and I dreamed of you every night. "We were in Tuscany. On a farm," I managed to say.

"What kind of farm?"

"Sheep."

"Huh." Another minute passed, in which there was nothing but city lights twinkling in the distance and the sound of the wind in the tree branches arcing over our heads. And then, "I'm not really sure what either of us is doing here. Well, me, I'm a sucker for punishment, but I don't get you. Seth told me that you didn't want to come out tonight."

"Is that what he told you?" I said. Is that what Phil had said to him? I recalled what I'd told her about Giovanni's test, and began to feel sick. "That's not true. I thought you had to study!"

"Is that why you haven't called me in a week? Didn't tell me you were leaving town? And when I see you, it has to be because Seth and Phil plan it?"

"No—"

"What's your story, really?" Now he sounded angry. "Seth tells me one thing, and you tell me something totally different. I have no idea what to believe."

Believe *me*. But of course, he couldn't. I was the one who'd disappeared. I was the one who'd lied to him about the unicorn. I was the one who'd tried to seduce him, then had barely touched him since. I was the one who hadn't called for a week. No wonder he was angry.

"First he said you were joining a convent. And you say you're supposed to, but you don't want to. Fine. But you also say you grew up over your uncle's garage, and now I hear you and Phil are heiresses that are being shoved into a convent so you can't claim your fortune. I didn't even know that was allowed. Is it true?"

I snorted. "Where the hell did Seth get that idea? Phil would never lie like that!"

"To be perfectly honest, I'm beginning to think this whole thing is a huge scam."

"What whole thing?"

He looked out over the city so I couldn't read his eyes. "You. Phil. All of it."

The tiramisu in my stomach turned into rock. I studied his profile, deep in shadow but clear enough to read his expression. Anger. Distrust. I was afraid to open my mouth, afraid what might come spilling out if I did. But looking at him there, I knew I'd lost him already.

"No. We're not heiresses, but we are stuck here, and my mom wants me—at least—to stay. I just want to go home. More than anything, I want to leave. And if I act like I don't want to see you, it's only because I don't want to get confused about leaving. Because, Giovanni, you're the only good thing about being in Rome."

Before I could draw breath to go on, he was kissing me, cradling my face in his hands, his heartbeat pounding beneath my fingertips, which had somehow found their way to his temples. For a few exquisite moments, there was nothing beyond that—our breath, our mouths, our hands in each other's hair—and the cells in my body sang with it. Forget the jitters I'd felt after the unicorn hunt; this was the only high I ever wanted.

Make that the only *great* thing about being in Rome.

Giovanni pulled away and his eyes were laughing, and for a second I thought I'd spoken that thought aloud. But then he cocked his head behind me. I looked, and back on the patio of the restaurant, the waiter putting chairs up on tables for the night was giving us both dirty looks.

Collina degli innamorati, indeed.

"*Vieni con me*," Giovanni said, tugging my hand. *Come with me.*

We escaped into the surrounding park, and as the trees closed in behind us, Giovanni's hand slipped to the small of my back.

"I'm sorry. I should have asked you. But you didn't call. . . ."

"It's been hard," I said. Now that I'd started confessing, I wanted to tell him everything. Where to start? "You know all those news stories about wild animal attacks recently?"

"I think we'll be safe in a city park," he said, and swung me around until my back was against a tree.

"That's not what I meant—"

"Let me get this out." One of his hands was braced on my waist, the other on the tree near my head. "I have been just as unfair. If everything works out at my program, and I can go back to school, what then? Maybe that's why I assumed the worst when you didn't call."

I leaned my head against his hand. "Don't listen to Seth anymore."

"If I hadn't listened to him tonight, I might not have seen you again."

I lifted my head. "But he's making it up. Phil doesn't have to lie to make boys interested in her."

"You don't, either." I could feel his breath against my throat. Was that true? He smelled so good. I closed my eyes, remembering those nights in the tree in Tuscany, my back against the same rough bark, my arms aching in equal part from hanging on to the platform and because I couldn't reach forward and put them around the guy I was picturing in my mind. And here he was, right in front of me. I hugged him close and thrilled.

"I'm glad," I said, "because there is something I need to tell you."

"Tell me anything. Tell me something so I don't have to listen to anyone else." His hand traced the hem of my shirt, and he pressed his palm flat against my stomach. I could barely remember what I was saying.

"So you know how, a long time ago, there were crusader monks? Religious orders who taught their members to be warriors and stuff?"

"Like the Knights Templar?" He brushed my hair off my neck with his other hand and cupped my jaw.

"Yes. Well that convent of mine, it's one of those."

"Right. Those kick-ass nuns of yours." He began to kiss my neck. "Good thing there are no more crusades."

"Oh, but there are."

He paused, then lifted his face. "Are you telling me you're training to be a soldier, Astrid the Warrior?"

I nodded. "More like a . . . hunter, though."

"Like an assassin?" The space between his eyebrows crinkled up. A Giovanni frown.

If only it were as easy as sitting on a rooftop and shooting at unicorns with sniper rifles. "No." Maybe I should backtrack. "You've probably seen stuff in the news about the wild animal attacks?"

He looked confused. "Not really. I've been doing so much studying, I haven't really been watching the news."

This may make things a bit more difficult. "Well, there have been these wild animal attacks. And we're supposed to stop them."

"Wildlife Control Nuns?"

"Yeah."

"And your mother is forcing you to quit school and do this?"

"Yeah."

He laughed. "I agree, Astrid. You need to get out of there.

That's the craziest thing I've ever heard."

And I hadn't even gotten to the nutty part yet. The part about the unicorns and the magic and the panacea that would cure everything if we only found out how to make it. I mean, if Gordian found out. We were Wildlife Control Nuns sponsored by a drug company. It got weirder by the second.

Giovanni kissed me then, and I pushed those other thoughts away. I couldn't tell him the truly crazy stuff. And every time I started talking he stopped kissing me and listened. Who wanted *that*?

He pressed into the tree and me, and my hair tangled against the bark, but I didn't care at all. I was barely standing on my own, supported in his arms and against the thigh he'd somehow wedged between my legs. Heavenly, butterfly-light touches of his fingertips on the skin of my stomach battled with heavy, hard kisses. He was holding himself back, but my heart was beating so fast, I thought my veins might pop. "More," I whispered, and he sighed, a near moan.

"Astrid." He rested his forehead against mine, breathing hard. "*Ti voglio bene.*"

I caught his hand against my heart. "No fair using Italian I don't know. What does that mean?"

He shook his head. "I'll never tell." But from the expression in his eyes, I got a pretty good idea. My skin turned to fire under his gaze, and every hair on my body stood at attention when he kissed me again. Our hands were still clasped between us, through my shirt, but then his slid from my grasp and pressed, palm flat against my sternum, fingers splayed wide across my breasts.

Giovanni didn't even cop a feel like other boys. I couldn't catch my breath, couldn't think. I sensed everything too much—the whispers of the leaves, Giovanni's heartbeat, the sound of our cloth-covered thighs rubbing against each other, the soft touch of his mouth on mine, each infinitesimal shift of his hand as his fingertips slipped beneath the edge of my bra. My blood seemed to vibrate with a strange and terrible chord. This rush, this careening, amazing feeling. I loved it. I loved it all—

No.

I stilled within his arms. This hyperawareness, I knew it. It wasn't me and Giovanni. It was a unicorn.

"No," I said aloud, and he pulled away. I bit my lip to keep from crying out, half from loss, half from fear. Several unicorns. Here. Close. And me without a weapon. Without backup. Could Phil sense them? Where was she?

"Astrid?" Giovanni said. "You okay?"

No, I wasn't. Because something else, something new, had started, as if some accelerant in my blood had ignited. It burned, it stung. My eyes watered and my nostrils and throat clogged. I stared down at my arms, almost expecting to see the skin crack and peel. What was this? I tried to list the symptoms, but my mind was too focused on the position of the unicorns.

"Damn!" Giovanni rubbed his eyes. "What the—it's like mace. Let's get out of here." He started pulling me back the way we came, but I shook my head.

"No. Not . . . that way." Just opposite the unicorns. They were moving fast.

We stumbled on, deeper into the park, and then we saw Phil and Seth. The latter seemed to be having trouble breathing. Both were disheveled. I noted that Phil's shirt was on backwards and inside out.

"Did you see them?" Phil asked.

I shook my head. "You?"

"No. What was that—"

"Burning?" I finished. "No idea. Is Seth all right?"

"I think he got a big lungful of whatever it was," Giovanni said. Seth was sitting with his back to a tree. I hoped he'd be able to run if he had to. The unicorns were fading now, but the burning lingered.

"Should we follow?" Phil asked.

"I think we should run. We're not prepared."

Giovanni was watching both of us. "Ladies, we should get Seth back to the restaurant. He's having some kind of allergic reaction."

"Won't they come for us, though?" Phil asked.

"That yearling didn't, but he was outnumbered." The unicorns were nearly gone, and I could breathe clearly again. "I think they decided against it."

Seth had started coughing, a phlegm-filled hacking that clearly gave Phil the willies. Giovanni helped him to his feet, and I tugged on the shirt tag underneath Phil's chin.

"Who needs a chaperone now?" I asked.

She brushed me off. "It's not what it looks like."

"Better not be. Two unarmed hunters alone in the woods is bad enough. But one?"

"I wouldn't abandon you, Asteroid." She squeezed my hand, then went to help Seth.

Giovanni joined me on the path back out. "I got pepper-sprayed once in high school. A canister went off in this girl's purse in the middle of math class. This felt like that."

"Really." I looked around but could see little in the dark. Of

207

course, who needed eyes when you could *sense* the unicorns?

"I've heard muggers sometimes use them to disarm their victims. Do you think someone was trying to rob us?"

Frankly, muggers had been the least of my concerns. Losing another purse would be nothing compared to a unicorn attack. That was it: no more making out with boys in the woods. It always ended badly.

"Astrid, *guardami*." He took me by the shoulders. "Look at me. Are you all right?"

His expression was full of concern, but I saw it only for a moment. For beyond him, at the edge of the woods, lay a pile of bodies.

At least, they may have been bodies. Kirin, once, from the look of the mangled bits of bone and hide that lay strewn around. My eyes burned again, looking at them.

"Oh, God," I whispered.

He turned around. "What the hell?"

One lay slit from tail to throat, guts spilling out over the grass. Another was in pieces, a thick coating of dark blood obscuring its brindled coat. If I hadn't spent time staring at a kirin corpse recently, I never would have recognized the species.

Before I could stop myself, I was standing in the middle of the massacre, circling the bodies in disgust and fascination.

Phil appeared beside me. "Who could have done this?" Her voice trembled. "No one at the Cloisters . . ."

The burning. I knew it. It was alicorn venom. I looked down at the drained white irises of the kirin corpse at my feet. "The third unicorn," I said, softly enough so the boys couldn't hear. "There was a third." We needed to call someone. We needed to figure this out. "Hunters are the only *people* who can kill a unicorn."

I raised my head to the path. Giovanni stared back at me, and there was nothing in his eyes but horror.

"But they can also kill each other."

15

WHEREIN ASTRID STRIKES A CHORD

THE SOUND OF METAL against stone resounded through the Cloisters, adding to the vibrations emanating from the wall and increasing my budding migraine. I'd begun building up my resistance to the chapter house, but this situation with the metal spikes and the sledgehammer was not ideal.

Neil gave the metal spike on the right another wallop, then lowered the hammer and stepped back. "Philippa," he said, practically bowing out of the way.

My cousin stepped forward, a kirin horn cradled in her hands, and laid it across the two protruding spikes in the wall. In the side of the alicorn, she'd carved her name in crude, triangular letters.

PHILIPPA LLEWELYN

"Is it fair," Cory said at my side, "that I have nothing on the Wall of First Kills?"

"If you'd like," I replied, "I can clean out Bonegrinder's grooming brush and you can hang up one of her hairballs. You've killed her plenty of times."

Cory snorted, Phil curtseyed and grinned, and even Neil failed to hide his smile. When Phil noticed that, she twirled her arms in the air and presented the horn again like she was a game show host. Grace whispered something I'm pretty sure was snide to Melissende, who took everything in and didn't change her expression at all. Rosamund looked longingly at the piano.

Another day at the Cloisters.

It had taken more than two weeks for Gordian to return the horn of the kirin to us so that Phil could post her entry on the Wall of First Kills. I still didn't know what kind of tests they did on the animals, but there was some part of me glad that they'd switched their focus to corpses rather than live specimens like Bonegrinder.

I'd called Gordian about the killing in the park on Monte Mario, and they sent out a team to collect the remains, but the alicorn venom was too overwhelming for non-hunters to approach, and in the end, they just torched the entire area and called it a fire. This was the story that we heard on the news the following day—a fire. No dead unicorns at all. I didn't know what the benefit was of keeping the situation under wraps, but when I tried to bring up the subject with Cory, she seemed mostly interested in the idea of fire. She wondered if napalm might be an effective weapon against unicorns.

I wondered why unicorns would turn on each other like that.

After the ceremony at the wall, such as it was, we were granted a bit of downtime. Melissende and Grace were icing their bowstring arms after a grueling day spent at the targets— the former was determined to join the hunter ranks on our next

211

outing, and the latter was still in major guilt mode for her failed shots. They huddled in the corner by the weapons, heads bent close together, gossiping.

Ilesha and Ursula, who had actually hit it off, decided to play chess on the chapter house's board, which was, as you may have guessed, made of unicorn. In the chess board's case, it was white re'em and dark kirin bones carved into playing pieces and inlaid in squares on the board.

I plopped down on the couch farthest from the Chair and the Wall of First Kills, and debated whether it would be worth it to go upstairs for a cool cloth to put over my eyes. How could the others stand it in here? Rosamund spent half her time in this gloomy, cavernous space, plonking away at the piano keys, totally ignoring the ambient vibrations in the wall, which I'm sure clashed terribly with whatever piece she was trying to play.

Cory went back to Neil's office, no doubt armed with yet another sheaf of yellowed archives, trying to track down more hapless victims of Alexander the Great's promiscuity to bring into our hunting fold. Maybe I'd join her in a bit and try to find some more information about unicorn behavior.

Valerija was sitting in a chair, staring into the middle distance. Dorcas was parked on the other couch, braiding Zelda's hair. Rosamund played on. Her choice today reminded me of springtime and dancing, like the painting Giovanni had shown me of Diana and her huntresses, laughing and gathered together to celebrate a successful hunt.

Maybe in earlier times, the huntresses here were like that. I tried to picture the girls around me partying post hunt. Nothing.

Of course, it didn't help that Ursula and Melissende had

started squabbling about Melissende's archery stance. I couldn't really make out much of the German, but judging by body language the younger girl had a problem with the way her older sister was placing her feet. Since Ursula had been the one hitting all her marks of late, it would probably behoove Melissende to listen, but I doubted that would happen. Ursula, in between moving her rooks and pawns, was calling out suggestions to her sister, and Melissende was shouting back something I didn't need to understand the language to know was *shut up*.

I laid my head against the armrest of the couch and tried to concentrate on Rosamund's music—the clear, frosty high notes and rumbling lows—but I couldn't get the image of that painting out of my head. Diana stared, stern and triumphant, from the backs of my eyelids. The men in the bushes awaited their doom. The hunter beckoned, smug and knowing. I lay here, trapped under the earth in a cage of unicorn bones.

Couldn't Rosamund play something else? I couldn't take it anymore. The longer I listened, the more the music seemed to blend with the way the walls rang. That awful chord echoed in my skull, even sharper now, as if the addition of Phil's horn had added to the clamor.

I opened my eyes and looked at the wall. How strange was that? I'd noticed nothing last month, when they added Valerija's horn. I stood and walked over to the wall, cringing slightly as I got closer. I traced my hand over femurs and jawbones, ribs, and pelvises, each resounding with the same vibration. I closed my fingers around the kirin's horn with Phil's name. All the same. I let my fingers trail further, and closed my hand over Valerija's trophy.

And felt nothing. Dead space. I lifted it from the spikes on the wall and examined it, turning it over in my hands. This one made no noise, no vibrations, either on the wall or off. I returned to Phil's horn and weighed them both in my hands.

Odd. I looked up and caught Valerija staring at me. I waved and quickly replaced both horns. Why were they different? Was there some process the old hunters had performed on the horns that Gordian might have inadvertently stumbled upon? If only I knew what kind of tests they were doing.

Was I the only one who noticed it? Phil had unhooked Bonegrinder from the chain that attached her to the masonry hook in the wall, and they had departed for points unknown. I longed to kidnap the horn to show her, but Valerija was still watching me, suspicion flaring in her eyes. Fine, have your stupid horn. There would be time later.

Instead, I wandered up to the courtyard to find Phil grooming Bonegrinder. The zhi was currently in her equivalent of heaven, pressed close to Phil's side, while tiny tufts of unicorn coat fell from the brush and drifted across the courtyard like little white tumbleweeds. I sat down nearby.

"So," Phil said brightly, "I'm an official unicorn hunter now." She cocked her head. "Feels . . . pretty much the same." She resumed brushing the zhi. "Which I guess is good. That I don't feel like a murderer or anything."

"How much longer do you think you'll stay here?" I asked.

"What do you mean?"

"You don't like hunting, you don't like the philosophy, you don't like sharing your room with Valerija . . ."

"How long will *you* stay?"

"I'm out of here the moment I turn eighteen," I said with surety. "Or sooner if I can get your dad to sue for custody."

"Yeah, but you'd ruin all the fun for both me and your mom. My dad would flip if he knew either of us was here," Phil said. She pulled hard at a snarl in Bonegrinder's coat, and the zhi bleated in protest. "I don't hate everything about hunting. I could do without the part where we actually kill the unicorns. But this little monster isn't so bad. And, to be honest, I like when we chase them. I like how that feels."

"You like the powers, then."

"You like them, too, Astrid. Don't lie."

I couldn't deny that. Since arriving at the Cloisters, it had almost become second nature to sense the unicorns. In the park with Giovanni, I wasn't sure what he was making me feel and what were my hunter powers springing to life. I loved that snapping-band feeling, right as everything slowed down. I loved how strong I felt whenever I chased a unicorn. I even loved how Bonegrinder bowed before me if I gave her half a chance. I could, however, live without attracting the monsters to me. I could live without the vibrations in the chapter house walls.

I changed tactics. "I bet Seth wouldn't like to see you flirting with Neil like you do."

Phil tossed her head and looked at Bonegrinder. "Seth and I aren't all that serious."

I practically choked on my own tongue. No denial? No *I wasn't flirting with Neil*? I'd been half joking before, but now I was in shock.

"Does Seth know that?" I asked, even as I was wondering what Neil knew.

Now she looked at me. "Does Giovanni think this is serious?" she asked. "Can it be, if you're going to stay in the Order for another two years?"

"He's going back to college in a few months, anyway."

"Well, so's Seth."

"And you?" I pressed.

Bonegrinder squirmed as Phil started tugging on a particularly stubborn knot. The zhi nipped at Phil's fingertips, and she swatted the unicorn's muzzle. "No bite!"

Bonegrinder's limpid blue eyes were filled with contrition and adoration, and Phil melted. "Monster," she said with a chuckle. The zhi's coat glistened in the sunlight. No wonder people had been fascinated with these creatures for millennia. They were so beautiful and so terrible all at once. Such an amazing source of strength but capable of such horror.

Like the virgin hunters themselves.

"Phil," I said, "I noticed something downstairs on the Wall of First Kills." I told her briefly about Valerija's alicorn.

"Weird," Phil said. "Let's go check it out." She brushed zhi hair off her pant legs, looped Bonegrinder's chain around a column, and accompanied me inside and back down the stairs.

We stopped dead on the threshold. Grace had Ilesha pinned to the weapon wall, holding a giant sword pointed at her throat, while Melissende was backing Ursula ever closer to the alicorn throne.

"Stop it!" Phil shouted.

"Or what?" Grace said. "You'll tattle to Neil? I'm trembling." Actually, she was, for she could barely keep the sword upright. Ilesha whimpered. I swallowed hard and started to edge toward the two of them.

"Go on," Melissende coaxed the younger girl in a voice as cold as ice. "You aren't afraid to just sit down, are you? Aren't you as brave and strong as your friend Ilesha over there? Don't you both have dozens of trophies on that wall? Just do it. Stop being a baby." She took another step forward. Ursula flinched, stumbled back, and put her hand on the armrest, then yelped and leaped away as if burned.

"Guess you *are* a baby," Melissende said. In English, no less. Humiliating her sister in front of everyone, showing off for Grace.

"Get away from them," Phil said, rounding the couch and closing in on Melissende.

Melissende didn't even turn around. "Why? She's my sister, and she thinks she's hot stuff as a hunter. So I asked her to prove it."

Ilesha began to slide down the wall as Grace's arms wavered. The sword was clearly too big for her. It was practically taller than she was. Grace seemed to be having trouble holding it aloft, and lowered the point to the floor as she turned her attention to Phil. I sidled over to the Wall of First Kills and grabbed the nearest alicorn off its stand.

In the corner, Rosamund wrung her hands, flummoxed, but there was no time to be freaked out. Grace had pulled a sword on another girl. If she took another step toward my cousin, I'd pull the alicorn on her.

Valerija stared impassively at the scene, apparently too strung out to even notice what was going on. Dorcas and Zelda were nowhere to be seen.

"Get away *now*," Phil repeated.

"Make me," Melissende said.

Phil grabbed her arm and swung her away, placing herself between the two Holtz girls. "Don't get near her again, or you'll deal with me."

"Tough words from the don's pet. How sweet." Melissende rubbed her arm. Phil glared at her.

But I was still watching Grace, who'd narrowed her focus to Phil's back. The tip of the sword dragged on the ground. "Phil," I warned.

Grace looked at me and gave a tiny shake of her head. Apparently, I was no threat. My fist tightened around the horn, but I knew I'd never be able to use it. Grace was right.

Phil turned toward Grace. "Mighty big sword for a little thing like you," she said softly. "Really think you can wield it?"

Grace sneered. "It's the claymore of Clothilde Llewelyn." She struggled to lift it again. "Do you think *you* can?"

Phil shook her head. "Don't you get it? This isn't a competition."

Grace laughed. "Of course it's not. After all, you're winning." She took a deep breath and began to lift the claymore. My hesitation shattered.

I rushed at her and slammed my foot down on the blade. The hilt was torn from Grace's grasp and clattered against the stones. Grace staggered backward, and even Valerija seemed to shake out of her stupor as the metallic din echoed from wall to wall, caught and magnified by every bone in the chamber. All the girls stared.

"If this was Clothilde's," I said, "I doubt she'd want it aimed at one of her own."

16

Wherein Astrid Revels in the Night

"**Y**ou're a badass, Cuz," Phil said, when we were standing in the chapter house alone. Somewhere upstairs, Melissende and Grace were being lectured at, threatened with calls to their parents, made to feel the full weight of their "irresponsible and violent actions." Ilesha and Ursula had been hustled to their room by a shaken Rosamund and were probably being cosseted and fed bonbons this very moment. Cory, no doubt, was listening at Neil's door. And I couldn't calm down. My foot still tingled from hitting the sword. I can't believe I did that.

"I'm not." I rubbed one ankle against the other and cast a glance at the claymore, now lying still and silent on the stones. "I was just trying to stop her." A badass move would have been actually using the alicorn I'd been holding in my hands. So I kicked a sword. Big whoop.

"Well, you stopped her!" Phil said. "Stopped everyone. I think Neil even heard you upstairs."

I shrugged. That would be another miracle to chalk up to the acoustic anomalies of the chapter house. I restored the alicorn in its rightful spot on the Wall of First Kills, wincing slightly as the vibrations grew stronger. The bones on the wall seemed to ripple in place, and I turned away before I felt sick.

"Let's put this room in order and then go back to the courtyard." I needed sunshine, and air untainted by the scent of fire and flood.

"You got it." Phil gave a little giggle and righted a chair. "After all, I wouldn't want to get on your bad side."

"Why do you keep saying stuff like that?"

She shook her head and started reassembling the chess set. The pieces had scattered during the altercation. "Because you should have seen your face, Astrid. Like Judgment Day had come and you were an avenging angel about to sock Grace Bo into hell. I was even scared of you for a second."

"I don't know what came over me."

"I do. They were threatening the youngsters. Llewelyns don't roll with that."

I dismissed her with a sniff. "So then you're tough, too."

"You bet I am." She flicked a lock of hair behind her shoulder. "Watch." She tiptoed over to the throne of bones and poised her finger over the armrest.

"Don't do it," I said, smiling.

Her hand descended in slow motion, while Phil kept up a running commentary. "Will she do it? Can she?"

"Is she a moron?" I asked.

"Closer . . . cloooooooser . . ."

I rolled my eyes.

"ZAP!" Phil shouted.

I flinched, and Phil started laughing. "Yeah, we're both *real* tough."

I shook my head and went to pick up the sword. It was much heavier than I'd expected. How had Grace held it aloft at all? I tried to lift the sword entirely off the ground twice before I managed to get it horizontal. Straight up, with the point against the stone, the hilt of the claymore rested right below my chin. I had newfound respect for good old Clothilde, if she could wield this monster sword on a regular basis.

"Hey, Phil, come help me hang this up." She bounded up the steps to the weapons wall, and together we wrestled the claymore back into its stand.

"Still pretty sharp," Phil said, examining the edge of the blade. "You have to admit, seeing this stuff is unbelievably cool."

I cast my eyes over the other weapons stored here. "I think I prefer our newfangled bows, with their state-of-the-art sights and levels and release aids."

"True." Phil twanged one of the bowstrings on the wall, which set off a whole new wave of vibrations from the bones opposite. "Lino did say that finger releases could throw off our aim."

Below the claymore hung a small, highly curved dagger made from a single piece of carved alicorn. It was a curious piece, different from almost every other weapon on the wall.

I looked back at the Wall of First Kills. There was no trophy for Clothilde Llewelyn. Could this alicorn knife be from her first kill? I lifted it from the wall, surprised that the hilt felt so warm in my palm.

"I say we get out of here tonight," Phil said, still running her fingers over the weaponry.

What would such a small dagger be good for? In my fist, the blade curved like a scythe. Maybe skinning a dead unicorn? "You mean call the guys?"

Phil shrugged. "Eh. Not unless you want to see Jo." Phil had taken to calling Giovanni that, in imitation of Seth. "But maybe we can convince Neil that we all need a night out. Clear the air, so to speak."

I took a couple of practice swipes with the blade. "Like a Cloisters field trip?"

"Sure! I think we're all going a little stir crazy in here. Melissende just feels left out. She didn't get to go with us to Tuscany; she's stuck being a bitch while the rest of us are fabulous all the time. That's got to be depressing."

I laughed, then switched hands. "But all those hunters in the same place are bound to draw in some unicorns." I shuddered, remembering the scene in the park. Why had the unicorns fought each other? Why were they there to start with? Had they been coming for us when they started to fight? Had it been a battle for rights—who would get to eat the unarmed hunters? And if so, why did the surviving unicorn retreat? I stared down at the alicorn blade. There were no markings on the hilt or pommel to indicate the name of the hunter to whom it had belonged. I wondered if, like the sword it hung beside, it belonged to Clothilde. I liked the way it felt in my hands.

"I think we'll be fine if we stay in populated areas. No dark, quiet make-out spots. No unicorn is going to come at us in the middle of a piazza." Phil put the arrow she was examining back on the wall. "Come on. Let's go ask Neil."

I wasn't entirely sure this whole scheme didn't revolve around Phil having a night on the town with Neil, but I didn't know how to ask her that, so I simply followed as she headed up the stairs toward his office. It wasn't until I passed the tableau of Clothilde and Bucephalus that I realized I still held the dagger in my hands. I hid it beneath Clothilde's billowing skirts, then caught up with my cousin.

Neil showed zero interest in squiring a bunch of teenage girls around Rome's night spots, and Cory worried that an evening out now would be tantamount to rewarding bad behavior.

"Well then how about just Ilesha and Ursula?" Phil asked. "Cheer them up?"

"Then who will police the others?" He shook his head. "I'm the don here. I have to have some rules."

Yes, his supervision had been marvelously effective down in the chapter house.

"Besides, they're children, Pippa. Not coeds. I can't allow these girls to go running about the streets of Rome at will."

I snorted. They all looked at me. "Please," I said. "Valerija was a homeless addict before she showed up on our doorstep. I doubt she needs protection from you."

"What about Ilesha and Dorcas and Ursula?" Neil asked. "What about Grace?" He shook his head. "Parents put me in charge of their children. I have to do what I think is best for them."

"So it's okay to endanger their lives by sending them off to chase man-eating unicorns, but you can't risk letting them go out for gelato?" Phil asked. "It may be time to rethink your system."

"It's not safe," he said. "Every time you and your cousin go wandering around the city, you get attacked by a kirin."

Phil threw her hands in the air. "And left to their own devices, these girls almost sliced each other up with swords right here in the Cloisters! What's more dangerous? I'm talking about a movie or something. Get some fresh air."

"Things have been a bit slow around here," Neil admitted, "what with the loss of our trainer. I suppose boredom is part of the reason the girls have taken to picking on one another."

"We still haven't gotten a new assignment from Gordian?" Cory asked.

"No," Neil said, his tone clipped and frustrated. "It's aggravating, to say the least. We need more equipment, more training. The hunters have been doing phenomenally well by themselves, but we had an agreement with Gordian, and it's not keeping its end of the bargain. I don't know how far Cory and my resources will stretch without the company's assistance."

"Marten Jaeger's a jerk," Phil said.

"Don't say that," Cory said. "He's made it all possible. He's responsible for everything we're doing."

"'Everything we're doing' amounts to driving an endangered species back into extinction so he can get his hands on a drug that will make him richer than he already is," Phil replied. "If he really wanted to do some good, how about finding a sustainable way to deal with the unicorn problem? He's as bad as those poachers hunting tigers in Asia." Phil stopped. "Actually, *we're* as bad as them. We're poachers."

"Poachers," Cory corrected, "are hunters who steal game from other people's lands. Unicorns are not game, and we were invited onto that farm. Ergo, not poaching."

"We're something, then, and it's not good." Phil crossed her arms and looked at Neil. "No opinion at all?"

"Poaching," he said, "can also be defined as hunting a species it is illegal to hunt *according to law.*"

Phil glowered, then turned away from the Bartolis altogether and tried to win me. "Marten Jaeger's *also* a jerk, Astroturf, because he doesn't give you enough credit. I've seen the way he blows you off every time you try to talk to him about his research."

"What should he be giving me credit for? The fact that I come to the same conclusions that his staff did months ago?" I was lucky he was encouraging me at all.

"Well, you told him about Brandt, didn't you? The only living human to have received a dose of the Remedy?"

True. I wondered if Marten had ever tracked him down and tested him, or if my ex had run away from home before he'd gotten the chance. I doubted Brandt would be an eager volunteer. And maybe the Remedy worked like standard anti-venom, and was metabolized by the body after use along with the venom it "soaked up." I sighed. I didn't know enough about any of these topics to really make myself useful to someone who had an entire pharmaceutical company at his beck and call. I wasn't good for much more than my aim and my unicorn proximity radar. Since I hadn't brought down a unicorn of my own yet, and my first instinct when I sensed a unicorn was to run in the other direction, I wasn't even good for those.

Satisfied she'd made her point, Phil turned back to the subject at hand. "The hunters need to get out of here for a few hours. This isn't good for anyone."

"How many of the girls speak enough Italian to understand a film?" Cory asked.

"An action movie, then, so dialogue doesn't matter." She glared at Cory. "Or just wander around a piazza for a few hours. Get away from the whole hunting scene for a bit. No wonder they feel competitive and pressured. This is all they've been doing for weeks." She caught herself. "All we've been doing."

If Neil noticed the slip, he gave no indication of it.

"And we'll be in a group," Phil was arguing now. "We can even carry weapons, if that will make you happy."

"Oh," Cory said. "Very inconspicuous, climbing the Spanish Steps with a longbow strapped to your back?"

"Then what do you suggest?" Phil asked. "You know all the history. What did hunters of yore do?"

"Stayed inside where they belonged," Cory replied.

"Well *I* don't belong locked up in here." Phil lifted her chin. "None of us do."

My cousin pouted to beat the band, and Neil called her "Pippa" no fewer than four times, and in the end, Cory, Phil, and I were charged with escorting the other girls to a movie and a gelato parlor, then straight back to the Cloisters before ten. Alone.

The first thing Phil did was call Seth and ask if he wanted to join us. We were standing in the courtyard at the time, watching Bonegrinder tear a shank of pork to pieces while the afternoon sun slanted down and made the twisting marble columns glow white. I marveled at the zhi's enthusiasm for her dinner. She was acting awfully ferocious, considering the meat was already dead. How different, I wondered, was Bonegrinder's behavior from that of a zhi raised in the wild? If food were scarce, would she cannibalize her own kind? Was that what we'd seen that night in the park? But why would a unicorn attack another unicorn when there were loads of unarmed, tasty people about?

Phil shoved her phone at me. "Giovanni wants to talk to you."

"Astrid the Warrior," he drawled when I picked up. "How's life in the Wildlife Control Nun business?"

"Frustrating." At least he was joking about it. He'd seemed a bit shell-shocked after seeing those corpses a few days ago.

"I thought we talked about this habit you have of waiting for Phil to make plans before you'll see me."

Phil, leaning close enough to hear both sides of the conversation, raised her eyebrows at me.

"What can I say?" I replied. "I don't have my own phone."

"I think you like playing hard to get."

"Ouch." Hard to get? I'd thrown myself at him!

He went on in that same mocking tone, "So, you're deigning to see me tonight, I hear?"

I turned away from Phil and walked a few columns down. "I *want* to see you tonight. I'm sorry I didn't call myself, but I've—"

"Been busy with those wild animals. I get it."

My throat started to burn again, but it had nothing to do with alicorn venom. I'd never heard him like this before. "What are you talking about? Giovanni—"

"—not wild enough for you," he was saying, as if I wasn't even there. I looked over at Phil, who was staring back, every bit as clueless as I was. "Baby, you've got no idea."

"Are you drunk?" I asked, and Phil's eyebrows shot skyward again.

Seth came on the line. "So, we'll see you both at Piazza Navona tonight?"

"No," I said. "I don't think it's a good idea." The last thing I wanted was for Giovanni and I to get into a fight in front of the other hunters. I'd lived through one public breakup. I didn't need another.

"Nonsense, mini Phil!" he said with a laugh that set my teeth on edge. "We'll have a blast. Bring all your little friends, too." He hung up.

I looked up at Phil. "This was a mistake. Let's not meet them."

"Stand them up? Is that how I raised you? Come on. Seth knows all the best places. It will be better for showing the girls a good time."

I shook my head. "No, something's weird. I've never heard Giovanni talking that way. He sounded . . . mean."

Phil's brow furrowed. "I hope he doesn't end up being a jerk to you, Astrid. I'd hate to have to feed him to a unicorn. Boys can be such losers sometimes."

Out in the yard, Bonegrinder was happily gnawing away at her latest bloody conquest. Weird as it sounded, I thought I'd rather spend the evening with her.

In the end, we didn't bring longbows with us, but I did retrieve the dagger from inside the Clothilde figure's skirts and stuck it in my purse. Though I didn't want to calculate our chances against a kirin without ranged weapons like bows and arrows, I felt better knowing that I had something more than my fists if we did run into a unicorn.

Ilesha, Ursula, Zelda, Dorcas, and Rosamund joined us, but Valerija declined after hearing that we'd be meeting up with some boys, and Melissende had slammed the door in Phil's face as soon as she and Grace saw my cousin on the other side. Frankly, I was happy to avoid their company for a few hours.

Piazza Navona was packed, as always, and I kept my purse slung across my body, doubly determined not to lose it because of the ancient—no doubt priceless—weapon I'd hidden inside.

We got our gelatos, then stationed ourselves by the huge Bernini fountain of the Four Rivers, eating ice cream, shouting over the rush of water, and people watching as the crowds passed by. Ilesha and Ursula seemed to have completely recovered from the trauma of the afternoon; and even though Dorcas was trying to act as cool as Zelda, who'd only gotten a small cup of lemon sorbet, she couldn't stop staring at the towering piles of multicolored gelato on top of Ursula's cone.

Cory was telling Rosamund about a small portfolio of sheet music she'd come across, and they were discussing old-fashioned methods for transcribing melodies, and how that might affect Rosamund's ability to play them. Phil was trying to decipher movie listings in an Italian newspaper and becoming increasingly frustrated that the titles weren't direct translations of the English films.

"Just pick something with a martial arts star in it," I said at last. "You'll be golden."

"There you are!" Phil was swept up off the edge of the fountain, and her paper and gelato cup slid to the ground. Seth spun her around and smacked his lips against her mouth. "Mmmmm, you taste like a cherry."

"Enjoy it while it lasts," Phil said. "That was all of it."

"Oh, I will." He turned toward the other hunters and pretended to doff a cap. "Ladies. Good evening. Seth Gavriel, at your service."

While the hunters introduced themselves, I looked behind Seth, but I didn't see Giovanni.

"You have a boyfriend, Phil?" Dorcas asked, eyes wide. "Does Neil know?"

"Ah, the famous chaperone!" Seth grinned at his audience.

"Too bad he's off duty tonight, huh?"

"Why 'too bad'?" Cory asked, oblivious to Seth's charms.

"Because I'd like to get a look at this guy you all spend so much time with. See what the big deal is."

Was that a note of jealousy in his voice? I wondered briefly how much Phil talked about Neil.

"Hey, mini Phil," Seth hissed at me. "Don't bother looking for your boy. He was too much of a wuss to show."

I bit my lip and pretended I hadn't been craning my neck to peer into the crowd.

"So," Seth said. "I have the perfect plan for the evening. There's a big outdoor concert in the Baths of Caracalla."

Cory looked up from where she was trying to wipe gelato off the newspaper. "That's all the way across town near the Cloisters."

"Why did we come out here to turn around and go back?" Ilesha asked.

Zelda shrugged. "I'm up for a concert. I don't even care who's playing." She stood, then brushed imaginary dust off her skirt. Rosamund was so excited, she bounced on her heels.

So to the Baths of Caracalla we went. On the bus, Cory justified it to herself by saying that at least it would make for an easy walk home after the concert, and the youngsters seemed excited that their night out would include more than ice cream cones. I did my best to hide my disappointment about being stood up. I wished I could talk to Phil about the situation, but she spent most of the ride with Seth's tongue down her throat, so I never got a chance.

The Baths of Caracalla, it turned out, were the enormous brick ruins near the Circus Maximus. Though little remained now aside from a few crumbling walls, arches, and vaults, it was still impressive. Massive, hundred-foot walls lit by amber spotlights soared above our heads, forming an imposing backdrop for the concert. The audience had assembled on a grassy hill in front of the ruins, lounging on blankets or in lawn chairs, while vendors walked among them and food and drink carts lined the street beyond.

I traced the outline of the dagger through my purse. Another Roman park? Perfect. The baths themselves seemed abandoned, but I wondered how secure they were. Would a quiet, dark little corner make a good hiding space for a kirin? The unicorns had to sleep somewhere, didn't they?

"This will be perfect," Seth said. He reached into his backpack and pulled out a folded tarp. "Not too close to the crowds, nice and dark . . ." He pinched Phil's side, but rather than yelping or giggling, she gave him an incredulous look.

"Is he always such a git?" Cory said to me under her breath as she helped me smooth out the tarp.

"I don't know what that means," I whispered back, "but he *is* usually nicer than this." And so was his friend. Where was Giovanni? He'd love something like this. I bet he'd be midway through a whole lecture on the architecture of the baths. I felt torn between relief that he hadn't shown up in his bad mood and depression that I was snuggling up with Cory to listen to the concert rather than with Giovanni.

The girls spread out on the tarp, armed with sodas, snacks, and glowing bracelets and necklaces they'd bought from one of the vendors. Chatter filled the warm evening air, and I began to relax. Perhaps Phil was right. Boys were jerks sometimes, and I shouldn't let it ruin my night. The weather was beautiful; I was out of the Cloisters, hanging out with friends, about to listen to music on a hillside in Rome . . . things were great.

A young couple in front of us had their dog on the blanket with them. The family next door sent their toddler over with a treat, and the dog rolled over, showing its belly to be rubbed. The move reminded me of Bonegrinder and her bottomless need for the hunters' attentions.

Cory noticed me watching and translated. "They're talking to the other family about all the dogs gone missing recently. Apparently, the baths are usually home to many strays. All gone in the past few months."

Bile rose in my throat as I thought of this cute pooch as a meal for a kirin. "I know you don't have any papers on this, and Gordian doesn't seem the least bit interested, but I can't help but think we'd be doing a lot better if we started researching their behavior. Feeding patterns, mating cycles, group or family structure, where they sleep, preferred diet—"

"Body language when they attack and when they feint," Cory finished. "I agree. If you want to gen up with me, I'm all for it, Astrid. I could use the help." She smiled. "That is, if you can spare the time off being one of the great *Llewelyns*."

But this time, I knew she was joking, and tossed a blade of grass at her. "Why is everyone so hung up on the families? You've been, too, you know you have."

Cory took a drink of her soda. "Makes sense, doesn't it? Did to me, at least. Leandruses were supposed to be whizzes at admin, and we are. My mum had all sorts of brilliant books and such. Your family were all the ace hunters, and Clothilde Llewelyn killed the karkadann."

"But now what do you think?"

"Dunno, really. Phil's best at targets, but Grace did just as well shooting that kirin in Tuscany, and Valerija took one single-handed. Melissende is a Temerin, beastly through and through, but her sister and Rosamund are dolls. And you—"

"Not as good a hunter as you and Marten think I ought to be?"

"You're better than I am."

"But not as good as you wish I were."

Cory said nothing. The concert began, and our conversation ended. I leaned back on my elbows and closed my eyes, letting the music wash over me. Unlike Rosamund's playing, there was nothing here that held the slightest stench of unicorn. Pure beats and rhythms, without that chord in the Cloisters wall or the twang of bowstrings. I breathed, and smelled nothing but grass and people and snack food. The crowd around me whispered and rustled. I let my eyelids flutter open. Rosamund tapped her fingertips on the blanket, silently playing along. Dorcas and Zelda danced at the edge of the group, twirling, their hands open to the stars that had begun to sprout in the pale blue evening sky.

I joined them, weaving in and out between them, spinning to the beat of the drums on the stage, clasping hands with Dorcas to create an arch for Zelda to shimmy through, dipping and swirling with the other girls and then back to twirling, letting the skirt I'd borrowed from Phil ruffle around me, a little wheel of color that flapped and rippled in the wind.

We danced for several songs; and Cory, Ursula, and Ilesha joined us in turn, whirling and leaping and undulating to the beat as the night closed overhead and the field turned violet, then midnight, then black save the amber spotlights and the hundreds of tiny, neon glowsticks. Sometimes I forgot about

Giovanni altogether for several bars. I didn't notice when Phil and Seth wandered off.

I did, however, notice when she came back. "Time to go," she said, appearing beside me, still as a rock in the river of music.

"What's wrong?" I asked. "Where's Seth?"

"Sent him away. He was being a jerk." She looked at the tarp. "Guess we have to lug this back with us."

"Come on," I said. "Stay for a few songs more. Dance with us."

She shook her head. "It's getting late. We promised Neil."

"Since when are you so worried about the rules?" I took her hands and tried to pull her into the dance, but she shook me off.

"Astrid, stop being so childish. Time to go home."

I stopped dancing, and the world jolted back into place. "The Cloisters isn't my home."

She bent over and started yanking up the tarp, dislodging empty soda bottles and candy wrappers. "Yeah. Keep telling yourself that."

"What is that supposed to mean?"

"That Aunt Lilith dumped you here and all your fantasies about going home are just that. Fantasies."

I reeled back as if slapped. Phil's face fell.

"Oh, Asterisk, I'm sorry." She reached for me, but I shied away. "Don't listen to me. I'm tired and frustrated. I didn't mean it."

"Doesn't matter if you meant it," I said dumbly. "It's true."

"No, sweetie . . ."

I grabbed the other end of the tarp and started folding it. "Gather up the girls."

Just because we'd left the baths didn't mean the dancing had

234

stopped. The other hunters twirled their way back through the park and over the Celian hill toward the Colosseum and the Cloisters of Ctesias. Their songs ricocheted off the marble walls of churches and echoed through empty archways of ruins and apartment houses fronted by gated courtyards. Rosamund's clear soprano rang above the others, broken only by occasional giggles as the girls chased one another through the streets. Even Cory seemed to be having a good time.

Phil was the only one who remained silent. I walked beside her. "What's going on?" I asked, slipping my hand around her shoulder.

She hugged the tarp to her chest, but leaned into me nonetheless. "You were right. We shouldn't have met Seth tonight."

"What happened?"

She pursed her lips and studied our feet. "He was being a loser."

I squeezed her shoulder.

"You know how our folks are always like, 'They're only interested in one thing?'" She gave a tiny, mirthless laugh. "Sometimes I wonder if that's true."

"I think sometimes it is," I said. "That's what it was like with Brandt. Every time we went out was like some complicated game. What he'd try, when he'd try it, and how I'd stop him without making him mad or doing something I didn't want to do. That's the only thing I thought about every time we were together. Not about the movie we were watching or what we were talking about. Just waiting for him to make a move. It wasn't dating; it was preparing for battle." Maybe that's what we really needed combat training for.

"And with Giovanni?"

I blushed and hoped she couldn't see in the dark. "I . . . wanted to sleep with Giovanni. At first. I thought if I did, I could leave."

Phil nodded. "I figured as much. What happened?"

"He wouldn't do it. Guess it's too late, now." And too bad, too. Dating Giovanni hadn't been like it had with Brandt. "I don't know why he didn't show tonight."

"Me neither. I'm sorry, Cuz. I—"

She cut off, but I knew why. We all felt it, but not one of us was prepared.

There was a pounding beneath my feet, like the ancient cobblestones were shaking loose from their foundation, and then Ursula screamed.

I turned around. Even in slow motion, the unicorn was almost a blur. Enormous, dun colored, like marble splashed with mud. A re'em. He was the size of a bull, of a bison, and the girls shied away. There was something on his horn, a scrap of fabric, a tiny bundle, but then he shook it loose, and as it crumbled to the pavement, I saw.

Ursula.

Cory shrieked and smashed her soda bottle to the ground. It shattered in her hand and she rushed at the creature, clutching jagged glass edges in her bloody fist.

They barely scratched its hide, and the unicorn butted at her. She went flying into the wall, and slid, and was still. Dorcas let out a little squeak and rushed over to her.

"Run," Phil whispered. "We have to run."

"He'll catch us." I fumbled in my purse, closing my hands around the hilt of the knife.

Zelda took off, racing for the busier streets ahead, screaming like a banshee. The unicorn turned to give chase, then shied back as two Vespa motor scooters wheeled up the alley, revving their little engines for the climb. The riders slowed, then stopped, and I could see them staring.

"*Chiama la polizia!*" Zelda yelled. She paused, then picked up a small metal pole lying at the base of a scaffold. I saw one of the riders fumbling in his jacket pocket for a phone. The unicorn pawed at the ground with his hoof, and Zelda approached him, gripping the pole like a baseball bat.

Rosamund was crouched over Ursula, her English deteriorating in proportion to her terror. "*Sie blutet stark. Hilfe! Hilfe!* She bleeds much!" She lifted her hand, soaked in red.

Ilesha had balled up her long skirt and was kneeling in the spreading pool of blood. Over them all, my hunter's hearing could make out Ursula gulping and weeping, gasping for breath and crying almost inaudibly for her mother.

I swallowed. Immunity to the poison wouldn't do her much good if she bled out before the wound closed. Should I help her? I probably knew more first aid than either of the other two girls.

The knife hilt felt warm beneath my fingers, and the world narrowed to the form of the unicorn, its enormous, twisting horn shiny with the blood of my friend. I pulled the dagger from my bag and started creeping toward the unicorn from behind. "Phil, get my back."

"With what?" She held up the tarp, powerless.

"I don't know, but we have to help Zelda!"

Zelda was standing in front of the bikers now, shouting at them to ride away, but Italian men are too macho for that.

"You're going to get killed!" she hissed. I wondered if they even understood her.

The unicorn was impossible to mistake, however. Every muscle in its enormous body screamed death and pain and blood. I heard Cory moan on my right, and breathed a tiny sigh of relief that she was at least alive. I nodded at Zelda, who tightened her grip on the pole and raised it higher. What I wouldn't do for a bow and arrow right about now. He had to know I stood behind him, another hunter. A few feet more and I could jab with my dagger.

Then Dorcas let out a battle cry and catapulted herself onto the animal's back. The beast lunged and reared, huffing and grunting as Dorcas hung on for dear life and pounded her fist repeatedly against his flanks. I ran forward, too, but couldn't get close as the animal spun, kicking out with its hooves and tossing its deadly, blood-spattered head.

"Dorcas!" I screamed. "What are you doing!"

"Go for the neck!" Phil shouted from behind me. "The carotid artery!"

And then I saw it. In her hand, Dorcas clutched a pitiful little pocketknife, barely two inches long. Each tiny puncture wound healed as soon as she lifted her fist for another lunge.

The unicorn probably felt nothing more than the pinpricks of an insect.

Zelda found an opening and attacked, slamming the metal pole against one of the creature's legs. He roared, then stumbled, hopping to regain his balance. As soon as I could, I rushed in from behind, jabbing the knife hard under the beast's rib cage. A gush of hot blood spilled over my hand; and the animal bucked, dislodging Dorcas at last. She fell softly, like a flower on the breeze, then crunched against the cobblestones, her arm at an impossible angle.

The beast wrenched away from me and my dagger and charged Zelda, spearing her through the side and scattering the bikers. She screamed as she was lifted on the tip of his horn, then, somehow, braced her feet against his face and kicked free, smashing back to the ground, then scuttling into the shadows, her arm pressed to her bleeding side.

The unicorn faced me, blood dripping down its horn and over its muzzle, its eyes focused on the knife in my hand. Blood still streamed from its side and down its foreleg.

"Hey!" Phil yelled, and the unicorn swiveled toward her. She swung her arms wide, and the tarp went flying out, covering its face. "Now, Astrid!"

I didn't think, I just leaped. This unicorn had no mane to grab; instead, I gripped ropes of muscle and shoulder blades wider than my head. It bucked beneath me, more massive and rumbling than any kirin, and the tarp whipped around us both, tangling and sliding in a flood of fiery blood.

He still bled. How was that possible? I fisted the dagger and fought for purchase on the creature's neck.

"Astrid!" Phil was shouting, but I had no idea what she wanted. How could I kill a giant with a dagger? I thought of the statue Giovanni had shown me of David and his sling. How could anyone do such a thing?

The unicorn tossed its head again and the tarp slipped, hanging only from the beast's horn. I lunged up his neck and grabbed the horn with my free hand, yanking back hard. The unicorn's face shot skyward, and I reached down and plunged the dagger deep within his throat, angling hard and drawing the concave edge all the way across. His flesh tore beneath my hand, the muscles convulsed, then released, and the unicorn stumbled down.

I rolled off his back to the ground, and let his blood wash over me like a river.

17

Wherein Astrid Lies Low

PHILIPPA SHOOK ME AWAKE as the ambulance arrived. I insisted I wasn't hurt, but between our lack of Italian and the blood on my body, it was quicker to let them take me away. The body of the re'em still sat in the middle of the street, and as they shut the doors of the ambulance, I saw a small knot of priests emerge from the crowd and circle it.

I recognized at least one from the church next door to the Cloisters.

We were all rushed to the Ospedale San Giovanni. Ursula was taken directly into surgery. I'd just finished showing the nurses that none of the blood was my own when Melissende sprinted into the emergency room, face white as any statue's, panting like she'd run all the way up the hill from the Cloisters. She probably had.

I stopped her at the door. "She's lost a lot of blood, but it's an alicorn wound."

"Understood," Melissende snapped. "Let me see her. Let me see my sister."

"I don't know what will happen if they give her a transfusion of regular blood."

Melissende slumped against the wall. "Maybe it won't heal?"

"I have no idea." Cory was still unconscious. Phil, fielding regular phone calls from Neil, told me they'd tried to call Marten and Gordian three times apiece, but there had been no answer.

"Will they let me give her my blood?" she asked. "Just in case?"

I doubted the hospital would countenance a direct blood transfusion without a good reason, like a rare blood type that only Melissende and her sister shared. "I don't know, but—"

Melissende shoved past me and into surgery.

Zelda had escaped with what, by the time the ambulances arrived, looked like relatively minor wounds to her torso. She'd also gone to the hospital, but they released her soon after with a neat line of stitches up her abdomen, like a McBurney's appendix incision on the wrong side.

"My mother will kill me if this scars," Zelda said, holding her shirt up to examine the stitching.

She was a lucky one. Dorcas had broken her arm in two places, while Cory had a three-inch gash on her head. They'd had to shave off a hunk of her hair to sew it up. Neil arrived and remained at the hospital, watching over his niece. According to him, the clergy and laymen of the church next door had overseen the transport of the re'em into our building. Apparently, the locals were not as ignorant of the purpose of the Order of the Lioness as I'd assumed. Finally, the uninjured and the ambulatory hitched a ride with a nurse finishing her shift back down the hill to the Cloisters. In the east, the sky was already growing light.

The corpse of the re'em lay, exsanguinated, in the center of the rotunda. As we entered, Valerija and Grace were examining it, their expressions filled with wonder and confusion. They looked up, their faces fresh scrubbed and innocent next to our battered, bloodstained bodies. Every inch of me crackled and flaked as I walked.

"Is Ursula going to be all right?" Grace asked.

"We don't know yet," Phil said. The younger girl bit her lip, nodded stiffly, then turned around and left the room.

Valerija seemed at a similar loss. "I'll put on the kettle." She also vanished.

I almost asked her to share her pill supply. We all needed something that would take us away right now. Six hunters stared wordlessly at the massive body of the re'em, then Ilesha flew forward and started punching it.

"You bastard!" she screamed, slamming her fists down like a child in a tantrum. "You bastard!"

Rosamund drew her away, clucking softly. "Come now. Come."

"Why did they bring it here?" Zelda asked. "Doesn't Gordian want it?"

"We can't get in touch with Gordian," Phil said. "Marten either."

Dorcas wavered on her feet. "I think I need to sit down."

Valerija returned from the kitchen. "Yes. Neil told Grace and me to make beds. Downstairs. In case—" She gestured weakly at Zelda and Dorcas.

"Thank you," Zelda said. "The doctors said not to climb stairs for a few days."

Phil put her arms around Dorcas. "I'll help put you to bed." She looked at me. "You okay, Asteroid?"

I nodded, still transfixed by the sight of the re'em. His short, pale coat was caked with dried blood. The wound at his ribs looked wider than I remembered, though it was nothing to the jagged, gaping maw at his throat.

The others left, and I barely noticed. We stood there alone, hunter and corpse, beneath the statues of Clothilde and Bucephalus, all silent, all still. Like the kirin yearling, the re'em seemed smaller in death. I walked around the body, taking in every detail that I'd missed during the fight. The tail was tufted like a lion's. His head was broader than it was long; with wide, flaring nostrils; rounded ears; a mouthful of fangs; and a short, curly beard about three inches long and slightly gray in color.

I looked up to see Bonegrinder standing in the doorway, her head cocked. She minced into the room, looking fearfully from the body on the floor to me.

"It's okay," I said.

Bonegrinder sniffed at the corpse, then shied. She approached me, hesitant, suspicious, then knelt and bowed before me.

I dropped to my knees.

I had to do it. I had to. Just like Phil did, with the kirin yearling. It would have killed us all. I reached out with a shaking hand and touched its coat. Cold. So cold.

Bonegrinder butted against me and licked my bloody palm, and I lowered my head, wishing I could weep.

"—very height of irresponsibility!"

"But we were ambushed!"

"And you knew that was a likelihood!"

The angry voices echoed through the emptied dormitory floor. I woke up and tiptoed to the door. Bonegrinder, curled up near my bed, followed. I didn't remember letting her in. I looked down at my arms, at the fresh set of pajamas and carefully combed out, slightly damp hair. I barely remembered anything after I'd washed that blood off.

A flash of memory. Me slumped against the shower wall. *Shhh, Astrid, you can't lie there in your towel . . .* Phil. Of course. And now she was shouting at Neil in the courtyard. I opened the door and went into the hall. The overcast sky made it impossible to tell the time.

Valerija stood against the parapet, her finger on her lips.

"So we just stay indoors for all eternity? Hide away in here? Is that your solution?" Phil was saying now.

Neil whirled on her. "If that's what it takes to keep them safe, yes."

"That's bull."

Bonegrinder jumped up and rested her front hooves on the edge of the parapet.

Phil went on. "If we're not safe because we're hunters, then we shouldn't be hunters anymore. That's the part that's dangerous. Whether we're walking down the street or going on a mission, it's being a unicorn hunter that puts us in the line of fire."

"Being hunters saved several of their lives this evening."

"But it also caused our lives to be in danger." A new voice, Cory's, coming from under the aisle. "That was no random attack. Just like it wasn't random when they came for my mother and me."

"And so your suggestion is that we hole up in here for

what? Forever?" Phil asked.

"At least it's safe," was Cory's reply.

"I can't live like that," Phil said. "I won't. And neither will a lot of those girls—" She gestured toward the dormitory, then stopped when she saw us standing by the parapet. "Astrid. You're awake."

I hurried down the stairs, Bonegrinder clopping at my heels. A moment later, I was in the courtyard, the stones cool against my bare feet. Morning. Had I slept all day and all night?

I went first to Cory. Her curly hair lay in stringy, flat mats around her face, and there was white gauze wrapped around the crown of her head. "Are you all right?"

"Concussion."

"Contusion," Neil corrected.

She waved her hand at him. "I'm a little fuzzy."

"And the others?" I turned to Neil and Phil.

"Resting, mostly," Phil said. "Grace and Melissende are still at the hospital with Ursula. She came through the surgery all right, but she lost one of her kidneys."

I sat on the steps. "Oh, no."

Phil glanced at Neil. "The real problem is that the healing . . . it slowed down after she had a blood transfusion."

This is what I'd feared. "She didn't start to react to the venom, did she?"

"No. But Zelda is completely healed now. We cut the stitches out of her today so they wouldn't get lost in her new skin. With Ursula, it's like any other injury."

"And it was an especially serious one," Cory said. "She's still in the woods."

"Some of the hunters went to the hospital today to give blood,"

Valerija said. "For Ursula. We think, maybe she gets more hunter blood, she starts to heal again."

"What does Gordian say?"

Neil's mouth was set in a thin line. "We've been unable to contact anyone from Marten's staff. Marten himself has gone away on business. I regret not having in place some sort of procedure for emergencies—some sort of all-hour hotline to Marten. I never thought we'd have an unplanned battle. We never intended to put hunters in play unless Gordian staff were on call. I'm going to drive up to Tuscany tomorrow and try to get hold of someone in person. At the very least, we cannot leave that corpse in the rotunda to rot."

"I don't want it going to them," I said abruptly. "I don't want them to have it." If they couldn't be bothered to answer our calls, why should we keep our end of the bargain?

"Astrid," Neil said, "this is part of our arrangement. They're allowed to claim all of the kills—"

"I don't care. We had a major emergency and they can't be bothered to deal with us? Marten fires our trainer, then drags his feet getting us a new one? They take our kills and never tell us anything—"

"It's not your decision to make," Cory said. "Marten's been wonderful to us."

Valerija snorted but said nothing.

Cory got back on topic. "I firmly believe that, given this tragedy, we need to take more precautions. No hunters wandering around without adequate weaponry and backup. I think what this attack shows is that any unicorns hiding in the city are aware of our concentration in the Cloisters. That an attack can occur a few blocks from here, on a busy city street . . ." she trailed off.

"She's right," Neil said, as Cory struggled to collect more thoughts in her addled brain. "That re'em had been hiding out in the adjacent park. We cannot let hunters outside anymore."

"What about the ones visiting the hospital?" I asked.

"When they decide to leave, they'll call and we'll make sure they are safely escorted home."

"And how will you ensure that?" Phil said. "Crossbows or cars?"

"Both, if that's what it takes," said Cory.

Phil turned to Neil. "And you're okay with this? Go out and gather up more and more young women to stash away in here, cut off from the whole world, so they'll be *safe*?"

"What are our options, Pippa?"

There were none. Not if we were hunters. We were in the middle of the city, and we were still attracting wild animals. We all knew it. But Phil and I were the people the new rules would most affect. We were the ones always sneaking out.

Of course, if Giovanni had dumped me, it didn't matter as much. I'd barely thought of him since the attack. Amazing how being bathed in arterial blood can wash out any lingering romantic disappointments. Extraordinary how seeing a friend gored before your eyes can make you forget all about your dating life.

I rested my head in my hands, and the argument went on above me.

Later that afternoon, when Phil and I were alone in my room, she held up her cell phone. "Twenty messages from Seth. Voice mails, texts, everything."

"Did he apologize?" I was lying on my bed, combing grass seeds from Bonegrinder's coat, while Phil wore grooves in the floor with her pacing. Strange, I'd never been one to cuddle the zhi much before. That had always been Phil's job. But feeling her warm little body curled close to mine was somehow comforting now.

"A million times."

"A million times in twenty messages? Wow. Must be long messages." I smiled ruefully. "Have you called him back? Told him what happened?" But these questions weren't the ones I really wanted to know the answer to. Twenty messages from Seth. Did any of them mention Giovanni? Did Giovanni mention me? Didn't he care enough to admit that he'd been acting like a jerk, too? Would he do the same, if I had my own phone?

She shook her head. "He wants to meet."

I sat up, dislodging Bonegrinder, who bleated in protest. "Are you looking for me to give you permission?"

"No!"

"To come with you, then."

Phil pressed fists to her temples. "No! Astrid, I thought you'd understand." She sat down beside me and laid her head on top of Bonegrinder's tummy. The zhi was in heaven, sandwiched between us. "I need to get out of here. This past day and a half, it's been torture. Nothing to do but sit here and think about all the things I could have done to prevent this—"

"There's nothing you could have done," I said. "It was an ambush, like you said. We barely knew that re'em was there until he was on top of us."

"I need to get away from the Cloisters for a little while. Clear my head."

"Maybe you can go with Neil when he takes his trip up to Gordian."

She turned her face into Bonegrinder's hair, so her response was muffled. "Nnoo. Mmeed to leaf somva here to watch you gguys."

"I think Cory and I can hold down the fort." Contusion or no.

"An adult." She lifted her head. "Besides, I bet Gordian will call back today and it won't be necessary for him to leave the Cloisters at all. It won't be necessary for any of us to leave, ever again." She stroked her fingers through Bonegrinder's coat, and the zhi beamed at her in adoration. "And I can't wait that long. I'll go mad if I have to stay here another hour. Don't you feel it?"

Usually, but I was still wiped from my fight with the re'em. I understood now why Phil had been so out of it after she killed the kirin yearling. "I don't like it. It's dangerous."

"Asteroid," Phil groaned. "You sound like one of *them*."

"Sorry. But it's true. I don't want you hurt. I couldn't bear that." I remembered Melissende's face in the hospital. Frantic, horrified. She and her sister may not have gotten along, but she still loved Ursula.

"Then come with me. We'll carry weapons. There's safety in numbers."

There was also a greater attraction to the unicorns that were lying in wait. I scratched Bonegrinder behind the ears, bowing my face forward so my hair hid Phil from view. "I . . . don't want to. Please, Phil, don't think I'm a coward. I just can't. Not yet."

I felt the mattress lift as Phil stood. "Fine. I'll pretend it's because you don't want to play third wheel to Seth and me."

That, too, but it was far from the top of my list. And I still couldn't look her in the eyes. I glanced instead at the bedside table, where the alicorn dagger sat, nice and clean. I picked it up, and Bonegrinder started in my lap.

"Take this," I said, and held it out to her, eyes still downturned.

She grabbed the hilt. "I was thinking a crossbow, but it doesn't hurt to have a backup weapon."

I watched her examining the knife, turning it over and over in her hands. "It's weird," I said. "That first stab wound I gave the re'em? It didn't heal."

She shrugged. "Maybe it didn't have time to before you cut its throat."

"Maybe." But the kirin had healed pretty quickly after it had torn Grace's arrow from its shoulder. "And I suppose it bled out too quickly for the neck wound to heal, either?" But then, the kirin yearling's wounds also seemed to knit, even after death. Were re'ems different somehow?

Phil made a few practice swipes with the knife. "I don't know, Asterisk. You were always better at the science stuff than me." She leaned over and gave me a quick kiss on the forehead. "I expect you'll have it figured out by the time I get home tonight. I'm going to go call Seth."

I grabbed her knife hand. "Please be safe, okay?"

"You got it."

She headed for the door, and Bonegrinder leaped up off the bed to follow her, bleating pitifully.

"No, no, sweetie, you stay here and keep Astrid company, okay?" She ruffled the thicker fur on the zhi's neck. "I'll be home to play with you later." She waved at me. "Sleep tight, Cuz."

She closed the door, leaving Bonegrinder and me to stare after her in dismay.

By the evening, I was going stir-crazy myself. Much as I may have wanted to, I couldn't spend the rest of my life hiding in my room with Bonegrinder. After all, if the zhi got any hungrier, I might begin to look tasty. I headed downstairs and found Cory in Neil's office, reading.

"The others are in the chapter house," she said when I knocked. "I get too much vertigo when I try to navigate the stairs, so I'm stuck on the ground floor for a few more days."

"Are you sure you're supposed to be straining your eyes to read those old documents?"

"On the contrary, I'm under physicians' orders not to." She smiled and turned a page.

"Are Melissende and Grace still at the hospital?"

"They came home a few hours ago. Grace said Melissende hasn't slept at all. Looked it, too. She's apparently been after the doctors nonstop to give Ursula our blood."

"Even if we designate our donations for Ursula, they still have to go through the same screening process. It will take time." I sat beside her. "Did they ever experiment with your blood at Gordian?"

"Hmmm?"

"Testing whether hunter blood has something to do with the Remedy. Transfusing our blood into a non-hunter and seeing if that gives them immunity to the alicorn venom."

"Would be difficult to find a volunteer to test it on," Cory said. "If it didn't work, they'd be done for."

"True." And it wasn't like they could transfuse our blood into animals and carry out a trial like that. Could it be as simple as our blood, though? Maybe the Remedy made by hunters was not a product of the unicorns they killed, but a product of the hunters themselves?

But as soon as the thought occurred to me, I dismissed it. That was ridiculous. If it was hunters' blood, there wouldn't be such a secret surrounding the production of the Remedy. The hunters in the Cloisters wouldn't have needed an entire laboratory to create it. And the histories would have been filled with stories of hunters kidnapped and drained dry, rather than breathless depictions of unicorn battles.

Besides, hunters weren't invincible. Cory and Dorcas were proof enough of that. It was only when we were wounded by an alicorn itself that we saw the same regenerative powers evident in the unicorns and recipients of the Remedy. And Cory had already been the subject of an experiment where alicorn venom had been dripped into an incision made by a steel scalpel. Nothing happened. So it couldn't be a mix of our blood and alicorn venom, either.

"Cory," I said, "are there any instances in the histories that describe a hunter receiving a dose of the Remedy? Not as a cure to alicorn poisoning but for an illness or some other injury?"

"I can't recall any offhand, but you're welcome to look through our archives."

Hint, hint. Well, it was about time to put my money where my mouth was. I'd been complaining for weeks that we didn't have enough information about the unicorns. That we should look into this history or that theory. But shuffling through musty old papers—only half of which were written in English and an even smaller percentage of which were decipherable—was the last thing I wanted to do after I spent the day shooting arrows until it felt like my arms would fall off. They reminded me too much of my mother's strange, mildewed books, filled with their crazy theories and pseudoscience.

On the other side of that door, lying in the rotunda, was a monster. A giant, venomous, deadly monster. A shark, a snake, a panther, and a rampaging hippopotamus all rolled into one. And I'd killed it. Me, who'd never killed anything bigger than a cockroach. And all these ancient, ignorant old archives would tell me was that the reason I was able to do so was because I had some sort of magical genetic predisposition for killing unicorns.

I longed to know the truth, but it wouldn't be found here. So I got chills every time a unicorn came near. That was called survival instinct. So I didn't understand the distortion in time perception when we went into battle. I'm sure half a dozen papers had been written about a mind's increased ability to process information in an emergency situation. How about the unusual aim, strength, and speed? Well, I had been doing nothing but training for weeks on end. And I shouldn't discount the placebo effect. Tell a bunch of teenage girls that we have special powers hunting unicorns and see what we can make of it.

Every don, every hunter, bought into the magic, relied on it, believed that because you were a member of one family you were capable of tracking, and because you were a member of another family you were capable of hunting. They didn't seek to understand why that was. They just believed it. Predestination. The will of God. Whatever. If it ain't broke, don't examine it.

Tell that to the girl lying in the hospital on top of the hill.

"Actually," Cory said, "I think there might be something in

254

the account of the Jutland Campaign." She pointed at a modern, bound set of photocopies on Neil's desk. "We just got our hands on the records when I was researching into the alicorn throne from downstairs. A lot of hunters died in those battles. The Danes gave us that throne as a memorial. They apparently made a similar one for their monarch."

I picked up the spiral-bound manuscript. "It's in English?" And typed?

"We borrowed an English translation from the Vatican archives. They were fascinated with Magrete the First of Denmark—never more so than when she called the entire Order up north to help rid her land of the scourge of unicorns. And there's not much mention in the archives of this, but I think the Vatican was afraid of losing the Order of the Lioness to her. Powerful women sticking together and all."

Science or not, I wanted to hear this story.

Very late that night, Phil returned from her date with Seth. I didn't even know she'd come back until Valerija knocked on Neil's office.

"Astrid?" she asked. "Philippa is in our room. You see her?"

I shook my head. "No, why?"

Valerija's face was drawn. "I think you go see her. She is . . . sad."

Cory and I exchanged quick glances and then we both followed Valerija up the stairs, head injury and all.

Phil was curled up on her bed, facing the wall, hugging a throw pillow to her chest. The lamp on the desk cast soft, yellow light on her blond hair, her wrinkled denim skirt, her pink tank top, and her golden summer skin.

"Phil?" I sat down beside her. "Are you all right?"

She nodded but said nothing. She hadn't even taken her shoes off, and they were leaving dusty smears on her coverlet. In fact, she was pretty dusty all over.

"Were you in a fight?" I asked. "Did you get attacked by a unicorn?"

"No. Asteroid, I'm really tired, okay?"

By the door, Cory leaned over to Valerija. "Fetch Neil, would you?" Valerija nodded and was off. I glared at Cory. Fetch Neil so he could scold her for going out against his recommendation? Yes, that would make her feel grand.

But, much to my surprise, Phil didn't protest, just curled into an even tighter ball.

I tried to brush the tangled strands of hair from her face, but they stuck to her cheeks. I saw dried tear tracks.

"Phil, honey, look at me. Did you argue with Seth?"

She nodded, squeezing her eyes shut.

A small knot of hunters had gathered outside the door. Perfect. I'd hated breaking up with Brandt in front of everyone, and now Phil was faced with dealing with the aftermath of her breakup while the whole Order looked on.

"Astrid, it's late, I'm tired, can you just leave me alone?" She turned her face toward me, and I saw her eyes, red and puffy.

And then she looked beyond me. "Neil."

I turned around. The don was standing on the threshold, while the other hunters clustered around. "Good God, Pippa, are you all right?"

She sat up then and shook her head miserably as he joined us on the bed. "I'm so sorry, Neil."

She reached out her hands, and he took them in his and looked at her, long and hard.

"Cory," he said very carefully. "Close the door."

"Come on, everyone," Cory said, bossy as ever. "Let's leave her alone. Stop staring." The girls began to disperse and head back toward their own rooms.

Phil began to cry, crouching forward, her head drooping beneath her shoulders. I reached out to put my arm around her and she shuddered.

"I'm so sorry."

Sorry for what? For going out? "Shhhh, honey, it's all right."

"Close the door, Cory," Neil said, more forcefully this time. But Cory had also left. Valerija, leaning against the wardrobe near the threshold, suddenly straightened.

And then I heard it, the unmistakeable clatter of hooves on stone. Bonegrinder, galloping toward us.

"Close the door!" Neil shouted. I stood, but I was too late. Through the doorway, I saw a flash of white, and Cory, struggling to run, with her hand to her head. Valerija grabbed the door handle and shoved hard.

A microsecond later, Bonegrinder slammed against the wood, growling and shrieking like the bloodthirsty beast she was. I heard splintering as her horn scratched the door, as her hooves scrabbled against it, then a high-pitched yelp as someone on the other side dragged her away.

Phil buried her face in her hands.

18

WHEREIN ASTRID MEETS A MONSTER

I F MY HUNTER POWERS make my body move faster than normal, do they do the opposite for my brain? That was the only explanation for how long it took me to understand what had just happened. One minute, I was caught in the grip of a hunter's desire to subdue a raging unicorn, and the next, I was staring at my cousin in shock.

Bonegrinder had wanted to attack her.

"No," I whispered.

"Astrid, go away!" Phil cried, but this time, she wouldn't meet my eyes. "Please, go away." She glanced at Neil. "All of you."

He stood, his jaw clenched as tightly as the hands by his side. "Are you hurt? Just tell me, are you hurt?"

Phil gave a tiny, miserable shake of her head. "Go. Away."

"Well, you're not happy about it, and that worries me. Were you *ever*?"

My heart seemed to implode in my chest, and I reached out blindly for the edge of the desk, for anything to support myself. Valerija stood at the door, her expression impassive. She might have been blind, deaf, like the marble fountain in the front courtyard. Everyone was so silent, and I wanted to scream.

"Philippa, I couldn't care less about the Order. I care about you." Neil's voice almost cracked on the words. "Tell me. *Was this your choice?*"

I'll be home to play with you later. That's what she'd said to Bonegrinder.

Phil's head drooped farther forward, and her reply was inaudible. It didn't matter.

"Who was he?"

Phil didn't respond. Neil looked at me.

"Her boyfriend," I said immediately. Neil's eyes flickered slightly at the word. "Seth Gavriel. He's doing a language program at a boarding school in Trastevere." I told him the name.

Neil nodded. "I'm calling the police."

"No, Neil," Phil said. "Don't."

"But, Phil," I said, incredulous. "If he—"

"Astrid!" she screamed. "Get out!"

My eyes burned stronger than alicorn venom, and I headed for the door. Neil put his hand on my shoulder and I shook him off. Valerija exited with me, but as soon as I hit the hall, I broke into a sprint.

Down in the rotunda, I saw Cory exiting the door to the lower levels. She'd braved the stairs after all.

"I shut Bonegrinder up in the catacombs," she said. "We should really consider doing that more often. We cleaned it up specifically for her and then we spoil her rotten, letting her stay above all the time—" she looked at my face. "Are you all right?"

"No." At that moment, I thought I'd never be all right again.

I stared at the carcass, at the tableau, at anything. My hands clenched, my fingers strained. I wanted to claw his eyes out. I wanted to kick his face in. Didn't he know we were hunters? Didn't he know what we were capable of?

All of a sudden, I understood what Melissende had said about the ancient hunters, sending out packs of zhi to cut down Actaeons. There was nothing I wanted more than to sic Bonegrinder on Seth Gavriel.

No sooner had the thought occurred to me than I found myself climbing upon the dais. I wrenched the sword from the mannequin's hand. I checked the blade. Still sharp. Not the real claymore of Clothilde Llewelyn, but it would do.

"Astrid," Cory said in horror. "What are you doing?"

I hopped down and crossed to the carcass of the re'em. I raised the sword over my head, then brought it down hard against the unicorn's horn.

The clanging echoed through the hall as I hacked away. It took five strokes, but at last, I sliced through the tip of the horn. I hoped it was still fresh enough. I dropped the sword on the remains and lifted the alicorn. It lay heavy and hot in my fist. Still powerful. Maybe still venomous.

Cory stepped in front of me. "Have you gone mad?"

"Yes." I said. "It started when I came here, and now it's full-blown." I turned toward the door.

"Astrid, wait! Where are you going?"

"He raped Phil, Cory. I'm going to kill him."

It only took two hours of wandering the streets of Rome to realize what a horrible idea that was.

Perhaps it was the fact that I hadn't brought my bus pass

nor any money, and walking to Trastevere—even running, as I'd done for the first twenty minutes—did a lot to burn off my rage.

Nothing seemed to have changed beyond the doors of the Cloisters. Still the same loud motorbikes, the same happy diners clustered around sidewalk café tables, the same people watchers and gelaterias with their candy-colored displays and pop music. No one knew what had happened to her, to me. The world was inconceivably as it had ever been.

I'd even run past the spot of the re'em attack on Via Claudia. There was blood in the cracks between the cobblestones, but nothing else to reveal the terror and violence of that night. A rainstorm or two, and it would all be gone. I wondered how many more bloodstains had been washed away in the thousands of years since this city's founding. Gladiators and sacrifices, assassinations and executions, battles and protests and even accidents. What was one act of violence to generations of death? Why did it feel like my world was falling apart?

At last, my feet slowed near another ancient stone wall on the north side of the city. Where was I now? The neighborhood seemed oddly familiar. That's right—the Villa Borghese, the beautiful park where we'd first seen Seth and Giovanni again. Phil had arranged it; happy, lighthearted, fun-loving Phil. The park was almost unrecognizable in the dark. Every memory I had of this place was now blackened by my new reality.

There was the fountain where Seth and Giovanni had waited for us. Here was the path where we separated when Giovanni took me back to Trastevere. I never should have left her alone. I never should have stayed inside the Cloisters today. Was it my fault? Was it me?

She wouldn't even speak to me tonight. Wouldn't look at me. Made me leave the room while she talked with Neil. She must blame me. If I'd gone with her today . . .

All my life, Phil had protected me. She came to Rome to be with me; she stayed on, even once she decided that she disagreed with the idea of hunting; she had my back, always, whether I was fighting with the Bartolis or a unicorn. She held me when I was scared, comforted me when I was sad, loved me more than anyone I'd ever known.

And the one time I could have protected her, I'd failed.

My legs gave out beneath me and I collapsed, exhausted, on a bench. Of course she couldn't trust me tonight. She couldn't trust me ever! Look at me, penniless, on the streets of Rome with a sawed-off alicorn in my hand. I'd gone running into the night with no plan. No knowledge of where to find Seth; no idea what I'd do to him when I found him; no sense of what, in fact, had happened to Phil, other than that she had lost her virginity and it hadn't been by choice. Had he hurt her? Threatened her? Drugged her?

Had any of us known that he was capable of something like that? Phil? Giovanni? Did Giovanni know what his friend had done? I wanted to hear the awful details—the truth—and yet, I dreaded it with every fiber of my being. Perhaps Phil had been right to throw me out.

I began to sob, boiling hot tears overflowing from eyes that had held them in far too long. I cried for Ursula and Phil, for the terrified look in the eyes of the yearling Phil had stabbed to death, for the photo of Sybil Bartoli that stared up at me from Cory's desk every day. I shed tears for Lilith, who'd had no idea what she was doing when she sent me to Rome, and for Neil, who had no idea what to do once we'd gotten there. I wept for Bonegrinder, whose love was so conditional, and for myself, whose love was anything but.

I cried until my eyes burned like brands, and beyond, until my whole body was aflame, lungs and throat and nostrils and skin and flesh. It was only then, when I could barely move from the pain, barely lift my eyelids to look, that I realized I was not alone and it was not my tears that seared my flesh.

There, less than a dozen feet away, stood a karkadann.

Massive beyond all imagining—an elephant, a tank, a battering ram of tightly coiled death, the monster stood and stared at me, shifting its giant head with the graceful slowness of all great animals. Its enormous chest expanded as it inhaled; and when the nostrils flared with exhaled breath, my body started to sting anew.

Why wasn't I dead yet?

I don't know how long I remained like that, in agony, too terrified even to move. The living karkadann before me made the one in the rotunda seem like a stuffed teddy bear. Each of its long, wiry hairs carried with it more menace than a dozen kirin; than ten re'ems; than a million white, fluffy zhis. Its eyes glowed orange and black, like banked coals, and frothy, pink-tinged saliva dripped from its enormous fangs. I couldn't bring myself to look directly at its horn. The ground trembled beneath me as it shifted its weight on its colossal hooves, and I knew why the armies of Asia had succumbed when they saw Alexander astride a creature like this.

I sat, frozen in numb terror, and waited for the end.

It didn't come forward. Slowly, through the burning, I slid to the side. It made one step, blocking me. I slid back. It did the same. I stayed perfectly still, and it waited.

"Please," I whispered. "Kill me, but don't mock me."

The kirin, torn to pieces on Monte Mario as Seth choked on the stench of alicorn venom. Me, lying sick in bed in our apartment back home as my mother pressed a cool and comforting hand against my fevered cheek.

Was my life flashing before my eyes? If so, what a strange group of images for it to choose.

Grace holding aloft the claymore of Clothilde Llewelyn. Me hacking away at the carcass of the dead re'em. Bonegrinder gazing at me in adoration then kneeling before my feet.

The karkadann stared at me.

My mother. Me. My mother. Me. My mother. Me.

I pressed my fists against my aching eyes. I'd snapped. My mind was incapable of processing its imminent death. That was the only explanation. But, if so, what were the chances I'd actually be able to recognize it for what it was?

My mother, me. My mother, looking at me, touching me, my mother, me, my mother, and me . . .

Her Daughter.

The word formed in my mind, and then the images shifted, slid, became a series of statues I knew well, of paintings of battles, of conversations I'd had with Cory. *Alexander the Great.*

Daughter of Alexander.

I opened my eyes and looked at the karkadann. It was still standing, head lifted; its terrible, deadly horn pointed like a spear at the stars.

Daughter of Alexander.

It stamped its foot.

"Yes," I said, as the world I knew burned to ashes. "I am."

I was beaten, broken, utterly insane. Unicorns were real; I'd accepted that. I was a hunter, immune to the venom, endowed with special abilities as part of a cosmic, genetic joke. I'd even allowed for that. I'd rolled my eyes when they talked about burning temples and the goddess Diana and the marvelous career of a young Macedonian prince and his trusty, one-horned warhorse, but I went along with it. I'd seen the effects of the Remedy firsthand. I'd stood by and watched a zhi yield to a hunter, then attack someone who wasn't. I'd accepted so much of the Order of the Lioness and its magic.

But as images rose in my mind, unbidden, shifting and sliding in a bizarre puzzle of word association, I began to wonder if all the magic that came before was merely a prelude.

I could *not* be talking to a karkadann.

Daughter of Alexander, it said to my mind, and then I saw again the dead kirin on the mountain.

"That was you," I said. "You killed those kirin the other night. Why?"

Why did I think it could possibly understand me? Was this why they said that Alexander had been able to talk to Bucephalus? If I stared very hard at the unicorn, would I be able to force images into its mind? What kind of thoughts did a unicorn have, anyway?

Ugh. Happy ones, I realized, as I suddenly got a very vivid picture of the karkadann devouring the kirin. Gross.

The karkadann snorted and tossed its head. Pride? Was that pride? I put a hand to my pounding brow. It hurt too much. "Why . . . does it burn?"

Alicorns alicorns alicorns . . . and professional wrestlers. Huh?

I was embarrassed to realize that my word association for *strength* was a guy in a metallic Speedo and face paint. Karkadann venom was strong. Strong enough to sense from afar. Strong enough to affect even a hunter.

"Why did you kill the kirin? Food?"

Giovanni with his hand up my shirt. I grimaced. *A camera.*

They were spying on us. The kirin were *spying* on us?

"Why aren't you killing me now?"

Daughter of Alexander.

"No," I said, in too much pain to be anything but blunt. "Daughter of Clothilde Llewelyn."

Laughter.

"I kill unicorns," I said. "That's what I am!"

A chemistry set. A Band-Aid on a scraped knee. The figure of Clothilde Llewelyn. The statue of the hunter in the fountain in the entrance court.

"I don't understand you." Did those words just come out of my mouth?

What, Lassie? Did Timmy fall in the well?

I no longer knew which thoughts were my own and which had been dredged up by the monster. Was it toying with me before it attacked? Was it making a joke?

It lowered its head and shook, and I flinched. Apparently, this conversation was every bit as frustrating to the unicorn.

"I take it Alexander was better at this," I said.

It growled, and I shied away. Was Alexander also able to withstand the stronger poison? How in the world could anyone bear to go near something like this? How did Clothilde have the wherewithal to raise a weapon against it? I could barely breathe, let alone stand.

Daughter of Alexander. Danger.

Images of Lino, aiming at one of our practice targets while Marten looked on. The figure of Clothilde Llewelyn. Phil, stabbing the kirin yearling. Me, slitting the re'em's throat. The kirin who'd waited for us outside the courtyard. The two kirin who'd watched us on Monte Mario.

I pressed my hands against my temples and let out a hoarse scream. The images poured on. Relentless, shifting, sliding, until at last they began to make sense.

Daughter of Alexander, danger. The kirin watch. The kirin remember. The Llewelyns decimated the unicorns. The Llewelyns are forbidden.

"Forbidden from what?"

The Cloisters of Ctesias. The chapter house. The Wall of First Kills.

From being hunters? Tell that to—well, everyone. The Bartolis, Marten, and my mother all seemed to think we were the best ones. How could we be *forbidden* from being hunters if it was our destiny?

"Well, it's a good thing that the kirin don't decide, isn't it?"

In my mind's eye, *Marten watched Phil draw her bow. Her form was perfect, the shot true. Technicians bustled around the body of the kirin yearling. Valerija held aloft the head of the other kirin. The Wall of First Kills shuddered beneath my hands—all but hers.*

The karkadann stiffened suddenly and whipped his head to the side. A fresh wave of fumes caught me, and I struggled to stay upright on the bench.

Bonegrinder, frolicking in the courtyard.

I followed its gaze, and indeed, there was a zhi by the gate to the park. The little unicorn minced forward, and I saw it wasn't just any zhi. A pink bandanna was tied around its neck.

"Bonegrinder!" I called, and pushed to my feet, wavering slightly.

The karkadann lowered its horn in warning, and I froze. Bonegrinder cocked her head, hesitant, then took a few steps forward, looking from one of us to the other.

How had she gotten loose? Cory said she'd shut her in the catacombs!

Tunnels. Freedom.

Bonegrinder came close enough to sniff at the karkadann's leg. The karkadann opened its mouth.

"No!" I said. "She's mine!"

Laughter. Chains. Whips. Prisons. Alexander.

"I don't understand you. You mean that she's domesticated?" Hardly, I corrected myself. I'd seen her go after Phil tonight.

Bonegrinder pawed at the karkadann's enormous hoof, then bowed before it, as it did to me.

Servant.

The karkadann seemed to sneer.

The two kirin lay dead on the hillside, while Marten watched Phil shoot practice arrows.

Bonegrinder rose and looked from me to the karkadann, clearly confused. Well, that made two of us. The karkadann was growling now, a rumbling so low I felt rather than heard it. It resounded through my bones like I was the trophies on the Wall of First Kills. The karkadann was angry. Furious, in fact. Any second now, it would tear us both apart. I fell back against the bench.

Suddenly, Bonegrinder was standing in front of me, facing the giant unicorn, making her little, high-pitched, bleating growl. Her legs were placed wide, her limbs bent, ready to spring.

Servant! No! Never!

Alexander, riding into battle. The dust of a thousand dead soldiers. Bloody jaws, teeth and skin broken on a copper bit, spears, scars, endless marches through deserts. No water. No food, but for another rotting carcass of a soldier who hadn't survived, tossed like a scrap to a dog. Alexander marched on.

The kirin on the hillside, and then . . .

Marten Jaeger, enormous, shadowed in harsh white light. Pain . . . so much pain. The sound of Cory crying, "Stop!"

The karkadann quit snarling and straightened, staring at the little zhi.

I stared, too. Was that last one . . . *her* thought? Bonegrinder's memory of the time she'd been a lab rat at Gordian?

Bonegrinder kept making angry little yips. Her fluffy white coat stood on end, shaking slightly as she faced off against the monster. The karkadann tilted its head back again, angling its horn away from us both, and she relaxed.

In my mind, I saw tiny Ilesha drawing her bow against the yearling. I saw Dorcas attacking the re'em with a pocketknife. I was getting better at translating.

Brave little thing.

Bonegrinder stepped forward and sniffed at the karkadann again. When the giant unicorn made no move, she began to frolic again, weaving in and out of the karkadann's legs.

I wondered if I was the only human ever to witness this interspecies unicorn interaction. Should I be taking notes? But would I even be able to lift a pen, let alone defend myself? My sight was beginning to go black at the edges. I was losing consciousness, suffocating from the fumes. My hands slipped on the bench until I was resting on my elbows. The karkadann was killing me by inches.

Bonegrinder?

"Yes," I said. "That's what we call her."

She likes it. Not her name, but good.

"What is her name?" I choked out. "She has another?"

A barrage of images, but I had no more screams in me tonight. Finally, they coalesced:

All slaves do.

I lay gasping for breath on the stone.

Daughter of Alexander, do not die yet.

"Why not?" I whispered. My eyes watered, my nose ran. The park swam in my field of vision. Bonegrinder whined, nervous, her breath warm and soothing on my raw face. "You like your food live?"

Laughter. No. Not food.

"Then what?"

Giovanni's voice: "Astrid the Warrior."

It *was* mocking me. This was all a game. Torture the hunter to death. And not just any hunter: the Llewelyn.

I need you. Freedom.

"From what?" I barely had breath to push the words past my lips. "You a slave, too?"

Once. Never again.

The darkness whirled now, beckoning me closer. Each breath was ragged, flat. My lungs were torn balloons.

And still the karkadann whispered inside my head.

They called me Bucephalus.

19

Wherein Astrid Awakens

My back was cold. My T-shirt kept riding up, exposing my skin to the night breeze. I curled forward more, hugging the warmth deeper into my chest.

The warmth bleated.

I opened my eyes with difficulty, as they seemed glued together by dried, crusty bits of sleep. Gray, watery dawn light filtered in, slightly blurred. The park. The bench. And Bonegrinder in my lap, burrowing her face into my shoulder so that her horn jutted painfully against my arm.

I was alive.

I sat up, careful not to dislodge the sleeping zhi. Alive or not, I wasn't sure I was up to a chase. I ran a hand over my face, then grimaced when I saw the mess of dried blood and mucus in my palm. I didn't even want to know what I looked like. Part of this might have been from my crying fit, but I was sure even more was due to—

That hadn't really happened, had it? I froze, halfway to the fountain across the clearing. My nice little chat with the karkadann? It was a dream, a nightmare. Perhaps my sore eyes and throat were products of my crying, of my running through the city in the grip of a murderous rage.

But the nosebleed, and Bonegrinder there on the bench . . .

No. It was a dream, born of too much stress and too many days spent staring at that tableau in the rotunda. Bucephalus! Right. Last night I talked to a twenty-three-hundred-year-old unicorn. Not even trees lived that long.

I rinsed my face off in the fountain, then drank a few mouthfuls from the spring water spigot nearby. Thank God for Rome's ancient public works. I hesitated for a moment, then plunged my whole head under the faucet, letting the frigid water wake me up and cool my burning skin. My face and neck were sensitive to the touch, the skin on my arms and hands dry and flaky.

A glance back at the bench had me on my feet again in a flash. Bonegrinder was gone! But not far; I found her a few trees away, sniffing the ground, possibly tracking a squirrel. How would I get her home through the streets of Rome without having her attack someone? Especially if she was hungry.

I gathered up the alicorn from where it had rolled under the bench and raided a nearby trash can for supplies. Plastic shopping bags, a bit of shredding twine—Bonegrinder had escaped from steel cages and catacombs. How would any of this hold her?

I heard a chorus of squeaks from the trees. Great. She'd caught breakfast at least. Now, if only I could get her out of here before we ran into any joggers or maintenance men.

Bingo: a bicycle chain. I gathered up my findings and whistled to the zhi. She trotted over, bits of brown tail fluff still sticking to her fangs. I knelt down and began knotting the plastic bags together into thick ropes. Of course, Bonegrinder could gnaw through steel locks, but maybe that was only if she got her teeth around it. I remember reading once that an alligator can snap its jaws closed with great force, but that you can hold the jaws closed relatively easily, I wondered if that would work for zhi.

I looped the bicycle chain around her snout, and she flinched as the links pinched her skin. Suddenly, I got a flash—a copper bit and muzzle, crusted with dried blood. An image from last night. An image from my nightmare. Bonegrinder looked up at me, her eyes more blue and limpid than ever, and I slid the chain off her face. Maybe the plastic would be a bit gentler. She balked when I tried to slip the carefully knotted loops of plastic around her head, but eventually I got the whole contraption cinched up tight. Her jaws were secured by a rope of plastic bags, which led back to the bandanna around her neck. I used the bicycle chain as a leash, with a secondary restraint made of bags tied around my own waist, and my free hand firmly gripping her horn. I'm sure we looked ridiculous, but since I was about to walk a unicorn through the streets of Rome, whether or not our trashy accessories would be noted as a fashion disaster was at the bottom of my list of things to worry about.

"Now be good," I warned Bonegrinder. She strained against my hand, trying in vain to free herself from my grip. This was going to suck. We walked, awkwardly, toward the gates of the park, and I began to realize how very impossible a task this would be. I couldn't leave her here, and I couldn't contact anyone at the Cloisters to come get us unless I started begging for spare change on the street corners so I could use a pay phone.

Bonegrinder stiffened, and her fur bristled. Oh no. I tightened my grip on both leash and horn as she began to growl. Was it a jogger? A janitorial crew? A pastry cart?

And then she took off, and I began to sprint to keep hold of her. We flew down the street, and in the midst of my weird, hunter time warp, I saw the solution. We'd run.

And I'd steer.

Miraculously, we reached the door of the Cloisters without mishap, and in record time, too. I wasn't even out of breath, though I hadn't been able to run half that distance the previous evening, and that was before my lungs had been ravaged by—

No. I'd decided that was a dream. Or at the very least, I'd decided I wasn't going to think about it until I'd gotten Bonegrinder safely back to the Cloisters. Which I had, so maybe now it was time to examine my memories of last night a little more closely.

They called me Bucephalus.

Yeah, that had to have been a dream.

Inside the rotunda, the re'em had begun to grow a tad ripe. Even Bonegrinder crinkled up her nose at the stench. We walked past the tableau, and I shuddered, expecting any second for the karkadann on the dais to move, to breathe, as the one in the park had. Terrifying as the stuffed version was, nothing could compare to the real thing.

I mean, the one in my dream.

Now, where to put Bonegrinder that would be safe and

274

secure? How often had she been escaping from the Cloisters to go romping through the streets of Rome? We hadn't been keeping that close an eye on her, and she usually slept with Phil.

Never again. My chest began to ache.

But last night, she'd remained safe in my lap the entire time I'd been unconscious. Perhaps the solution would be to keep her close until we could find a more permanent place to put her. A more permanent place to put Phil.

I wondered how my cousin was doing, but after last night, I didn't know if I could face her. I cast a glance at the staircase to the dormitory floor. If she was upstairs, asleep, I couldn't risk bringing Bonegrinder past her door on the way to my room. The zhi might go ballistic again.

So instead I went down to the chapter house. Today, the vibrations from the wall didn't seem as grating. Maybe I'd grown used to them, or, more likely, in light of everything else that I'd been dealing with in the past few days, the buzzing was nothing more than a slight annoyance. It was almost soothing, in fact, like a white noise machine.

There was a collar and chain sunk into the masonry in the wall, and I secured Bonegrinder, then let her join me on the couch. I threw a hand over my face, curled my body around the zhi, and let my eyes drift shut once more.

It may have been only minutes later when I heard a soft voice in my ear.

"Asteroid."

I jolted awake. "No, Phil! Bonegr-*scmunnnnf.*" She pressed me to her chest.

"Honey, why do you smell like garbage?" She pulled away, her nose wrinkled.

"Long story." Bonegrinder was near the wall, eyeing Phil warily. I looked back at my cousin, and she waved her hand at me. Neil's ring glinted from one of her fingers.

"I'll be fine with this on," Phil said. "He thought I should have it. Thought I should have a lot of things, really. Like a physical at the hospital and a nice chat with the police and the American consulate." She sighed and looked down at her hands.

"Oh, God, Phil, I'm so sorry."

"Me, too."

My sore lungs felt like they were being crushed anew. "This is all my fault. Are you hurt? Are you going to be—"

"Whoa. All your fault? Say that again and I'll slap your face." She stood now and wandered away.

"But if I hadn't let you go out alone . . ." I began from my position on the couch.

"I'm out alone plenty. And when I'm out with you I still manage to get in private time with my dates. You had nothing to do with this." She trailed a tentative finger along the armrest of the alicorn throne. "Huh. Watch this." She plopped down in it. "Comfy."

I was momentarily stunned into silence.

"I feel like a queen," Phil said, lifting her chin. I said nothing, and after another moment, she slumped. "Please, Astrid. Don't you be weird, too."

Don't be weird meaning don't talk about what happened? Don't be weird meaning don't run around Rome, then roll around in garbage, then go to sleep in the one spot I've been trying to avoid up until last night? Don't be weird meaning don't

276

have long, involved conversations with imaginary, thousands-of-years-old monsters?

Too late, Phil.

"I'm really sorry for throwing you out of my room last night," she said at last. "I wished you were there so many times. Just to hold my hand. Anything. Neil is nice, but it's not the . . . same."

"Phil." I rushed toward her, then stopped just in time. My thigh brushed against the throne, sending shockwaves of pain rippling up and down my leg.

"Watch it," she said flatly. "You're still a live wire."

"Now I'm going to slap *you*." I sat on the floor. "Talk to me. Tell me what happened."

"I had sex with Seth."

"He forced you."

She looked away. "This is as bad as the police."

I touched her knee. "I want to understand."

She was silent for a long time. "Me, too, Astrid. Me, too. I want to understand why I didn't stop him. It was all so quick, I don't even know. One second, we were fooling around, and the next . . . he was . . . *inside*."

I clenched my jaw and my fists. "Did he hurt you?"

She shook her head miserably. "Physically, but nothing compared to how much we've been smacked around while hunting. As soon as I felt him, I tried to push him away, but . . ."

"But what?" I asked.

Phil practically hissed and flew up from the chair, sweeping past me and over to the other side of the room. I rose, too. Perhaps I shouldn't be pushing her.

"This is the problem!" she said. "You all keep saying stuff like 'rape' and 'force' and 'hurt' and 'fight,' and it makes me wonder . . . if I *didn't* fight, maybe it *wasn't* force. If he didn't hold me down, if he didn't smack me around . . ."

"No, Phil—they're just—the words I know. I don't think—"

She faced the wall of weapons. "Like maybe it was all some horrible mistake. Like he didn't mean to. Because I really liked him. And he liked me. So I don't . . . think he wanted to hurt me." She leaned her hands, palms flat against the wall, but I knew she felt no vibrations from the weaponry, no humming from the bones. "I pushed him and said stop, but it was . . . over. He was done. That was it."

I swallowed past the lump in my throat. It was nothing like I had been imagining last night in the grip of my murderous rage.

She took her hands from the wall and stared at them. "But that was enough. For whoever decides these things. Alexander. Or Diana. Or Bonegrinder. Who knows?"

I stared at her, incapable of putting my thoughts into words, terrified that speaking at all would clam her up for good. If it hadn't been for the hunting, for the eligibility, for the trial by zhi, would she have told us at all?

"So what do you think of that?" she asked abruptly, and turned to look at me. "I like him. I still really like him. What do you think of that?" Her tone was a dare.

"What does it matter what I think?" I asked. "The only thing I care about is you. What you think. What you feel. I'm glad you aren't hurt—"

"I *am* hurt," she snapped. "Incredibly hurt. Just not the way . . . people think I should be. No bruises. No blood."

I bit my lip.

"Because here's the part you're gonna love," she said after a minute. "I didn't want to. You know that. I wanted to stay here, with you, with Neil, with the others. So of course I wasn't going to have sex. And he knew it, too, because we talked about it. The other night, at the concert, he wanted to, kept asking, over and over, and I kept saying no. And he backed off. That's what you do, right? You make a choice, together. And until you both make it clear you've changed your mind about having sex, the matter is closed."

I nodded. I'd taken the same classes in school as Phil.

"So as much as I'd like to think he just made a mistake last night, wasn't thinking in the heat of the moment, hadn't realized that I didn't change my mind . . ." She took a deep breath. "I know the truth. He didn't make a mistake. He planned it. Because when he pulled out . . ." She grimaced. "He was wearing a condom, Astrid. Had been wearing one the whole time, I guess, because I sure as hell didn't notice him putting it on!"

She laughed now, but there was no humor in it at all. I could only imagine the response she must have gotten at the hospital, at the police station. Safe sex rape? Right.

"And *that's* when I got really mad. Would you believe it? When I saw that. Before that, I'd been angry at myself, sad, scared. . . . But now I was furious at *him*. Not happy that I wasn't going to get pregnant, that I was protected—all that. Because it meant he knew exactly where it was all headed. No matter what I'd said, no matter that I'd told him I didn't want to sleep with him. He knew what he was going to do. And I'd been thinking such generous thoughts—like he was all out of control or something, and it just *happened*. What kind of crap is that? And maybe, because I was thinking that when he was doing it, maybe that's why I didn't fight? Maybe I could have stopped him?"

"No," I said. "Don't think that."

"What's the alternative? That I've been seeing this horrible, violent guy for all this time? That I've been dating a monster?"

"What did you do?" I whispered from my place across the room.

"Hit him." Her mouth became a thin line, as straight as her spine. "Wish there'd been a unicorn nearby, I could have really whaled on him. Or not, I guess. At that point."

"What did he do?"

"Called me a bitch and walked away." She shook her head. "Like he was done. Like he had what he wanted." Her voice caught. "And you know, that's the one thing I *never* wanted. This whole time, I wasn't waiting for something in particular. Just someone who wanted me. Not sex. But me."

My feet propelled me toward my cousin, my arms enfolded her. And she wasn't so much bigger at all. She smelled sweet, like a dozen bars of soap, and her eyes were as red as mine, and she buried her face in my shoulder and her body shuddered against my chest, like she couldn't breathe at all.

"So tell me, Astrid. Do you call that rape?"

I squeezed her tighter. Did I? Hell yeah. Would the police? Would the courts in Italy? Would Seth? But then I realized I didn't care what anyone else called it. Phil hadn't made the choice—and Seth knew it. He knew it, and so he took her choice away from her.

It was rape. It was horrible.

And on top of all that, I'd lost her. Who made these rules? Who decided what virginity was? Had it been Diana? Stupid ancient goddesses and their warped, patriarchal ideals. Nothing about Phil had changed. She was the same as ever. It wasn't fair.

"Tell me," she mumbled into my shirt. "Tell me what to do now. Tell me how to stop thinking he's an okay guy anyway. Tell me that Neil is right, and he's the worst bastard ever born. Tell me what I do when Neil gets back from Gordian and there's only one ring. Tell me how I'm going to sit here and watch you play with Bonegrinder, watch you shoot bull's-eye after bull's-eye. Tell me how I'm going to handle going home and never feeling that power again."

More shuddering, and then we stood there and wept together, arms wrapped so tightly around each other that I thought for a moment that we were the same person, that any second, my power would flow into her and we'd both be whole.

But all the magic in the world, all the magic in that room, wouldn't make things work that way.

Eventually, she pulled away and wiped her hands against her tear-streaked face. "Sorry," she said. "But you really do kind of stink."

I gave her a weak smile. "It was necessary, trust me. Bonegrinder got loose last night, and I had to raid a trash bin to tie her up and get her home safe."

"You went out alone?" Phil's brows furrowed.

I bit my lip. "Yeah. I . . . it's a long story."

"Did you see anything?"

Yes. I saw a karkadann. He poisoned me from afar, to within an inch of my life. And then he left me unconscious on the park

281

bench. Oh, and I think we might have had a conversation. Me and the unicorn.

"No," I said. Phil had more than enough to deal with.

We headed upstairs together. Apparently, while I'd been asleep, Lucia had arranged to have the re'em moved from the rotunda to the catacombs until the people from Gordian came to retrieve the body. The only sign it had ever been in the rotunda at all was a few smears of blood on the mosaic floor.

I took a shower that was all too short, and had just finished combing my hair and changing into a fresh set of clothes when Phil came bursting into my bedroom, holding her cell phone and shaking from head to foot.

"It's him," she said. The readout on the phone's display showed a half dozen missed calls. "All while I was downstairs talking to you. What do I do? What if he comes here?"

I took the phone from her and clicked it off. "You're not to speak to him. Nobody here will let him in. We'll call the police and it will be fine."

And for a while, I thought it could be. Phil sat down and started braiding my hair in that cool, backward French braid she knew, and we talked about the time she set up a volleyball court in the backyard and ruined her parents' new sod. That went on for about fifteen minutes. Then there was a knock at the door.

Grace came in. "Excuse me, Phil? There's a boy downstairs in the outer court who wants to see you. He says it's extremely important. Neil's still out. What do you want to do?"

Phil's hands froze on my head. I grabbed the elastic band off the coverlet, wrapped it around the base of the braid, and stood up. I may not be armed with an alicorn, but I could still take that jerk if necessary. How dare he come here?

"You stay," I said. "I'll handle it."

Back down the stairs I went and through the rotunda, where a whole knot of hunters had gathered, waiting. "Is he outside?" Ilesha asked as I marched past.

"Not for long," I growled.

I pulled open the bronze doors and stopped dead. There, on the threshold, stood Giovanni.

"Astrid," he said. "You have to help me."

I started to close the door.

"Wait!" He shoved against the bas-relief. "Please. It's Seth. He's missing. Left his cell phone, everything behind. I've been calling Phil on it all day, and she's not answering either. I need to find him."

"And why is that?" I asked with a sneer.

"Because the police are looking for him."

Go figure. "Maybe he did something wrong." I went back to trying to push the door closed.

Giovanni shook his head and wedged his foot against the base. "Please. He's in trouble! Do you have any idea what that's like?"

I froze for a moment. Giovanni certainly had. But this wasn't the same. Not nearly.

Giovanni stopped pushing against the door, taking my hesitation for acceptance. "Do you know when Phil last saw him?"

"Yeah," I said. "When he raped her. Good-bye."

"What?" Now Giovanni threw all his weight against the door, and it was too much. It flew open, and we both stumbled

283

into the rotunda. The hunters screamed.

Giovanni regained his balance, and looked around in wonder at the marble, the statues, and most of all, at the enormous stuffed karkadann in the tableau at the center.

"So it's true," was all he said.

20

Wherein Astrid Uncovers the Enemy

"G ET OUT," I SAID, and my voice had never sounded quite so deadly. "Get out *now*."

Giovanni looked at me as if he'd never seen me before; and for a moment, I was glad there were no weapons nearby, because that's how little I trusted my own muscles. The re'em was gone, but its blood seemed to flow through my veins, burning brighter every moment.

He walked back through the doors, then turned on the threshold. "Okay. I'm out. Now will you talk to me?"

I said nothing, just stood there and glowered. The girls looked back and forth at us.

"Astrid, please."

How could I have ever been on the verge of sleeping with this guy? How could I have thought he was the answer to my prayers of escaping this place? How could I have thought I ever loved him?

He looked at the hunters behind me. "Fine, will any of you help me? I'm trying to find my friend. He's about six foot two, blond hair—"

"We met him," Zelda said, running her finger over the spot where the re'em had gored her. "And we don't know where he is now."

Giovanni sighed and looked at me again, his eyes like a stranger's. "I know you're angry at me. And I have no idea what happened with Phil and Seth. But you clearly want him located as much as I do. Five minutes. Just talk to me for five minutes, and then you can go back inside your convent and spend the rest of your life hunting unicorns for all I care."

His words hit me like a punch in the gut. I stepped outside and the bronze doors banged shut behind me.

"How do you know what we do?" I asked, stepping away from the doors and out into the open. The golden afternoon sun was already hitting the courtyard at a hard slant. I squinted and moved toward the fountain, where the air was slightly cooler. Giovanni followed me, his face hard.

"To be frank, I thought it was a joke. But you people are evidently serious."

I bit back a groan. He sounded so much like me a few months ago. "Deadly serious. I'm a Wildlife Control Nun, remember?" He said nothing, offered no apology. "What do you want?"

"Is it true, what you said about Seth and Phil?"

"Yes."

Giovanni closed his eyes for a long moment, and when he opened them, he seemed to have come to a decision. "I'm going to be completely honest. You probably can't hate me more than you do now anyway."

"Probably not," I agreed coldly. "You were mean to me on the phone, then you stood me up, then your best friend assaulted my cousin, and now you just threatened me on my own doorstep."

"Oh, it gets worse."

"Bring it on."

He took a deep breath. "Okay, after that night, when we first met, and we went to that club?"

And I'd jumped on the kirin and gouged out its eyeball? Yeah. I'd never forget that night.

"So we left you guys, and we went to a café. I was really nervous, because I thought I'd been drugged, remember? This guy came up and started talking to us. He was very friendly, talked about how he'd been a student once, didn't have any money either, blah blah blah. So we get a bottle of wine, and we're all talking, and he tells us that he's your uncle—"

Uncle John? Giovanni took in my shocked expression.

"Yeah, I thought it was a little weird, too. He had an accent, and I knew you guys were American. Anyway, he says that you two are these heiresses, with the rights to this price-less fortune—that's exactly how he put it, too, a 'priceless fortune'—but that if you joined the convent, the whole thing would be turned over to the Church as part of your vows."

"That's a load of crap from front to back."

Giovanni shrugged. "He was buying us wine. Or Seth, anyway, since I was too freaked out to drink. Anyway, he said he was trying to protect the family fortune, and if we'd agree to go out with you girls, convince you not to join the convent, he'd cover the costs of wherever we took you and a little extra besides. Whatever we wanted."

It had been premature to say I couldn't hate Giovanni and Seth more. They had been *paid* to take us out? My fingers itched to tear the alicorn on the fountain from its moorings and shove it through Giovanni's sternum.

"What was his name?"

"Alexander."

I let out a bark of harsh laughter. Give the guy credit! Our uncle *Alexander*! It was almost funny. Almost. "And what did 'Alexander' look like?"

"I don't know. Normal?"

"Last name?" Could it have been The Great? Or Magnus?

Giovanni shook his head. "I don't know. I didn't get it. And I thought the whole thing was a load of BS anyway, so I didn't care. But Seth kept going on and on about how it was a no-lose situation. You were cute and you were apparently rich and it was all being paid for and what was the harm?" He looked down. "So I finally said yes, but I thought the whole thing was kind of creepy. But then, at the museum, you didn't act like a nun at all—"

I blushed, recalling how very nunlike I was *not* on that day.

"And you said all this stuff about how your family was pressuring you into it. So then I started to think maybe that Alexander guy was right, and you were being forced to give up everything . . ." He trailed off, and I knew we were both remembering the lounge chair.

"So then why didn't you sleep with me when I asked you to?" There it was, right out in the open. What did it matter? I didn't care what he thought anymore.

"Astrid, everything I said to you that night was the absolute truth."

My throat and eyes began to sting, or kept stinging, this constant, buzzing burn that was almost second nature by now. "Except that you didn't like me. You were being paid to go out with me."

"I liked you *and* I was being paid. I couldn't afford that huge dinner all on my own!"

"Oh, well. I see. All forgiven." I looked away. "Your five minutes are up."

"No. Listen to me!" He grabbed me by the shoulders.

I glanced down at his hands, then up at his face. My blood boiled like I was hunting, and the air crackled with fire and flood. Maybe it was the horn from the fountain. There were no unicorns nearby.

I yanked away from his grip. "Touch me again and I'll tear your arms off."

My own shock was reflected on his face, even as I said it. How bloodthirsty had I become? I hugged my arms across my chest, for everyone's protection.

He regrouped. "I thought it was incredibly sketchy, for the record. I mean, every time I was with you, it was easier to forget how weird the whole thing was. I just thought about you."

I just thought about you. My very bones began to ache.

"But when we were back at school, or when the things you said didn't add up, I couldn't shake my suspicions."

"That's the smartest thing you've said so far."

"I mean, *Wildlife Control Nuns?*" He took a few steps away, stuck his hands in his pockets.

I wondered if it was to help him resist the impulse to reach for me. My entire body tingled where our skin had met. I wished he'd never touched me, wished my last memory of Giovanni's body was when he held his hand against my heart.

"I started thinking the whole thing was some kind of scam, some massive con that we were too young to understand. You do not get paid to take out beauti— girls like you. It's bizarre."

Agreed.

"But last week, it got superweird. Seth was the one who always did all the arrangements, called the guy, got the money, whatever. Anyway, he comes back and says that Alexander told him it was down to the wire. That you two were about to take vows."

"But, Giovanni, you knew that I wouldn't have—" I bit my tongue to keep from saying more. He knew how much I wanted to leave. He knew the only thing tying me to Rome was the fact that he was there. He knew because I'd told him, then kissed him like he was the last man on earth.

Giovanni's eyes seared right through me and he was silent and still, hands deep in his pockets, standing with the space of the fountain between us, and tugging on me with the force of an imploding star.

After a minute, he began to speak again, slowly now, with great difficulty. "He told us that the convent was a bunch of crazy people, who thought they had special powers to hunt unicorns. Unicorns!"

Now that *did* sound like Uncle John.

"He said we had one chance now. If you had sex, then you couldn't join. I believed that much—you'd pretty much said the same thing to me in Trastevere that night. But he wanted us to . . . do it. Sleep with you both."

"Bet you were sorry you missed your chance, then."

Giovanni didn't even take the bait. "He offered us ten thousand euros each for . . . proof that we'd slept with you."

I gasped.

Giovanni pressed his fists against his forehead. "I . . . was . . . I was horrified. Here I was, trying to straighten my life out, and I felt like I'd somehow become tied up in some sort of

290

sting operation. Like any second Interpol was going to bust in and arrest us all for . . . I don't know what. Running an escort ring or something. I freaked out." He paused. "But Seth was excited. He thought you'd be—" he cut off. "I'd told him, you see. About that night."

"He thought I'd be easy," I filled in, my voice toneless.

Giovanni nodded without looking at me. I didn't blame him. All he'd see in my eyes was murder. "But Phil had apparently told him she didn't go all the way. And when I refused to ever have anything to do with you again, he even . . ." He trailed off, but I could fill that bit in as well.

Seth had wondered if he could trade girls.

"Anyway, he got me drunk, to try to convince me to go in on it. Kept talking about how I could pay a year of tuition with the money, and how we weren't doing anything wrong if you and I wanted to have sex, anyway—"

My gasp of breath must have been loud enough for him to hear over the sound of the fountain, because he flinched, eyes still downcast, so I couldn't read him at all. Was that the truth? Were his feelings that strong? He hadn't moved an inch closer, but my flesh seemed to singe where it faced him, like I stood too close to a fire. I wanted to cry, to shout. I wanted to throw things at him. And more than anything, I wanted him to touch me again.

But I couldn't. I held my breath until I was sure I could trust my voice enough to say, "And that's when you decided you didn't want to see me."

"I was so angry at you," said Giovanni. "I thought everything you'd told me was some giant lie, some huge scam. I mean, unicorns?"

He met my eyes now, and my resolve faltered. I struggled to keep my chin from quivering. Yeah, unicorns.

"And that was the last thing that happened. Seth went out with you and Phil, and I stayed home. And I've been studying a lot, so I haven't really gotten a chance to see him much in the past few days. Then the police showed up."

"And you thought it was a sting?" I scoffed.

"I had no idea what it was, but I thought I'd give talking to you and Phil one last shot, because you'd always seemed like nice people, no matter what might have been going on." He looked back at the Cloisters. "But . . . there's a giant unicorn in that place."

"Yes."

"And you say Seth . . . that Seth and Phil . . ." He couldn't seem to bring himself to say it. I understood the feeling. It was inconceivable and true.

"Yes."

"And you don't know who that guy who paid us was?"

"You're going to have to give me something more than 'He looked normal' for me to tell you that." All I knew is that it wasn't Uncle John. He'd never have gone to such disgusting extremes. If he wanted us out, he'd march right through the front door and drag us bodily from the premises. I'd seen him do as much one night when Phil was at a house party past curfew.

He threw his hands in the air. "I don't know. It was a while ago, and I was distracted. I thought I'd seen a unicorn on the— Jeez, that was real, wasn't it?"

"Yes."

"And you . . . attacked it?"

"Alexander?" I prompted.

"He was older. White hair. Really pale eyes."

I narrowed my eyes. "Tall, clean cut, maybe a business suit?"

"Kind of old-world European, I guess. Yeah."

"Oh, God. Marten."

"Who is that?"

"Our sponsor." But why would he be trying to get rid of Phil and me? It made no sense. All he ever talked about was how great the Llewelyns were at hunting, how we had extraspecial super hunting abilities, how we'd make our ancestors proud. He liked us. He *wanted* us to hunt!

Giovanni was waiting for me to go on, still a safe distance away, still keeping his hands deep in his pockets, but listing, ever so slightly, in my direction. I, too, was leaning toward him. I rolled back on my heels.

"Okay," I said. "Where did you meet this Alexander? Where did he drop off your money?"

Giovanni shook his head. "All handled by Seth."

"You know nothing about it?"

"I didn't want to know. It was sketchy."

"But you took the money anyway." A heavy silence hung over us both. Was it Marten? Why in the world would he want us gone? And did he have any idea what his little proposition had engendered?

"For the record: I'm sorry I did it. I know that means nothing to you now."

"You're right," I lied, then got control of myself. "My best guess is that your friend, having . . . done what was asked of him, is collecting his reward." I shuddered. "I have no idea where that might be, but we can track down Marten. There are some things I'd really like to know the answer to as well." Like how

293

dare he, and who does he think he is, and did he really want to take us all on, after he'd taught us to use swords and crossbows and knives? "I'll ask Neil when he gets home."

"Ask me now." We looked toward the entrance arch to see Neil Bartoli standing there. Giovanni backed up a few steps.

"Neil, I think you should listen to this. This is Giovanni Cole. He's a classmate of Seth's, and he says the two of them have been receiving money from Marten Jaeger all summer in return for taking us out."

Neil looked at Giovanni like he was junk on the bottom of his shoe. "Curious. Almost as curious as the fact that when I arrived at the Gordian office today, it was completely shut down. I've still been unable to get in contact with anyone there or with Marten himself."

"No!"

Neil nodded curtly, his face drawn with concern and frustration. "I can't account for it. Marten has always been a phone call away, always eager to show up at odd times, to be involved in the running of the Cloisters . . . and now, I have injured hunters, an ineligible hunter, a body rotting in the rotunda—" He noted Giovanni's stricken expression. "A *unicorn* body."

"Of course!" Giovanni practically snorted.

Neil beckoned to me. "Come along, Astrid. We clearly have no information this young man will find useful. When we know the location of his friend, we will be informing the police."

"Astrid." Giovanni's voice was nothing but plea, but there was no shape to it, as if he didn't even know what he wanted to ask from me. I understood completely. Walking away from

294

him was the worst kind of torture.

But I did it anyway.

Neil's news was received with the appropriate amount of shock and dismay by the other hunters, but it was nothing to compare with what he told Phil, Cory, and me privately later on.

"I'm afraid we may have made a very grave mistake," he said.

"No kidding." I stood against the door of Neil's office, arms crossed over my chest. Cory and Phil were seated on the chairs in front of Neil's desk. "I think we trusted a real sicko. According to Giovanni, he was soliciting volunteers to deflower us."

"According to your ex-boyfriend, the friend of the man who raped Phil?" Cory said. "Yes, he sounds like an extremely trustworthy sort."

"Guys," Phil warned. She turned to Neil. "No one at the Gordian labs would tell you anything about how to contact Marten?"

"No one was *there*." Neil clarified. "The place was abandoned. I contacted the landlord, and found that his number for them had been disconnected as well. They are paid for three more months, so he wasn't particularly concerned."

"And you guys have no other contact information?" I asked. "No other address?"

"This is all my fault," Neil said, his posture stiff. "I've endangered the hunters under my care and I've been counting on support from a source that has proven unreliable."

"This must be some horrible mistake," Cory said. "He's been so supportive of me—of us—all this time. I'm sure there's a reasonable explanation—"

"Like what?" I asked. "'I closed my business and skipped town. Oops, meant to tell you?'"

"I never trusted him," Phil said. "He fired Lino and never replaced him or our weapons."

"You never liked Lino," Cory snapped. "And you don't know if he had a good reason for his actions then."

"Neither do you," I said. "We weren't able to get an answer out of Marten. Just. Like. Now."

"Why would Marten be trying to sabotage you?" Cory pressed. "He's been doing nothing but encouraging you to hunt. Half the girls here hate the constant stream of Llewelyn this and Llewelyn that."

"Then maybe you shouldn't add to it," I grumbled. "Giovanni described him to me."

"Described a distinguished middle-aged European business-man in Rome?" Cory said. "Imagine how uncommon they are."

"Men who know about Phil and me?" I replied. "Who know all about the unicorns? How likely is *that*?" I left Cory to ponder the improbability on her own.

"Look," Phil said. "I know I don't have any status here anymore. I'm not a don, I'm not a trainer, I'm not a hunter. I should probably just pack up and go home."

Neil blinked. Hard. And I wasn't the only one to notice it, judging by the way Cory's head turned in his direction.

"It's dangerous for me even to be inside this building," she went on. "We only have one ring, and we have a very slippery little zhi on our hands."

Which reminded me—someone should go check on Bonegrinder, chained up in the chapter house. Just to make sure she didn't escape.

"And it's no secret that I don't like Marten Jaeger and never have," Phil said. "But I also can't imagine why he'd want either of us out of the hunting business."

"Maybe he wants us all out," I said, "but we were the only ones with boyfriends he could bribe."

"Then why wouldn't he just cut funding to the Cloisters?" Cory asked.

"Well," Neil said, "he *has* disappeared off the face of the earth. Perhaps that's what he's doing now." He shook his head. "But that still won't stop us. We still have our ties to the Church. We'd have to change some of our policies, but the Order would survive. There would still be hunters."

"It still doesn't answer the question of why," Phil said. Cory looked vindicated. "Maybe everything Giovanni told you was true, Astroturf, but why? Why would he want to get rid of us?"

I shrugged. "I don't know. Because we hunted them to extinction last time, and he needs them to make his new superdrug?" But how many unicorns would he need, really? And how many would we actually end up killing before he found a better solution?

"Besides," Cory said, "you can't permanently get rid of us. There are always more being born."

"True," said Phil. "Short of killing off the family lines . . ."

Neil cleared his throat. "This is all speculation, anyway. Right now, I will continue trying to contact Marten Jaeger, and until I have, I don't want anyone to leave the Cloisters without my knowledge and permission. Bonegrinder will be confined to the lower quarters until we figure out how to deal with the presence of multiple non-hunters. I'm going to start calling everyone's parents right now, to inform them that the situation has moved beyond our control. Ursula and Melissende's parents are already on their way. And"—he cleared his throat—"I will be leaving at once to look for Marten at the other Gordian offices in Europe. If he doesn't answer his phone, I'll beard the lion in his den. He can't have vanished into thin air."

"Leaving!" I gasped.

"After what Giovanni told you, Astrid, I believe very strongly that when we find Marten, we will find Seth or the means to locate him, at the very least." He looked at Phil. "I will not allow either of them to get away with this."

"And what about the rest of us?" Cory said, with a quick, harsh shake of her head that made her curls fly. "You can't just leave me—us here."

Phil spoke up. "We have an idea, actually, of someone who could step in and watch over the other hunters, while Neil conducts his search." She exchanged a glance with Neil.

"Someone familiar with the history," he added. "Sympathetic to the cause."

"Like who?" I asked. There weren't a lot of unicorn experts around.

Neil looked at me. "I was thinking of Lilith Llewelyn."

21

Wherein Astrid Clashes with Her Elders

"Look at it this way, Asterisk," Phil said, nocking another practice arrow on her string. "You know how much crap the teachers' kids get away with at school? It's the same thing. Only with unicorns." She let the arrow fly. It went way wide. Phil sighed.

I marked another zero next to Phil's name on the sheet, then took the bow and quiver from her. At least she was still able to draw the string. It was a bright, sunny morning, and I was conducting an experiment in the Cloisters courtyard.

"Maybe, but I'd rather any of our teachers than Lilith." Ready, aim, fire. Bull's-eye. Again. I handed the bow to Cory, then marked the data down on the sheet. Besides, I wasn't quite sure what kind of "unicorn crap" I could potentially pull off. You might lie about having lost your homework, but I wouldn't be able to pretend I'd killed a kirin if I hadn't.

And Lilith wasn't the most lenient taskmaster, either.

Cory pulled the last arrow from the quiver, then got set up in her stance. "What is so wrong with your mother, Astrid? I know that your family didn't put much credence in her studies before. But now you must admit she was right."

I think Cory would be a much better archer if she weren't always so concerned about the exact placement of her feet. It's as if she needed to line up on little markings on the ground every time she went to take a shot. *Twang. Thunk.* Still, not bad. Not a bull's-eye, but she hit the target.

And that was without the unicorn.

"Her mom's not bad," Phil said. "She's a little intense maybe, but it could work for us. I talked to her the other day about . . . things."

I whirled on Phil. "You didn't tell me that!"

She shrugged. "Well, it's not like I could call my dad."

I shook my head and shouldered the bow. "Okay, bring in the zhi!" I called. The door near the rotunda opened, and Bonegrinder came bounding out, trotting toward Cory and me and giving Phil a wide berth. My cousin pretended not to notice and went to retrieve the arrows.

Only once had she forgotten herself and tried to pet the unicorn. Bonegrinder had almost bitten her fingers off.

We started again, and I moved to the "with unicorn" column on the spreadsheet. Phil's aim was the same. Arrow after arrow missed the target and clattered against the masonry at the far side of the courtyard. I shot another series of bull's-eyes. But this time, so did Cory.

"Amazing," Phil said, turning Neil's ring around and around on her thumb, which was the only finger on which it would stay. "What I want to know is why I'm worse than you normally, even *before* Bonegrinder came out. When did you become such an ace archer?"

I shook my head. "I don't know. It could be the ambient unicorn influence here. Or the months of practice."

"But we've all been shooting nonstop since we got here. Shouldn't I have at least developed some natural skills?"

I shook my head at the data. It was true. Phil had always been a much more capable athlete than I. "Maybe you never really developed your natural skills. Just relied on your hunter powers. Like people who suddenly lose one sense and then realize how hard they have to work to develop the others?"

Though it still didn't make sense. Cory had more experience than either of us, and she wasn't as good a shooter as I was, whether or not Bonegrinder was present.

"Close your eyes and do it," Phil said. "I want to see if you can bull's-eye without concentrating."

"I don't think that's how it works," Cory said. "It's not like I can just shoot an arrow in the air and it will hit the target. It's almost as if—" She hesitated, searching for the right words. "The power comes over me, and the target is all I can see. Like we're connected."

"I agree." I yanked the arrows out of the target. "Like I can't help but concentrate. There's nothing in the world except me and the monster."

"True," Phil said. "I never thought of it that way. It just seemed natural. Like zeroing in on a spiked ball." Her face fell. "You don't think I was somehow using my powers to play volleyball, do you?"

"Not unless we had unicorns in the school gym," I reassured her. Did that mean Phil was leaving? Heading back home to college and her volleyball team? Could I blame her?

I ran the experiment with all the hunters who were well

301

enough to shoot, which included everyone but Dorcas, still in her cast. Ursula had been dismissed from the hospital two days ago, but she remained confined to a bed downstairs. As predicted, her healing had begun to accelerate again as her own blood overtook the donated, non-hunter blood in her system. The doctors were mystified.

What mystified *me* was that no one from Gordian seemed even remotely curious about the re'em, the attack, the changing pace of her recovery, and what any of it might mean for their own research into the Remedy. Neil continued to wait in vain for a return of any of our messages. As soon as Lilith arrived, he planned to leave Italy and search for clues as to Marten's whereabouts.

The police hadn't found Seth either. I was pretty sure he'd left Italy.

Since we'd been restricted to the Cloisters, I had decided to spend some time studying the nature of our powers. These were things that none of the ancient hunters knew about. They didn't run trials testing the relative powers of each hunting family, nor the powers of hunters versus non-hunters, like Phil. If I was going to be stuck here, I'd at least attempt to add something to the faulty, anecdotal, incomplete data we had on file.

Maybe it was magic, but that didn't mean I shouldn't try to understand it.

The early data conformed to what we already knew. Each hunter was a better shot when Bonegrinder was present, but proximity to a unicorn made no difference in Phil's archery talent. When Bonegrinder was not present, the hunters exhibited a range of talent, but there seemed to be little to no relationship between their natural skill and their hunter powers. A bad natural shot could be a good hunter—better, even, than a good natural shot. And certain foibles of each hunter were present whether or not they were accessing their powers. Cory still had her bizarre stance ritual. Grace was still very susceptible to performance anxiety. She usually got off her first shot just fine, then buckled. Sometimes she couldn't even draw the string to take a second shot.

"I lose all my focus," she explained curtly, then went off to sulk and refused to stay for the rest of the test.

I also couldn't figure out where I'd suddenly acquired my own mad skills.

Maybe there *was* something to be said for the ambient unicorn presence inside the Cloisters. I wished I could repeat the test somewhere in the open, really test the proximity variable. But that might prove dangerous to the public. I wondered if it would work with a unicorn *corpse* . . .

Phil interrupted me while I was lost in thought, planning hunting crusades where each hunter wore a coat of unicorn fur. What had come over me the last few days? I'd gotten downright bloodthirsty ever since I'd killed that re'em. At least, that's when I think it started. It had been a busy few days. But I wasn't the same girl I'd been in the United States. Not the same person who flinched when Giovanni had grabbed the suspected pickpocket. Not the same as the one who'd almost lost her lunch when Phil had stabbed the kirin in Tuscany.

Like it or not, I'd become a hunter. Astrid the Warrior, indeed.

"Asteroid."

I snapped out of it, then became promptly appalled by my

line of thought. "Sorry," I said to Phil. "What?"

"She's here."

As you might expect, Lilith was very pleased with the Cloisters. After our quick reunion and an introduction to the other hunters, we got her settled into her room. Neil still occupied the don's quarters, and no one mistook my mother's pursed-lipped smile for joy at that fact, but at least she didn't complain out loud. As anxious as I'd been about her arrival, it was nice to see my mother again, to hug her and smell the scents of home. Phil was curious about her parents, and Lilith gave us a brief update on news from home, but it was clear that she wasn't the slightest bit interested in anything outside the unicorn hunting world. She'd come to the Cloisters at last.

So we gave her the tour, and as Cory talked nonstop, I watched my mother preen beneath the tableau of Clothilde and the karkadann that may or may not be Bucephalus. I watched her touch the alicorns labeled Llewelyn on the Wall of First Kills in the chapter house, pointing out which hunters were from our direct line and which were from other branches. Cory ate it up.

"I didn't know you had so much genealogical information, Lilith. Perhaps you can help me fill in some of the gaps I'm dealing with—"

"Ah, the throne!" Lilith swept past Cory to the central column and began examining the alicorn chair. "Astrid, do you know what this is?"

"A torture device?" I said.

She shot me an exasperated expression. "It's from the Jutland Campaign. This is how I first discovered the hunters."

"I know," I said. Cory looked enthralled. "I was just reading up on that the other day."

"I'm not surprised," Lilith said. "It's one of the only times in history that the hunters were really in the mainstream. So many of them died in the battle against the unicorns massing there. Lots of Llewelyns. That's how I found them. I was studying cemetery records, and I wanted to know why there were so many young Llewelyn women buried in some random town in Denmark. Where were their families? What were all these young women doing by themselves?" She ran her hands along the armrest. "The truth changed my life forever."

And mine. "Well, that's a lot closer than any of us hunters can get to it. It hurts us to touch it."

Lilith raised her eyebrows. "Really."

Cory cut in. "Lilith, would you mind if I showed you some of the paperwork I'm having difficulty translating? You seem to have a much greater understanding of—"

"Of course," Lilith said, waving her hand benevolently at Cory. She sat in the throne, and disappointment flashed across her features so quickly that anyone who didn't know my mother might have missed it entirely. But for that moment, she reminded me of Phil. "Just bring it down here. I would like to have a private word with my daughter."

Cory scampered off. I turned to my mom, feeling suddenly like a supplicant before a great queen.

"It's so good to see you again, Astrid," she said.

"You, too."

"I was a bit disappointed to hear from Neil on the drive over here that you'd killed a re'em. Why didn't *you* tell me?"

I hung my head. "I meant to. I just . . . everything happened so fast. The hospital, and then Phil—"

"I'm incredibly proud of you," she said, as if she hadn't heard. "A re'em. And barely armed, I'm told! I knew you had it in you." She eyed me. "You don't look happy about it."

"Well, it wasn't exactly a celebration," I said. "Ursula almost died, and then—"

"I don't think your ancestors would think like that. Victory is victory. There are always casualties. But you're still the best hunter here."

I shook my head. "No, I—"

"Of course you are. The Llewelyns always were." She glanced around the room. "I can see, though, that we have our work cut out for us. Between you and me, the way Neil has been running this place is positively shameful. I listened to him jabber the whole way back from the airport about his ridiculous isolationist policies. Does he honestly believe he's protecting you by keeping you here, festering and atrophying? No, he's just making you all that much weaker, letting you indulge in your fear. It's going to be so much harder to get those younger girls to go back and hunt now."

"Ursula is barely out of the hospital—"

"As I said, casualties happen. You girls are going to have to get used to it." She gestured to her seat. "Every horn in this throne killed a hunter, Astrid. Jutland was a massacre. But they persisted, and eventually they were victorious. The way Neil is acting, you've already surrendered. Did you think this was going to be a piece of cake?"

"No," I whispered. Far from it. I knew the dangers in coming here. That's why I hadn't wanted to do it.

"Good. At least I didn't raise a coward." She leaned back in the chair. "Now, the other issue. Your cousin's despicable behavior—"

My mouth dropped open. "Phil did nothing wrong!"

Lilith rolled her eyes. "Nothing wrong? What business does a hunter—any hunter—have dating? Neil has informed me that you had a little boyfriend yourself. Is this true?"

"Yes, but—"

"It's over," Lilith ordered.

"It already was," I said through clenched teeth. "But Phil—"

My mother waved me off with her hand. "I couldn't care less about Phil. At least she's not in your way anymore."

"In my way!" I gasped.

"Of course. You're the Llewelyn, here, Astrid. The only one now. And I'm going to see to it that people begin to recognize that."

"No!" I stared at her in horror. "Mom, there are already plenty of problems here with cliques and favoritism. We don't need anything to add to it. If you would look at the research I've been doing, you'd see that there's no discernible difference between a Llewelyn hunter and one who—"

"Astrid," she said, laughing and shaking her head, "trust me on this, okay? Why don't you ever trust me?"

I swallowed heavily. It's not that I didn't trust her. I just didn't agree with her.

"Things are getting worse out there, Astrid. People are already starting to realize the truth about the Reemergence. These aren't just any wild animals: they're unicorns. And they can't be killed by wildlife experts or national guards or SWAT teams. Just hunters. And when the public realizes that, they'll turn to us. They'll turn to you, the descendant of Clothilde Llewelyn."

"Or as close to it as you can get," I said. "Since Clothilde didn't have kids."

Lilith smiled and sat back in her seat.

"So that's what you want?" I said wearily. "For me to be a spokesperson for Unicorn Hunters R Us?"

"I wish you wouldn't be so cavalier about our birthright, sweetie." She held out her hand to me. "It's time for you to stop complaining and start accepting. Take this boy thing. Even if you weren't a hunter, I don't think you've shown the best judgment when it comes to dating. First, that silly Brandt, who was a waste of the Remedy, if you ask me. We save his life, and his response is to humiliate you and then run away from home?"

"They still have no idea where he is?" I asked, and took her hand.

"No. The men of this world are getting themselves lost left and right, if you ask me. Brandt, that Marten Jaeger man, the boy who was dating Phil." Her grip turned firm. "I want you to promise not to get mixed up with any of them ever again."

"Ever?" I said as lightly as I could. "Come on, Mom. Don't you want grandkids one day? More little unicorn hunters?"

"Promise!" She slammed my hand against the armrest.

My blood ignited, and stars exploded behind my eyes. "Stop!" I cried.

"Promise." Lilith's voice was calm, almost quiet. "I can't lose you, Astrid. I've waited too long."

I whimpered and dropped to my knees as my mother slowly ground my hand against the ridges of the alicorn. Images flared to life behind my burning eyes: *girls sprinting across a sea of mud while a hundred hooves shook the earth and the sound of inhuman screams rent the air. Blood and venom mingled in the tiny, red streams running through a wasteland filled with bodies of both unicorn and hunter.*

Jutland.

What was happening to me? I fought the pain, as I had that night on the bench with the karkadann, but control slipped through my grasp like the slippery, water-weed hair of a kirin.

A hunter screamed as her face was splashed with blood. Another, on the ground, struggled to breathe as the giant head of a re'em loomed over her, his face blotting out the sun. The metallic clang of sword hitting horn echoed, and the cries of the dead and dying could hardly be discerned from those still battling.

The invading visions piled up, overlapping and tumbling around one another in my head until they found a free place to rest.

One hunter, her blond hair almost obscured by mud and gore, tore a sword from the dead hand of her comrade, then whirled around and gutted a charging einhorn. She straightened, pushed her hair out of her face, and stared at me. "Promise."

And from far away, I heard the sound of footsteps on stone. Cory skipped into the chapter house, her arms filled with papers. "Here they are— Astrid?"

I yanked my hand back so hard the skin tore on the edge of an alicorn. I fell hard onto the floor and gasped for breath. Lilith looked up at the intruder, her face a mask of geniality.

The wound on my hand closed up tight, and I saw my mother smile.

I had not believed that my mother could have instituted so much change in so little time, but in the week following Neil's departure, the Cloisters became a different place. We were roused well before dawn, made to do calisthenics and Pilates for three hours, then given breakfast. Afterward, we were put to work learning to preserve the hide of the re'em, and then it was another two hours of target practice. Since we were low on modern weaponry, Lilith had authorized use of the ancient bows and arrows lining the walls in the chapter house. These bows were harder to hold, harder to draw, and harder to aim. Two hours shooting them felt like forty. After that, we had lunch.

I don't even want to talk about the afternoon.

"I don't know," Phil said one evening, watching the hunters limp around the dormitory floor after Lilith had locked us upstairs for the night. "I don't want to trash Neil, but Aunt Lilith is superfocused. Maybe this will be good for you guys?"

Phil had been very careful not to use the word "us" when referring to hunters, after the first time my mother had heard her and made it perfectly clear that Phil only remained in the Cloisters by the grace of Lilith.

"We *are* becoming better archers," I said at last, taking in Phil's hopeful expression. "Grace has nerves of steel these days. You're right. Maybe this is . . . good for us."

Phil looked relieved, and inwardly I cringed. Nowadays, it seemed as if the moment dinner was over and my mother sent us upstairs, I wanted nothing more than to go to sleep. I had little time to think of my half-finished experiments, of the still-missing Marten Jaeger and Seth, of my strange karkadann dreams, or of Giovanni.

I was also having Giovanni dreams. They usually got me through my second round of crunches.

Cory's gaze flashed toward mine and away. We'd never

310

spoken about Lilith's little trick with the chair, but that moment marked the beginning of the end of Cory's infatuation with my mother. The real death blow came when my mother had assumed responsibility for all archives, and Cornelia Bartoli, renovator of the Cloisters, founder of the newly formed Order of the Lioness, was relegated to second-class status within her own walls.

Melissende and Grace were in heaven—Neil's favorites displaced, and a donna who also seemed to long for the good old days. At the same time, my mother's supposed "favoritism" of her own daughter amounted to little more than extra sets of push-ups and an increasingly watchful eye. I hobbled toward my bedroom door, eager to slip beneath the covers and shut the world away.

It was not to be. I'd barely crossed the threshold to my room when Lilith bustled into the hall and began issuing orders.

"There's a report of an attack in the suburbs. It's clearly a unicorn. I think it's time for a field exercise."

Everyone groaned.

Phil shook her head. "Look at them, Aunt Lilith. They're exhausted. You can't mean to send them out now, after everything you've put them through today."

Lilith ignored her and turned to Cory. "Please gather up the weaponry. I want at least six recurves and full quivers but throw in a few crossbows, too, as backups. I'm sending out all eight of you."

"Do you even have an idea how many unicorns there are?" Phil asked. "Last time we went hunting, it took six of us to bring down *one*."

"I don't see us as having much of an option," Lilith replied coldly. "I'd like to have more hunters on my roster as well, but it's out of both our hands."

Phil shut her mouth.

Lilith turned to the other girls and raised her voice. "Back into street clothes, ladies. I want you downstairs and ready to go in ten minutes."

Around me, the other hunters were grumbling and heading into their rooms to get dressed, but I hadn't changed yet, so I followed Phil and Lilith down the stairs.

"I think I should come along," Phil was saying. "Be support staff."

"Absolutely not," Lilith said. "You're a liability."

"When we went hunting before, we brought our archery trainer along. He never got in the way of the unicorns, and he was able to coach us during the hunt."

"I don't really care how you did things before, Philippa. I'm the donna now, and I will plan our strategies."

"With what experience, Aunt Lilith?" Phil asked as the three of us arrived at the lower landing and exited into the rotunda. "Did I miss that time you were in the army? That time you had any field practice hunting at all?"

Lilith turned around and raised her hand, and for a moment, I thought she was going to slap Phil across the face. The don's ring glinted on her finger. "Did I miss that time that you were stripped of your hunter powers through your own poor decisions and irresponsible behavior? The time that you put my daughter in a situation where she was regularly associating with a rapist?"

"Mom!" I cried, appalled.

She whirled on me. "Astrid, I don't want to hear from you.

I'm your mother, and you and your cousin have been sneaking around behind my back for months, flouting my rules as well as the rules of the people I entrusted to care for you."

"Your rules!" I shouted. "You said go to Rome and be a hunter. Well, here I am!"

"Yes," Lilith said drily. "Dating. Sneaking around. Who knows how far things would have gone?"

"So what?" I said. "It's my choice."

"But it isn't always, is it?" Lilith hissed, looking at Phil.

"That's really uncalled for," Phil said.

"Is it?" Lilith folded her arms over her chest. "Guess I'm just not like perfect, easygoing Neil, who is far too polite to say the things that need to be said. Well, maybe it's not proper, but if you stayed inside, *where you belonged*, this never would have happened."

"Enough!" I shouted so loudly that the words reverberated off the mosaic walls. Phil's chin was high but trembling. "How can you possibly talk that way to her, knowing what she's been through?"

"Because Philippa knows full well she'd get a hell of a lot worse from her father. Why do you think she's staying here rather than going home?"

Phil wouldn't meet my eyes.

Okay. New tactic. "And I think Phil's right. She has some experience at this, Mom, and she can coach the girls who don't. As long as she stays out of the way—"

"When I want your opinion, Astrid, I'll ask for it. Phil, go upstairs."

"Do not tell me what to do, Aunt Lilith," Phil said, in a low, dangerous voice. "As you are so fond of pointing out, I'm not a hunter anymore."

313

"Go to your room," Lilith repeated, "or I'll let Bonegrinder out of her cage."

For a moment, everything was silent, then Phil turned and headed back up the stairs. I glared at my mother, then ran after my cousin.

She was a few steps up the spiral stairs, leaning against the curved wall and looking out of the slit windows at the street beyond.

"Phil, I'm so sorry—"

"I'm leaving, Astrid." She kept her eyes on the window. "I thought I could stay a bit, make this easier for you, laugh about your mom, like always, but . . . I can't put up with that. She makes me feel like dirt."

"She's full of it," I said. "She's always been full of it."

Phil shook her head, and I could see tears glistening in her eyes. "Not about everything. She was right about the unicorns, remember? And she's right about you. You're something special." She swallowed hard. "And maybe she's right about that other thing, too."

"No, Phil, how could we have known?"

She shrugged. "I don't think we could have. But it doesn't make what she said any less true. If I'd stayed inside, I'd be . . ."

"You'd shrivel up," I said. "We aren't going to live in a cloister, Phil. Neither of us. I don't care what she says."

Phil nodded. "That's why I need to go. But not home. I'm not sure yet. Maybe I'll try to help Neil find Marten Jaeger. I have a couple of questions I'd like to ask the guy." She straightened. "You better go back down there. Your ten minutes are almost up."

"There it is." My words were a breath on the night wind to the knot of hunters huddled on the edge of the highway. Given the

314

presence of policemen, journalists, and onlookers, it had been no small feat to sneak our weaponry out of Lilith's rented car. It's not like you can slip a longbow into your purse. We'd been forced to drive pretty far away from the actual crime scene—a car dealership by the side of the highway in which four salesmen and a mechanic had been found torn to pieces—in order to find a discreet place to unload. We'd immediately turned away from the highway and toward the surrounding area. Both buildings and tree cover were sparse, but there was a small knot of woods over the next hill that was our best bet. And, sure enough, as we drew closer, I caught a flash of darkness on darkness, and a whiff of ashes and mold.

"I can't see it," Melissende said by my side, "but I can feel it."

"Me, too," said Grace. "Think it feels us?"

"If it doesn't," Cory said facetiously, "it hears us." That would matter in normal hunting. With unicorns, it made no difference.

"Fan out," I said. "Not too far. I don't want any of us in an angle of fire." Why was it just standing there at the edge of the woods? I could barely make out an outline now. Perhaps it hoped that if it stayed frozen, we wouldn't be able to see it at all. "Stay in pairs so you have a backup ready if the unicorn string-jumps your first shot."

"Who do you think you are?" Melissende said. "We've got it."

But they followed my suggestions anyway. Arrow on the string, we began to stalk. Fifty feet, and the kirin remained frozen. Forty, and I could feel my world narrowing, focusing on the midnight-brindled coat, the sweet spot just behind the heart. It was almost too perfect—the kirin angled broadside to me. How soon should I risk a shot? When would it flee?

At thirty feet, I knew the other hunters felt the same way, saw their hesitation from the corner of my eyes. Once one of us moved, we'd all need to be ready. This would work; it would actually work. Never mind that we didn't have our high-tech bows, with their balanced sights and their geared strings, and their perfect, synthetic-fletched arrows. We had something even better—skill and a perfect shot. Perhaps this would be Melissende's first kill. That would get her off my back for a while. Or maybe Grace, to ease the bitterness of the last hunt.

My blood began to sing that now-familiar chord, and the scent of unicorn rose with every breath. Who would shoot first?

With my hunter quickness, I caught sight of Melissende. She raised her crossbow, lowered her head over the sight, and let loose. The unicorn sprang into the brush.

The woods are filled with golden eyes.

On either side of me, the hunters rushed forward, but I remained rooted to the spot.

"No!" I shouted, but it was too late.

From all around they came, a dozen, maybe more, their horns lowered, their teeth bared, their coats flashing the colors of midnight as they shot through the darkness.

Ambush.

I saw Ilesha go down, whether by horn or hoof, I couldn't tell. Rosamund was firing her crossbow into the pack, and when the bolts were gone, she threw it and ran. Two kirin followed her, and I shot arrows at them both, hitting one in the flank and the other in the neck. Neither would be enough to kill.

In my mind's eye, I saw the field of mud, the dying hunters, the bloody sky. I shot every arrow I had, and when the last flew from my bow and found its mark in the eye of a kirin, I threw down my bow and grabbed my curved alicorn knife.

"Retreat!" I heard Cory cry. Valerija was screaming, half draped across the back of a kirin, and slicing hard at its legs with a long knife. Melissende was still discharging her crossbow, but she'd soon be out of bolts. Grace spun in the center of a group of rearing kirin, a light sword all that stood between her and their horns. Zelda must be down, for I saw her nowhere. The hunters still on their feet were running for the highway now, the kirin racing back toward the trees.

"Help me!" Valerija was hanging from the back of a kirin as it ran for the woods, dragging her with it. "My arm! My arm!" Somehow she'd become tangled in the unicorn's mane. I rushed forward, alicorn knife in hand, as it disappeared between two trees, with Valerija bumping behind.

We zigzagged through the undergrowth, Valerija screaming in pain and panic, the kirin grunting loudly. My legs flew over the ground, leaves and branches blurring as I charged forward; and then I was flying, landing on the beast and hacking away with my knife.

The kirin's head snapped up as I sliced through its mane and Valerija slid to the ground. She scrambled up in a hurry, cradling her elbow in her other hand.

She was unarmed.

"Run," I gasped, as the kirin bucked. "You're dead with no weapon—" The unicorn threw me off, and I spun in midair, landing in a clumsy half crouch. The unicorn lowered its horn at me and, even in the darkness, I could see blood pouring from its many stab wounds.

No, I could *smell* it. How weird was that? Even weirder, they weren't closing. Just like with the re'em that night.

"Run!" I repeated to Valerija. I tugged at her shoulder, trying to pull her toward the clearing before the unicorn charged.

Her eyes grew huge and round and then fire exploded all along my back. I tried to breathe but could not, and my mouth filled with hot, bitter blood. I dragged my eyes from Valerija's horrified face to my torso. What was that bump sticking through my shirt? It looked like an alicorn.

How strange.

Valerija ran, and the world went black.

The scent came first: fire and flood. The odor of apocalypse.

A moment later, there was nothing but pain. No air, no light, no sound but my own heartbeat, loud and slow.

There was grit between my fingers, sticky, wet. My vision blurred when I tried to open my eyes, and when I tried to speak, my mouth was caked and dry.

As for breathing, it hurt too much to try. Each shuddering gasp sent sharp, fiery arrows through my lungs.

I struggled to turn my head, my hands digging in the dirt to steel myself for the torment of moving an inch. Had Valerija left me to die in the woods like an animal? Was she here, too, dead or dying? Where were the others? Were we all . . .

A croak of despair escaped my throat, and it hurt so much that I almost passed out again. So this is how it ends. Alone, in the dark. No mother, no Phil, no chance. The darkness began to grow fuzzy again, and I tamped down the instinct to inhale.

Daughter of Alexander.

I froze, face down in the muck that I now realized was a puddle of my own blood.

Daughter of Alexander, breathe. You will be well. Your lung works once more.

I choked again, and the air felt like fire. It seemed as if an age passed in pitched battle, me against my lungs, with weapons of oxygen and agony. And then, I coughed, blood and sputum flying from my mouth, and I found that I could breathe. It hurt terribly, but I inhaled.

Do not move.

Yeah, no kidding. I blinked and breathed, content for a moment to have that tiny privilege restored. Air. Oh, air. I'd never before appreciated you!

Several minutes later, I turned my face to the side. A foot away lay the bodies of two kirin, one whose horn was drenched in blood. That must have been the one that had attacked me. This seemed familiar, somehow, like the pictures piling up in my head.

A Band-Aid, a crossbow, a bonfire. Giovanni and me in the woods; the eviscerated unicorns; the tableau in the rotunda; me, on the ground, with a giant hole in my back . . .

He'd saved me. He'd saved me again.

A microphone, a waiting audience . . .

Daughter of Alexander, can you speak?

"Yes," I said, in a voice like a toad.

The karkadann stepped from the trees.

You are getting better at this.

22

Wherein Astrid Puts the Pieces Together

THE NIGHT PASSED, and I drifted in and out of consciousness, while the karkadann watched over me in colossal silence. I could feel the waves of venom pouring off his horn, and yet they didn't bother me as they once had. Perhaps I was growing used to it, building up a resistance after each exposure. It had almost killed me on the park bench, but here, next to a near-fatal wound, I hardly felt it. Or perhaps the venom was connected to the Remedy after all.

"Does it help?" I asked aloud.

A beaker in my chemistry lab back at school. My lab notebook covered in my scribbles.

You are the scientist. You say.

And then, much later:

"The others—they're all dead, aren't they?"

No hunter perished this night.

Then why was I alone here? They wouldn't have left me for dead, would they? And even if they thought I'd been killed, they would have come looking for my body. I choked and coughed.

And then, in my mind's eye, I saw a kirin running with a giant lump on its head. My body, impaled on its horn.

A trophy.

"They . . . took me?"

Fireworks. Dancing. The figure of Clothilde Llewelyn.

"To prove they killed me. The Llewelyn." I shook my head. Perhaps I was better at translating the images when I was losing consciousness. "But I'm not so different from the other hunters. Why do they care?"

Vengeance.

"Against whom?"

Against the hunters. Against me.

"Why you?"

Laughter. Then a pop quiz. Then kirin.

I almost groaned, until I realized how much it would hurt. Why wasn't it Cory here instead of me? She could give him an encyclopedia's worth of knowledge about kirin.

They were from Asia. That part I knew. And they had spread through Europe by the time of the first extinction. They hunted in packs, and the prevailing legend was that they appeared around the time of a great leader. Like Confucius. They were tough as hell to see at night, which may be why the ancient drawings of them were covered in clouds, and they fought like demons. In olden days, people worshipped them, sacrificed to them as if they were gods.

Yes. The kirin desire man's worship.

A walled city, a barred gate . . . Exile, I translated.

Exile does not please them.

Exile? The truth bubbled up inside. That century and a half when we thought they were extinct? To them, it had been exile.

These were more than simple beasts, quietly surviving in the wild pockets of the world. Unicorns had been *hiding*.

Had they gone into hiding after Clothilde killed that karkadann? Did they know their days were numbered then? Cory had always described Clothilde's karkadann kill as the Last Hunt. I'd certainly never heard of anyone killing unicorns after that.

I was so thirsty.

Into my head came the vision of a schoolgirl, walking along a road with a brown lunch bag in her hand. Very close, and very vulnerable. A meal for him carrying a meal for me.

I could get you food and drink, but you would not like my methods.

"No." I tried to lift my head from the ground, but the flesh of my back boiled as I shifted. Was I healing? Unlike Ursula, I hadn't gotten a transfusion of non-hunter blood. I had no idea how much I'd lost, but I was still here, still alive. Perhaps I still healed. As the gory images of the schoolgirl faded, I risked speaking again. How could he be treating me with such kindness and act bloodthirsty to another girl? "Why don't you kill me?"

I need your help. Like last time.

"In the park?"

No. With Clothilde Llewelyn.

I closed my eyes. Right. The karkadann who thought he was Bucephalus. Talk about delusions of grandeur! "How have the last two thousand years been treating you?"

Not bad.

I tried to laugh then, and was rewarded with a flash of fresh pain. Well, what did I expect? For the talking unicorn to be *reasonable*?

Pop quiz: Karkadann, I thought, since I didn't have the strength to speak. Alexander's warhorse, Bucephalus, according to all accounts except my mother's, had died, mid-campaign, in what is now Pakistan. In his mourning, Alexander named a city after his greatest companion: The "horse city" Bucephala was now known as Jhelum.

True. But I did not die there.

That's what my mother said. She said Bucephalus had escaped, and that Alexander had made up the death story to save face.

According to the legends the unicorn hunters passed around, Bucephalus lived for another two thousand years, until Clothilde Llewelyn came along and finally defeated him, the last surviving unicorn, in an epic battle that had cost them both their lives.

I did not die there, either.

No, *he* didn't. It was different karkadanns, each time. A few animals could live a hundred years—I think we learned in bio class about birds of prey—and a few plants could reach into the thousands. But a two-thousand-year-old, battle-tested unicorn? He looked awfully spry for his age.

Besides, I'd seen the unicorn in the rotunda, the one Clothilde killed.

There is only me.

Then what's the thing in the rotunda?

The karkadann began to growl, and the earth itself trembled beneath my palms, chest, and cheek.

Do you doubt me, Daughter of Alexander?

I was in real trouble now, if my thoughts were no longer my own. I was used to keeping my mouth shut in front of my mother. With this karkadann, it wouldn't help.

I wondered about the other hunters. Where were they? Where was I, for that matter? What did they think had happened to me? Did they think I'd been eaten? Did they think I was dead?

Do you want them to?

The thought was so clear in my mind that, for a second, I thought it belonged to me alone.

"No!" My mother, and Phil . . . they'd be so upset.

Are you sure? It is very nice, being dead. No more hunting. No more being hunted.

"You'd know, *Bucephalus*," I said, "what with dying twice now."

Laughter. You must be getting stronger. I felt him shift above me, and the corresponding wave of venom-filled air. *It is almost closed now.*

I got a flash of my back: my shirt, torn to shreds and stained brownish red with dried blood. Beneath it, a glimpse of a horrific, enormous wound.

I recoiled from the vision in my head. How had I survived? No one could live through a wound like that, not even a hunter. I'd have bled to death or stopped breathing or—was it possible that the horn had missed all major organs? No, I couldn't breathe. My lung must have been pierced, at the very least. But it had healed, too.

The karkadann snorted. He was growing impatient, standing here. I could tell. You'd think that a few millennia would chill a guy out.

I will have all the time in the world when the rebel kirin are defeated.

"You need my help?" I glanced at the body of the nearest kirin. "I think you're better at killing them than a hunter is."

For now. You get better. Besides, I do not want to kill them all. I want to free them.

"I don't understand."

A rush of images flooded my brain, each more confusing and muddled than the last. *The burnt scriptorium of the Cloisters; Marten watching Philippa at target practice; the head of the kirin that Valerija had killed;, the Wall of First Kills; the alicorn throne; the claymore of Clothilde Llewelyn, the golden, blown-glass vial that my mother had used the night she'd saved Brandt's life—*

"Stop," I gasped. "Please."

A Band-Aid; a crown; an endless, barren wasteland; the scent of hot horse and dying men; the bronze bit in my mouth, tearing, tearing—

I tried to rise, but I blacked out.

When I woke again, the pain in my back had subsided a lot, and I risked pushing myself to a sitting position. The corpses of the kirin were gone, and I shuddered to think what had happened to them. I didn't see the karkadann, either.

"Karkadann?" I whispered into the woods. The quality of the light through the trees made me think it was late afternoon. "Um . . . Bucephalus?"

Daughter of Alexander, are you well?

Yes, I thought. Where was he?

Near. Your skills have increased.

My skills at reading his mind? He couldn't be too close—I didn't even sense the venom.

325

Yes, you grow better for me. Better to withstand me. Better to listen to me. Better to hunt.

"Hunt you?"

Laughter. Try it.

Gingerly, I reached behind me and touched my back. My skin felt rough and rippled beneath my fingertips, and I cringed, coughed again, and felt dizzy.

The ground trembled, and the karkadann emerged through the trees. He stood above me and dropped three small, slightly squashed oranges to the ground near my feet.

Good?

I picked one up, ignoring how sticky my hand felt, how it was spattered with blood and dirt. "Yes. Thank you." It was wet and slimy to the touch, and the caked mud and dirt stuck to the rind. Gross. Unicorn spit.

I tore into it anyway, then sucked at the juice as best I could without eating the dirty parts. How far had I come from the hospital aide who would never dream of eating food without freshly washed hands?

I guess once you spent the night in a mud pit made with your own blood, you relaxed the rules a bit.

"Okay," I said, between mouthfuls of orange. "You saved my life. Now tell me about the kirin."

Not all kirin but some. They have been deceived. They think they will find a new glory among men. But all they shall find is slavery. They do not listen.

"Well, I can't talk to them . . . can I?"

No. But your sword can.

I lifted my arm. It hurt. "I doubt I'll be doing anything with a sword anytime soon. Besides, you saw what happened last night. We hunters are no threat to more than one unicorn at a time."

You will be now. You are better all the time.

I shook my head. "The ancient hunters had years to learn their craft. We've had a couple of months. They had experienced people to train them. We have no one. They understood their powers. We do not."

The last is true.

"Do you . . . understand the powers?"

Daughter of Alexander, I am teaching you now. When the kirin gored you, he taught you. When you pet your—Bonegrinder?— she teaches you. When you stand in your prison, surrounded by bones that sing and horns that scream, it is all a lesson.

Being around unicorns made us better hunters. If our abilities manifested themselves only when we were around unicorns, it would make sense that prolonged exposure could enhance the powers. That I could understand. And it explained the bones in the wall just fine. But it didn't tell us how to take on a pack of kirin.

Alexander and I were with each other all our lives. We were born at the same moment. He was best of all. But he was lost without me. Hunters are different. It took me thousands of years to understand. And then I met Clothilde.

"And killed her!"

No. Clothilde Llewelyn died in bed surrounded by her grand- children.

"That's impossible."

Is it? You too are dead, Daughter of Alexander.

And all at once, I understood. I didn't even need the images the karkadann placed in my mind. *A young woman stood in a field, her hunting clothes torn to shreds, her wounds closing as she strode forward, past the bodies of dead einhorn and kirin, her claymore held high. Her fair hair wasn't long, like in the tableau, but shorn short, the better to show off the scar that ran vertically across her scalp.*

She stood before the karkadann, her face battle weary and drawn, pointed her sword tip into the earth, and said, "The world changes, unicorn. The fences rise, the forests fall. There is nowhere to hide and nowhere to hunt that does not rob from men. This world is not for you. And neither is it for me."

"You made a deal," I whispered. "Exile."

Yes.

"Where?"

Secret.

There had been no extinction, no Last Hunt. There had been no great battle between Clothilde, the greatest of all unicorn hunters, and Bucephalus, the greatest of all unicorns. It was all a lie. And Clothilde "died" so that no one would know the secret. So she could stop hunting. And she got married, and she had children. And the hunters never knew! Talk about a line of lost Llewelyns! Cory would flip. That is, if she still thought there was anything special about Clothilde's lost descendants once she knew the truth.

Her descendant has been found.

The golden vial appeared in my mind's eye. The golden vial Lilith had procured from the man who'd been my father. The very last remnant of the Remedy.

"Shut up."

Why do you think I come to you?

"I honestly couldn't say."

You are the only one I trust not to kill me on sight.

"None of us would," I insisted, "because we can't. We aren't good enough at hunting."

Did you think you could kill that re'em? You can do anything. It is your choice.

"I choose to remain dead, then. Like Clothilde."

The karkadann growled again, and I could tell that he regretted his slip. But if he could talk to me, he could talk to the others, right? I'd been granted a reprieve. A single, perfect chance. I could have died last night. Could die the next time I was sent on a hunt. I can't do it anymore. I won't.

I rubbed my hands together, and the grime began to ball up and flake off. Before, Phil would have been all over this unicorn conservation plan the karkadann and Clothilde had dreamed up. I bet Ilesha and Rosamund would go for it as well. Cory, not so much, but—

Daughter of Alexander, I need you. You have also been harmed by this false Alexander. This upstart. But it is nothing to what shall become of the unicorn. The kirin begin to sense the cage door closing. They think when they kill all hunters they will be safe. Last night was an ambush. The kirin believe you are weak, now. No Llewelyns. Now is the time.

The false Alexander? I remembered what Giovanni had told me about the man who called himself Alexander in the bar. "Do you mean Marten Jaeger?" A less likely latter-day Alexander the Great I could not imagine. Alexander had been a young, strong warrior. Marten Jaeger was an old man with a nice manicure and a sleek car.

The world changes. Now, one needs no army and no sword to conquer the world.

329

"But he still needs unicorns." The Remedy. A drug that could save the world or seize it. But it still didn't make sense. "Marten is not a hunter. How can he interact with the kirin at all?"

I do not know.

God, why was I listening to this? It was crazy. Bucephalus! Alexander the Great! Magic I could learn just by sitting here soaking up unicorn venom! It was all ridiculous. The only remotely useful thing he'd told me was that Clothilde got away with feigning death and quitting the Order of the Lioness.

I should follow in her footsteps.

You will not help me. The karkadann seemed to growl. Again, the earth shook, and the birds grew quiet in the trees above.

"Will you kill me for real if I don't?"

Kill me then, I thought at him. For I'm dead if I go back to the Cloisters. I'm dead every time I pick up a bow and arrow and go after a unicorn. We're all dead. Clothilde was right. The only way to avoid death is to embrace it—and run.

He lowered his horn and parted his jaws. I sat trapped, on the ground, incapable of standing, pinned between a tree and a monster. I don't know how long it went on, but at last, the beast turned and galloped away.

And I breathed free.

"Mi scusi," I said to the startled shopkeeper in my tourist Italian. *"È un'emergenza. Per favore, posso usare il suo telefono?"* He just stared at me, eyes wide. I hoped I'd said it right. It was all the Italian I could think of at the moment.

Of course, what else could it be other than an emergency? I was standing on the linoleum across from his tabacchi counter, covered in blood and grime, holding my torn shirt together with both hands. He handed me the telephone. I prayed that I recalled the number correctly, and dialed.

"Hi. It's Astrid. I need your help."

23

WHEREIN ASTRID CHOOSES DEATH AND LIFE

THE SHOPKEEPER THREATENED to call the police, after he'd gotten me settled in a chair with a blanket, some wet towels, and a lemon soda. I was never so thankful for Italian hospitality. The walk out of the woods had sapped every last bit of strength from my body, and I was fighting to remain conscious.

I couldn't understand much of what he was saying to me, but he seemed to think I was the victim of either a hit and run or a really bad mugging. He also wanted to take me to a hospital, but I insisted I wasn't injured. Then he started getting suspicious, which I understood just fine, language barrier or no. If the blood staining every inch of my skin and clothing wasn't mine, who did it belong to?

Through the window of the shop, I saw a passenger van pull up outside, and a familiar figure jump out of the driver's seat. He'd come. Giovanni had come.

The bell over the door jangled as he ran inside, ten feet away, then eight, then five. I could feel his arms around me already.

Four feet away, with nothing but the corner of the counter between us, and he stopped dead.

"Astrid. My God, what happened?"

When I rose, hands extended, he recoiled. I fell back on the bench, deflated. I bet I looked like a monster. I bet he was relieved he'd gotten out when he'd had the chance. "What do you think?" I croaked.

"A"—he lowered his voice—"unicorn attack?"

I nodded miserably, and shut my burning eyes.

Next thing I knew, Giovanni and the shopkeeper were engaged in a fast-paced debate. Giovanni's Italian had certainly improved over the summer.

"He thinks we should take you to the hospital," Giovanni translated for me at one point, and then, a bit later, "I'm trying to convince him this isn't gang related." Finally, he interrupted the shopkeeper's tirade with an upraised hand, turned to me, and said, "Do the people at the convent know where you are?"

I thought of the karkadann's plea as I said, "Why do you think I called you?"

Giovanni seemed no more sympathetic than I had been to Bucephalus when he replied, "I'm trying not to ask myself that question right now."

It was no more than I deserved. I held out my arms again. "Giovanni, look at me. You have no idea what happened to me today. I should be dead. I can't go back to the Cloisters. Please, please, just—"

The shopkeeper watched all this, then said something else. He rummaged in a drawer, and emerged with a set of keys.

Giovanni's translation was delivered in a flat voice, and he refused to meet my eyes. "He says there's a room upstairs he rents to students in the winter months. He wants us to go up there, so you can wash off. He says you are scaring the customers."

Because I looked like I'd walked off a horror movie set. "Oh. Okay." I stood up. I followed the shopkeeper up the stairs, stumbling only twice, and he led us into a plain, modestly furnished studio. The bathroom didn't even have a real door on it, just a cornered-off partition with a toilet and a showerhead over a drain in the sloped floor. The kitchen consisted of a sink, a cabinet, and a single-burner stove. There was a bed in the middle of the room and a single chair by the door.

The shopkeeper whispered something else to Giovanni and left. "He says he's got some spare clothes downstairs you can wear. And some linens and soap for . . . your shower."

"Thank you," I said. "*Grazie!*" I called after the man.

Giovanni looked around the room, then parked himself in the chair. I went over to the sink and started running the water, plunging my hands beneath the faucet and marveling at how the stream turned black, then red.

The shopkeeper returned with a stack of towels and sheets, soap and shampoo, a shirt and a pair of drawstring pants, a brush, a packet of tea, and a can of what looked like soup.

"*Grazie,*" I said again, taking the supplies from him, humbled immensely by his generosity. "*Grazie mille. Come si chiama? Mi chiamo* Astrid Llewelyn."

"Salvatore Basso."

Salvatore. *Savior.* Well, he'd certainly saved me. "*Signor Basso, molto, molto—*"

"*Dio la benedica, signorina.*" He said, patted my mildly cleaner hand, and left.

Giovanni still wouldn't meet my eyes, so I dropped the linens and clothes on the bed, then took the soap and towels with me into the bathroom stall. I stripped off my disgusting clothes and threw them out into the main room, then turned on the water to the shower before using the toilet. That experience was astoundingly gross, and even knowing from my hospital volunteering that stuff like—ick, *this*—was pretty common after major incisions hadn't prepared me for the shock of it. I bit back a cry.

"Astrid?" Giovanni's voice from the other side of the partition. "Are you all right?"

"Fine," I gasped. I touched my back again, feeling the tender, new skin there. How would I be able to wash it? Did I dare ask Giovanni to help?

"I'm putting some water on for tea," he said. "Is there anything else you need right now?"

Yes. I thought. I need you to come sponge off my back. I stepped into the spray and undid the rubber band securing my braid. I let the hair unwind, there, under the shower, careful to keep the length falling forward on my shoulders. Rivulets of water poured down my thighs and calves, stained scarlet.

"Like money?" he said. "Or a ride back to . . . wherever you're going?"

Standing underneath the shower, I choked, and almost vomited up the soda that Signore Basso had been good enough to give me. "You're . . . leaving?"

Silence.

"Giovanni?" I strained to listen above the sound of the shower, the sting of the water on my raw back, the swirling suckle of the

335

drain beneath my toes. "Are you still here?"

"Yeah," came the whispered reply from the other side of the partition. He was a few inches away. "Right here." There was a soft thump against the wall. I put my hand up, picturing him on the other side, resting his forehead against the plywood.

"Don't leave me," I begged. I pressed hard against the wood, as if I could push right through it and touch him.

Eons passed in silence. And then, "I won't."

I scrubbed my face, then my arms and legs, bending over carefully so as not to stretch the skin of my back. I washed my neck, belly, chest, and between my legs. There was a small, shiny pink mark, shaped a bit like a double helix, where the unicorn's horn had burst through my front, right below my bottom right rib. I marveled again that I'd survived.

Okay, enough stalling. I clenched my jaw and reached behind me. A new rush of red-stained water pooled at my feet, and I bit my lip. Flakes of dried blood bigger than euro coins broke off in my hands, but if I tried to run my fingers over the skin, I—

"Ow!" I spat out, and my legs began to shake. I pushed out into the walls with both hands to remain upright.

"Astrid? Are you all right?"

I took several deep, shuddering breaths, then turned off the shower. "Yes. I just—" I groped for a towel, then wrapped it carefully around my midsection. "I'm coming out now."

"Thanks for the warning."

By the time I got around the corner of the partition. Giovanni had returned to the stove area, where he was pouring out two mugs of tea, his back turned, his head tilted resolutely toward the teacups.

I sat on the edge of the bed and let the water from my hair drain into my lap. "I, um . . ." Another deep breath. "I can't wash my back."

He straightened, but didn't turn around. "Why not?"

I swiveled away from him, then let the towel slide down to my waist. "Look."

I don't know when he turned. I didn't want to know. But then, suddenly, there was a sharp intake of breath from across the room.

"What does it look like?" I asked, and there was a terrible catch in my voice. I dared not turn around to see the horror I felt reflected on his face.

And then, his hand touched my back, warm, and solid, and impossibly gentle. He traced a strange, jagged shape between the bottom tips of my shoulder blades. "Don't tear my arms off, now," he said, in a tone so low I could hardly hear it.

That's right. I'd once threatened to do so if he ever touched me again. "I couldn't if I wanted to." My voice shook with every syllable. "What does it look like?"

"Like a star. Like a giant, twisted, many-fingered star." He hesitated. "What happened?"

"I was gored," I said. "Straight through."

"But . . ." I knew every question in his mind. Knew it because I had them, too. How did you survive? How can you walk at all? How did it close up in such a short time? "It's almost healed."

"I heal quick, if it's a unicorn-inflicted wound."

He lowered his hand. "Are you saying you're a superhero? You're like Wolverine or something?"

I swallowed. "If there's a unicorn around, then, yes."

I felt the bed shift as he rose. "I'm going to clean off your back." His tone gave no indication whether or not he believed me. "Is that okay?"

"Please." I heard him rummaging around in a cabinet, and then running the sink. He returned to the bed and I felt his hand on my shoulder, and a soft, warm cloth on my back, dabbing away at the edges of the wound. We sat in silence for several minutes as he washed my back. Outside, the sun set, and the room grew dark around us.

"Do you want to turn on the light?" I asked at last. "Make it easier to see?"

"It's actually easier like this," he said. "Easier not to . . . see."

I balled my hands in my lap and hunched my shoulders as much as I dared. "It's that bad, huh?"

"Astrid," he said, and sounded as if he was fighting for breath. "You're *naked*."

I laughed then. I couldn't help it. All this time, I thought he'd been appalled, and really, he'd been trying his best to be a gentleman. I turned to face him, with my damp hair spilling down over my shoulders and veiling my breasts. He stared at me, his expression a mixture of awe and concern, and I stared back, completely unmindful of everything but this boy, this moment. Last night, I died. Today, I'd been reborn. Who was I now? Astrid the Warrior, as Giovanni liked to say, or Astrid the woman, whom Giovanni could actually have?

I took a deep breath. "You need to know . . ."

A split second of hesitation, then he breathed out, *"What?"*

"The way I feel about you—it never changed. I tried to hate you, but . . . I couldn't. I can't. And I don't want to."

He sighed in relief, leaned forward, and kissed me hard—

nothing more than his mouth against mine, but it felt like a full body embrace. He cupped my face in his hands, and though I wished for all the world for him to crush me in his arms, I knew my back could never take it.

He drew away at last, panting a bit, and buried his face against my neck. "This week was hell. I deserved everything you said to me at the convent that day. I was so awful. And when you walked away from me, I knew how badly I'd messed up. Again. It made everything that happened at school seem like nothing more than bombing a problem set. I'd been trying so hard to be good again, and I was worse than ever."

I threaded my hands through his curls, caressing his scalp.

"When you called today, I didn't care why or how, I just knew I needed to get to you. I stole that van from the school. They'll kick me out for sure, now. First Seth disappearing, then me . . . but I didn't care, as long as I saw you again. Even if you hated me. Even if the only thing I could be for you was the guy who translated the Italian and made the tea. Even if I had to stand there on the other side of the shower wall, not knowing if you were bleeding to death in there. Just knowing that you had no clothes on, and we were in a room with nothing but a bed, and I could never, ever touch you again."

"You can," I said, "if you want to." And for a second I thought he would—that we both would. Then I winced, as an arrow of pain shot through my torso. "Just not right this minute, maybe."

He nodded and pulled away. It didn't matter, though. I was dead now. I had all the time in the world to be with Giovanni. "You get dressed," he said. "I'll make fresh tea."

He flipped on a light as he went, and I changed into the pants and loose shirt while his back was turned. The combination of lamplight and nighttime transformed the apartment's window into a mirror, and I lifted my shirt and peeked over my shoulder to look at my back. It was as Giovanni had said. A starburst of fresh scars more than a hand spread wide radiated from the center of my back. Each ray coiled in on itself, crossing and recrossing, like a braid or a dozen figure eights laid end to end. I remembered Kaitlyn's description of the mark on Brandt's leg. Why hadn't I seen this before, on Ursula, or on Zelda, who'd also gotten an alicorn injury? But they'd also both gotten stitches. When the kirin in the courtyard had scraped my arm, I'd closed it up with bandages. Today, I'd healed naturally, Brandt through the Remedy. Was it connected?

Giovanni cleared his throat, and I whipped my shirt back down. "Have pity on me, at least," he said.

But he wasn't asking me to do anything. It wasn't at all like Kaitlyn had once told me, about what guys expected and what you owed them. Giovanni broke every rule I'd understood about girls and boys. He defied every expectation I'd ever put in place.

We sat on the bed and he handed me a mug, and in between sips, I told him everything. I told him about Alexander the Great and his warhorse, about the goddess Diana, about the temple fire and the vestals and the Cloisters and the Jutland Campaign. I told him about my mother, about Brandt, about Bonegrinder and Cory and Neil and Gordian. I told him about killing the re'em and getting attacked by the kirin. I told him about Bucephalus and what the karkadann had said about Clothilde, what he'd said about me.

"Do you think I'm crazy?" I asked, when I was done and the tea had gone cold again.

He shook his head. "We're in Rome, Astrid. Between the ancients and the Church, what you're saying sounds like a comparatively minor miracle. Talking unicorns and wounds that close on their own? I can point to half a dozen places in the Bible—"

"Forget the Bible for a second," I said. "Do you believe me?"

"I believe my own eyes." He gestured to my back. "So, yeah. Man, I wish I could watch you shoot sometime. When you were describing it just now—I've never seen you look so alive."

I drew back, aghast. "That's not true!"

He held up his hands. "Whoa, what did I say? It was just an observation."

"Don't say that. Hunting was awful. I'm so relieved to be free of it." I lay down on the bed, resting on my side so as not to put pressure on my back, and tried to forget his words. He was wrong. Plain wrong.

Yet bowstrings twanged and swords clashed inside my mind.

Giovanni scooted up next to me. "Why do you think you're free?"

"Because all the other hunters think I'm dead."

"Your family."

I was quiet for a moment, imagining what it would be like not to see Phil again. Or even my mom. "It will be okay."

"Hmmm." He curled his body to match mine, leaving a few inches between my back and his front, and caressed my arm. "I'm not sure. That doesn't sound like you, leaving those girls to fend for themselves. Didn't you say some of them were twelve or even younger? Remember the night we met? You

341

wouldn't even let me thrash that gypsy kid who stole your purse."

"That was different." In my head, I pictured Ilesha, falling as the kirin charged. I didn't even know if she was okay. Bucephalus had said none of the hunters had died, but the karkadann wasn't omniscient. I wondered if anyone else had been seriously injured.

The information the karkadann had given me—would it help them? Would it protect them the next time they went on a hunt, save them from another kirin ambush? Did they even understand that it had been an ambush?

"What are you thinking, Astrid?" His hand traveled up and down my arm, but no farther.

"How nice it is to lie here with you."

He made that unconvinced little harrumph again.

"Why?" I asked. "What are you thinking?" Sex, probably. We were lying on a bed, after all. And I'd taken my clothes off in front of him. And he was a teenage boy.

But Giovanni surprised me again. "I'm thinking about how you're not really free. From everything you told me, it sounds like you draw unicorns to you, just by dint of who you are. That's dangerous, isn't it?"

"It stops when I'm . . . not a virgin."

"Really tempting request," he whispered into my hair. My entire body seemed to tingle, and the scars on my back burned like a brand. He exhaled hard against my skin. "*Really.*"

I rose on my elbow and looked down at him, his head making a dent on the beat-up pillow, his skin, dark against the sheets, his big brown eyes and the little hollow beneath his Adam's apple where his pulse fluttered so fast I could hardly tell one beat from the next. I twisted and lowered myself until I was lying across his chest, and we started kissing. Our bodies meshed together, mine damp and raw and sensitive to every touch, his warm and solid and human and wonderful. I grabbed handfuls of his shirt, clinging to him as my heartbeat raced to catch up to his, as our lips and tongues touched and everything seemed so perfect I wanted to cry out in triumph. I slid over, just a few inches, until I was lying more completely on top of him. He reached up to pull me in close, and I whimpered in pain. His hands dropped to the side.

No! Stupid wound.

"If you could do it now," he said softly, lying utterly still beneath me, as if he was terrified of hurting me again. "Tonight. Would you?"

"I don't know. I would want to."

"And if it wasn't me, would you want to still?"

I knew what he was asking, really. Was it freedom, or was it him? I kissed his chest through his T-shirt, breathed him in—the fresh, living scent of Giovanni, untainted by any touch of unicorn, any whiff of fire or flood. "No. It's you."

"It's you, too, Astrid the Warrior."

I pulled away. "Stop calling me that."

"Why? It's true, isn't it? It's what you are."

I slid off the bed, crossed the room to the window, and stared out at the night. Even Rome was far vaster than what I knew of my little neighborhood near the Cloisters. How could he expect me to return there, knowing how isolated it was? Knowing how dangerous?

"That unicorn, the one that talked to you—"

"Bucephalus."

"He said that it was especially bad for the other girls now. For anyone with your . . . abilities. That those other unicorns were trying to hunt you down and would go after the other girls when you were gone. He said you could stop that. Make it safe again. And then you could do whatever you wanted."

I looked over my shoulder at him. He was sitting on the bed, looking amazing and warm and oh, so out of reach! "Like you?"

"You think I do what I want?"

"No. I think what I want to do is you."

He laughed, but then got serious again right away. "Astrid, look at your back. You could have died. Should have died. That you didn't is a miracle. Do you want to mess with that? Considering there are man-eating monsters out there?"

I looked out the window again. Somewhere in the dark, the karkadann waited. I couldn't hear him anymore, but I could still tell. It was such a part of me now, this unicorn sense. To lose it would be like going blind.

Giovanni went on. "Do you want to . . . sideline yourself, knowing how bad it is for your friends?"

I swallowed, defiant. But Clothilde had done it, and no one blamed her.

Had she, though? Clothilde hadn't abandoned the other hunters to their doom. When she ran away, she'd first struck a deal with the karkadann that would protect everyone from the unicorns. Hunters and laymen alike. And what's more, she'd protected the unicorns from mankind as well.

Astrid the Warrior, Daughter of Alexander, descendant of Clothilde Llewelyn, unicorn hunter—these were the names everyone else had given me. Were they my names? Were they *me*?

Could I turn my back—my scarred, unicorn-marked back—on them even if I wanted to? Even tonight, so sure I wanted to vanish from that world forever, I couldn't stop thinking about the Remedy; couldn't stop recounting to Giovanni in breathless, excruciating details what it had been like to slit the throat of a rampaging re'em; couldn't stop scanning the countryside, even now, for a glimpse of a unicorn in the darkness.

I *was* a hunter—in bone, in flesh, in blood, in fact.

I needed to return.

24

Wherein Astrid Faces Her Family

Boys are curious creatures. The second you give in and offer them what they've been hounding you for, they start to question it. Thus it was that as Giovanni drove me to the Cloisters the next day, he was no longer so certain that we'd made the right decision.

"I've been thinking about it," he said, navigating crazy Roman traffic and narrow streets. "And I'm worried about your safety. Sure, you survived the last goring, but what about the next battle? I don't know what I'd do if something happened to you."

I smiled at him. "That's sweet."

"Also, what about us?" He swerved around a Vespa and ran a yellow light. I gripped the jump bar. "If you commit yourself to this, can you—? Can we—well, what *can* we do?" He honked angrily at a pedestrian and downshifted. I marveled that a kid from New York knew how to drive at all.

"You're just horny this morning, aren't you?"

He didn't answer that. He didn't need to. We'd spent the

night wrapped in each other's arms, kissing some, talking some, but mostly just lying there, making sure our bodies touched as much as possible through our clothes. We knew, perhaps, it would be the last time. My mother was still in charge at the Cloisters, and she was adamant that there would be no men in her hunters' lives, in any capacity. And there was still that very real possibility that death would catch me the next time I drew my bow.

The morning light was soft on the front courtyard's mosaics as Giovanni pulled up outside. Sunlight sparkled on the water in the fountain. The stone girl stood there, stoic as always, dipping her alicorn into the basin and announcing her sacrifice to anyone who cared to read the Latin inscription at her feet. Smug bitch.

"Here we are," he said, and let the car engine idle. "Do you want me to go inside with you?"

"That's dangerous, until we know where Bonegrinder is." Or, you know, my mother, whom I wouldn't put it past to sic the zhi on any intruders or potential Actaeons.

He nodded. "Right, the little pet . . . unicorn." In the light of day, he seemed to have a tougher time saying the word. I didn't blame him. "So." He played with the keys dangling from the ignition. "You'll call me?"

"Yes. As soon as I know what's going on." I looked down at my hands. "Do you have any idea where you'll be?"

"At school if they don't figure out I stole the van and kick me out. With my mom's family if they do. Either way, I'll have my cell phone. I'm not leaving Italy anytime soon." His tone gave little away, but I understood nevertheless. He'd sacrificed a lot to come to me last night. His position at the school, maybe even his future. And he didn't even get sex out of the deal. Didn't even get a girlfriend, since I was going back to the Cloisters with no clue what would happen next. Most incredible of all, he'd encouraged me to do it.

I slid out of the passenger seat and stood there, hand on the door, unsure what to say next. Giovanni stared straight ahead, gripping the wheel in both hands. "It's right," I said. "I'm sure of it."

He nodded curtly. "Be careful, Astrid. Just—" he broke off. *"Ti voglio . . . ti voglio tanto bene."*

"What does that mean?" I asked. He'd said it before, on the hillside, but now, it sounded as if his heart would break.

He hesitated. "It means everything. It means I love you. It means I want you. It means I want you to be okay. It means everything."

Yes, it did. *"Ti voglio tanto bene, Giovanni."* I shut the van door and after a moment, he drove away, and I faced the Cloisters alone.

The rotunda was dark and silent. I went first to Lilith's offices, but they proved empty of both my mother and the haphazard piles of documents that had been lying around during Neil's tenure. My mother had been more of a pack rat than either of the Bartolis. Where did everything disappear to? Her room was also empty—her bed didn't even look slept in.

"Hello?" I called, as I exited back into the rotunda. Nothing. The door to the underground area—the scriptorium, chapter house, and catacombs—was closed, and the cloistered court-yard was empty. I looked toward the second level, but there was no sign of life upstairs either. Was it possible that they were all out on a hunt this morning? And where was Phil? I know she had been planning on leaving, but I'd hoped she would delay her trip a day or two if I turned up dead.

There was a scratching at the closed door to the stairwell. Bonegrinder! I opened it, and the zhi came bounding out, bleating happily and gamboling around me. "Where is everyone, girl?"

Bonegrinder stopped mid-cavort, then headed up the stairs, looking back every few steps to make sure I followed. What, now she obeyed orders? Curiouser and curiouser.

The dormitory hall was chaos. Half-packed suitcases warred for space with rolled-up rugs and garbage bags stuffed with Cory's carefully chosen throw pillows and comforters. I knocked on Phil and Valerija's door.

"What?" came a groggy voice inside. "The first train's not till noon, so—" Phil threw open the door and stopped. My hand tightened on Bonegrinder's collar until I saw the ring on Phil's thumb.

"Oh my God, Astrid." Her red, shadowed eyes grew wide and filled with tears. She went as if to hug me and I stepped back.

"Careful. My back."

"You're alive!" she cried. "How? Val said—" Behind her, Valerija sat up in bed now, rubbing her eyes. I waved at her. Her mouth dropped open. "She said the kirin got you."

"They did," I replied. "It's a really long story, but the quick version is I spent a day lying in a pool of my own blood in the middle of nowhere and then I walked out."

"Hey, everyone! Astrid's alive!" Tears were running freely down Phil's face. She grabbed my hands in her own. "Oh, Astrid, we thought—your clothes. What are you wearing? Why didn't you call?"

Another really long story. Down the hall, doors opened and faces peeked out, filled with shock and joy. Cory and Rosamund came running, Zelda, Dorcas, and Ursula following after. Even Melissende and Grace seemed happy to see me. I backed against the parapet, leery of being trapped in a bone-crushing hug. My back felt better this morning, and Giovanni had said the scars looked less livid then they had the previous evening, but I knew I wasn't a hundred percent yet.

"Why can't I hug you?" Phil said. "I need to hug you." She grabbed my head in her hands and squeezed. She kissed my forehead, my cheeks, my nose. "Thank God, thank God, oh, Asteroid, you have no idea—" she stopped. "Have you seen Aunt Lilith?"

I shook my head. "I couldn't find her."

"No, well, you wouldn't, would you?" Cory said.

"What? Why?"

Phil tugged on my arm. "Come here," she said softly. "I'll fill you in." To the group, she said, "All right, everyone, back to packing. Astrid's safe and sound."

"Packing?" I asked, as Phil pulled me into her room and shut the door.

Phil told me everything. The kirin ambush had taken its toll on the hunters. We'd lost three bows, two knives, *me*—and Ilesha was currently in the hospital with a crushed femur and a cracked pelvis. She'd been trampled. When Lilith had heard about what had happened to me, she'd broken down completely, tearing off her ring and falling to her knees in front of Bonegrinder. It had been Cory who'd tackled the creature to the floor before she could attack.

350

"I talked her down," Phil said. "But I don't know if that was worse." Lilith had then announced that the Cloisters was closing, and sent everyone to pack while she called all their parents and made travel arrangements. Phil had tried to call Neil to complain, and Lilith had confiscated her phone. Later, Phil had found her down in the chapter house, ripping the trophies off the Wall of First Kills.

"What?"

"She was screaming like a banshee, Astroturf. I tried to stop her, but she pushed me out the door, then locked it. She's been in there all night."

"And you left her there!" I cried. "With all those weapons, in that state of mind—" I flung the door to Phil's room open and started to run.

"Astrid, wait—" Phil called after me as I sprinted down the stairs. "Don't you think we tried? But by the time I got a hunter to help me, she'd shoved—" Bonegrinder, sensing an imminent chase, bounded along beside me. Phil's voice faded, and the zhi and I sprinted into the rotunda. "We've been trying to break down that door—"

I threw a glance over my shoulder at the door to the lower quarters. Phil skidded to a stop at the base of the stairs. "No ax to be had in this place?"

Cory bumped into her from behind. "She locked them all in with her."

"So?" I cried. "Rip a bone from the wall." I started down the stairs, Bonegrinder hot on my heels, and the other girls following at whatever pace they could manage.

"Mom!" I screamed. "Mom, it's Astrid!" Please, please let her be thinking clearly. I reached the bottom of the stairs. The skeletal kirin's head above the door leered at me as I raised my foot to kick. The door showed signs of splintering but stood firm. The first attack splintered it further, but it didn't collapse. She had barricaded herself in.

"Mom!" I called again. "Open the door!"

Cory materialized by my side. This time she had a unicorn femur with her. "Here," she said. "But be careful. She's shoved the throne up and it'll hurt you if you touch—"

"Motheeeerrrr!" I shrieked and battered at the door until the bone shattered in my hand. "Open the door! It's all right! I'm alive."

From within, there was no sound at all. *No . . .*

"Mommy! Please!" I placed both hands against the door to shove.

"Astrid, no!" Cory said, but it was too late.

The field of mud rose in my mind's eye, the wormy, smoke-filled sky, the stench of mold and ashes, of blood and human waste and death. Unicorns and hunters screamed, bows twanged and swords clashed with horn and skin and bone. Fangs tore at flesh, and hooves crushed skulls. Human voices shouted in foreign languages and galloping monsters sounded like thunderclaps in the desolate air.

But there was no pain.

"Phil!" I said. "Help me!"

"It doesn't hurt you?" Cory asked as Phil took her place by my side, but I was too busy pushing to answer, ignoring the visions and the renewed agony in my back and putting all my weight against the broken door, against the bits of alicorn throne that showed through, against the ghosts of hundreds of dead hunters who shouted above it all.

Once I had a foot or so of space, I climbed through the wreckage. "Mom!" I called again as I stumbled onto the floor, free of the chair, and the visions evaporated. I limped forward, conscious of the excruciating pain in my back. The room was a wreck, as Phil had said. All the trophies had been torn down and strewn across the floor. Tables and chairs were overturned, the piano was lying at a crazy angle. My mother stood before the weapon wall, the claymore of Clothilde Llewelyn in her hands.

"Astrid?" she said. She looked at me, her eyes hollow and haunted, her lips and cheeks pale. And for the first time, I knew what it would look like if my mother really *were* crazy. She'd spent the last night insane with grief. "Oh, honey, is it really you?" The sword clattered to the floor and we met in the middle of the room. She enfolded me in her arms, but I barely noticed the sting of her hands on the tender flesh of my back. "Oh, Astrid, Astrid."

"Didn't you hear me yelling for you?"

"I didn't . . ." She shook her head and started crying again. "I didn't know what to think. They've been trying to break in all night long."

I looked around the room. "Mom, what did you do?"

"I sent you to your death, sweetheart. I killed my daughter. My daughter!"

I shook my head. "No. I'm right here."

"It's a miracle!" she gushed. "And one I'm not risking again. Just making you come here, and the other girls . . . It's too dangerous. There's no way we can fight them. It's all a lie. The ancient hunters trained their whole lives. I make you train for a few weeks, a few months, and I somehow expect you to survive? It's impossible."

I nodded. "I know, Mom. I've been saying it all along. It's dangerous. It's terrifying. But at least here, if we draw them, we're somewhat prepared. We're not like Cory or I were when we each met the zhis in the woods—no weapons, no nothing."

She pointed to the trophies strewn about the room. "These hunters . . . they may have been successful at first, but in the end, they all fell."

"Not all of them, Mom." I pulled away, crossed my arms in front of my chest. "There was Clothilde."

She stared at me.

"Why didn't you tell me about my father—that he was a Llewelyn? That he was descended straight from Clothilde?"

She turned and retrieved the sword from where it had fallen. "I did," she said. "You don't remember, but when you were young, you knew. You used to run around the house with a tinfoil sword." She smiled wistfully. "You were so adorable then. And when you stopped listening to me, when you started trusting John over me, it was just another thing you chose to forget. All the magic. All the fun we used to have together. So, yes," she said, lifting her chin. "Then I kept it to myself. My own secret, my own revenge. I didn't want you to have another crazy story to hate me for or claim it was incest or some other nonsense."

Please. Way too many generations had passed for it to be incest. If my mom had ever paid the slightest bit of attention to a genetics book published after Mendel first started breeding pea plants, she'd know that.

"But you didn't tell the Bartolis, either," I said. Were the rest of the hunters outside the door, listening to this? Did I care? "They could have found other hunters . . . a whole line! Why?"

My mother kept her face down. "Because, sweetie, I wanted

it for you. Llewelyn from both sides—Clothilde Llewelyn, even. The greatest hunter ever. The one who killed the karkadann!"

But she hadn't killed the karkadann. Or didn't my mother know that?

"Your father's family—they don't even know who they are, honey," my mom said. "They didn't deserve it, like you."

"Didn't deserve being sent off to die?"

"You're right," she said. "They don't deserve that. None of us do. I understand that now. I didn't before—I was just thinking about glory. It's the only thing we have, Astrid. The only thing that makes us special."

"That's not true."

"But this isn't special. It's terrible. When you called me last month, I didn't understand. But now—" She held her hands out to me. "Come on. Let's go home. Let's just leave this place. When I saw that poor little girl, her body all broken—"

"Her name is Ilesha, Mom."

"—when I thought of you—dead, torn apart, *eaten*—I couldn't bear it. I can't bear to let it happen to any other mother's daughter either."

"So you throw yourself in front of the nearest zhi? What about all these people? They're counting on you!" That's why I'd come back. I didn't wish for death—either literal or metaphorical.

"I don't know what I was thinking—I was crazy with grief," Lilith said, and looked sincerely contrite. "This place, these monsters—it's too much. It's nothing like the books I read. Even if there were casualties, it wasn't—real. It wasn't someone I loved. And the hunters still won. But last night, I lost you, we lost the battle . . . Please, Astrid, let's go home. It's what you always wanted. What *you* wanted, sweetie. I want it now, too."

It was. I couldn't lie. But things had changed. "I can't do that."

"Of course you can. We'll pack up and go. If the kirin are chasing us, we'll run. We'll find someplace they can never get to. Manhattan. A Caribbean island. Anywhere."

There was a scraping behind us, and the door shoved inward another inch.

"Astrid, darling, listen to me."

And another. "Astrid!" came the muffled tone from the other side. "What's going on in there?"

What was going on? My mother was offering me the life of my dreams and I didn't want it.

No, that's not true. I wanted it. Desperately. Manhattan. Giovanni lived there. If we went to New York City, we could be together. For real. I could have my old life back, but better. Lilith and I could be on the same page for once.

But I couldn't take it. I needed answers, closure, vengeance. For Phil. For the hunters. For the karkadann. And for me, too.

Phil squeezed through, leaped over the throne, and glowered at us both. "Asterisk, do you have any hips at all?" She started pulling at the throne. "Help me with this."

I steeled myself against the visions and started tugging. Inch by battle-bloodied, Jutland-scream-filled inch, the throne moved out of the way. As soon as there was enough space, the other hunters poured through the hole. Cory held Bonegrinder fast by the collar, then hooked her up to the chain in the wall, where she strained and gnashed her teeth at Lilith.

"Are you done packing?" Lilith asked Phil.

Phil simply looked at me. I nodded at her, and understanding passed between us. "I'm not going anywhere, Aunt Lilith."

"Well, you can't stay here. I'm closing the Cloisters."

"No, you're not," Cory said. "I opened this place. I won't watch you destroy it."

Lilith turned to her. "I'm trying to keep you safe."

"We'll keep ourselves safe," I said. "Hunters have done it for thousands of years. And the really smart ones, like Clothilde, do it on their own terms."

It was true, and it had been what Phil was talking about all along. Clothilde, too, had rebelled against the society that had bound her as a hunter for all her life. She'd faked her own death to escape it. We wouldn't do that. It would be a choice, to hunt. A choice I made on my own.

My mother, here, gripping the claymore as if it were one of the tinfoil swords from my childhood, had no concept of what we were doing. To her, unicorn hunting was a story in a dusty old book. She wanted me to be honored, but she didn't understand the risk such honor entailed. She hadn't seen her own death not like Ursula and me. She hadn't killed anything herself, like I had, like Phil had. And when Cory had watched someone she loved die, it had awakened in her a desire to fight. All my mother wanted to do was flee.

"You can't lead us," I realized aloud. "You're not one of us."

"Astrid—"

I shook my head. "Mom, you're right. I think it's time for you to leave the Cloisters of Ctesias. I swear to you, the Order of the Lioness will be in good hands." I turned to Phil. "Want to be donna?"

"Second the motion," Cory said, shocking every Llewelyn in the room.

Phil blinked at me, then at Cory. "Are you guys sure?" She

looked around the room at the other hunters, most of whom were nodding vigorously. Melissende bit her lip and looked down, and her sister elbowed her hard in the gut. Melissende shrugged.

Phil's eyes turned glassy, but she lifted her chin. "Okay. I'll do it." She raised her hand, and the red ring glinted in the light. "After all, I really like the accessories."

"You're children!" Lilith said. "I can't allow you to make this kind of decision for yourselves."

"No, Mom," I replied sadly. "We're not children. We're warriors. Just what you wanted us to be."

25

Wherein Astrid Attunes the Hunters

It was surprisingly easy to convince Lilith to leave after that. I think my mom knew when she'd been outclassed. She'd already packed most of her things, but I followed her to her room anyway, and we made awkward small talk while she closed up her suitcases and Phil made arrangements to move Lilith's flight home up a day. "Strange, huh?" Lilith said, as she zipped up the last suitcase. "A few months ago, I was helping send you off. Things certainly have changed, haven't they?"

I stood by the window, my eyes scanning the streets. There was something tickling the edge of my senses, some whisper of unicorn awareness, but nothing close enough to cause me any real concern. "Yes," I said at last, turning to face my mother. "They certainly have."

"You know I only want the best for you, right, sweetie? That's all I ever wanted."

I nodded, hoping Phil would come soon and save me from this unwanted tête-à-tête. When she did, we rode with Lilith to return her car, then dropped her off at the train station. She said she could go on her own, but for some reason, I wanted to see her out of Rome. I wanted to know she was both safe and gone.

"Listen up, people," Phil said, when the meeting convened in the chapter house later that afternoon. We'd spent the day cleaning up, unpacking the necessary implements, and canceling travel plans. I don't know how it was that Phil sweet-talked the hunters' parents into letting them stay after everything that had happened, after Lilith's hysterical announcements and doomsday predictions to the adults. She'd spent a full hour on the phone to Neil, hashing out a strategy. At the moment, he planned to keep searching for Jaeger, then return to the Cloisters as soon as possible to help out. In the meantime, my guess is that no one's parents knew they'd just placed the safety of their children in the hands of a teenager. Either that or the next few days would bring a phalanx of angry parents descending on the Cloisters to carry their daughters away.

"As you know, we've seen some big changes around here, the most important of which is a move to a more fair and democratic Order of the Lioness for all."

"Do we have to recite the Yankee pledge of allegiance now?" Cory mocked.

Phil stuck her tongue out at Cory. "First, I want to say that I really appreciate your vote of confidence—"

"Or you could look at it as a vote of no confidence in your aunt," Grace said, her smile somehow simultaneously sweet and venomous.

"Whatever way it happened, it happened," Phil said, returning the smile with an equal amount of sugar and punch. "Also, I want to say that I appreciate your hard work this afternoon, cleaning up the chapter house and the wall. I know it wasn't easy to figure out where all the bones were supposed to go—"

Dorcas, scratching underneath the edges of her cast, said, "They're dead. I don't think they care where they hang on the wall."

Cory cleared her throat and made a wrap-it-up gesture to Phil.

"We're going to get to some policy stuff in a bit, but first, let's turn the floor over to my cousin, the amazing, death-defying Astrid." She mocked a crowd cheering as I stood up and faced the others. Apparently, you can take the girl out of the volleyball team, but you can't take the volleyball team out of the girl.

"Thanks. I, um . . ." Where to start? I spent yesterday talking to a karkadann. I found out that Clothilde Llewelyn never killed him, that unicorns were never extinct, that me and mine were in danger of ambush every second unless we found both Marten Jaeger and the pack of kirin who had pledged loyalty to him? "I wanted to show you guys something." I turned around and lifted my shirt.

The room filled with gasps.

"This is what happened to me the other night. How I survived, I don't know. I came to on the ground, but for hours I couldn't move. The kirin who gored me was dead. He'd been killed by another unicorn."

"Why?" Zelda asked.

Here's where things started to get wonky. I lowered my shirt and faced the group. "There seem to be . . . factions."

Melissende snorted. I was losing them.

"The other night was no accident. Those kirin ambushed us. They knew we thought there would only be one of them.

I"—I'd been told? By a unicorn?—"believe that these kirin are somehow in league with Marten Jaeger, and if we don't find them, if we don't find out what's going on, there will be more ambushes. More surprise attacks."

Melissende rolled her eyes now. "Unicorns working with a man? A non-hunter? It makes no sense. How could he get near them? How could he even talk to them?"

"I don't know," I said. And neither had the karkadann.

Cory was biting her lip. "Astrid, that's madness. I've been in the Gordian labs, and I've worked with Marten for several months. I know that boy told you all sorts of horrible stories, but, honestly, it's impossible. Marten couldn't even keep his hands on a zhi unless I was there helping him."

"Maybe he has other hunters," Dorcas said. Everyone stared at her. "What? Is that weird?"

"Yes!" Cory said. "Why would he bother funding the Cloisters if he planned to keep his own hunters?"

"But it was *you* who came to *him*, Cory," I said. "He knew you were gung ho about the Order. Maybe he agreed to help you so that he could keep a close eye on what you did?"

"To what end?" Cory said, jumping up. "Why would he do any of the things he's done? Why would he disappear now if he wanted to watch us?"

"Control," Phil said softly. "He's always wanted to control us. He gave us a trainer, then took him away. He bribed some guys to sleep with me and Astrid when he thought we were getting too good. And then, when things went south there, he left town before he could get in trouble. Maybe he thinks we're no threat anymore."

"Even if what you say were true," Cory went on, pacing now,

362

"It doesn't put him in league with some kirin to hunt us all down. I don't think he wants to hurt anyone. I don't think it was his idea that Seth force you against your will."

"I don't either, but it's the result, anyway," Phil said.

"The kirin *are* trying to hunt us down," I said. "And they are in league with Jaeger. I have it on very good authority—"

"Whose?" Melissende asked.

I hesitated. "Just believe me, okay?"

"I think not," Melissende scoffed. "My little sister almost died last week. I think I need more than your word to risk putting her in harm's way again."

"It is true," said Valerija from the back of the room. She'd been sitting apart from the rest of us, picking at her nails and glowering. Now she rose. "What Astrid says. The kirin and Jaeger are one. And Dorcas says truth, also. I was a hunter for him."

We all lapsed into silence and stared at her. "He found me in town. No money, no house. One day I see unicorn, like Bonegrinder, and it does not hurt me. I think people talk about this, and he finds out. So he finds me, gives me pills. He is very nice to me. I think maybe he wants to screw me, but no. He takes me to a house. There are many unicorns, all in a row. Like a farm. There are many scientists. They are very scared. One of them died, maybe many, before I came there. Jaeger says with me there, no one will die."

Dorcas looked smug. The rest of us, shell-shocked.

"He says I stay as long as I like. He gives me bed and food and anything else I want. But I have to take tests. Some hurt, very bad. Hurt like that chair—" She pointed at the throne, and shuddered. "But he gives me more pills, then."

"How long did you stay there?" Phil asked.

Valerija shrugged. "Long enough. Then one day, he says I must leave. We get in a van. They tell me what to say, what to do. Say if I do it right, you will feed me, give me a bed, too. If I do it wrong, unicorn will kill me. And if I tell you, unicorn will kill me." She crossed the room, to where her alicorn hung on the Wall of First Kills, and pulled it down. "Do you hear this? It makes no noise." She tossed it back and forth between her hands. "I wonder why, many days." She looked at me. "You wonder, also?"

"Yes," I said. "I did." But I'd been too afraid to ask Valerija why.

"I know. You always think, every day. Like the scientists. I see you think, and I am scared if I talk to you, you think until you know the truth. Why do you think it makes no noise?" She waved the horn in the air.

"I think you didn't kill it," I said, after a moment of consideration. "I think the magic only works if it is a hunter's first kill."

She nodded. "Yes. They gave me head in bag. A unicorn kill it, they say."

I wondered if it was Bucephalus. If he was protecting me, even then.

"But that was the kirin Astrid attacked," Phil exclaimed. "The one we saw the night of our first date with Seth and Giovanni. Maybe it was the kirin that reported back to Marten. Maybe it was the kirin who showed him who to look for when he met the boys in the bar!"

Valerija ducked her head. "I am very sorry, Phil, because you are a good person. That night, when you came home, I call the people at Gordian. I tell them Neil is calling police."

Phil blinked, hard. *"But I shared my room with you."*

"He says to report anything weird that happens. I report. I think it is why he went away, why he does not call, why Neil can't find him."

"How could you do that to me?" Phil asked, her voice breaking.

"I am scared. I am scared unicorn will come to kill me."

"So why are you telling us all this now?" Grace asked. "Aren't you afraid the unicorns will kill you?"

"Yes," Valerija said. "Very afraid. But when unicorn tried to kill me in Tuscany, you protect me, Grace. We both almost died, but you protect me. So I think I will try to be a hunter, for you. When unicorn try to kill me two days ago, Astrid protect me. Astrid die for me."

"Well, I didn't really die," I said with a blush.

"What you say is true. Marten Jaeger is with kirin. Many, many kirin. I know where he is. I know where they are. I can lead you. And I want to. Because now I know that unicorn come to kill me either way. And you are the only one trying to stop it."

"Don't trust her," Phil hissed. "She's a liar and a spy."

But what she said coincided pretty well with what Bucephalus had told me. And what's more, it explained how Gordian was keeping kirin—they had hunters with them. Were there other girls like Valerija being blackmailed or manipulated into being guinea pigs at the labs?

"I'm serious," Phil said, when no one backed her up. "I will not have this, this *traitor* under my roof!"

"*Your* roof!" Melissende cried. "Didn't you just finish talking about how democratic we would be now?"

Grace looked at her, incredulous. "You *want* the drug-addicted spy to lead us someplace?"

Melissende frowned.

Rosamund spoke up. "Valerija may be telling the truth, but what difference does it make? If the other night proves anything, it's that we do not have the skill to hunt many unicorns at once."

"Yet," I said. "I think we can learn it." I looked at the alicorn in Valerija's hand and at the wall, which still let out its faint, buzzing chord. The magic worked because all the bones on the wall were made from unicorns that a hunter had killed. I turned my head and looked at the throne, still sitting awkwardly near the remains of the door to the chapter house.

The throne was made from the horns of unicorns that had killed hunters. The first time I touched it, it burned like alicorn venom, like being near the karkadann. But the next time, I saw a vision of the unicorns' last battle along with the pain, like the first time I'd talked to the karkadann, when he'd almost killed me with his images and his poison. And now—

I walked over and placed my hand against the armrest. The vision of Jutland swam up in my mind, and I clenched my jaw and swatted it down until it was there but not overwhelming. No pain accompanied the images, the sounds, the smells. It was pure.

Like my last conversation with the karkadann. Had I built up a resistance to the poison? Had I gotten stronger, somehow? Did the throne work the same way?

Daughter of Alexander, I am teaching you now. When the kirin gored you, he taught you. When you pet your—Bonegrinder?—

she teaches you. When you stand in your prison, surrounded by
bones that sing and horns that scream, it is all a lesson.

This throne, this room, this entire building. It wasn't a torture chamber. It was a training tool.

I needed to test it. "Ursula," I said, "do me a favor and sit on this throne."

"What?" the younger girl cried. "No! You're crazy!"

"I don't think it will hurt you."

"Astrid!" Phil said. "What are you doing!"

"Or maybe it will, a little. But it will stop. Look!" I plopped down on the seat, and the dead hunters started fighting again. I smiled through gritted teeth. "See?"

Melissende shook her head. "Absolutely not. I think I recall a week ago, almost getting my head torn off for suggesting the same thing." She turned toward her sister and began speaking in German.

"I won't," Ursula announced, and crossed her arms over her chest.

"But you're the only one who has had a similar experience to mine," I argued. "The only one who's been exposed to enough alicorn venom to start building up the resistance. It's going to be too much of a shock to the others."

Ursula shook her head vehemently, and Melissende wrapped her arms around her. "Leave her alone. She's been through enough."

"I will do it," Valerija said. "I go through many tests at the farm. Many poisons. And in Tuscany, I got stabbed by kirin, remember?" She tugged at the shoulder of her faded black shirt, pulling it down until we could all see the double helix markings gracing the hollow beneath her clavicle. "I will do it."

I stood up, and she joined me in front of the throne and squeezed my hand, hard.

"It is going to hurt, at first," I warned her, "but just stick through it. Concentrate on what it makes you see."

"Oh, so now it's a hallucinogenic chair?" Cory asked.

Valerija nodded, took a deep breath, and dropped onto the chair.

Then she screamed.

"No!" Phil shouted. "Astrid, help her, stop it!"

What had I done? Now I was experimenting on people, following the nutty theories of a half-mad unicorn who thought he was an ancient war hero? Watching her writhe in pain was more than I could stand.

I grabbed Valerija's hand to try to pull her off the throne, but she shook me away and gripped the armrests tightly. She began to shudder, and her screams died off into a whimper as her eyes rolled back into her head. An endless minute passed, and half the girls in the room were hiding their faces or peeking through their fingers with horrified eyes. Then, almost inaudibly, Valerija whispered, "The battle. The blood. So many dead. There is one of mine. A Vasilunas. She looks like me." She blinked several times. "It is gone. The pain. Now, only the visions."

She stood up and rubbed her arms as if cold. Every hair on her body seemed to stand on end, and her skin almost glowed. She was breathless, exhilarated.

"I feel . . . strong."

"*Scheiße! Nein!*" Melissende shouted, standing up. "*Ich glaube das nicht.* This doesn't prove anything. You are not a better hunter because you sit on a chair."

"Yes," Grace said. "How shall we prove it? Take turns shooting

Bonegrinder and see who kills her faster?"

We all looked over at the zhi we'd chained to the wall in the corner.

She wasn't there.

"Damn escape artist!" Cory shouted. "She must be in the Cloisters still."

"Not necessarily," I said. "There was a time the other week when we locked her in the catacombs and she escaped. With the door to the chapter house unsecured—"

"When?" Cory asked me.

"It was the night that Phil—" I gave Cory a look of apology. "I'm sorry. So much was going on, I forgot to tell you."

Phil furrowed her brow at me. "Was that the morning you went out and came back smelling like garbage?"

"Was that the morning after the night you swore you'd kill Seth?" Cory snapped, clearly unhappy at being left out of the loop.

"Excuse me?" Dorcas said. "Shouldn't we be looking for Bonegrinder?"

"See?" Melissende said. "What kind of super hunters are you if you can't even keep a baby zhi captive?"

We adjourned back to the stairwell, taking a quick left into the entrance of the catacombs. As the hunters spread out through the uneven, dirt-covered space, skirting the empty wall niches where the bones of ancient hunters had once rested, I paused and looked at Valerija. She was also frozen in place, head lifted, focusing on something that no one else could see or hear.

Bonegrinder was drinking from the fountain in the front courtyard.

I saw it clearly, felt her choke as she slurped up a fly floating on the water, felt a sneeze building up inside her muzzle when she drank too fast. Valerija's eyes met my own. She saw it, too, I knew it. She raised her eyebrows at me. I nodded, and she turned around and took the stairs.

This was the power, this was the sensitivity that we'd so imperfectly understood. This was how I'd known there'd been a zhi in the Myersons' backyard, a kirin hiding among the potsherds, a yearling hunting sheep. This was how I knew there'd been a pack of kirin lying in wait for the hunters to attack. Our native abilities could tell if there was a unicorn near—and once attuned, we could pinpoint them exactly. See through their eyes, understand their thoughts. Know where they would move before they knew themselves.

I felt Valerija's hands close around the zhi's torso, felt Bonegrinder's disappointment and frustration at being captive yet again. "Val's found her," I announced, and smiled at the disbelieving faces around me. "So, who's next for the throne?"

I'm not going to say the evening was a pretty one. Grace was the next volunteer for the throne, and the process took its toll on her. She leaped up from the chair involuntarily several times, and in the end begged Melissende to hold her down until the pain became more bearable. Ursula went next, and, as I'd suspected, had an easier go of it, given her increased exposure to the alicorn venom. Ditto for Zelda. Dorcas flatly refused to try. Rosamund threw up the second she sat down on the throne, then bowed out and retreated to her piano, where she played simple scales until her hands stopped shaking.

"I'll try again later," she said.

I looked at Cory, whose expression showed equal parts terror and determination. "Hold my hand?" she asked me.

"Absolutely."

Rosamund segued into an unfamiliar piece while Cory and I joined each other in front of the throne. This tune was mournful yet frenetic, like the battle in the visions. The trophies on the wall behind us hummed along, and Cory squeezed my hand so hard the bones crunched together.

"It's going to be okay," I whispered. "I promise; it's better than a hole in the back."

"True," she said, and drew a deep breath. "For my mum."

I nodded. Then she sat.

Unlike the others, Cory did not scream, but she gasped, and her eyes bulged. Phil, who'd looked on the verge of tears all night, hid her face in her hands. Cory wrenched my arm almost out of its socket, and every muscle in her body seemed to tense.

"You can do it, Cory," I said. "Concentrate on the music."

"I'm fine," she hissed. "I do what it takes." And she always had.

Rosamund, across the room, paused, mid-melody. "Do you want me to stop?"

"No!" Cory shouted, and began to writhe. Rosamund, taken aback, played on.

A minute later, it was done, and I helped a shaky Cory out of the chair and onto the floor, while Phil rushed over with soda and crackers.

"That was horrid," Cory said, when she'd recovered somewhat. "What a barbaric idea."

"How do you feel now?" Phil asked.

"Like the others," Cory said. "For instance, even now, Bonegrinder is plotting how to attack you despite the ring. It may become a problem. She thinks your calves look delicious."

Phil's mouth dropped open. Cory laughed.

Melissende jumped up and strode over to the throne. "My turn."

After all the hunters but Dorcas had been attuned, Melissende insisted on giving their newfound abilities a test run. I was nervous about the endeavor, but Phil agreed and tapped Melissende to lead the hunt. I had a sneaking suspicion that my cousin would end up being a very diplomatic donna.

Melissende took with her the seven freshly attuned hunters—Dorcas's bum arm and my still-healing back kept us both out of commission—and together with Phil, we two left-behinds raided the Cloisters' larder and played a game that Phil called What Will Bonegrinder Eat?

"So that's a no on broccoli rabe, eggplant, garlic bread, and honeydew," Dorcas said, reading the list.

"And a yes on prosciutto, sausage, salami, ham, raw minced lamb, anchovies, and dried calamari," Phil said. "As well as the wrappers of all the above. And, apparently, my calves."

"I think Cory was kidding," I lied. Phil had nice, toned calves, and Bonegrinder was a connoisseur.

Of course, all the fun and games were merely to distract ourselves from the paralyzing fear that I'd made a horrible mistake. What if there was another ambush? What if the chair didn't really give us extra sensitivity when it came to hunting? What if I'd just sent seven girls to their deaths? What if I'd convinced each one of them that they could take on a pack of kirin apiece and they were, even now, bleeding to death in the streets and cursing me with their very last breaths—

Bonegrinder lifted her head, cocking her ears forward.

"They're back!" Phil said. The four of us ran from the kitchen and into the rotunda, each filled with trepidation and anticipation.

Seven hunters stood lined up on the mosaic floor, battle worn, covered in cuts and scrapes. Their clothing was torn and dirty, spattered with blood and gore. They looked exhausted and exhilarated.

"Well?" asked Phil.

One by one, they each held out an alicorn and smiled.

26

Wherein Astrid Prepares for Battle

FIVE DAYS LATER, I sat in the courtyard in the darkness before dawn, waiting to speak to the two most important males in my life. In the last week, my experiment had proved valid under every test. Zelda single-handedly, with only one wasted arrow, brought down a pack of five zhi who'd been wreaking havoc in a local schoolyard. Melissende and Grace had successfully stalked and killed a lone re'em with nothing more than a sword and an ax.

And my back had completely healed, leaving only a raised magenta starburst scar in the center of my spine. It didn't even twinge anymore. Last night I'd been sparring in the practice courtyard with Grace, and I couldn't feel it, even when I lifted the claymore that was fast becoming my close-range weapon of choice. Every time I touched it, I felt a little closer to Clothilde.

Daughter of Alexander.

Of course *he* would come first. I supposed it was better this way. Giovanni might pass out if he got near the karkadann. I cast a glance over my shoulder at the Cloisters. The others were

374

still asleep, getting as much rest as they could before the big day. Could they hear the karkadann as I could? Was he even now invading their dreams?

I stepped out of the courtyard and into the street, since Bucephalus was too big to squeeze through the archway. Somehow, the night made him seem more massive and yet more ethereal. I wondered how he navigated the streets of Rome without being noticed. I wondered if people saw him and attributed their vision to too much grappa. He stared at me through giant, half-lowered eyes, and tilted his horn away from me, a courtesy I no longer required but appreciated nonetheless.

"You know what I'm doing?"

Yes. You confront the kirin.

I unfolded the map. "Can you read this? Do you know where we are going?"

He snorted and stamped his foot. *Foolish girl. I have conquered half of Asia. And I know the kirin. I know where they hide.*

"Then why didn't you tell me?"

You did not say you would help until now. I will not beg a human. Ever! The karkadann growled, and the stones rumbled beneath my feet.

"But you've been watching me. You knew what we've been planning."

And you watch me, too.

It was true. I'd been searching for him ever since we made this plan, calling out to him the only way I knew how. I'd spent the last week terrified that he would refuse to aid us after I'd rebuffed him last time. Or worse, that one of the scouting parties would happen upon him before I did and try to kill him before I'd had a chance to explain.

It is a strange alliance.

"Is that what this is? An alliance?"

I felt the karkadann riffling through my mind. *I see your fear. I submit. I will not kill a hunter. I will protect them, as I have protected you.*

"That's all I wanted to know." I breathed a sigh of relief. The safety of the hunters was my first duty. His vengeance against the rebel kirin was his. We had very different goals in mind, Bucephalus and I. But now, today, they were aligned enough so we could work together. After he'd ended the association between the kirin and Gordian, he didn't care about the other unicorns, had no opinion about the Reemergence at all.

I *had* to have an opinion. It was my role in life. I just wasn't sure yet what that opinion was. Hunt these endangered creatures? Capture them and send them into exile again? What would Bucephalus say if I suggested that?

The karkadann shook his head, turned, and galloped away.

Fight hard today, Daughter of Alexander, and I will slaughter by your side.

That gruesome image was still knocking around in my head when the headlights of Giovanni's van turned up the street.

I climbed into the passenger side. "Hi."

"Where's your bow?" Giovanni said with a nervous laugh. "How can you hunt anything without a weapon?"

I pulled the alicorn knife from its sheath on my belt loop. Valerija had saved it for me, retrieving it from the spot she'd seen me last while they'd spent time searching in vain for my body.

"Here," I said, my tone matter-of-fact. "I'll load up the rest in a minute."

Giovanni's eyes went wide. Oh, he'd been making a joke. I'd clearly spent too much time recently dealing with the practicalities of carrying as many large weapons as possible without hampering movement or speed. I doubted it was anything his other girlfriends had ever thought about. I also doubted any of his other girlfriends had ever whipped out a giant knife from the next seat over.

"The others will be along soon, but I wanted a few minutes alone." I said. He gave me a hopeful look, but I wasn't angling for a predawn make-out session. "Are you sure this is still okay? Me tapping you as driver? We're without a car now."

"Sure," he said, patting the steering wheel. "I've always wanted to see Cerveteri."

"This isn't a tourist trip," I said. "That's why I wanted to talk to you before we started. We need some ground rules."

"No sex. Got it." He winked at me.

"Some ground rules for the battle," I clarified, though I felt my entire body flush. "As I told you, the unicorns are drawn to the hunters. It's part of the gig. I don't know how soon they'll know we're there. We may have to park pretty far away from their actual hideout."

"Understood."

"And whatever happens—whatever you see, whatever you hear—do *not* leave the van. If they come at you, get away from the windows, keep the doors locked, duck down as far as possible."

"Aye, aye, captain." He gave me a mock salute.

"Giovanni, this isn't a joke. I can't have you as a liability. I know you. I know you like to get involved. You can't in this situation. I need you to stay somewhere safe."

He was quiet for a moment. "Would it be easier if I just gave you the keys and got out of here, General? Because I certainly wouldn't want to do anything that would be construed as getting in your way. Or, you know, *saving you*. I know how much you've hated it when I've done that in the past."

"Don't," I said in a low tone.

"Don't what?"

"Cast that in my face." I closed my eyes for a moment, taking stock like a hunter of the whole situation, collecting every bit of data. We were both nervous, and neither of us knew what would come next. "You know I couldn't do without you. I wouldn't even be here if it weren't for you. And I appreciate it all, more than I can say." I opened my eyes and turned to him. "I need you."

For a moment, he stared at me without saying anything, examined my face, searched my eyes until I almost ducked my head. What did he see when he looked at me now? Was I still the girl in the towel on the bed? Or had the knife scared that image right out of his head? "I know all that," he said at last. "I'm just worried about you. About the fact that there's absolutely nothing I can do."

I pulled him close and kissed him. "You're doing it already. I promise." I looked at the empty seats behind us. "By the way, how did you convince them to let you borrow the van again?"

"It's four A.M.," he said, and popped the trunk. "They don't know I have it, just like last time."

The door to the Cloisters opened, and eight figures stepped out into the courtyard. All carried weapons—bows and crossbows, swords and knives, axes and arrows—all culled from the weapons wall in the chapter house. Phil brought up the rear with two bags, one stuffed with first aid supplies, the other with food and drink.

"Whoa," Giovanni said, slipping out and around the back as the hunters began loading the van. "This stuff is hard-core." He picked up the claymore. "Can you guys even lift this sword?"

Phil bit her lip to suppress a grin. "That one's Astrid's."

Giovanni dropped it on the pile. "Oh."

The hunters laughed, which didn't help the situation at all.

As everyone climbed into the van, I turned to Phil. "Sure you don't want to come?"

"To what end?" she asked bitterly. "Either I stay out of the way, and I'm nothing but deadweight, or I forget myself, get involved, and end up being one more helpless person for you to worry about."

"I worry about everyone," I said. Didn't matter if they were helpless or not.

"Exactly," Phil replied. "And I worry about that most of all. Besides, I need to watch over Dorcas and Ilesha." She gave me a hug. "You be careful, Asteroid. No new piercings, okay?"

"Got it."

She glanced over my shoulder at Giovanni, waiting in the driver's seat. "Is he cool?"

I nodded. "He's doing his best. It's really hard to understand from the outside."

"I know." Phil scanned the horizon. "You better take off."

In the rearview mirror, I noticed that she watched us all the way to the end of the street.

"How is she doing?" Giovanni asked me, as we drove. "With . . . everything?"

"Still really pissed at your friend," I said, looking out the window.

"I'm really pissed at him, too."

"And as for the rest, I don't know how long she'll end up staying here. She was doing great in college. She has a volleyball scholarship, you know. I think she should go back after . . . after this is over."

"Aren't *you* going to go back after this is over?"

I risked a glance at Giovanni, who was staring intently at the road out of town. "I don't know what I'm going to do."

He nodded, but didn't take his eyes off the road. At least his driving was on a more even keel than it had been last time. The other girls were chattering softly in the back, but I wasn't fooling myself that this was a private conversation. Cory, at least, had to be listening.

"I'm going back," he said softly.

"To where?" Melissende asked from the front-most bench seat. She was always ready to make an awkward moment worse. Giovanni cursed under his breath.

"Mind your own business!" I hissed at her, twisting in my seat.

She grinned and lit a cigarette.

"Oh, there's no smoking in the van," Giovanni said, but Melissende merely laughed and puffed in his direction.

"Condemned prisoners get last cigarettes," she said. "I might die this morning."

No one felt like talking much after that.

The roadways remained clear at this early hour, save the occasional garbage or delivery truck, and cabs or Vespas transporting their occupants to and from late-night trysts. I wasn't sure if the other hunters were trying to sleep or going over fighting strategies in their mind—or praying. Valerija, in particular, looked like she might be sick. This concerned me more than anything, as she alone had seen the gathering of unicorns we were facing this morning. I knew there'd be a lot. How many, though, no one was quite sure. It was possible we were headed to a massacre.

According to Valerija, the compound she'd been staying at was located in the village of Cerveteri, a quaint town less than an hour northwest of Rome in a lush, green countryside surrounded by farms and vineyards. Jaeger had kept her in a large villa outside town. It was surrounded by a tall fence topped with barbed wire. The kirin, she said, hid underground.

"Like, in a bunker?" Phil had asked at the time, but Valerija didn't know.

Fortunately, the standard tourist guidebooks did. Apparently, Cerveteri's one claim to fame was the giant network of underground Etruscan tombs honeycombing the bedrock of the entire area. In ancient times, well before the Romans settled in Italy, the ruling Etruscans had built a vast city of the dead in Cerveteri—a necropolis. There were acres and acres of unexplored tombs beneath the fields and pastures, but the ones that had been excavated were giant, beehive-shaped mounds carved directly from the earth, their chambers replete with columns and shelves and even beds and furniture, all hollowed out from the tuffa in a single piece inside these massive hills. From what I could tell, it was a bit like the pyramids in Egypt, had they been built someplace where grass, trees, and time could burrow in and bury the tombs under eons of history, until no one knew any longer who'd been laid to rest there or why.

How close had the hunters come to sharing the Etruscans' fate? Those nameless hunters whose lives had been taken by the monsters whose horns now made up the throne, even the hunters who had carved their names into the trophies on the wall—we modern hunters knew so little about any of them! And the world knew so little about us.

My mother had done her part to keep the legends alive, but few people knew we'd ever existed. Even now, in the wake of increasing reports, sightings, and attacks, almost no one understood the true nature of unicorns. To most of the world, they were the fluffy, innocent magical creatures of myth and bedtime stories.

To us . . . I shifted in my seat, feeling the tug of scar tissue along my back. To us, they were something else entirely.

Cory leaned forward and grasped the back of my seat with both hands. Her knuckles were split and bruised from the fights of the past few days. "Do you feel that?"

I nodded. On our right, in the shadows of the road's shoulder, there'd been traces of a unicorn. It had found a hitchhiker on the edge of the road—a young woman. "Two hours ago?" I asked. Venom still mixed with her blood on the road.

"Think so," she replied through clenched teeth.

I covered her hand with mine. "We'll get them. I promise."

Giovanni flashed me a look. "You're freaking me out."

Cory sat back in her seat. I wondered what part scared him more—that a person had been torn to bits and eaten on the side of the road, or that we could tell, hours later, exactly what had happened.

Soon, all the hunters were noting the traces of unicorn in the fields around us. And Giovanni saw the destruction himself.

Slaughtered remains of dogs, sheep, and other farm animals gathered flies and carrion birds all over the pastures. That would be an interesting study when all this was over. How long did the venom linger after death? Were crows and vultures immune as well, or did unicorn leftovers result in the kind of death piles common in other instances of animal poisonings? In other words, if a vulture ate the poisoned remains of a unicorn's prey, would it die, too?

Finally, we pulled off the highway and onto a local road winding up a hill into the center of town. Shops and restaurants lined the streets, and a wide, tree-filled park ran down the middle of the road. Pretty. Picturesque, even, if you ignored the bloodshed I could sense on every corner. Every telephone pole was plastered with a lost dog poster. Cory blinked back tears as we drove by one that looked like her puppy, Galahad, back home.

"Val," I called into the back seat. "You're on."

"What," Giovanni muttered, "you can't just use your spider sense to direct us?"

"Not here," Zelda said. "This whole area is crawling with unicorns."

"Left at the top," Valerija broke in. "A small road . . ."

Giovanni followed Valerija's directions in silence. The road wound over a hill, following signs for farms, restaurants, and historical sites, and then hit another straightaway.

"Here," Valerija said. "On the left." The villa came into view. It looked pretty. Peaceful, even, with its brick balconies and terra-cotta roof tiles. There was a garden and a fountain in the yard, a tiny vineyard, a stone terrace overlooking a little pond.

And five mean-looking German shepherds patrolling the

fence line. Strange—there'd been a marked lack of animals anywhere else in town. Apparently, Marten's deal with the kirin extended to his pets as well.

"Here?" Giovanni asked, slowing.

I shook my head. "A little farther."

Cory leaned forward again. "Won't they know we're here?"

I gripped my knife handle and took a deep breath. "They'll know soon enough."

As the edge of the sky began to catch fire, eight hunters lined up beside a gravel road. Before us was a low wooden fence; beyond lay the field of battle.

Well, *field* was a bit misleading. Below us lay a sunken, mazelike path riddled with grass-covered mounds, dead ends, blind alleys, sharp corners, collapsed tombs and archways, high walls, and other disadvantages. Here and there, giant, spear-shaped Italian cypresses shot skyward like unicorn horns or sharpened swords. Mist gathered in the nooks and crannies of the paths, making the largest tombs look like islands floating on a roiling gray sea, their grassy summits silver and violet with dew. I hadn't planned on such a reduction in visibility. I hadn't realized we'd be hunting in a labyrinth.

The kirin had chosen well.

At my side, Cory shouldered her bow and consulted an archaeological map she'd scored from the museum in Rome. "The Xs mark the tombs big enough to house a kirin, but keep in mind that they aren't necessarily hiding inside. As we talked about before, if you're feeling overwhelmed, circle back to Rosamund, who will be remaining at the fallback position here"—she pointed with one finger to a place marked on the map—"which is where that pine tree sticks out of the wall along the main drag . . ." She spotted it through the mist and pointed again. "The Via degli Inferni."

"The Path of Hell," Giovanni translated. I turned around. He was leaning out of the driver's side window. "Are you sure you don't want me to get on top of the van, work as a spotter?"

The hunters stifled their giggles. A spotter! For kirin!

"Stay inside and stay down," I repeated. "Please. Don't even watch."

He scowled, rolled up the window of the van, and scrunched down in the driver's seat.

I turned back to the sunken, fog-filled warren. This was it. I'd brought us here. Now I had to get us through it. I breathed deep, smelling dew and dirt, undercut with the acrid scent of unicorn. When I closed my eyes, I could feel them, like pulse points spread out over a body. I knew the hunters felt them, too, dozens of kirin, blood drunk and sleeping, nestled tightly inside ancient tombs meant for a people long gone.

I hoped to make their slumber permanent.

At my side, Rosamund's head was bowed, and she clutched the cross at her throat and prayed. I grabbed her free hand and bowed my head, too, and before I knew it, Ursula slipped her palm against mine. German, French, English, and Romanian blended together as the hunters joined in a circle, murmuring our most fervent wishes: that we'd be triumphant, that we'd survive. After a moment, Rosamund lifted her head and smiled at us. "Do you hear it?" she asked. "The chord, like the wall. It beats in my blood."

In the circle, the hunters began to nod, the revelation changing each of their expressions from terror to determination.

My blood sang with a hunter's power. We could do this.

"Let's get started," I said, and I watched the first hunters descend into the maze.

I turned around. Giovanni was staring at me through the window of the van. I walked over and pressed my palm against the glass. He mirrored me from the other side.

Go, he mouthed. *I'll wait for you.*

"Now our turn," Cory announced. I stepped over the fence line and into the path of hell.

27

Wherein Astrid Leads an Army

THE DREAMS OF UNICORNS are not pretty. The one nestled in the tomb on my right was remembering uncovering the den of a wild pig and her seven piglets. I dispatched him while their death squeals still echoed in my head. The one on my left woke from a dream of two campers in a pup tent a split second before my first arrow pierced his eye. He died before he could rise.

I continued down the corridor; and the hillocks rose around me, blocking my view of anything but the narrow, grassy tunnel on every side. Up ahead, I sensed two unicorns, very close together. A mother and a colt.

A baby unicorn? Could I? Could I kill a nursing mother?

Then, in the distance, the sound I'd been dreading—the clash of steel against horn. All at once, like a wave, they awoke. I heard them growling, then roaring; and the air was suddenly filled with shouts and the twang of bowstrings.

I turned away from the mother and colt and bolted down a side street, flying past tomb entrances I hoped were empty, scrambling up the side of the nearest scalable mound to get a better view. The mist had thickened with the coming dawn; and now it swirled beneath me like a stormy sea, as the half-invisible kirin darted to and fro down the alleys and in and out of the ruins, pursued by hunters who looked like little more than dark blobs in the soup.

I waved at Rosamund, our lookout, but she was too busy firing into the maze to respond.

"Help!" I heard Zelda cry from nearby, and I hurried down the hill, leaped the last few feet, and dropped to the ground. A kirin whizzed past, and I shot from five yards as it quartered away. The arrow passed cleanly through both lungs and clattered against the tomb wall on the far side. I took off in pursuit, but the animal didn't make it more than another ten or fifteen steps before it dropped, motionless, to the ground.

I stopped short, almost tripping over the body. What? I'd gotten a pass-through. Those wounds should have healed right up. I examined the entrance wound. It still bled freely. Had I hit its heart?

Zelda screamed again, and I hopped over the body and kept running. I found her at the end of a blind alley, fending off a pair of kirin with a small ax while trying to climb backward up a hillock whose ancient stones and red earth crumbled beneath her feet.

There wasn't enough room to shoot. If I got another pass-through, I might hit Zelda. I shouldered my bow and pulled out the claymore, raising the sword high and rushing forward as the unicorns' attention was focused on her.

I wasn't quick enough. One kirin turned and reared just as I reached it, knocking its hooves hard against my arm. The sword flew out of my grasp and tumbled away. As the unicorn landed, the tip of its horn sliced hard down my chest and left forearm, ripping through my shirt and my flesh. I shouted in pain as it lifted its head again and slammed me back against the stone. I felt his horn scrape the stone near my cheek, then slide into the soft tuffa. He'd missed, but I was trapped beneath him.

Blood poured from the cut on my arm, and the unicorn gnashed its teeth in my face and kicked, trying desperately to free its horn from the side of the hill.

"Zelda!" I yelled over its roars. "Help me!"

"*Un moment*," she yelled back, as metal severed the morning air from her direction.

Its fangs were in my face, its breath hot and reeking of ashes and rot. I tried to read its mind, but the only word I could see was *kill*. I tried to slide out of the way, but my shirt was caught, and the kirin kicked and reared with hooves like sledgehammers. My arm was healing, the wound knitting and the blood slowing a little more with every breath. I shoved at the kirin's muzzle, and it snapped its jaw in my face, digging its horn another inch deeper into the stone in order to get close enough to bite my head off.

My knife! I reached down toward the sheath with my right hand, gripping the handle tight. With one firm thrust, I shoved it up under the kirin's jaw and straight into its brain.

It slumped, and I pulled out, palming the blade with hands drenched by blood—mine and the unicorn's. Zelda still fought. I ran toward her, cupping my injured arm. There was no way I'd be able to shoot a bow right now, and the two-handed claymore was out of the question. But I still had my knife.

I'd almost reached her when the other kirin knocked the ax from her hands and reared up for the death blow. Zelda threw up her arms to protect her face and I raised my own knife, knowing I was too far to reach.

Above us, a giant shadow covered the dawn sky. I froze. The karkadann stood on the summit of the hill, horn lowered at the kirin, who dropped abruptly to all fours and stared.

For a moment, the world stopped, a slowing that made my hunter sense seem, by comparison, like a speeding train. The karkadann dared the kirin to test his wrath. And the unremitting bloodlust that poured from the kirin in waves gave way, for just a split second, to defiance. It charged.

So did Bucephalus.

The karkadann caught the kirin up by the belly, lifting the smaller unicorn on his giant horn and tossing him in the air like a dead leaf. Zelda cowered as the beasts clashed over her head, and then the kirin was dashed against the wall and rolled to the ground. It tried to rise once or twice, but its legs would not support it, and it began to whine, as blood and substances that were not blood poured freely from the hole in its gut.

I stood like a statue in the middle of the path. The karkadann tilted its head back at me, then galloped off. I rushed to Zelda.

"You okay?"

She nodded, then said thickly, "And you?"

I wiped blood off on my pants. "I'll be fine."

"Was that a . . . karkadann?"

"Yeah." I braced for the next question. The part about how it didn't kill us.

She cocked her head at the dying kirin, whose whines had now turned to high-pitched squeals of agony. I knew just how it felt. "Why isn't it . . . healing?"

"I don't know," I said, retrieving my bow and sword. "Maybe

it's susceptible to karkadann venom."

"No," Zelda said. "The others, too. That I shot with my arrows. All of them—they didn't heal." She picked up her ax, walked calmly over to the kirin, and brought the blade down on the creature's neck. The ax didn't make it all the way through its spine, but it was enough to put the unicorn out of its misery.

I watched her, dumbfounded. "That happened to me, too. I got a pass-through and it went right down. I thought I'd hit it through the heart or something."

"What's wrong with these kirin?" she asked.

I fingered the alicorn-tipped arrows on my quiver. "Maybe it's not them. That night, in the grove near the highway—those unicorns bled, too. And the re'em . . ." I remembered slitting its throat with my alicorn knife. Maybe the reason we'd had a harder time before was that we hadn't been using the old weapons, the ones made with alicorn. Maybe an alicorn wound healed on a hunter, not on a unicorn.

The ground rumbled, and the hunters' screams echoed down the alley. There was no time to talk. Zelda and I started to run.

The sky was now light enough to see beyond the next few feet, and over the top of the mist, I caught sight of unicorns leaping from hill to hill like chain lightning over thunderheads, their brindled coats rippling twilight and black, manes crackling around them, fangs bared, hooves pistoning as they rampaged over each rise.

Near the pine tree, Rosamund shouted directions to the hunters still in the trenches, shooting arrow after arrow into the back of any unicorn close enough to give her a clean shot. Melissende, too, had taken refuge on high ground, standing astride the monumental keystone of a tomb's entrance arch, her crossbow zinging away. Two kirin with severed horns ran past, and Grace chased them, swinging her katana and screaming at the top of her lungs. They barreled up the rise toward Rosamund, who stood her ground and kept shooting, then suddenly ducked as one leaped clear over her body and landed on the far side of the fence.

Near the van.

"No!" I shrieked and ran forward as they began to butt and kick at the sides and windows. "Stop!"

The windows shattered in the onslaught, and the little van began to rock on its wheels as the two unicorns kept up their attack.

Rosamund had regained her feet but seemed unsure about shooting at the battered van while Giovanni was hiding somewhere inside. I crawled up the hillside, hampered by my weapons and bum arm.

"Stop them!" Stop them!" I screamed. "For the love of—"

Daughter of Alexander, they are distracting you.

I whirled around and looked into the Via degli Inferni, where the six remaining hunters were in the midst of a frenzied battle against more unicorns than I could count. And there, just over the next hillocked tomb, I could see the massive back of the karkadann. Through his eyes, I saw him killing kirin as they poured from the alleys and into the main road.

Cory was fighting four on her own, using a long and short sword combo; Melissende was running out of bolts; Ursula had followed her sister's lead and climbed to higher ground to use her bow; and Valerija was trying her best to stay out of sight until she was close enough to assist another hunter with her knife. In the midst of the fray, I saw two flashes of silver.

Zelda and Grace, with ax and katana.

And they'd all die.

"Stay down, Giovanni!" I screamed at the top of my lungs. I looked at Rosamund. "Shoot high." Then I jumped down into the mist again.

My alicorn knife flashed white in the light of the rising sun, and I began to cut a swath through the gathering kirin. The air was filled with shrieks and blood and the overwhelming crush of bodies, slamming against one another, crashing to the ground. I slid on the damp grass and dirt, and for a moment, I forgot I was in the Italian countryside on a beautiful summer morning. This could be the mud plain of Jutland.

Every battle was the path of hell.

I'd almost reached Cory's side when I heard Melissende shout over the roar, "The big one! Shoot it!"

"No!" I cried, but there was no way she heard me all the way up there. I saw Ursula raise her bow and aim away from the crush, and I yelled and waved my arms, but her focus had shifted to her prey. She released the string.

A massive roar shook the earth, and kirin and hunter alike seemed to freeze for a second and hunker down. Ursula lowered her bow, and even from this distance, I could see the look of dismay on her face. Hooves the size of manhole covers thundered up the hillock toward her. The karkadann's horn was lowered, and Ursula's arrow protruded from its flank.

"No!" I screamed again, and swiped at a charging kirin. "No! No! You promised!"

The karkadann roared again.

Treachery! Treachery, Daughter of Alexander!

At this, I saw every hunter still. They'd heard him, too.

The karkadann paused, then raised himself on his hind legs, towering over Ursula's head, half as high again as the mound upon which they both stood.

"No!" With all my voice, all my heart, all my soul. "She doesn't know!"

He came crashing down, feet from Ursula, and the tomb crumbled beneath his weight, Ursula shrieked as the ground gave way under her feet and she slipped into the darkness below.

"Ursula!" Melissende wailed, then aimed her crossbow at the karkadann, balancing on the wreckage.

Try me, Daughter of Alexander. The karkadann faced her flat on.

She paused, in shock, then lowered her weapon. "*Wie bitte*?"

Of course. It made words in our heads. Melissende's words would be German.

Grace, nearest to the tomb, was shouting. "She's inside. She says she's stuck! Someone help me move the rocks!"

But the kirin had started up again, and now the tone of their thoughts had changed. Threaded through the murderous rage was an element of . . .

Treachery?

"They're moving!" Rosamund called out from the pine. The battlefield was emptying, kirin sprinting off in ever-greater numbers.

Cory made the victory signal and shouted, before whirling and slicing off the head of a yearling racing by.

No. They weren't retreating. They were discovering another target. The karkadann's eyes met mine and he jumped down from the collapsed hill and began to chase the others.

Treachery comes in every human face.

I scowled and sprinted after him.

"Astrid!" Cory's voice came from behind me. "We did it!"

I ran, hardly even sure where we headed, but certain that it was far from over.

The path narrowed as it moved farther away from the tombs, and the deep banks on either side of the excavation gave way to low, gentle slopes and tree-covered wilds. I couldn't keep up with the animals, hard as I tried, and as their lead increased, I found I couldn't keep up the inhuman hunter pace, either. I began to shed my heavier weapons. The claymore. The bow and quiver.

Every hundred yards or so, I came across another dead kirin. Bucephalus was taking them out as he came upon them. The trail of dead was enough for me to follow, and I soldiered on; but then I could find no more bodies, and my hunter sense was scattered and vague. I couldn't sense the karkadann at all, and I knew every kirin had fled. I was ready to stop altogether, when the house came into view. The chain link gate separating the path from the yard had been battered to smithereens.

I put on a fresh burst of speed, clambering over the broken gate and rushing into the yard as fast as my tired legs would take me. There were two dead German shepherds near the building, and three dead kirin on the terrace. No sound came from the building.

Near the back was a sliding glass door, now as smashed as Giovanni's windshield. The furniture within had been knocked about or flattened, and there were two more kirin bodies bleeding out on the floor. I followed the trail of destruction, though I knew it was too late.

There was a large hallway lined with empty cages big enough to hold zhis. Beyond this, the building opened into a large central courtyard. Here I saw the final kirin facing off against the karkadann.

"What are you doing?" I screamed with what little voice I had left, but he did not answer me, just pounced on the smaller animal and ran it through. I stared, appalled, as he gutted the kirin, dragging out its entrails and stomping them into mush against the stone.

She was the leader.

The karkadann's explanation slammed into my brain like a punch. She had betrayed him, condemned who knows how many of her own kind to lab rat slavery for some supposed chance of glory. Bucephalus wasn't happy, and he clearly didn't appreciate my reaction to his gruesome show of power. I wasn't allowed to judge their monstrous ways. He faced me, horn lowered.

And now, for the human.

"What?" I tightened my hand on my knife, though I doubted it would be a defense. Talk about treachery! "You said—"

And then I heard it. A pathetic little whimper from behind me. I risked a glance. Marten Jaeger, in a sweat suit, cowered behind a potted plant.

Treachery.

Marten hadn't gone back up north. Neil was wasting his time. He'd been here all along, hiding a few miles outside Rome in his secret unicorn hideout, perhaps continuing his testing. And the kirin must have thought he was responsible for tipping us off to their location. All of a sudden, the rapid retreat and chase made perfect sense. They weren't angry at the karkadann. They were angry at their false Alexander.

"Astrid," Marten whispered. "Thank God. Do something. Kill it."

Get out of my way, Daughter of Alexander.

"Where have you been?" I asked him. "Why—why did you do this to us?" My voice cracked on the words, and fresh, hot tears poured down my blood-spattered face. "To Phil!"

Out of my way. I shall kill this pretender.

"I was trying to protect you!" he said, his words garbled with terror. "If you weren't hunters, you'd be safe. Alive. That's all I intended. Those boys, they were your ticket out! I didn't want anyone hurt."

"You're lying."

"I swear! When the kirin saw Llewelyn hunters, they wanted you dead. They brought me dead blonds until I understood."

My hand flew to my mouth.

"It's like—like they know about Clothilde, and they do not want a Llewelyn anywhere near a bow."

So then he didn't know the truth about Clothilde, even if the kirin did. If they even did. I no longer knew what I could trust about the karkadann's story, nor could I imagine what he'd told the other unicorns to get them to agree to exile. I stared Marten Jaeger down. "But then—why didn't you just convince us to go home?"

"I tried, in Tuscany. Remember? But you said it yourself, you'd still be hunters, no matter where you went. It wouldn't be enough for them. I did the only thing I could think of."

The karkadann growled behind me, and I could feel the venom pouring off his body.

Move!

Marten's face was turning red, his eyes watering, and his

breath coming in short, shallow pants. "Help me, Astrid!"

Help him. How he'd helped us? How he'd plotted against us, hurt us, risked all our lives? Imprisoned Valerija, abandoned us all, kept us in the dark about the danger we faced? Help him. Help him what? Protect him from a behemoth with bloody murder emanating from every pore? With my single tiny alicorn knife? Choose him over the creature who'd saved my life again and again?

"Why did you do this to us?" I sobbed, refusing to move, despite the karkadann's repeated orders in my head. "To all of us?" The hunters, the unicorns. Everyone he'd manipulated and hurt.

Marten stared at me in disbelief. "For the Remedy. I needed the Remedy. I needed to find it. I—had to." He coughed, as the alicorn venom seeped into his lungs. "So many lives saved. It was worth it, Astrid. And . . . I did it. I know the secret. We can save everyone, cure everything, change the world. Help me."

I almost collapsed where I stood. The Remedy. He'd found it. Everything inside me wanted to sing in exultation. Astrid the Warrior and Astrid the healer merged for one brief, shining moment, and I pictured humanity transformed. What was vengeance in the face of that?

I turned around and faced the unicorn. "Please," I said. "It's over."

No.

"You've stopped the kirin. That's enough."

No.

"For me!" I clasped my hands together in front of my chest.

I have already spared one life for you today.

His massive head swept to the side and I flew several yards

and landed hard against tiled steps, cracking my skull on the floor. For a moment, starbursts filled the air, and when I looked again, it was over. Marten's face was twisted and purple, veins protruding from every angle. The tiny hole in his chest hardly bled at all.

And the karkadann was gone.

The walk back to the necropolis seemed miles longer than I'd remembered. The sky went from silver to periwinkle to blue during my hike, and the sun burned off every trace of mist.

Bucephalus had barely touched Marten. With the kirin leader, he'd shown no compunction over decimating and defiling her body. With Marten, who'd been complicit in the entire scheme, he'd only punctured him enough to kill. I didn't understand it. Perhaps I never would. The karkadann possessed his own scales of justice.

I retrieved my weapons from where I'd dropped them, but the claymore was pretty much dragging in the dirt behind me as I rounded the last corner into the Via degli Inferni.

Ursula and Grace sat near a pile of unicorn corpses. Grace was binding Ursula's arm in a sling and holding her own leg at an awkward angle. They both looked up as I approached.

"Where is everyone?"

"Looking for you," Grace said. "We thought you'd been dragged off again." She turned her head and called for Rosamund, who was rounding the hill with Melissende, each dragging a kirin corpse by the legs. "Get them back! Astrid's here!"

I checked out Grace's leg and Ursula's arm. Were these our only injuries? Were there any casualties?

"We killed dozens," Grace said matter-of-factly, finishing her first aid. "But even more managed to escape. Should we burn the corpses, do you think?"

One by one, I saw Cory, Zelda, and Valerija come running. They looked scraped up, and Cory had an enormous bloodstain on her leg that made me think she'd been gored. But nothing major. I breathed a sigh of relief.

"Did you get it?" Melissende asked. On the hill, Giovanni emerged from his van and saluted me. There was a nasty bruise forming on his brow, but he looked otherwise unharmed. I waved him down, but he seemed to hesitate.

"Get what?"

"The karkadann."

I shook my head. "No. I don't know if he can be killed."

"Well, he certainly doesn't like being shot," Ursula said.

"He saved our lives," Zelda said. "Isn't that weird?"

"No," I repeated. "He's saved my life a few times now." I bit my lip, weighing my words carefully. I needed to tell them about the karkadann, about Marten Jaeger, about the Remedy. But an official debriefing might be beyond my ability right now. There would be time back at the Cloisters, once we regrouped, bathed, slept, healed. Once I talked to Phil.

Or cried on her shoulder.

"I'm glad you didn't get him," Melissende said abruptly. "He's like our own Bucephalus, eh?" Then she turned around and went back to preparing the pyre.

She is a smart girl.

The thought was a whisper.

And ferocious. I like.

Where was he?

Far away, and farther still, Astrid Llewelyn.

He called me by name now?

You deserve a name. You are your own. Not Alexander's. Not Clothilde's. Not even your mother's.

I wandered away from the group, away from their chatter, worried somehow that they'd hear him as well. "Are you going into exile again?" I murmured. Was this the new last hunt?

Our exile is gone. We have no choice. And so, I know to stay far from any hunter, far from danger. Far from anything that would give you cause to hunt me down.

I drew a shuddering breath. We would not have survived this morning without him. There were too few of us, and the unicorns were so strong.

The image of the Myersons' sparkly, silly little bedtime story resurrected itself from the depths of my brain. *"I will never really leave,"* said the unicorn. *"I will always live in your heart."*

My weapons clanked against my side, and my clothes were turning sticky with dried gore. My blood burned and sang, and my fingers itched to shoot something. Power and bloodlust coursed through every strand of my DNA. I breathed, smelling fire and flood, blood and death, and knew he was right. The unicorn would be inside me forever. There was no going back.

"Hey," Giovanni said from behind me. I turned, wiping tears from my eyes. "You okay?"

"Are you?" Better not to answer.

"I'm in much better shape than the van," he said. "I'm going to get kicked out of school for sure this time." He pointed behind his shoulder. The van looked more like a crumpled newspaper than anything you'd drive around in.

"Giovanni, I'm so sorry—"

He shrugged. "I'm used to it by now." He was silent for a moment, looking over the carnage-strewn path. "So you weren't kidding about the danger."

"I told you."

"Or about the superpowers." He shook his head. "I suppose it's safe to admit now that I peeked a few times. You know, before they started playing Whac-a-Mole with my vehicle. You're . . . amazing, Astrid. I've never seen anything like it."

"Thanks." Amazing, huh? Covered in blood, bristling with blades, and smelling like a butcher shop.

"And I've come to a decision."

I blinked. "You have?"

"I think it's *vital* that we do not sleep together. You know, for the safety of the world." His eyes sparkled and there was just a hint of a smile at the corners of his mouth.

"Okay," I said, and smiled back at him. "But kissing is allowed, right?"

"Oh, definitely," he said, and pulled me close. "After all, the warrior always wins the heart of the fair young . . . man."

ACKNOWLEDGMENTS

*R*ampant would be more endangered than unicorns if not for the patient, insightful efforts of master marksman Kristin Daly, who loves killer unicorns almost more than I do; the strong, hunter instincts of Deidre Knight; the friendship of Anna Hays, who heard about this from day one; Lauren Perlgut, who still thinks I should be calling this book *The Horn Identity*; Mackenzie Baris, who made me Astrid the Unicorn Hunter action figures; and the deadly accurate critical aim of fellow writers Justine Larbalestier, Marley Gibson, and Carrie Ryan.

Thank you to everyone on the HarperCollins team who shepherded this book through the wilderness: Alessandra Balzar, Donna Bray, Corey Mallonee, Ruta Rimas, Jon Howard, Laura Kaplan, and Barbara Fitzsimmons and the design team at HarperCollins Children's Books.

As always, I am grateful to my supportive friends and family, especially my father, who loves science, medicine, and fantasy adventures; my uncle Chuck, who gave me a bow to practice on; and my brother Luke, who has steadily fed my unicorn habit.

I owe a deep debt of gratitude to bow hunter Tara Quinn, who was patient and highly creative while I pestered her during the research for this novel. Her knowledge about hunting animals both real and imaginary was indispensable to the creation of this story. She's a great hunter; any mistakes are my own. Also, thank you to her husband, Sean, for his demonstrations of both bow and taxidermy, and to my father-in-law for introducing me to both of them.

A special shout-out to my friends and colleagues who encouraged me to make the genre leap: Julie Leto, C. L. Wilson, Erica Ridley, TARA, WRW, Libba Bray, Holly Black, Cassandra Clare, Cecil Castellucci, Margaret Crocker, and Scott Westerfeld, who kept asking about Bonegrinder.

Speaking of inspirations, thank you to those who have portrayed and created warrior women of film and literature. Astrid would not exist were it not for Princess Leia, Sarah Connor, Ripley, Eowyn, Aravis Tarkheena, and Buffy Summers, all of whom taught me that women are powerful and loving, and showed me whom I should write about.

And finally, thank you to Dan, who was there when I woke up from my dream of being chased by a killer unicorn, explored the depths of Etruscan burial grounds by my side, stood beneath me as I balanced in a tree stand, and hugged me when I wrote "The End." This one's for you.